A WORD
KELLEY ARMSTRONG . . .

Some series begin with a grand, sweeping plan. Others with a single story. In my case, that single story was *Bitten*, which I wrote as a standalone novel, perhaps to be revisited in a few years with a sequel, but certainly not intended to launch a series. When the possibility was raised, I was thrilled by the opportunity to spend more time with those characters. But I couldn't foresee a long-running series centered on my werewolves. Having my Pack face an annual threat would get very old, very fast.

The solution was to expand my fictional universe. Not only would I bring in other supernatural types, but I'd spin off to new narrators, weaving a world that widened with every book.

It sounded like a great idea. Little did I realize that by the time *Stolen* came out, my readers would be happily settled in, wanting to follow Elena Michaels and her Pack on countless more adventures. They didn't want me changing narrators, especially not switching to Paige, the overconfident young witch they met in *Stolen*.

Dime Store Magic got off to a bumpy start, but I feel it was actually the book that truly launched the Otherworld as a series. It brought in a fresh crop of readers who were more comfortable with witches than werewolves. Most of the original readers stuck around, too, once they discovered that Paige wasn't as bad as they feared.

By the time I returned to Elena in book six—*Broken*—I could see where I wanted the series to go. I could also see where I wanted it to end. So I began tipping in clues. It was another five books before I launched the end-game with *Waking the Witch*, continuing it into *Spell Bound* and, finally, wrapping it up now with *13*.

While some would say it would have been fitting to return to Elena for this final story, I've always had another plan. Back in *Stolen*, I introduced twelve-year-old Savannah, and I dreamed that the series might run long enough for her to become an adult narrator. And so Savannah grew up in the series, wending her way through the lives of all the other characters, slowly maturing until, with *Waking the Witch*, she was ready to begin the journey that would, with *13*, cement her place as a true "woman" of the Otherworld.

And yet I haven't forgotten where it all began, and with whom. So before we begin the final journey, I'd like to take you for a quick trip into the past, back to Elena, to the prologue that launched the Otherworld series.

BITTEN:
THE PROLOGUE

I have to.

    I've been fighting it all night. I'm going to lose. My battle is as futile as a woman feeling the first pangs of labor and deciding it's an inconvenient time to give birth. Nature wins out. It always does.

It's nearly two A.M., too late for this foolishness, and I need my sleep. Four nights spent cramming to meet a deadline have left me exhausted. It doesn't matter. Patches of skin behind my knees and elbows have been tingling and now begin to burn. My heart beats so fast I have to gulp air. I clench my eyes shut, willing the sensations to stop, but they don't.

Philip is sleeping beside me. He's another reason why I shouldn't leave, sneaking out in the middle of the night again and returning with a torrent of lame excuses. He's working late tomorrow. If I can just wait one more day. My temples begin to throb. The burning sensation in my skin spreads down my arms and legs. The rage forms a tight ball in my gut and threatens to explode.

I've got to get out of here—I don't have a lot of time left.

Philip doesn't stir when I slip from the bed. There's a pile of clothing tucked underneath my dresser so I won't risk the squeaks and groans of opening drawers and closets. I pick up my keys, clasping my fist around them so they don't jangle, ease open the door, and creep into the hallway.

Everything's quiet. The lights seem dimmed, as if over-powered by the emptiness. When I push the elevator button, it creaks out a complaint at being disturbed at so ungodly an hour. The first floor and lobby are equally empty. People who can afford the rent this close to downtown Toronto are comfortably asleep by this time.

My legs itch as well as hurt and I curl my toes to see if the itching stops. It doesn't. I look down at the car keys in my hand. It's too late to drive to a safe place—the itching has crystallized into a sharp burn. Keys in my pocket, I stride onto the streets, looking for a quiet place to Change. As I walk, I monitor the sensation in my legs, tracing its passage to my arms and the back of my neck. Soon. Soon. When my scalp starts to tingle, I know I have walked as far as I can, so I search for an alley. The first one I find has been claimed by two men squeezed together inside a tattered big-screen TV box. The next alley is empty. I hurry to the end and undress quickly behind a barricade of trash bins, hide the clothes under an old newspaper. Then I start the Change.

My skin stretches. The sensation deepens and I try to block the pain. Pain. What a trivial word—agony is better. One doesn't call the sensation of being flayed alive "painful." I inhale deeply and focus my attention on the Change, dropping to the ground before I'm doubled over and forced down. It's never easy—perhaps I'm still too human. In the struggle to keep my thoughts straight, I try to anticipate each phase and move my body into position— head down, on all fours, arms and legs straight, feet and hands flexed, and back arched. My leg muscles knot and convulse. I gasp and strain to relax. Sweat breaks out, pouring off me in streams, but the muscles finally relent and untwist themselves. Next comes the ten seconds of hell that used to make me swear I'd rather die than endure this again. Then it's over.

Changed.

I stretch and blink. When I look around, the world has mutated to an array of colors unknown to the human eye, blacks and browns and grays with subtle shadings that my brain still converts to blues and greens and reds. I lift my nose and inhale. With the Change, my already keen senses sharpen even more. I pick up scents of fresh asphalt and rotting tomatoes and window-pot mums and day-old sweat and a million other things, mixing together in an odor so overwhelming I cough and shake my head. As I turn, I catch distorted fragments of my reflection in a dented trash can. My eyes stare back at me. I curl my lips back and snarl at myself. White fangs flash in the metal.

I am a wolf, a 130-pound wolf with pale blond fur. The only part of me that remains are my eyes, sparking with a cold intelligence and a simmering ferocity that could never be mistaken for anything but human.

I look around, inhaling the scents of the city again. I'm nervous here. It's too close, too confined; it reeks of human spoor. I must be careful. If I'm seen, I'll be mistaken for a dog, a large mixed breed, perhaps a husky and yellow Labrador mix. But even a dog my size is cause for alarm when it's running loose. I head for the back of the laneway and seek a path through the underbelly of the city.

My brain is dulled, disoriented not by my change of form but by the unnaturalness of my surroundings. I can't get my bearings and the first alley I go down turns out to be the one I'd encountered in human form, the one with the two men in the faded Sony box. One of them is awake now. He's tugging the remnants of a filth-encrusted blanket between his fingers as if he can stretch it large enough to cover himself against the cold October night. He looks up and sees me. His eyes widen. He starts to shrink back, then stops himself. He says something. His voice is crooning, the musical, exaggerated tones people use with infants and animals. If I concentrated, I could make out the words, but there's no point. I know what he's saying, some variation of "nice doggy," repeated over and over in a variety of inflections. His hands are outstretched, palms out to ward me off, the physical language contradicting the vocal. Stay back—nice doggy—stay back. And people wonder why animals don't understand them.

I can smell the neglect and waste rising from his body. It smells like weakness, like an aged deer driven to the fringe of the herd, prime pickings for predators. If I were hungry, he'd smell like dinner. Fortunately, I'm not hungry yet, so I don't have to deal with the temptation, the conflict, the revulsion. I snort, condensation trumpeting from my nostrils, then turn and lope back up the alley.

Ahead is a Vietnamese restaurant. The smell of food is embedded in the very wood frame of the building. On a rear addition, an exhaust fan turns slowly, clicking with each revolution as one blade catches the metal screen casing. Below the fan a window is open. Faded sunflower-print curtains billow out in the night breeze. I can hear people inside, a room full of people, grunting and whistling in sleep. I want to see them. I want to stick my muzzle in the open window and look inside. A werewolf can have a lot of fun with a room full of unprotected people.

I start to creep forward, but a sudden crackle and hiss stops me. The hiss softens, then is drowned out by a man's voice, sharp, his words snapped off like icicles. I turn my head each way, radar searching for the source. He's farther down the street. I abandon the restaurant and go to him. We are curious by nature.

He's standing in a three-car parking lot wedged at the end of a narrow passage between buildings. He holds a walkie-talkie to his ear and leans one elbow against a brick wall, casual but not resting. His shoulders are relaxed. His gaze goes nowhere. He is confident in his place, that he has a right to be here and little to fear from the night. The gun dangling from his belt probably helps. He stops talking, jabs a button, and slams the walkie-talkie into its holster. His eyes scan the parking lot once, taking inventory and seeing nothing requiring his attention. Then he heads deeper into the alley maze. This could be amusing. I follow.

My nails click against the pavement. He doesn't notice. I pick up speed, darting around trash bags and empty boxes. Finally, I'm close enough. He hears the steady clicking behind him and stops. I duck behind a Dumpster, peer around the corner. He turns and squints into the darkness. After a second he starts forward. I let him get a few steps away, then resume the pursuit. This time when he stops, I wait one extra second before diving for cover. He lets out a muffled oath. He's seen something—a flash of motion, a shadow flickering, something. His right hand slips to his gun, caressing the metal, then pulling back, as if the reassurance is enough. He hesitates, then looks up and down the alley, realizing he is alone and uncertain what to do about it. He mutters something, then continues walking, quicker this time.

As he walks, his eyes flick from side to side, wariness treading the border of alarm. I inhale deeply, picking up only wisps of fear, enough to make my heart pound but not enough to send my brain spinning out of control. He's safe quarry for a stalking game. He won't run. I can suppress most of my instincts. I can stalk him without killing him. I can suffer the first pangs of hunger without killing him. I can watch him pull his gun without killing him. Yet if he runs, I won't be able to stop myself. That's a temptation I can't fight. If he runs, I *will* chase. If I chase, either he'll kill me or I'll kill him.

As he turns the corner down a connecting alley, he relaxes. All has been silent behind him. I creep from my hiding place, shifting my weight to the back of my foot pads to muffle the sound of my nails. Soon I am only a few feet behind him. I can smell his aftershave, almost masking the natural scent of a long day's work. I can see his white socks appearing and disappearing between his shoes and pant legs. I can hear his breathing, the slight elevation in tempo betraying the fact that he's walking faster than usual. I ease forward, coming close enough that I could lunge if I want to and knock him to the ground before he even thought to reach for his gun. His head jerks up. He knows I'm there. He knows *something* is there. I wonder if he will turn. Does he dare to look, to face something he can't see or hear, but can only sense? His hand slides to his gun, but he doesn't turn. He walks faster. Then he swings back to the safety of the street.

I follow him to the end and observe from the darkness. He strides forward, keys in hand, to a parked cruiser, unlocks it, and hops inside. The car roars and squeals from the curb. I watch the receding taillights and sigh. Game over. I won.

That was nice but it wasn't nearly enough to satisfy me. These city backstreets are too confining. My heart is thudding with unspent excitement. My legs are aching with built-up energy. I must *run*.

A wind gusts from the south, bringing the sharp tang of Lake Ontario with it. I think of heading to the beach, imagine running along the stretch of sand, feeling the icy water slapping against my paws, but it's not safe. If I want to run, I must go to the ravine. It's a long way, but I have little choice unless I plan to skulk around human-smelling alleyways for the rest of the night. I swing to the northwest and begin the journey.

Nearly a half hour later, I'm standing at the crest of a hill. My nose twitches, picking up the vestiges of an illegal leaf fire smoldering in a nearby yard. The wind bristles through my fur, chill, nearly cold, invigorating. Above me, traffic thunders across the overpass. Below is sanctuary, a perfect oasis in the middle of the city. I leap forward, throwing myself off. At last I'm running.

My legs pick up the rhythm before I'm halfway down the ravine. I close my eyes for a second and feel the wind slice across my muzzle. As my paws thump against the hard earth, tiny darts of pain shoot up my legs, but they make me feel alive, like jolting awake after an overlong sleep. The muscles contract and extend in perfect harmony. With each stretch comes an ache and a burst of physical joy. My body is thanking me for the exercise, rewarding me with jolts of near-narcotic adrenaline. The more I run, the lighter I feel, the pain falling free as if my paws are no longer striking the ground. Even as I race along the bottom of the ravine, I feel like I'm still running downhill, gaining energy instead of expending it. I want to run until all the tension in my body flies away, leaving nothing but the sensations of the moment. I couldn't stop if I wanted to. And I don't want to.

Dead leaves crackle under my paws. Somewhere in the forest an owl hoots softly. It has finished its hunting and rests contented, not caring who knows it's around. A rabbit bolts out of a thicket and halfway across my path, then realizes its mistake and zooms back into the undergrowth. I keep running. My heart pounds. Against my rising body heat, the air feels ice-cold, stinging as it storms through my nostrils and into my lungs. I inhale, savoring the shock of it hitting my insides. I'm running too fast to smell anything. Bits of scents flutter through my brain in a jumbled montage that smells of freedom. Unable to resist, I finally skid to a halt, throw my head back, and howl. The music pours up from my chest in a tangible evocation of pure joy. It echoes through the ravine and soars to the moonless sky, letting them all know I'm here. I own this place! When I'm done, I drop my head, panting with exertion. I'm standing there, staring down into a scattering of yellow and red maple leaves, when a sound pierces my self-absorption. It's a growl, a soft, menacing growl. There's a pretender to my throne.

I look up to see a brownish yellow dog standing a few meters away. No, not a dog. My brain takes a second, but it finally recognizes the animal. A coyote. The recognition takes a second because it's unexpected. I've heard there are coyotes in the city, but have never encountered one. The coyote is equally confused. Animals don't know what to make of me. They smell human, but see wolf and, just when they decide their nose is tricking them, they look into my eyes and see human. When I encounter dogs, they either attack or turn tail and run. The coyote does neither. It lifts its muzzle and sniffs the air, then bristles and pulls its lips back in a drawn-out growl. It's half my size, scarcely worth my notice. I let it know this with a lazy "get lost" growl and a shake of my head. The coyote doesn't move. I stare at it. The coyote breaks the gaze-lock first.

I snort, toss my head again, and slowly turn away. I'm halfway turned when a flash of brown fur leaps at my shoulder. Diving to the side, I roll out of the way, then scramble to my feet. The coyote snarls. I give a serious growl, a canine "now you're pissing me off." The coyote stands its ground. It wants a fight. Good.

My fur rises on end, my tail bushing out behind me. I lower my head between my shoulder bones and lay my ears flat. My lips pull back and I feel the snarl tickling up through my throat then reverberating into the night. The coyote doesn't back down. I crouch and I'm about to lunge when something hits me hard in the shoulder, throwing me off balance. I stumble, then twist to face my attacker. A second coyote, gray-brown, hangs from my shoulder, fangs sunk to the bone. With a roar of rage and pain, I buck up and throw my weight to the side.

As the second coyote flies free, the first launches itself at my face. Ducking my head, I catch it in the throat, but my teeth clamp down on fur instead of flesh and it squirms away. It tries to back off for a second lunge, but I leap at it, backing it into a tree. It rears up, trying to get out of my way. I slash for its throat. This time I get my grip. Blood spurts in my mouth, salty and thick. The coyote's mate lands on my back. My legs buckle. Teeth sink into the loose skin beneath my skull. Fresh pain arcs through me. Concentrating hard, I keep my grip on the first coyote's throat. I steady myself, then release it for a split second, just long enough to make the fatal slash and tear. As I pull back, blood sprays into my eyes, blinding me. I swing my head hard, ripping out the coyote's throat. Once I feel it go limp, I toss it aside, then throw myself on the ground and roll over. The coyote on my back yips in surprise and releases its hold. I jump up and turn in the same motion, ready to take this other animal out of the game, but it scrambles up and dives into the brush. With a flash of wire-brush tail, it's gone. I look at the dead coyote. Blood streams from its throat, eagerly lapped up by the dry earth below. A tremor runs through me, like the final shudder of sated lust. I close my eyes and shiver. Not my fault. They attacked me first. The ravine has gone quiet, echoing the calm that floods through me. Not so much as a cricket chirps. The world is dark and silent and sleeping.

I try to examine and clean my wounds, but they are out of reach. I stretch and assess the pain. Two deep cuts, both bleeding only enough to mat my fur. I'll live. I turn and start the trip out of the ravine.

In the alley I Change then yank my clothes on and scurry to the sidewalk like a junkie caught shooting up in the shadows. Frustration fills me. It shouldn't end like this; dirty and furtive, amidst the garbage and filth of the city. It should end in a clearing in the forest, clothes abandoned in some thicket, stretched out naked, feeling the coolness of the earth beneath me and the night breeze tickling my bare skin. I should be falling asleep in the grass, exhausted beyond all thought, with only the miasma of contentedness floating through my mind. And I shouldn't be alone. In my mind, I can see the others, lying around me in the grass. I can hear the familiar snores, the occasional whisper and laugh. I can feel warm skin against mine, a bare foot hooked over my calf, twitching in a dream of running. I can smell them: their sweat, their breath, mingling with the scent of blood, smears from a deer killed in the chase. The image shatters and I am staring into a shop window, seeing nothing but myself reflected back. My chest tightens in a loneliness so deep and so complete I can't breathe.

I turn quickly and lash out at the nearest object. A streetlamp quavers and rings with the blow. Pain sears down my arm. Welcome to reality—changing in alleyways and creeping back to my apartment. I am cursed to live between worlds. On the one side, there is normalcy. On the other, there is a place where I can be what I am with no fear of reprisals, where I can commit murder itself and scarcely raise the eyebrows of those around me, where I am even encouraged to do so to protect the sanctity of that world. But I left and I can't return. I won't return.

As I walk to the apartment, my anger blisters the pavement with every step. A woman curled up under a pile of dirty blankets peers out as I pass and instinctively shrinks back into her nest. As I round the corner, two men step out and size up my prospects as prey. I resist the urge to snarl at them, but just barely. I walk faster and they seem to decide I'm not worth chasing. I shouldn't be here. I should be home in bed, not prowling downtown Toronto at four A.M. A normal woman wouldn't be here. It's yet another reminder that I'm not normal. Not normal. I look down the darkened street and I can read a billet on a telephone post fifty feet off. Not normal. I catch a whiff of fresh bread from a bakery starting production miles away. Not normal. I stop by a storefront, grab a bar over the windows, and flex my biceps. The metal groans in my hand. Not normal. Not normal. I chant the words in my head, flagellating myself with them. The anger only grows.

Outside my apartment door, I stop and inhale deeply. I mustn't wake Philip. And if I do, I mustn't let him see me like this. I don't need a mirror to know what I look like: skin taut, color high, eyes incandescent with the rage that always seems to follow a Change now. Definitely not normal.

When I finally enter the apartment, I hear his measured breathing from the bedroom. Still asleep. I'm nearly to the bathroom when his breathing catches.

"Elena?" His voice is a sleep-stuffed croak.

"Just going to the washroom."

I try to slip past the doorway, but he's sitting up, peering nearsightedly at me. He frowns.

"Fully dressed?" he says.

"I went out."

A moment of silence. He runs a hand through his dark hair and sighs. "It's not safe. Damn it, Elena. We've discussed this. Wake me up and I'll go with you."

"I need to be alone. To think."

"It's not safe."

"I know. I'm sorry."

I creep into the bathroom, spending longer than necessary. I pretend to use the toilet, wash my hands with enough water to fill a Jacuzzi, then find a fingernail that needs elaborate filing attention. When I finally decide Philip has fallen back asleep, I head for the bedroom. The bedside lamp is on. He's propped on his pillow, glasses in place. I hesitate in the doorway. I can't bring myself to cross the threshold, to go and crawl into bed with him. I hate myself for it, but I can't do it. The memory of the night lingers and I feel out of place here.

When I don't move, Philip shifts his legs over the side of the bed and sits up.

"I didn't mean to snap," he says. "I worry. I know you need your freedom and I'm trying—"

He stops and rubs his hand across his mouth. His words slice through me. I know he doesn't mean them as a reprimand, but they are a reminder that I'm screwing this up, that I'm fortunate to have found someone as patient and understanding as Philip, but I'm wearing through that patience at breakneck speed and all I seem capable of doing is standing back and waiting for the final crash.

"I know you need your freedom," he says again. "But there has to be some other way. Maybe you could go out in the morning, early. If you prefer night, we could drive down to the lake. You could walk around. I could sit in the car and keep an eye on you. Maybe I could walk with you. Stay twenty paces behind or something." He manages a wry smile. "Or maybe not. I'd probably get picked up by the cops, the middle-aged guy stalking the beautiful young blonde."

He pauses, then leans forward. "That's your cue, Elena. You're supposed to remind me that forty-one is far from middle-aged."

"We'll work something out," I say.

We can't, of course. I have to run under the cover of night and I have to do it alone. There is no compromise.

As he sits on the edge of the bed, watching me, I know we're doomed. My only hope is to make this relationship so otherwise perfect that Philip might come to overlook our one insurmountable problem. To do that, my first step should be to go to him, crawl in bed, kiss him, and tell him I love him. But I can't. Not tonight. Tonight I'm something else, something he doesn't know and couldn't understand. I don't want to go to him like this.

"I'm not tired," I say. "I might as well stay up. Do you want breakfast?"

He looks at me. Something in his expression falters and I know I've failed—again. But he doesn't say anything. He pulls his smile back in place. "Let's go out. Someplace in this city has to be open this early. We'll drive around until we find it. Drink five cups of coffee and watch the sun come up. Okay?"

I nod, not trusting myself to speak.

"Shower first?" he says. "Or flip for it?"

"You go ahead."

He kisses my cheek as he passes. I wait until I hear the shower running, then head for the kitchen.

Sometimes I get so hungry.

13

BOOKS BY KELLEY ARMSTRONG

13

KELLEY ARMSTRONG

VINTAGE CANADA

VINTAGE CANADA EDITION, 2013

Copyright © 2012 K. L. A. Fricke Inc.

Published in Canada by Vintage Canada, a division of Random House of Canada Limited, Toronto, in 2013. Originally published in hardcover in Canada by Random House Canada, a division of Random House of Canada Limited, in 2012, and simultaneously in the United States of America by Dutton Books, a division of the Penguin Group (USA), New York, and in the United Kingdom by Orbit, a division of the Little, Brown Book Group, a Hachette UK Company, London. Distributed by Random House of Canada Limited.

Vintage Canada with colophon is a registered trademark.

www.randomhouse.ca

This book is a work of fiction. Names, characters, places and incidents either are the product of the author's imagination or are used fictitiously. Any resemblance to actual persons, living or dead, events or locales is entirely coincidental.

LIBRARY AND ARCHIVES CANADA CATALOGUING IN PUBLICATION

Armstrong, Kelley
13 / Kelley Armstrong.

(Women of the otherworld ; 13)

ISBN 978-0-307-35905-6

I. Title. II. Title: Thirteen. III. Series: Armstrong, Kelley. Women of the otherworld ; 13.

PS8551.R7637T55 2013   C813'.6   C2012-902029-X

Text and cover design by Terri Nimmo
Cover images: Buena Vista Images / Getty Images,
© John Evans | Dreamstime.com

Printed and bound in the United States of America

2 4 6 8 9 7 5 3 1

This book goes out to all the readers of the Otherworld.
For those who discovered it with *Bitten* a decade ago,
to those who just discovered it a month ago.
You took a dream and you made it real.
Thank you.

PROLOGUE

Typical guy. You fight through hell—literally, hacking through legions of beasts and zombies and demon-spawn—to sneak home and spend a few stolen minutes with him . . . and he's not there.

Eve grumbled as she paced around the tiny houseboat, multihued blood dripping from her sword. "Where the hell are you, Kris?"

Her angel partner, Trsiel, couldn't cover for her much longer, and she'd really wanted to check in with Kristof. He'd been keeping an eye on the living world for her, watching as his sons and their daughter got caught up in this mess. There really wasn't much a ghostly father could do to help, but the check-ins made them both feel better.

He wasn't at the houseboat, though. Nor was he at the courthouse. Eve had gone there to find the justice building shut down. The guard on duty had muttered something about magical wards needing repair, just regular maintenance. Which was bullshit. Afterlife court was closed because the higher powers were racing around commandeering forces to put out fires both on earth and in the afterlife. But they weren't telling the shades that their world was on the brink of war. No, that wouldn't do at all. Just pretend everything is fine. And if you see a monstrous beast racing down Main Street, it most certainly is not a hellhound that escaped its dimension. Er, but you should probably notify demon control anyway.

I

Eve walked into the bedroom and looked around. Their bed was made, the sheets drawn drum tight. Kristof had grown up with maids and cooks and housekeepers, and though he'd happily shed all those trappings after his death, he kept his world here just as neat and orderly as if he still had staff.

Eve wiped her sword on the gazillion-count Egyptian cotton sheets. For a moment, they were smeared with a satisfying rainbow of blood. Then it evaporated into the white cotton. She sighed and sheathed her sword.

"Fine, I'll leave a proper note."

She conjured paper and a pen.

> *Dear Kris,*
>
> *Heaven and hell are being torn asunder as angels and demons battle themselves and each other. In the living world, supernaturals continue to barrel toward a war between those who want to reveal themselves to humans and those who know such a revelation will destroy all we hold dear. The veil between the realms grows thinner with each passing moment as we plummet toward catastrophe.*
>
> *Hope all is well with you.*
>
> *Hugs and kisses,*
>
> *Eve*

She'd just finished when she heard a patter behind her and wheeled to see . . . nothing.

Another patter sounded on the polished hardwood floor and she looked down to see a white rabbit. It rose on its hind legs.

"Eve Levine," the rabbit squeaked. "Mighty daughter of Balaam, lord of darkness and chaos. I prostrate myself before you."

The rabbit attempted to bow gracefully, but its body wouldn't quite complete the maneuver and it flopped onto its belly. When it looked up at her, its pink eyes glowed with an unearthly light. Eve concentrated hard and a second shape superimposed itself on the rabbit, that of a toadlike lump with jutting fangs and eyes on quivering stalks. She blinked and the bunny reappeared.

"Nice choice of form, imp," she said.

"I considered a kitten, but that seemed unwise when meeting a dark witch."

"Witches don't kill cats. Especially not witches who've been recruited to angelhood." She grasped her sword and lifted it. "Rabbits, however? Rodents. Vermin. Nothing in the manual against that."

The rabbit backed up. "Please, my lady. Balaam has a legion of imps scouring every dimension for you. He is most eager to speak to you."

"Is he? And what could my lord demon father want from me?" She gasped in feigned surprise. "Wait . . . Does it have something to do with this big reveal I've been hearing about?"

"Yes, yes!" The rabbit thumped a back leg with excitement. "You have heard of the glorious plan, then? After centuries of hiding, supernaturals have finally found the willpower to reveal themselves and take their rightful place as rulers of the human world."

"About time."

The rabbit leaped up. "I knew you would agree. You will help your father, yes? You will join the fight here and you will persuade your earthbound daughter to do the same."

"Savannah?" Eve tried to keep her voice calm.

"Of course. She is a mighty spellcaster. Mighty indeed. And very well connected in the supernatural world. Lord Balaam has approached her himself, but she has refused his generous offer."

"Balaam went *near* my—" Eve stopped short as her sword glowed blue, infused with her fury. But the rabbit-imp didn't seem to notice. She took a deep, steadying breath.

"Foolish girl. Of course I'll speak to her. She listens to her mother. First, though, you'll need to tell me everything you know about my father's plans, so I can properly explain them to her."

The rabbit told her everything and she thanked it most graciously . . . then lopped off its head, which flew into the hall at the very moment the houseboat door opened. A tall, broad-shouldered figure filled the doorway. As Kristof Nast stepped in, the rabbit's head bounced off his polished Italian loafers.

"Eve?" he said, peering at his feet as she walked into the main cabin. Then he saw her and smiled. "If there are decapitated rabbit heads flying, there's only one explanation. Eve is back." He stopped as he saw her expression. "What's wrong?"

"It's Savannah," she said. "She's in trouble. Well, bigger trouble. We need to—"

Light flashed. Kristof disappeared. The houseboat evaporated and Eve found herself in another dimension, surrounded by misshapen beasts, Trsiel at her side, her sword still in hand.

"Oh, hell," she muttered as the beasts charged.

I led my half brother Bryce away from the rubble of the exploded lab, ignoring his protests, and ignoring Adam, who was sticking close and wincing every time Bryce coughed. I couldn't blame Adam for worrying. The Supernatural Liberation Movement had injected Bryce with something called a "vaccine against mortality," which sounded lovely, until you figured out that meant it contained DNA from vampires, zombies, and god only knows what other creatures the gang had rounded up for their experiments.

So I really didn't want to catch whatever Bryce had either. Before we'd escaped, the woman who'd injected him had suggested it was transmittable. I had to trust they weren't crazy enough to make it *easily* transmittable. And if they were? Well, then, I was already screwed. The only way out of the lab had been to drop into a pit of water connected to an underground sewer. Bryce was so weak he'd almost drowned and I'd had to help him. I'd stopped short of giving him mouth-to-mouth when he woke on his own, but we'd had plenty of contact. So I could be infected. But that was a concern for later. Right now, I was just happy to have survived, especially when the whole place had come down on our heads as the liberation movement blew up their own lab.

I'd never been so glad to be tramping—wet, smelly and dirty—down a New Orleans alleyway. Or to see Jeremy

5

Danvers, the werewolf Alpha, or Jaime Vegas, his necromancer girlfriend. Or Adam. Most of all Adam.

Bryce might be my half brother, but I've known Adam since I was twelve. Bryce? Well, let's just say we aren't close.

"We'll turn onto the road up here," Jeremy said. He was scouting the way, limping from the blast. "We should be far enough from—"

He stopped and tilted his head, werewolf hearing picking up something we couldn't. When he frowned, Adam moved up beside him and whispered, "Trouble?"

"I can hear a police radio. They're looking for two men and a woman seen leaving the blast site."

"Two guys covered in dust and bruises?" Adam said. "And a girl who looks like she went swimming in a sewer?"

Jeremy nodded.

I looked down at my soaked clothing. The only unscathed one was Jaime, who'd been blocks away when the building went up.

Jeremy said, "Anita Barrington set off an alarm, meaning there will be members of the reveal movement looking for all of us. You're going to need to hole up until Jaime finds us clean clothing. I'll go with her while she does."

"I'll be—" Jaime began, then cut herself short. As a necromancer, she had no innate defensive skills. As a fortyseven-year-old on the celebrity circuit, she didn't have any acquired ones either: All she usually had to deal with were hecklers. "I need backup, but I don't think it should be you," she finally said to Jeremy. "Bryce needs a guard with superhearing and superstrength. I just need someone to watch my back. Savannah can do that. She isn't battered and bruised. Her jeans are black and won't look wet from a distance."

Jaime gave me her jacket—a cute leather one that we'd bought on a trip to Milan. It was a little short—she's fivefive and I'm nearly seven inches taller—so on me it looked fashionably cropped. With the help of her brush and scarf, we tied my wet hair back and I stopped looking like a drowned rat, even if my sneakers sloshed with every step.

We found the guys a quiet spot to wait. Then we set off.

The Supernatural Liberation Movement. I gave them a vowel and called them SLAM. Their mission was to reveal the existence of supernaturals to the human world. There was a very good reason we hadn't done this already—because it was stupid. Every time the world found out about us, heads rolled—our heads. Even if we could argue that this wasn't the Middle Ages anymore, we weren't just different in gender, skin color, religion, sexual orientation, or any other equality issue. We had powers. Often deadly powers that gave us an advantage over humans. You can bet your ass we wouldn't be welcomed with open arms . . . except maybe by military research facilities.

So why was this movement gaining traction? First, the majority of supernaturals are not as tuned in to our world as I am. Through the Cabals and my connection to the interracial council, I had the advantage of seeing things from a global and historical perspective. Second, there are a lot of disaffected supernaturals out there, especially young ones who don't understand why the hell they shouldn't flaunt their abilities. For most of my twenty-one years, I'd have agreed with them—I had power, so I used it. All these young supernaturals needed was a man with a plan. And they found him in Giles Reyes—AKA Gilles de Rais—a charismatic leader who'd convinced them that a bunch of unusual events in our world—including me, a sorcerer/witch hybrid—fulfilled some kind of prophecy that declared it was time for the big reveal. It didn't hurt that Giles claimed he was really a fifteenth-century French nobleman who'd stumbled on immortality and had, after centuries of experimentation, found a way to grant it to all his followers. That was the "vaccine" he'd given Bryce. I thought of my brother, who was ready to keel over. Apparently it hadn't quite been perfected yet.

Now, because of us, Giles's vaccine had been destroyed before it *could* be perfected. He was going be pissed. I really wished I could stay to see that, but we had places to go, things to do, a world to save.

When police cars zipped past, sirens wailing, Jaime caught my arm and gestured wildly, laughing, as if sharing a juicy bit of gossip.

We were nearly to the commercial district when a police cruiser whipped around the corner, cut us off, and slammed on the brakes.

"Play it cool," Jaime whispered.

I hadn't planned to do anything else.

"Hey, guys," Jaime said as the officers—a slender, middle-aged woman and a stocky young patrolman—climbed out of the car. "We heard the sirens. What's going on?"

"A bomb was detonated a few blocks over."

"Seriously?" Jaime's eyes rounded as she scanned the rooftops. "Where? I have a blog, and if I could get photos, that would be—"

"Um, *bomb,* Jaime?" I cut in. "Normal people run the other way."

"Because normal people don't have a Twitter feed with a hundred thousand followers." She took out her cell phone and propped up her shades. "Do you know the address? I can foursquare it now, then tweet photos after we get there."

"We are not going to a bomb site—we are going to your interview." I turned to the officers, mouthed, "Hollywood," and rolled my eyes.

"Can we see some identification?" the woman asked.

"Absolutely," Jaime chirped, then giggled. "But the date of birth is between us, right?"

Gotta say this—Jaime has the ditzy C-lister routine down pat. The male officer seemed ready to hop back into the car, but his partner insisted on the ID.

Jaime showed her cards and offered to send autographed eight-by-tens. She explained who she was—Jaime Vegas, renowned spiritualist, as formerly seen on *The Keni Bales Show* and more. The male cop said he'd heard of her and that his sister-in-law would love a signed photo.

"That's . . . an interesting way of making a living," said the female officer—Medina, according to her badge. "You're free to go on to your interview, Ms. Vegas. It's your friend here who needs to come with us."

"What?" Jaime screeched. "No. She's not my friend. I mean, yes, of course you are, dear." A pat on my arm. "But she's my publicist. I need her for the interview."

"Then you'll have to reschedule, because she's coming with us. She was seen entering the bombed building before the blast, then leaving it shortly after."

"Wouldn't I need to have left *before* the bomb, considering I'm still alive?"

Medina's look warned me not to be a smart ass. "We just want to speak to you."

"Then speak here."

"Miss, we have multiple eyewitness reports. That's enough to arrest you on, but we'd like to give you the chance to talk to us first. Provide some insight into your co-conspirators."

"Co-conspirators?" I waved at Jaime. "This is the only person I've been conspiring with today. Does she look like a criminal mastermind?"

"You were seen in the company of two men."

"Two?" Jaime swatted my arm. "Oh my God, you're so selfish."

"What did these guys look like?" I asked.

The officers exchanged a look. The woman cleared her throat. "We have preliminary descriptions, but we're hoping you can add to those. It will certainly help your situation if you can."

In other words, the only "description" they had was the one Jeremy heard—two guys covered in mortar dust. Whatever they had on me was bullshit. Yes, I'd been inside that building, but I'd gone in through the roof, meaning no one had seen me enter. I'd exited through the sewer. I had a feeling their "witnesses" were members of SLAM.

"If anyone saw me near this building, there's an explanation. But I'll come downtown if that helps." I turned to Jaime. "You go on, do your interview—"

"Absolutely not," she said. "This young woman is my publicist, and you can't treat her like a terrorist. I came here to check out venues for a possible charity appearance. That's right—charity. New Orleans has been through hell, and if you want tourists coming back, you can't arrest them on the street . . ."

She continued her diva rant as Medina started leading me toward the cruiser.

"It's okay," I said to Jaime, trying to shut her up. "You stay here. Let Adam know I've been delayed. He'll have to postpone the interview. I won't be long and—"

"Take your hands off her!" Jaime yelled at the cop.

"She's not touching me," I said. "Listen, Jaime—"

She aimed a kick at Medina's shins. It didn't come close. Intentionally so—the one thing Jaime can do is kick with the precision of a stiletto-clad kung-fu artist.

The younger officer—Holland—grabbed her. "Cut that out," he said. "Or you'll be going to the station with her."

Jaime wrenched free. "Don't you dare lay your hands on me!" She feigned another kick and lost her balance, stumbling. "You tripped me!"

"Get her in the car, too," Medina said.

As Holland muscled her toward the car, Jaime put up

little resistance. Once in the backseat, she slid over, making room for me.

"What the hell?" I whispered as Medina shut the door.

"You're my backup and I'm yours," she said. "If they take one, they take both."

While I appreciated the support, I'd rather she made sure Jeremy and Adam got Bryce to a doctor. Before I could protest, the officers climbed into the front seat and we pulled away. Jaime handed me her cell and whispered, "Call Paige."

I didn't. I called Lucas. After he'd answered, I leaned into the gap between the front seats.

"I'm calling Jaime's manager to cancel the interview. That's okay, right?"

Medina looked ready to say no, but her partner nodded. "Just keep it short."

Lucas was waiting patiently, having realized from my comment to Medina that something was up. "Hey," I said to him. "Can you call Adam at the *Daily* and postpone that interview and photo shoot. Jaime and I . . . we kinda got ourselves arrested. Adam's waiting for us with the photographer. Bryce something-or-other."

"Dare I ask what's going on?"

"Mmm, better not. Seems someone thought they saw me near an explosion, which is total bullshit. I've been babysitting—" I cast a quick glance at Jaime, who faked a scowl. "Um, keeping Jaime company. Anyway, it's a big misunderstanding that I'm sure will amuse everyone at the office later. I'm hoping this will be cleared up soon, but tell Adam to wait no more than thirty minutes. I know he has important things to do."

"All right." Lucas paused, then asked, "Are you both okay?"

"We're fine. We didn't embarrass ourselves too badly, so no emergency intervention required."

Another silence on his end.

"Really," I said.

Medina twisted to look back at me. "A *short* call."

"Gotta go," I said.

"All right. Let me know if you need legal help."

"I'm sure we won't. It's just questioning."

Medina signaled for me to cut it off. I said good-bye and handed the phone back to Jaime.

CHAPTER 2

As we drove out of the city, I realized these were state cops. I suppose I should have noticed sooner. It seemed odd for an outside department to be involved in a big-city case, but maybe even years after Katrina, New Orleans was still in a state of bureaucratic upheaval.

We pulled into a small station on a regional road surrounded by forest and swamp. Medina got out of the car as Holland made a note in his book. She opened my door. As I started to climb out, Holland opened Jaime's door, then stopped dead.

"What's that?" he said.

I turned to see some kind of black powder smeared on my seat.

"Damn it," I muttered. "Did I sit in that?"

I went to wipe off my butt, but Medina grabbed my hands and yanked me into position so fast I barely had time to snap, "Hey!" before I stood spread eagled against the cruiser.

Jaime yelped, genuine now, and tried to get out, but Holland pushed her back in and slammed the door.

"Is that what it looks like?" he asked as Medina patted me down. "Something from the bomb?"

"Could be," she said.

It wasn't. Whatever ripped that building apart wasn't some low-grade blasting powder. But showing any familiarity with what had caused the explosion—or bombs in general—seemed unwise.

Medina patted my back pockets.

"Only thing in there is my wallet," I said. "But go ahead and check."

She pulled out the wallet. Then she reached into the other back pocket, stopped, and waved Holland over.

"What?" I said.

I tried to twist and look, but she slammed me against the car again. I craned to see, being careful not to move anything but my head. She was holding a folded piece of paper and a crushed cardboard tube sprinkled with black powder.

"That wasn't—"

She shoved me against the car again, then unfolded the paper. Holland leaned over to read it. He swore. His gaze lifted to mine, lip curled in disgust. "So you knew nothing about the bombing? Then why is the address in your pocket?"

"What? No. That wasn't in my pocket. Not the paper or that powder. Look at my wallet. Notice anything odd? It's soaked. Like my pocket. That paper and tube are dry, meaning it couldn't have been in there."

"Okay, so how did you get wet?" Holland asked.

"I . . . it's kind of embarrassing, okay? I fell in a puddle. Landed on my ass."

"Yes, that is embarrassing," Medina said. "But not as embarrassing as the truth."

"What do you mean?"

"Your wallet was in your back pocket. It probably fell into the toilet. I lost a cell phone that way once."

"No, my jeans are soaked—"

"Then I guess that bathroom accident was even more embarrassing. Or maybe you put these things in your pocket after you got them wet."

"I've been sitting on them, in wet jeans—they'd at least be damp!"

Medina gave me another shove, hard enough that my chin hit the car. My teeth caught my tongue and I tasted blood.

Holland took over, holding me still as Medina tugged my ID from my damp wallet.

"Savannah Levine," she said. "You're under arrest for . . ."

Medina arrested Jaime, too, despite the fact that they had no evidence to suggest she was involved. That's when I really knew this wasn't kosher, especially when Holland seemed surprised by Medina's decision. He didn't argue. She was the senior partner. But when we got inside and someone yelled that there was trouble with a guy in the holding cell, Holland volunteered to help and got out of there fast.

Medina called over a second officer, a guy barely old enough to be shaving. He took charge of Jaime, who hadn't said a word since we left the car. When I glanced at her now, she was blinking hard, eyes unfocused.

"Jaime?" I said.

She managed a weak smile. "I'm okay."

She didn't look okay. The officer had led her halfway down the hall when I heard a clatter and turned to see her doubled over, emptying her stomach onto the linoleum tiles.

"Oh, God," she said. "I can't believe I did that." Her voice came out thick, words slurred.

"Partying a little early today, were you?" Medina said.

"Wh-what?" Jaime struggled to look up at her, eyes refusing to focus.

I tried to get to Jaime, but Medina yanked me back. "Your friend is fine. She just needs to lay off the booze." She called to the young officer, "She's one of those Hollywood types. Probably spent the night on Bourbon Street."

"What?" I said. "No, we—"

"Should I send the mug shot to the tabloids?" the young officer asked with a grin.

"No, that's exactly what these people want. There's no such thing as bad publicity. I'll handle the processing. Just stick her in the drunk tank."

"Is that the charge then? Public drunkenness? For both of them?"

Medina nodded. I opened my mouth, but her look made me shut it.

She pushed me into the next open doorway and shut the door behind us as the other officer led Jaime to the cells.

"What the hell is going on?" I said, spinning on Medina. "First you question me about a bombing. Then you arrest me for it. Now you've switched to public drunkenness?"

"Would you rather the bomb charge?"

"There is no bomb charge. You—"

"There still might be."

She cuffed me to a chair, then sat across from me and took out her cell phone. After a minute, I realized the beeps I heard weren't from texting or e-mailing—she was playing a game.

I yanked on the chair. "You aren't processing me."

"Do you want me to?"

Part of me wanted to insist she charge me, just to see if she would, so I could confirm what I suspected was happening. But the rest of me said that was a very stupid idea.

So I seethed and writhed inside while she played her game.

"I want to make a phone call," I finally said.

"You did."

"That wasn't my official call. You're holding me, so I'm entitled to—"

"You're entitled to a call if I charge you."

I closed my eyes and concentrated. Find the core of stillness, then focus all my energy on casting—

"I wouldn't do that if I were you," Medina said.

"Do what?"

"Whatever you're doing."

I leaned forward. "And what would that be?" I met her gaze. "Oh, wait . . . You know, don't you?"

"Yes, I do."

Just as I suspected. "Who are you working for? The moronic liberation movement that bombed their own building?"

Her head jerked up. "Are you accusing me of being a terrorist, Ms. Levine?"

"Is that what you think they are? Good, then we're on the same page. Either way, holding me is a very bad idea. I'd suggest you reconsider and let me cut you a deal with the Cortezes."

Her eyes narrowed. "Are you trying to bribe me?"

"If that's what it takes."

She leaped up and slammed me and my chair against the wall. As she shoved, she grabbed my shoulder, fingers digging in as she leaned down to my face.

"I don't know who the hell these Cortezes are, but I can promise you that I'm not afraid of any gang. They can't buy me and they can't threaten me. Neither can you. I was giving you a break, Ms. Levine. Holding you on a lesser charge until I could consult with my superiors on the evidence we found in your back pocket. But if you want that charge—"

"No. I don't. I—I made a mistake."

"A very big mistake." She shoved me again, the chair clattering against the wall. "And it's not going to help your case. Since you don't seem to like it here, let's see if you prefer being in the drunk tank with your friend."

CHAPTER 3

I found Jaime curled up, shivering and pale, in a corner of the holding cell. I tried to rouse her, but she wouldn't open her eyes. When I said I was going to call a guard, she managed to murmur, "No. Don't . . . cause more trouble. Just give . . . minute. Food . . . poisoning."

I glanced around. The cell looked like . . . well, a cell. About eight by eight feet. A typical spot in a small station for holding people awaiting charges or the onset of sobriety. From the looks of it, more cells were needed. This one now had five occupants. Like Jaime, two were lying on the floor. Drunk, I guessed. At least they were quiet.

There was one bed, currently occupied by a chick with the kind of tattoos that scream "I got this once when I was really drunk." Except that, judging by the quantity, it was more than once. A lot more, which might suggest it was complete lack of taste rather than serial-drunken stupidity. Her blond hair was frizzled at the ends, as if she'd overused her straightening iron. She wore cutoffs with several rolls of pitted cellulite hanging out below. Her upper half hung too, tank top screaming for a bra.

In short, she was not the sort of person I was in the mood to deal with nicely. Still, I tried.

"Hey," I said. "My friend's really sick. Do you think she could take the bunk?"

"Go to hell, you skinny-assed bitch."

All the frustration of the last hour flared and when I grabbed her, my hands glowed white.

The woman shrieked. "You're burning me. You bitch, you're—"

I pushed her off the bed and she landed on the floor, half on top of an elderly homeless woman. I apologized to the old woman, but she seemed beyond hearing me.

The biker chick scrambled up and charged. I raised my fists. She put out her claws, scratching and spitting and yowling. A blow to the stomach stopped her before I got my hair pulled. When she staggered back, I downed her with a kick.

"You're going to regret this," she whined from the floor. "I know people."

"Men, you mean. Big, ugly men who ride big, ugly bikes." I loomed above her. "Word of advice? If you're going to trash-talk, get your ass off the bitch seat and learn to fight for yourself."

She whined and hissed a little more, then shut up. Beside her, the old woman straightened.

"Did someone call a lawyer?" she asked.

I turned to the bars. No one was there.

"Is that your lawyer?" she said. "Can he help me? I need to get out of here."

I followed the old woman's gaze to the middle of the room. Still no one.

Jaime moaned. I hurried over and helped her to the cot. Before she lay down, she glanced at it.

"I'm not sure I want to touch that," she said.

"You're washable," I said. "But on second thought . . ."

I pulled off my jacket and wadded it up for a pillow, so her hair wouldn't connect with whatever critters might be living on the mattress.

"Thanks," she said. "How much trouble are we in?"

I crouched beside her. "We haven't been charged with the bombing, but . . . something's fishy. That powder and note weren't mine, obviously. Neither of us was processed. Neither of us has been charged. But we're locked up."

"Medina works for someone," Jaime said, her words coming slow, as if it hurt to speak. "The movement or a Cabal."

"I thought so, too. I called her on it, and now she's convinced I tried to threaten her with a gang called the Cortezes."

"Maybe, but—"

She stopped and cocked her head. A frown. Then she peered around the cell and at the empty hall beyond.

"Ghost?" I said.

"I'm . . . not sure. I thought I heard . . ." She trailed off, shook her head, then paled, as if the movement made her stomach churn. "Oh, God. What did I eat?"

"Just a pastry and a coffee hours ago."

"A latte. Must have been the milk. I feel like—"

"Did someone call a lawyer?" the old woman warbled again.

I turned to see her staring at an empty spot with a look I recognized from all my years hanging around Jaime. She was seeing a ghost. It happened sometimes with the mentally ill.

"Is it my father?" I said to Jaime. "Is that who you think you heard?"

She nodded, eyes still closed.

"Can you look? See if he's here?"

A faint, pained smile. "If it was your dad, I'd hear him loud and clear. Kristof Nast does not allow himself to be ignored. He took off to hunt for you after the explosion." She frowned and opened her eyes. "I didn't hear back from him—"

She blinked, then stared at the same empty spot as the old woman.

"Oh," she said.

"He's there?"

"Yes, but . . . faint. Something's wrong." She pushed up and struggled to listen. Then another, "Oh."

"What's he saying?" I asked.

"He's barely coming through. Maybe because I'm sick."

Jaime tried her best to communicate, with no success. When she started getting frustrated, I stopped her and said, "You rest. I may have a second avenue of contact today."

I nodded at the old woman, who'd been following our efforts placidly.

"Mmm, not sure that's such a good idea," Jaime said. "She's crazy enough to see ghosts, but that also means she's not exactly coherent."

"Well, no offense, but you're not doing so hot yourself. Rest and I'll see what I can get."

The biker chick scuttled away as I sat down beside the old woman.

"Are you going to get me out of here?" the old woman said, staring up at the blank space above us.

"You can see him, right?" I said.

She nodded.

"Good," I said. "So now he's going to talk and you're going to tell me what he says."

"I want out."

"Which he'll do, as soon as you've helped me talk to him."

She turned her dark eyes to me. "So you can't hear him?"

"No."

She smiled. "Then I have him all to myself." She looked up and said, "Get me out of here."

My father managed to trick her into passing on a message, telling me to demand to call Lucas, but after that, she caught on. She whined at him that she wasn't stupid and he was supposed to help her, with me. Then she started to wail.

"Ignore her," Jaime croaked as I tried to calm the old woman. "I can hear him better now."

I got up and went over to Jaime. My father must have followed, because the woman let out a scream of frustrated rage. She flung her hands out and shouted something I didn't catch.

Then she smiled and lowered herself to the floor and started mumbling to herself.

"Shit," Jaime muttered. "She's not crazy. Or not only crazy. She's a necromancer."

"What?"

"She just banished your father."

"Without vervain?"

"She used a nastier method. One I've never learned because I don't want to be tempted to use it. It knocks a spirit through dimensions."

"Shit!" I leaped to my feet and looked around.

"Don't worry, Savannah. Your dad will find his way back. Or your mom will track him down."

"Can you let her know?"

She shook her head. "Not now. When she's on assignment, I can't call."

I wanted to argue that this was an emergency, but I trusted Jaime wouldn't let my father suffer unnecessarily. Okay, she might, but only if my mother wouldn't find out about it, which in this case, she eventually would.

"All right," I said. "My father was telling me to go ahead and demand my phone call. I'm not sure I like the sounds of that, but . . ."

"He wouldn't suggest that if it wasn't safe. So go ahead. Try to flag someone down."

The hall had been empty since I'd arrived. I walked over and leaned against the bars, but couldn't see anything. I started casting a sensing spell, then stopped. I shouldn't automatically reach for a magical solution when mundane methods would do the job. Now that I was the spell-powered equivalent of a twelve-year-old, I had to conserve all the juice I had. And, I suppose, it was a good rule in general.

So I called for a guard. When no one answered, I shouted. When still no one came, I started the sensing spell again. Stopped again. Walked over to Jaime.

"Do you have a mirror?" I asked.

"They took my purse and patted me down."

I stood there, waiting, until she sighed and pulled a necklace from under her blouse. It was a locket. I popped it open. On one side was a tiny picture of Jeremy. On the other, a mirror.

I shook my head. "With some people, it's hidden weapons. With you, mirrors."

She pulled a face.

"Watch it," I said. "Or I'll make you look in it."

"No, thank you," she muttered, raking her fingers through her tangled hair.

I angled the mirror to look both ways down the hall.

"I see a desk," I said. "But it's empty. Looks like pages scattered on the floor."

"Make a ruckus. You're good at that."

I yelled again for a guard. Then I grabbed Jaime's shoes and clanged the bars like a B-movie convict.

I looked again at those dropped pages—someone had left in a hurry. I remembered the biker chick shrieking during our fight. Then the old woman screaming when my father ignored her. If no one had come for that, they sure as hell weren't coming for my clanging.

I crouched and studied the lock.

"You gonna pick that with your hairpin, sweetheart?" the biker chick sneered.

"No, I'm going to pick it with hers."

I walked over to Jaime and held out a hand. She plucked two from her hair.

"See, you do come ready for trouble," I said. "Mirrors, stilettos, hairpins. I get the feeling you've been in jail before."

She flipped me off as she lay back on the cot.

I hunkered down by the lock again. Of course, there is no way in hell you can escape a jail cell with a hairpin. But it made a good cover story while I worked at the door with an unlock spell.

Two days ago I'd been told—by some mysterious other-world entity—that my spells weren't actually gone. My power supply had just been cranked way down. Like a neophyte witch, I could build power through practice, and so I'd been practicing.

I'd been able to successfully cast simple things like a light ball. And that flare of magic with the biker chick had reinforced something I'd experienced once before—that if I tapped deep enough into my power, I could cast on emotion, without even reciting a spell. That was serious mojo. If this temporary power drain meant I could reach that level someday, then it was worth it. But right now, I needed all the juice I could get. I was determined to open this door, however much time and concentration it took. It took a lot. Twenty minutes later I heard a little *click*.

"Finally."

I stood and pulled on the door. It moved about a quarter inch then caught, something inside grinding.

"You can't open a cell with a hairpin, you stupid twat," the biker chick said.

I turned to snarl at her, then gathered that frustrated anger and flung it at the door instead. Another click. When I yanked, it gave a little more, but still wouldn't open.

"You're getting there," said a voice behind me.

I turned to see Jaime, wobbling slightly. She squeezed my shoulder.

"You're getting it. Just keep—"

The door at the end of the hall flew open, a cacophony of shouts blasting through before it closed again. Silence. Then the thud of heavy boots.

A moment later, a man came into view. He looked like a

stereotypical cop, right down to the mustache and lantern jaw. He wasn't wearing a uniform, though. He was wearing blood.

Bare chested. Skin dappled with red. More blood dripping from his hands, which were dangling at his sides, his fingers stubby, nails thickened to claws.

There's not much I'll back away from. A werewolf partway into his Change is one of those things.

CHAPTER 4

I backed up into Jaime, my arms wide to shield her. She started around me, her chin going up, mouth firm, lower lip quivering slightly.

"I—I can handle this," she said.

"Jaime . . ."

"He won't touch me. I'm the Alpha's . . ." Her voice dipped, uncertain, then came back stronger. "I'm the Alpha's mate. He wouldn't dare touch me."

"Under normal circumstances, I'd agree. But I don't think this guy cares."

The werewolf stopped in front of the cell. If those partially changed hands didn't confirm something was wrong, his eyes did. Pupils so huge his eyes seemed black. The whites suffused with red. His breathing came hard, ragged.

"Drugged," Jaime whispered. "Who's stupid enough to drug a—?"

"Hello, ladies," the werewolf said, his voice a deep rumble, almost a growl, as if his vocal cords were changing, too. So was his face—nothing drastic, but the planes and angles were off-kilter, making him look disfigured.

"Wh-what's wrong with him?" the biker chick quavered.

The woman who'd been silent so far—a thirtyish blonde in a suit jacket and slacks—had risen to her feet. "Shut up," she hissed to the biker chick.

"Don't we have some pretty ladies here," he said, his gaze tripping over Jaime and me. "Pretty ladies in a cage."

"Which is locked," I said. "If you want in, you'll need to get the key."

"Yes." Jaime stepped closer to the bars and raked back her hair. "If you want to visit us, you need to find the key."

"Are you fucking—?" the biker chick screeched to a stop. Frozen. Caught in a binding spell.

"Nice one," Jaime whispered.

"That wasn't me."

The blonde stepped up beside Jaime and flicked open the top button on her blouse. "Go find the key," she said to the werewolf. "Then we can play."

He inhaled, nostrils flaring, then lumbered off.

When he was gone, the blonde whispered, "You know what he is?"

"Canis lupus," I said. "Human variety."

"And you are?"

"Savannah Levine."

"Sav—?" Her eyes widened. Then she nodded. "Good."

"Not so good. My mojo is on the fritz, so we're going to need to rely on you."

"What about . . . ?" she looked at Jaime. "Wait. I know you. You're—"

"Good on a stage," Jaime said. "Lousy in a fight. We've got another necro." She nodded at the old woman. "And I'm guessing one reasonably innocent bystander." A glance at the biker chick, now huddled on the floor.

"Keiran Courville," the blonde said. "My mojo's not much better. Been sick as a dog since they brought me in. Drugged, I think."

"Shit." I looked at Jaime. Not food poisoning after all. Either Medina or Holland must have injected her somehow. My money was on Medina.

So we had four supernaturals in a cage, three probably drugged. A drugged werewolf on the loose. What the hell was going on?

"You ladies fighting over me already?" a voice asked.

We all flinched as the werewolf sauntered back into view.

"You need a *key*," I said.

"Fuck the key—can't be bothered. I want in now."

He grabbed the door and yanked, neck tendons bulging, and the door snapped open.

I stepped in front of Jaime.

"Okay, big guy," I said. "You know you're in serious shit right now. That blood tells me someone's dead. And considering this is a police station, that someone is a cop, meaning—"

He grabbed me by the shirtfront. "You like to use that mouth, bitch? I'll show you where you can use it."

"Let me guess?" I said. "Here?"

I kneed him in the groin. Yes, it's a cheap shot, but I wasn't really concerned with fighting fair right now. Or with preserving his ability to procreate.

He dropped me on my ass. And he should have dropped himself, because it was a helluva blow. But he only snorted, then came at me as I scooted back.

"Hey, handsome," Jaime called. "Forget the little girl. I've got something you want."

He looked from me to her, then lumbered toward her. Keiran hit him with an energy bolt.

"What was that?" the biker chick screeched as the werewolf fell back, a scorched spot on his side.

I launched a fire ball—well, more like a firefly—but my aim was good and it hit him in the eye. He bellowed louder than he had when I'd gotten his crotch.

That shot of rage jump-started his stalled Change. His brow and jaw receded, mouth and nose jutting. Thick, black hair sprouted from his chest and back.

"What the hell?" the biker chick shrieked. "What the fucking hell?"

"Is that a werewolf?" the old necromancer said. "I've never seen a werewolf."

He charged her. I cast a binding spell. It didn't work. Keiran launched something and maybe it did work, but it didn't stop him. Didn't even slow him down. He grabbed the old woman by the hair and wrenched. Her neck snapped. He threw her across the cell. She hit the wall and collapsed like a rag doll.

The biker chick started to scream. Really scream. A high-pitched wail that caught the werewolf's attention like the squeal of a rabbit. He turned on her.

I tried another binding spell. When it failed again, I grabbed Jaime and shoved her toward the broken cell door, waving for Keiran to follow.

As we tumbled out into the hall, Jaime glanced back. Her eyes widened and she stopped. I pushed her along the hall, and she didn't struggle, just wrenched her gaze from the screaming woman and the werewolf and didn't look back again.

I didn't look back at all. Didn't dare, because if I did, I might go back and try to save her. If I tried, I'd lose the opportunity to get us out of there. So I didn't.

The biker chick didn't scream for long.

The door into the main part of the station flew open. I stopped short, arms flying out to keep the others back.

Medina shot inside, followed by Holland. Both were staring over their shoulders. Medina shut the door quietly, then leaned her forehead against it.

Holland's gaze stayed fixed on the door. His hands fluttered in front of his chest. It took a second to realize what he was doing. Crossing himself.

"It's okay, Rory," Medina murmured, face still against the door. "We're safe now."

Holland kept crossing himself and closed his eyes. I motioned for Jaime and Keiran to be still, then crept forward, and slid the gun from Holland's holster. I had it halfway out before he noticed. He grabbed for it, but I yanked it free. Medina's head snapped up. She went for her own weapon, but her holster was empty. Her lips parted in a curse.

When Holland opened his mouth, I motioned for silence, using the gun for emphasis. I waved for Medina to open the door. She shook her head.

I stepped forward and whispered, "Open the goddamned door or I'll—"

"I can't."

Jaime shouldered past, grabbed the handle and pulled. The door didn't budge.

"It's a time lock," Medina said. "It'll open in a few minutes. But you . . . you . . ."

"You don't want to go out there," Holland whispered.

Medina nodded. "We'll be safe in here. Just—"

A sickening crunch from inside the cell. Then a grunt. Medina went still, then snatched the gun from my hands and headed for the holding cell.

I could have warned her. But I figured she already knew something was going on. And she *was* a cop. Serve and protect the taxpayers. I was a taxpayer.

In front of the cell, she stopped dead.

"Oh my God. Oh my God."

A grunt. A snort. I ran for Medina. Didn't mean to. Jaime and Keiran even tried to grab me. I ran anyway.

The werewolf was on all fours, back humped, fur still sparse, a nightmare version of a wolf.

The biker chick was dead. And . . . no longer in one piece.

The wolf was over her, bloody froth and other bits dripping from his jaws. He growled, fur on end, his drug-hazed eyes fixed on Medina.

"Shoot him," I whispered.

"The—the bullets. They aren't . . ." She swallowed. "They aren't silver."

"Oh, for God's sake." I reached for the gun.

She yanked it away from me and stumbled back. "No, you'll only antagonize—"

The wolf ran for the cell door and I slammed it shut. It was broken and wouldn't lock, but the beast lacked hands, meaning sliding it open would be imposs—

The wolf hit the door. The whole wall shuddered. He took a bar in his jaws and yanked.

"The gun," I said, wheeling. "Give me—"

Medina started to run toward the time-locked door. I caught her by the leg. She went down. The gun flew. She twisted, trying to throw me off as the wolf—

Two staccato shots. I looked back in time to see the wolf collapse. Jaime stood there, gun clutched in her hands.

"I see Jeremy's lessons are paying off," I said as I got to my feet.

"When you're the Alpha's girlfriend, you need to know how to stop those guys."

She was spelling it out for Medina's benefit, putting a little extra emphasis on "Alpha" and sliding her gaze the cop's way. Sure enough, Medina paled.

"Seems she does know something about our side of the universe. Fancy that." I walked over to her, still huddled on the floor. "By that look on her face, though, she doesn't know nearly as much as she should. Like exactly who she was taking into custody. And who's probably on his way right now, tracking down his girlfriend, very pissed off about the situation and about to be even more pissed off when he sees that." I pointed toward the dead wolf in the cage.

"I—I—"

"That's the problem they were having in lockup when we arrived, wasn't it? You weren't just stupid enough to imprison a"—I glanced at Holland, still standing by the door, in shock. I had no idea how much of this was penetrating, but I shouldn't take chances—"a guy like that, but you drugged him, too. Intentionally released his inner animal."

"No." She scrambled up. "I just arrested him. That's my assignment."

"From the liberation movement?"

"Yes. I bring in people like us."

"Like us? What are you?"

"Acies," she said. A vision-enhanced half-demon, very mild powers. "They give me sedatives, then someone comes to bail the prisoners out and takes them to the lab. Sometimes I find the subjects on my own. Sometimes I'm tipped off. That's what happened with you. I got a call. My contact didn't tell me who you were—he just described you and where to find you. The sedatives have always worked." She glanced into the cell and swallowed. "It must be the latest batch. Everything was fine—"

"Yes, just fine. All you were doing was kidnapping our kind on false charges then selling us as guinea pigs in horrific experiments."

She bristled. "Those experiments will save us. They're benign—"

"Benign?" I clenched my fists so hard I heard the faint pops of my knuckles cracking. "Tell that to the subjects they dumped into a watery pit. Before they were dead! Those *benign*—" I lifted my hands for emphasis and sparks flew everywhere.

Jaime caught my elbow. "How about we skip the blame game. Jeremy will find me eventually, and this is something he shouldn't walk into blindly."

She was right. Most werewolves can't follow a scent when you've traveled by car, but Jeremy wasn't your average werewolf. He had an extra boost of kitsune blood, which helped him find his family when they were in danger. Jaime was family. He'd be on his way.

"Am I drugged?" I asked Medina.

She shook her head. "I only had enough left for one more. You seemed compliant enough." She gestured at Jaime. "She was the one who was fighting."

"When you came in here, what were you running from?"

She pointed to the cell.

"There's nothing else?"

She shook her head.

So the werewolf had been on the loose, and she and her partner ducked in here to escape it, only to trap themselves with it. Which I'd say was fitting, except that they weren't the ones who'd died for her stupidity.

"So as soon as that lock opens, we're free to go?" Keiran asked.

Medina nodded.

Holland lurched from his stupor. "N-no. There's paperwork. We have to do the paperwork. People can't just walk out of . . ."

He looked around, then caught sight of the blood sprayed across the hall floor. He stumbled toward the cell, Medina grabbing for his arm to stop him. Too late. Holland saw what was in there, doubled over and threw up.

He was still retching, Medina at his side, when the time lock on the door clicked. Keiran grabbed the handle. I jammed my foot in the way, stopping it.

Keiran glowered at me. "I'm leaving, okay? I don't care what the council says about this mess and my 'duty' to help clean it up—"

"I was just going to say to be careful."

I pulled my foot away and she slipped through. I was about to follow, but Jaime caught my sleeve.

"Not so fast," she murmured. She slid one stiletto into the door opening, then put her ear to the gap.

Medina marched over. She'd pulled her partner away from the carnage in the cage and left him sitting, slumped against a wall, head on his knees. She grabbed the door. When Jaime made a move to stop her, she snapped, "You stay here, until I make sure the witch is okay."

As Medina went through the door, Jaime gave me a questioning look.

"Hell, no," I murmured. "I've had enough of playing hero. We didn't send them out as bait. Their choice. Might as well take advantage."

We could hear Keiran's pumps receding along the hall, then the softer thumps of Medina's loafers. A murmur of voices as Medina caught up. The click of a door. We waited for another ten seconds.

"No screaming yet," Jaime said.

"Always a good sign."

We slid out.

CHAPTER 5

We crept down the hall. There were two doors at the end. The left one headed to the interrogation room; the right to the main office.

I cracked open the door on the right and listened. A week ago, I'd have been ashamed of myself for being so cautious, called myself a frightened little witch mouse. A week without powers has taught me that the only reason *not* to take that extra second was ego.

When we heard nothing, I eased open the door and went through first.

Everything was silent and still. I turned to give Jaime the all clear. Then I stopped.

Silent and still. In a police station that's just been ravaged by a werewolf.

"What's up?" Jaime whispered.

I lifted a finger to my lips and pivoted, straining to hear.

Jaime tapped my shoulder and I jumped.

"Let's just go," she whispered.

She was right. If losing my powers had made me careful, it had also nudged me to the edge of paranoia. A werewolf had just rampaged through an isolated police station where I'd only seen four officers, including Medina and Holland. The other two must be long gone. Or dead. Judging by the blood on the werewolf, I suspected option two. That would explain the silence.

We passed a quad of cubicles. Something crunched underfoot and I looked down to see a broken pencil. Pens were scattered off to my left. Papers blanketed the floor around the desks. Crimson blood dotted the pages. Only drops, though. Someone wounded and getting the hell out, scattering office supplies in his wake.

I took another step and heard the slam of a car door. I pictured a survivor sitting in the parking lot, gun drawn, waiting for someone—or something—to come out those front doors.

I turned back to Jaime.

"We should look for a side exit," I whispered.

She nodded. In front was the reception area. To our right, another door hung partially open. As we headed for it, I noticed more blood streaked on the linoleum. Still wet. From the werewolf, I presumed. I steered around it and kept going.

More blood ahead. Lots more. Smeared in front of the partly open door. Lines ran through it. Drag marks. Was the werewolf the only thing responsible for those blood trails? I wasn't sure enough to go through that door.

"Other way?" Jaime whispered behind me.

I nodded. As we crept back in the direction we'd come, I kept glancing back at the blood smears by the door. What if someone was in there, wounded?

I shook it off. As I'd said, I was done playing hero. While I was sure that Paige-and-Lucas-fostered self-sacrificing side of me would erupt again, it wasn't popping out while we had a dead werewolf in the back room. We had to escape. This was Medina's mess. Let her deal with it. Or let the Pack do it—after we got to safety.

"Hello?" a man's voice called from the reception area. "Is someone here?"

Jaime stopped and looked back at me.

"I want to file an accident report," he called. "Hello?"

I motioned for Jaime to follow and we backed up to a block of filing cabinets. As I tugged her behind them, I caught a flash of something across the room. Jaime gasped. I wheeled.

There was nothing there.

Jaime had her eyes half closed and was taking deep breaths.

"What'd you see?" I asked.

"Just a ghost. Some kind of—" Another deep breath. "A residual, I think. It startled me. Sorry."

A residual was a spectral image, usually the replay of a gruesome death, meaning Jaime had every right to look like she was five seconds from puking. But why had *I* caught a flicker of it?

The guy in reception called out again. I plastered myself back against Jaime. My heart kept thumping. I tried to calm down. It was just a guy. At worst I could play receptionist and get rid of him.

Yet the self-talk didn't help because it wasn't the guy making my heart race. I kept thinking about that flash. A niggling doubt in my gut told me to look again.

I peered out and jerked back so fast I elbowed Jaime.

"What—?" she began.

I clamped my hand over her mouth. My heart was thudding so hard now I could barely draw breath. She tugged my hand away and mouthed, "You saw it?"

I nodded. *What* had I seen? I didn't know. My brain was throwing out bits and pieces like a jammed movie camera.

Not human. No, not *humanoid*. That's what had my mind stuttering, because it wasn't human and it wasn't beast, and that wasn't possible. I lived in a world of monsters, but they were all recognizably human. Only werewolves could change form. This . . . This wasn't a werewolf.

Eyes. I'd seen eyes. Cold, unblinking, reptilian eyes scanning the room. Looking for us.

Forget what it was—it was looking for us now and when it found us . . .

Blood. I'd seen blood and gore dripping from misshapen jaws. I stared at the smear on the floor and now saw more than drag marks. I saw claw marks.

"Hello?" the man called. "Jesus Christ. Someone's gotta be here."

A creak. The door opening. A growl. An inhuman cry, half shriek, half snarl.

I leaped from my hiding spot. The thing flew at the man. Literally flew, leathery crimson wings billowing out. Its beaklike snout opened and it let out another horrible cry.

"Holy shit," the man said. "Holy fucking—"

I hit the beast with an energy bolt. Or I tried to. What came out was a spray of harmless sparks that showered the thing. It gave a screech, more annoyance than pain, and reared back. Four taloned feet flashed. All four grabbed the man. Grabbed him and ripped. Blood sprayed. An arm landed by my feet. The man was screaming. All that blood, and that arm lying at my feet, and the man was still screaming.

Jaime had to drag me a couple of feet before I snapped out of it. I pushed her along ahead of me as we ran for the second door. My sneakers slid and squealed on the blood. A grunt from across the room. The beast. The man had gone silent now. Thank God, he'd gone silent. But that meant the beast had heard my shoes.

Jaime wrenched open the door. We tumbled through. I yanked it closed. The beast hit it with a thud, the wall shuddering. I held it shut with both hands, my feet braced. It threw itself at the door, over and over, shrieking.

Jaime grabbed my shoulder. I lifted my hand to brush her off, then realized she was holding out a steel baton. We jammed it into the handle. The door rocked twice more. Then stopped. Talons clicked on the linoleum as the beast retreated.

I glanced at Jaime. She didn't ask what that thing was or how it got here. Right now, it only mattered that it *was* here.

"It's looking for another way in," Jaime whispered.

"Which means we need to find another way out."

I turned. We were in an office. The chief's office, I was guessing. Big, spacious, filled with natural light . . . all coming from skylights overhead. Barred skylights. No other exit.

There was a shout. Then an earsplitting screech. I spun toward the door.

"Holland!" I said. "We forgot about—"

A scream cut me short. The same kind of horrible scream I'd heard from the man who'd been torn apart.

Jaime gripped my elbow. "Too late," she said. "We need to find a way out."

I stood frozen as the scream was replaced by wet smacking and grunting as the creature devoured the young officer. Then everything went quiet.

I pressed my ear to the door.

Jaime tugged me back. "It just remembered there's a bigger meal in here."

I took a step, and nearly landed on my ass. I looked down at what I'd slipped on—the extension of the blood trail that came through the door.

It continued past the massive desk. I took two steps and leaned around to see what looked like rope on the floor. Another step. Not rope. Intestine, stretched out from what remained of a torso clad in . . .

"Medina," I whispered, seeing the name plate on her uniform shirt.

That was the only way I would have recognized her. Her legs and one arm had been ripped off. As for her head, it was still attached, barely. Where her face should be, there was a bloody crater.

Jaime stepped around the desk. I blocked the sight.

"There's someone behind her," Jaime whispered.

I looked behind the desk. There were bodies there. Two, maybe three. It was impossible to tell. One face stared up from the pile. The blond witch, Keiran.

"Okay," Jaime said, taking a deep breath. "We need—" She looked around. "Phone. We need to find the—"

Her eyes rounded. She lunged forward. "Savannah!"

Cold steel pressed against my throat.

CHAPTER 6

"I'd say, 'Nobody move,'" said a raspy male voice. "But I think the knife makes that redundant."

I started whispering a spell. The blade pressed into my windpipe.

"I'd call that moving," he said. "Another word and you won't be speaking. Or breathing."

"There's a thing out there," Jaime said. "Some kind of beast."

"Demon," he said. "Demonic, at least. I was testing out a particularly tricky new spell."

A sorcerer. One who knew witch magic, which explained how he'd appeared from nowhere. Cover spell.

"Who are you?" Jaime demanded, as if reading my mind.

He continued as if she hadn't spoken. "That beast wasn't quite what I hoped to summon, but I've sent it back now. With a full belly, apparently. Pity about Jackie Medina. A nice person to work with. So dedicated to the cause. So gullible."

"She wasn't drugging us to make us more compliant, was she?" Jaime said. "The drugs were supposed to drive super-naturals crazy. Why?"

"Is this the point where I explain my master plan? Um, no. Thanks, but I have more important things to do."

"Like cleaning up this mess," I muttered.

"That's not on my list either. I'm sure either the council or the Cabals have a crime-scene cleaning team on speed dial. And avoiding fallout . . . ?" He chuckled. "Definitely not part of the plan. As for the plan itself, let's just say it underwent a serious change when Ms. Medina called me and said she had Jaime Vegas and Savannah Levine in custody. The Fates must be smiling on me. Well, not the Fates, maybe, but someone is. I wanted a chance to test my spell, and you gave me a better one than I ever could have imagined. Now, Ms. Vegas, could you do me a favor and call Eve Levine? I know you have *her* on speed dial."

"I can't—" Jaime began.

"Yes, you can." He gestured at the knife against my throat.

Being told to call my mother or I'd die? Serious déjà vu. First Leah O'Donnell, the half-demon who came back from hell. Now this asshole. Everyone wanted Mom. Which meant, while part of me said I should be scared, I was really just annoyed. And impatiently waiting for this sorcerer to get caught up in negotiations with Jaime and relax his grip enough for me to escape.

"You can call her," he repeated. "And you will, because if you don't, I'm going to slit her daughter's throat and leave her on this pile of bodies."

"You don't understand," Jaime said. "Eve is out of contact. Someplace I can't reach her."

"You mean she's off on an angel assignment."

Jaime let out a squeaky laugh. "Um, no. Trust me, Eve Levine is no—"

"She's an angel. Ascended angel. Celestial bounty hunter."

I looked at Jaime, and waited for a real laugh, not that nervous titter.

Her mouth opened. Closed. She swallowed. She looked at me and blushed.

Angel? My mother was an angel?

I wanted to laugh. Only I couldn't, because it made sense to me—as much sense as the concept of my dark-witch half-demon mother as a divine agent could.

Leah had said my mother was on her tail. That Mom could keep her from going back to hell. Who could do that except an angel?

When my mother came for Leah, I'd seen her faint outline. I'd also seen something glowing at her side. Something she'd used to slice bloodlessly through Leah's host body and send her soul back to hell. What could do that except a celestial sword?

Kimerion—a demi-demon who'd been helping us—said Leah must have gotten divine aid to escape her hell dimension. He claimed it was a collaboration between the angelic and the demonic. Then he'd asked about my mother.

That's why Leah wanted her. That's why this guy wanted her. Because my mother had a direct line to the celestial.

I felt . . . Confused. Then that fell away and what took its place wasn't fear or pride. It was hurt. Hurt because this son of a bitch knew my mother was an angel, and I didn't. Hurt because I trusted Jaime—trusted her since I was fourteen years old—and now I realized she'd kept something about my mother from me, something important.

Finally, Jaime said, "If you know what Eve is, then you understand that she's not always at my beck and call. Six months of the year she's an angel. I can't summon her. I'm forbidden—"

"You can't?" he said. "Or it's forbidden? Those are two different things. If Eve Levine finds out that her daughter died and you didn't have the guts to try calling her, she'll reach through the dimensions and rip those guts out through your belly button."

"I can't—"

The blade slid across my throat. I felt the skin split. Felt blood run down my neck. Heard Jaime yelp. Tried to turn, but the blade was still there, cutting in deeper, his other hand wrapped around my hair now, wrenching my head up.

Mom!

My eyes bulged as I gasped for breath. I found it. Somehow I found it.

I could still breathe. Blood oozed down my neck. But it didn't spurt. I stopped struggling.

"Good girl," the sorcerer whispered. "Ms. Vegas, the ball is in your court."

She was already saying my mother's name, the words spilling out as she yanked off my mother's silver ring and clutched it. "Eve, I need you, please, Savannah needs you."

She paused for breath, and he dug the knife in again and I gasped, eyes rolling in pain, a scream caught in my throat, not daring to let it out, barely daring to breathe for fear it would press my throat harder against the blade.

The sorcerer was murmuring something. A spell?

Mo—

I stopped the thought. Squeezed my eyes shut. Don't call her. Don't call her.

Are you crazy? There's a knife—

I can't call her. I won't. My mother was an angel. A goddamned angel, and if people knew I could summon an angel, I'd have a knife to my throat every week. I had to trust Jaime.

"I—I think she's coming," Jaime said. "I feel her, and—"

"Tell her to cross over there."

He pointed. I tried to look, but the knife wouldn't let me.

"I—I don't under—"

"Tell her to cross there. Into the circle."

Circle? I didn't need to look now. It had to be something for binding a spirit.

"No," I said, wheezing. "Jaime, don't you dare—"

The knife bit in and I yowled. Couldn't help it, even if it made the blade dig in all the more.

I could barely see Jaime through a haze of red. But I glowered at her, pouring every bit of rage and betrayal into that glare.

Don't you dare let him bind an angel, Jaime. Don't you dare.

"I—I can't tell her where to cross over. It's not like that. She—"

"Eve!" His voice rose to a shout. "I'm sure you can hear me. You're going to cross into that circle or your daughter is going to die."

I closed my eyes and concentrated as hard as I could. *Do not cross into the circle.* I had no idea who this guy was or what he was up to, but he wanted to harness an angel, and with everything that was going on—the freedom group, the immortality vaccine—we couldn't let it happen.

I'd tricked Leah. I could trick him, too. I just needed enough time.

The sorcerer restarted his incantation, shouting the words now. I didn't recognize the spell. Didn't even recognize the language. Not Hebrew or Greek or Latin.

Something older.

As his voice rose, he pulled the knife away from my throat, tightening his grip on my hair. He flicked the blood-covered blade to the left. Toward the circle.

My fist went up, spell on my lips, but he slapped the blade back so hard my knees gave way, only his hold on my hair keeping me upright. He yanked me to my feet.

"The circle, Eve!" he shouted. "Cross into the—"

He stopped. And he laughed, a low, rasping chortle. "Yes. That's it. Thank you."

The knife eased on my neck enough for me to look over at the circle and see . . .

My mother. I saw my mother. Not a faint image or a shadowy apparition. I saw my mother, as real as she'd looked nine years ago, when she'd left our cell to find us a way out of the compound where we'd been trapped. She'd never returned.

"Eve," the sorcerer said.

She pulled something off her back. A four-foot-long sword, the metal glowing blue.

"Jaime? Tell him he has five seconds to drop his blade or I use mine," she said, her gaze fixed on him, dark eyes blazing.

I could hear Mom. *Why* could I hear her? But he could, too. His knife hit the floor with a clatter. He released me and I fell to my knees, hands going to my throat.

"Good," she said.

She kept walking toward him, but lowered the sword. I stared up at her.

I can see you. And he can see you too, can't he? Why can—?

My gaze dropped to the floor where my mother was leaving a trail of boot prints.

She shouldn't be able to leave boot prints.

The hell-beast. He'd summoned a hell-beast and it had materialized. It had crossed the dimensions and physically entered ours.

What had he said before he started the ritual?

I'm testing out a particularly tricky new spell.

"There," he said to Eve. "I've let Savannah go. I just wanted to bring you here, Eve. We have very special plans—"

My mother lifted her sword. Ready to send him to hell, as she'd done with Leah.

She swung the blade. One clean, effortless cut through the torso. The sorcerer's eyes bugged. His mouth worked. Then his upper half slid to the floor, blood spurting, the shriek dying in a keening gurgle as his legs fell over and he lay there, blinking, mouth still open, any noise he made drowned out by Jaime's screams.

"What the hell?" Mom whispered.

She backed up, sword held out, gaze fixed on it as if it had come to life in her hand. She slid on the blood and looked down at the floor.

"What the hell?"

She stared at her jeans and blouse, soaked with the sorcerer's blood.

"What the hell!"

I stood there, watching her and trying hard, very hard, not to look at that horrible, bisected body.

My mother blinked. Then she leaped forward, sword raised, and stabbed the still-blinking sorcerer through the heart, releasing him to death.

Jaime stopped screaming. At least, stopped audibly screaming, fist jammed into her mouth, eyes closed. Then she went rigid. Her eyes flew open and fixed on something I couldn't see.

"You—you called her," she whispered. "I don't know what you did but—"

She flinched and I knew she was talking to the sorcerer's ghost. My mother jumped forward, but Jaime lifted her hands.

"I-it's okay. He's gone." Jaime looked around. "I don't understand."

"I do." My voice came out soft, barely audible. Then I turned to my mother. "You're real. I mean, you're here."

I stepped forward and reached out. My fingers touched her sleeve. The fabric dimpled under them and then I was touching her. Her. My mother. "Oh, God."

My eyes filled and she reached for me. I swallowed. Fresh blood trickled down my neck. She stopped short, yanked at her shirt and wheeled on Jaime.

"First aid. Find a kit. Now!"

Mom ripped her shirt off, buttons popping, and pressed it to my throat. Then she led me over to a chair and made me sit. All I could think was *It's Mom. My mother is here. I can see her. I can hear her. I can reach out and touch her.*

I sat there, feeling no pain while she and Jaime tended to my throat. In shock, I guess. I dimly heard my mother say the cut was shallower than it looked—the sorcerer knew what he was doing, inflicting minimal damage while making it look serious.

I didn't care. My mother was here. Right here. I kept trying to process it, but my brain refused.

They taped me up. No one said much. I think we were all in shock, even Mom, who kept looking over at the bisected corpse as if she expected it to magically mend.

"How . . . how did he do it?" I whispered. "That's not possible." I looked at Jaime. "Is it?"

She shook her head. "Zombies, yes. A ghost inhabiting a living body, yes. Bringing back a ghost in corporeal form? It doesn't happen. Can't."

"Just like you can't manifest a hell-beast," I said. "But he did."

No one answered me.

"We need to go," Jaime said finally. "We can . . . figure all this out later. For now, we have to call—" She glanced at the phone, then at the bodies.

"No calls," I said, snapping out of it. "Or the first person the cops will track down is whoever received a phone call post carnage."

"Careful, baby," Mom said. "You probably shouldn't talk."

Baby. How long had it been since I'd heard that? Fresh tears made the room swim. I swiped them away as she leaned over, ignoring the blood as she hugged me tentatively, then tighter, when I didn't evaporate at her touch.

"It's okay," she whispered. "Everything's okay."

Only it wasn't. We were in a room with dead people. Dead people who'd been carved up and ripped up and chewed on, and at any moment someone was going to come through the station door and find blood and entrails decorating the chief's office.

Jaime was right. We had to get out of here. And, yes, that

meant that after eleven years, I couldn't stop to hug my mother, even though she might disappear back to the after-life at any moment. But that's how it was. Life isn't fair. Not when there are bodies to dispose of.

It took about thirty seconds to realize that we couldn't do it. Hiding the bodies was useless, given the sheer amount of blood. All we could do was take the first-aid kit—which we'd touched—look around and determine that we hadn't touched anything else except the baton in the door. Take that, too. Smear our footprints in the blood. Hope that my blood would go undetected. Pray we hadn't shed hairs—rather, pray they weren't found. Really, in general, we just prayed that the Cortezes could cover this up.

Could even a Cabal cover it up? I wasn't so sure. Didn't want to think about that.

Next we went into the locker room to find clean shirts for Mom and me. We grabbed a blouse and a gym top from Medina's locker. Jaime changed into Medina's sneakers. They weren't a great fit, but they'd do, though she insisted on taking her heels, too—they were her favorites. My jacket was back in the cell, remarkably clean. My wallet and Jaime's purse were in the front room. Mom found our processing papers hidden inside Medina's desk. We took those, too.

Last and maybe most important was video surveillance. But we got lucky there. The camera was an old tape one that only monitored the reception room. We'd never been in there. I grabbed the tape anyway.

Before we left, I borrowed Jaime's phone—which had been in her purse—and texted Adam. A simple *we're fine, don't come after us*. Last thing we needed was to have Adam and Jeremy show up right as the authorities discovered the bloodbath within.

I didn't even have time to put the phone away before he texted back. *Can u call?*

Mom leaned over to read the screen and shook her head. "Later."

I texted back *soon*.

CHAPTER 7

As I noted earlier, the station house was on a regional highway surrounded by swampy fields. So no easy escape. If a vehicle went missing from a house near the massacre scene, the cops wouldn't rest until they found it.

That meant heading back toward New Orleans on foot, through marshy fields of thigh-high grass, our shoes squishing in the mud. The sun beat down and humidity rose from the moist ground like a steam bath. When we made it to a strip of moss-laden cypress, I called Adam.

"Are you okay?" he said in lieu of a greeting.

"I'm fine. How's Bryce?"

"Holding up. The jet's almost here. He's going to Miami—at least temporarily. But about you . . . ?"

"Yeah, sorry for the cryptic text, but we wanted to make sure Jeremy didn't try to track Jaime down."

"He hasn't yet. Lucas called and said you two had been arrested and that he didn't want us going after you. He was very calm about the whole thing."

"Lucas is very calm about everything."

Adam chuckled. "Yeah, well I wasn't. Even Jeremy was getting antsy. But Lucas insisted we hang tight until there was a cause for panic. So everything's okay now? You guys are out?"

"We are. As for okay . . ."

I stumbled over a vine. Mom caught my arm and whispered, "Watch your step, Savannah."

"Who's that?" Adam said.

"Uh . . ." I looked at my mother. "Long story. Anyway, um, yeah, about the jail . . ."

"You broke out?"

"Er, not exactly. The officer who arrested us said we were free to go. After the rampaging werewolf episode."

"Rampaging werewolf?"

"He was drugged."

"Which explains everything." Adam took a deep breath. "Okay, full story later. Short version: rampaging werewolf and impromptu jail release. Which will take some council work to fix, but the main point is that you're out and—"

"There's . . . more."

A pause. "Do I want to know?"

"Probably not. The werewolf wasn't the only one snacking on cops. There was this hell-beast . . ."

I didn't get much further into my story before Adam had me on speaker phone, so Jeremy could listen, with Lucas conferenced in from Miami. I put Jaime's phone on speaker, too.

When I got to the part about the pile of corpses and the hell-beast slavering at the door, Lucas said, "That's . . ."

"Did I just lose the connection or are you actually speechless?" I said.

"I think he's trying to figure out if you got some of those drugs," Adam said.

"I didn't."

"Jaime?" Jeremy said. "You're all right? Are there lingering effects from the injection? I presume it was an injection."

"I'm fine," Jaime said. "But really, under the circumstances, that's not our first priority."

It was his, though, closely followed by the dead werewolf. As for the rest, that ball was in Lucas's court.

"Can the Cortezes clean this up?" I asked.

"Hold on," Adam said. "I'm still stuck on the part about a demonic entity manifesting in our world. That's next to impossible. There are accounts of it, but none less than two hundred years old, meaning none that have been verified. Are you sure—?"

"That the creature with bat wings, a beak, and butcher-knife talons wasn't just a really ugly police dog?"

"No, I just mean . . . You said it was a spell. Maybe an illusion. Like a sorcerer's trip wire. Those things are enough to scare the shit out of anyone."

"But they don't *rip* the shit out of anyone. It tore a guy apart, Adam. Right in front of Jaime and me. Ripped him limb from limb—"

Jaime looked ready to be sick again, so I stopped.

"I'm sorry," Adam said. "That wasn't clear and I—"

"Had to be clear. You're the research guy. I know."

Lucas cut in. "Right now, I need to mobilize forces. Give me all the details you can. Did you notice the station number or address?"

My mom whispered it, which I repeated. When I'd finished, Lucas stayed silent.

"There's someone with us," I said.

"Yes, I noticed. For a moment, it sounded like . . ." A long pause. "Never mind. That address again . . . ?"

"The person with us," I said. "You were going to say she sounds just like my mother."

Silence.

"It is," I said.

Silence.

"It's my mom. That hell-beast the sorcerer brought over? It was a test run for what he really wanted to do—which was summon my mother."

"You means she's . . . ?" Adam began.

"Right here. In the flesh."

More silence. At last Jeremy broke it, saying, "Hello, Eve."

"Hey, Jeremy," Mom said with a smile. "Long time no see. Well, I've seen *you* plenty of times, but maybe we'll finally get a chance for a face-to-face now."

"I . . ." Adam began. "I don't understand. How . . . ?"

"We aren't sure on the how," Mom said. "But we have a pretty good idea why I was brought over. I'm not your average ghost." She paused. "Jeremy, can you explain it after we sign off?"

I glanced over at Jaime.

"She didn't tell him," my mother murmured to me. "He figured it out." She raised her voice. "Jeremy will tell you why I'm such a valuable commodity. Now, we really should let you guys get to work on cleanup duty. Savannah is . . ." She glanced at my bandaged throat. "She really shouldn't be talking so much."

"What?" Adam said. "I thought she was okay. Savannah?"

Mom winced. "She's fine, Adam. Just a . . . blow to the throat. It'll be sore for a few days."

"Blow?" He swore under his breath. "Okay, tell us where you are. We'll be right there."

"We . . . can't do that," I said. "We need to lie low until we're sure no one links us to this thing."

"Then we'll lie low with you. If you're hurt, Jeremy should check you out."

Mom took the phone and clicked it off speaker.

"Hey, Adam," she said, as she put some distance between us. "I know you're worried about Savannah, but I promise she's fine, and she's right, we need to lie low . . ."

Her voice trailed off. After a few minutes, she came back and handed the phone to Jaime.

"Adam isn't happy, but Lucas agreed with us. He's recalling them to Miami on the jet that's coming for Bryce. We'll follow as soon as we can."

⚜

As we trudged through the forest after making the call, it finally hit me. Really and truly hit. My mother was here. Now. With me. I could hug her. Talk to her. Except I couldn't. Not really. I could talk and I could touch, but not the way I wanted to.

I wanted to take her hand and find a place for us to sit down and say to her, "Tell me everything." *Tell me about your new life. How did you become an angel? What's it like? Are you happy? How's my father? What was it like getting back together after all those years? Are you happy?* That was the big one: *Are you happy?* Of course I could have asked her that anytime Jaime contacted her for me, but I never did because I wouldn't trust the answer unless I could see her face. Now I could. And I still couldn't ask. It wasn't the time or the place.

How many times had I fantasized about this moment?

When we'd been in that underground cell together, and she'd figured a way out, she'd made me stay behind until she was sure it was safe. I remember sitting in my cell. Waiting. Waiting. Then our captors came and told me she was dead and I thought, *They're lying*. They'd caught her escaping and they were keeping us apart to punish us. But as days and nights passed in that tiny cell, I'd had to face the truth. If my mother was alive, she'd have moved heaven and earth to come for me. So she had to be dead.

Yet I indulged the fantasy. After I went to live with Paige, there were plenty of nights that I'd lie awake and imagine the door opening, my mother there, come back for me.

Now she had, and it wasn't anything like my dreams. Yes, she'd come back for me. Yes, she'd saved me. But I wasn't a child anymore. I didn't need my mother now to rescue me from a hellish life. My life was fine. It had always been fine—my issues with Paige had been ideological clashes and teen angst, long since worked out.

But this was still a dream come true. Maybe even better, because I didn't need anything from her now. I just wanted to be with her. Spend time with her. Private, quiet time . . . completely impossible under the circumstances. So I trudged along through the woods and snuck glances her way, reassuring myself she was still there, and watching her do the same to me. Keep moving forward. That was all we could do. That and pray that the Fates would let her stay long enough for us to have some time alone together.

The forest trek wasn't easy on Jaime, even in sneakers. Werewolf partner or not, she didn't spend a lot of time in the woods. I did—plenty of camping and hiking trips with Adam. And Mom was holding up fine. I kept expecting her sword to snag a tree, but she dodged and sidestepped obstacles, as if it was part of her anatomy.

"When we get to town, you need to get rid of that," I said finally, pointing at the sword.

It was slung on her back. Just slung there, stuck on a thin cord, as if magnetized. Physically impossible to do with a hunk of metal that big, but I guess the rules of physics don't apply for celestial gear.

"She can't," Jaime said. "Big no-no in the angel corps."

"Under the circumstances, I think they'd make an exception," I said. "We needed to take it out of the station, because it was a murder weapon. But now we're heading for civilization, and that ain't a pocket knife. You need to get rid of it."

"I know. It's just . . ." She nodded and stopped walking. "I'll try."

As she pulled it from her back, I stepped off the path and found a shallow gully filled with dead vegetation. She plunged the blade in sideways. When she covered it, I could still see a glimmer. I waded in and reached down to push it under.

Mom grabbed the back of my jacket and yanked me back.

"Uh-uh, baby," she said. "You're not touching that without oven mitts. Industrial oven mitts."

She pushed it down farther, covered it with more debris, then dragged a huge fallen branch over it. Seemed like overkill, but I left her to it. When she was done, she walked backward away from it, murmuring, "So far, so good."

"It's fine," I said. "If you have to return for it, it's marked. Now—"

A tremendous crack had me diving for the ground, arms over my head. As I dropped, I saw what looked like that massive branch sailing into the air, broken in two. A whirlwind of dead vegetation swirled up, then exploded, wet and stinking of rot. I clawed it from my face and looked around.

Jaime was crouched ten feet away. My mother stood where I'd left her. On her back, the sword glowed blue, so bright I had to look away.

"Damn," she said. "I was really hoping that wouldn't happen."

She helped me up and brushed the dead leaves from my clothes.

"So you can't leave it behind," I said. "Literally can't. That's . . . inconvenient."

Jaime stood, picking leaves from her hair. "You can hide behind a blur spell when we aren't alone. Probably a good idea. You're so used to being a ghost, you're liable to walk into walls and plow down old ladies."

That wasn't an ideal solution—Mom couldn't stay under a blur spell for very long at a stretch. We didn't tell Jaime that. We'd figure things out when we had to.

We set out again, and I fell in step beside my mother. "So how long have you had the sword?"

"You mean, how long have I been an angel?" Her voice dropped. "I'm sorry. I know this is a big shock."

"One that could have been avoided." I glanced back at Jaime, trudging behind us.

"No," Mom said sharply. She shook her finger at Jaime. "Don't give her that look and don't apologize."

"I—" Jaime began.

"You feel bad and you shouldn't." Mom looked back at me. "She couldn't tell you, Savannah. *Couldn't.* She would have been bleeped."

"Bleeped?"

"Cosmic interference. Yes, maybe she could have found a way around that, but if she tried, the Fates would have decided I couldn't be her spirit guide anymore. And no one wanted that, right?"

"Right." I glanced at Jaime. "Sorry."

She nodded. Still looked guilty, though.

"So how come that sorcerer wasn't censored?" I said. "He told me what you were."

"No idea. Same as I have no idea how he got me to materialize."

"It was a spell. I heard him doing the incantation. I didn't recognize the language, though."

"Hmm." She kicked aside a branch and murmured, "I find it hard to believe such a spell could even exist. Way too dangerous. Which could mean it's not just an old spell he dug up, but something . . ." She shook her head. "We'll work it all out later."

"If you're still here," I said. "When the Fates realized what happened, they'll recall you, won't they?"

You could disappear at any second. That's what I meant. I couldn't say it, though, as if putting it into words might make it so.

"I don't know," she said. She stopped. "Maybe we shouldn't be in such a hurry. We're far enough away from the station. Let's take a rest."

Let's rest. Let's talk. Let's just be together while we can.

God, how I wanted that. But I knew we shouldn't, and from her expression, she knew it, too. We'd left a massacre behind, one that reeked of the inexplicable and the supernatural.

"We'll have time," I said, and resumed walking.

"I'm sure we will." She reached up and ruffled my hair, then laughed. "Not as easy to do that now, is it?"

I nodded and my throat tightened. She put her arm around my shoulders, gave me a squeeze, and we carried on through the woods.

CHAPTER 8

We made it as far as the first motel, still a few miles from the city, and decided that was good enough. The place was a dump. But the desk clerk was happy to take sixty bucks cash and didn't ask us for ID, credit cards or even a name.

He probably took one look at Jaime and me and decided we were working girls. I didn't tell Jaime that. Her ego might not have survived. After being drugged and sick, seeing people torn to pieces and cut in half, then tramping through swampy fields for miles, she was not her usual glamorous self. I was worse. I don't even want to think about how the motel clerk figured I'd hurt my throat.

My mother hid behind the building while we checked in. We found her leaning against the wall, looking far more cool and collected than either of us. Medina's shirt was too small—Mom's a fraction under my six feet—but the Levine women aren't blessed with curves, so it fit snug and short. She'd come from the afterlife in a very unangelic pair of worn jeans and leather boots. Her straight dark hair hung to her midback. She looked exactly as I remembered her, which I suppose made sense. Ghosts don't age. But she looked, well, let's just say that seeing her now, I realized why everyone said we looked alike. I had slightly shorter hair and blue eyes. Better fashion sense, too—I was also partial to jeans and boots, but my tastes were more Fifth Avenue than

Walmart. Other than that, it was like walking toward a mirror.

She was gazing over the field, frowning slightly.

"See something?" I said.

"No, just . . ." She glanced at Jaime. "I'm surprised Kris isn't pestering the hell out of you by now. He must have gone straight to the Fates to plead my case."

"Actually, no," Jaime said. "He was around before you came, but there was a problem. Come on inside and I'll explain."

Mom tried not to be freaked out about my father's situation. "He'll find his way out. Eventually. The man is brilliant, but he has the worst sense of direction. Once, he promised me a trip to the beach and teleported us to the Sahara."

"It has sand," I said.

"Exactly what he said. To be honest, I had more fun there than I would ever have had at the beach."

"But if he has a *bad* sense of direction . . ."

"That just means he gets lost a lot. Meaning he has to get *un*lost a lot." Her fingers tapped the bedspread. Then she said, more emphatically, "He'll find his way back. Okay, kids, so the next step is . . ."

"Resting," Jaime said. "Please tell me it's resting."

"To rest, you need to actually sit down," I said. "You've been standing there since we arrived. The beds are reasonably clean. Just pull back the spread and keep your clothes on."

"Please," Mom said. "For once, keep your clothes on."

Jaime made a face at her. Mom tugged back the cover, then reached over and dragged Jaime to the bed, hard enough that she fell onto it.

Jaime rolled her eyes, but stayed put, and they bantered for a few minutes as Jaime got comfortable. Watching them was . . . odd. I knew Mom had been Jaime's spirit guide for years, and I guess I knew they were friends, too, but seeing them together, so comfortable with each other . . .

Was I envious? I don't know. But it did make me feel . . . odd. My mother once called me the center of her world. That wasn't maternal hyperbole. I really had been the center of her world and she'd been mine. We'd moved from city to city, never staying in one place for long. She had contacts and students, but I rarely saw them and they never saw her outside of business. Even her friends, she kept at arm's length. This relationship with Jaime was different. I was happy for her, though.

"Okay, we'll rest first, then call a cab and get a real hotel," Jaime said. "There, we have a plan."

"Well," Mom said, "as much as I hate to argue with my elders—"

"Hey, no age jokes. You're only two months younger than me."

"Mmm, did I mention I paid a visit to the big ol' hall of records in the sky? Seems there's a slight discrepancy in your accounting."

"If there is, blame my mother. I never lie about my age. I never give it unless necessary, but I never lie about it either."

When Mom didn't respond, we looked over to see her holding Jaime's cell phone.

"Hey, how'd you get—?"

"Shit, these have changed a lot in a decade," Mom said. "Don't worry, I won't send dirty text messages to Jeremy. You do enough of that anyway."

"I never—"

"Ghost, remember? I can see you even when you can't see me." She paused. "That doesn't sound good. Let me clarify that I never stick around when it goes beyond texting." She pushed a few buttons. "I wonder how many heart attacks I could cause by calling up a few folks, reminding them that they owe me favors?"

"They'd think it was Savannah."

"Damn."

"Back to the topic at hand," I said. "We can't rest—at least not for long. That's what Mom was about to say before she got distracted by the shiny twenty-first-century technology."

"Oh, yes, we can rest." Jaime reclined on the bed and shut her eyes. "Look, I'm doing it right now. It's so relaxing. You guys should try it more often."

"We—"

"—just escaped a bomb, incarceration, a werewolf, a hell-beast, a sorcerer, and Eve's really sharp sword. We have earned a break. Or I have. You guys can play along."

"We need—"

"Does it involve running? Fighting? Slaying? Uh-uh. Not for the next"—she checked the bedside clock—"six hours."

"One."

"Five."

"One."

My mother laughed.

Jaime glowered at her. "You think that's funny. Of course, you do. You raised her." She turned to me. "Four and a half."

"Two."

"Fine. Two hours. During which time we will do or say nothing—"

"We need to discuss what happened and plan our next steps. If you want to rest instead, I'm sure a few blankets will make the bathtub very comfy."

"Fine. Talk."

We started by piecing together what happened at the police station. Or a reasonable guess, based on what we knew. Medina had been working for the Supernatural Liberation Movement, sedating supernaturals and ultimately delivering them to the laboratory, where they'd become guinea pigs for the vaccine. Then sorcerer dude inserts himself into the equation. Either he wriggles his way into SLAM or he takes out Medina's usual drug supplier. He gives her drugs that will agitate the supernaturals in custody, making them everything from ill to crazy to psychotic.

Why? Well, that was the first of many questions. He hadn't seemed surprised by the reactions to the drugs. Why would a supernatural intentionally cause a scene that risked humans discovering our powers? Sure, that's what SLAM ultimately wanted, but this wasn't the kind of "reveal" that made us look like peaceful and productive members of society.

Whatever the reason, he gives Medina the drugs. Then she picks us up following a call from SLAM. He finds out. And he decides this would be a really, really good time to try that new spell he's been working on. Use Jaime and me to lure my mother, then conjure her into the world of the living.

Why?

"An angel is always handy," Jaime said. "Even in a fight between demons. Especially if you're also half-demon yourself. Eve gets hit up by more influence peddlers than any politician."

"I can see that," I said. "With Balaam leading the pro-reveal side, even *I'm* useful. He made a personal appearance a few days ago." I turned to Mom. "Turns out the reveal movement is harboring a couple of his lackeys. A real nice brother-sister duo named Sierra and Severin. Ice half-demons with a talent for torture. Balaam had them hold me hostage so he could propose an alliance."

"That son of a bitch." Mom's sword wobbled beside her, glowing bright blue. "I heard he'd spoken to you, but taking you hostage—"

"Um, Eve?" Jaime said. "Can we hold off on threatening a lord demon? Even if he is your father?"

"So he contacted you, too?" I said. "Or tried?"

Mom hesitated.

"It's okay," I said. "I'm a big girl. I'm used to being second choice. And also being kidnapped as a way to get to you."

Her expression made me regret saying that.

"I'm sorry, baby," she said. "I know you've gone through hell because you're my daughter. I never intended that."

I shrugged. "Honestly, the cost-benefit ratio comes out in my favor. I get a lot of mileage out of being your daughter and only the occasional threat on my life. Even that's just in the last week or so. Which I suspect isn't coincidental."

"It's not. The Fates have always been able to keep this angel gig a secret. If that's not the case anymore, something's broken down." She paused. "Actually, lots of things have broken down. It's hell over there. No joke intended."

"The movement," I said. "It's got the demons divided, and that's rippling through everything, isn't it?"

"Not just the demons. The angels are split, too. The ascended ones, at least."

"Are they supernaturals?"

"Most, but the divide isn't along those lines. Some—former human and supernatural—think exposure is the best thing for everyone. Others, like me, think it'll be a catastrophe. So it's chaos, with the Fates and everyone else trying to keep order and doing a damned poor job of it. Balaam has had imps and demi-demons out for weeks, scouring the dimensions trying to find me. I've been slaughtering them left and right. But a full-blood angel saw me talking to one. Next thing you know, the rumor's circulating that I'm a double agent for Balaam, which is what a lot of them believe anyway."

I remembered what Kimerion said. "They think you helped Leah escape, don't they?"

Jaime sat up. "Seriously? Oh, yes, you freed the bitch who tried to kill Paige, so she could go back to earth and give it another shot. Maybe take your daughter out, too."

"According to their theory, I wasn't really all that upset about what Leah did with Paige. Considering Leah was working for Kristof, I probably had a hand in it so he could get custody of Savannah easier. Later, I came to feel a little bad about Leah getting a raw deal. So I agreed to free her for Balaam, to help this liberation movement, with her promise that she'd stay away from Savannah. When she reneged on the deal, I dragged her back to her hell dimension before she could tattle."

"They believe that?" I said.

"In the angel corps, the ascendeds keep tallies of souls retrieved. Like notches on our swords. Trsiel"—she glanced at me—"my partner, keeps another tally for me. Enemies made. By this point, the lists are about equal. And I'm very, very good at my job."

She pulled her feet up to sit cross-legged on the bed. "The Fates know it's bullshit. But an angel *was* involved with Leah's escape. They know that, too. So they put me on the case, also knowing I'm pissed off and eager to clear my name. All this means that there are multiple reasons why this sorcerer might have brought me over. Maybe he wanted an angel for the fight. Or he wanted an angel for a hostage. Or he wanted Balaam's daughter. Or I was getting too close to finding out who freed Leah. Main point for now? He *did* bring me over. We need to find out who this guy was, which isn't going to be—"

I held up a wallet. "Dead sorcerer guy's wallet, complete with ID."

My mother smiled. "Smart girl."

"I'm a licensed PI, Mom, even if I do spend more time behind the reception desk than in the field."

"All right then," Mom said. "You and I can take showers, and then we'll hit the road. Jaime? You just keep on resting. You don't need to wash that blood out of your hair. It's red anyway. And I'm pretty sure that *isn't* puke—"

Jaime was in the bathroom, slamming the door, before she finished.

Mom grabbed the motel stationery and started writing. As soon as the shower started, she set the paper on the nightstand, got off the bed, and slung her sword onto her back.

"Let's go, baby."

"But . . ." I glanced at the bathroom door. "Oh."

"Yes, we're ditching the diva. I'd say she'll kill me later, but I'm pretty sure that's not possible, and even if it is, I'll only end up back where I was this morning."

"Someone has to—"

"Lucas has already sent a local operative. That's what I was doing with her phone earlier—texting the motel address to him. Now come on."

"Just a sec."

"We can't—" She began.

I grabbed Jaime's cell phone. "We may need this."

Mom smiled. "That's my girl."

The Cabal operative was due to arrive in five minutes. We were to meet him at the corner, where we could keep an eye on the motel until he arrived.

We didn't speak until we got there. Then Mom said, "I don't like tricking her either, Savannah."

"I never said—"

"I can see it in your face. Yes, I would have rather just told her to stay behind, but as much as she bitches about staying out of the action, she'd never have agreed."

"And if she came she'd be likely to get hurt. So it's better for her if we leave her behind."

"Exactly."

"And her lack of offensive powers means she's not much help in a fight, which means she'd just be an extra person to look after."

She exhaled. "Do you want me to deny that, Savannah? I won't. My main concern is her getting hurt."

I checked my watch, then eased back under the shade of a tree, in case Jaime decided on an uncharacteristically short shower and looked outside for us.

"You don't agree," Mom said.

A bubble of panic popped inside me. Of course I did. I always agreed with my mother. She knew best. She took care of—

I took a deep breath and silenced twelve-year-old Savannah.

"I . . . agree in principle, but I wouldn't have handled it the same way."

"Good," she said, so emphatically I jumped. "You aren't a carbon copy of me, Savannah. I don't want you to be. I want you to be your own person. In this case, I stick by my decision. We agree to disagree. And we push on. Unless you want to . . ."

She nodded back toward the motel.

I shook my head. "It's done now, and I'm guessing that's the Cabal guy's car turning the corner."

The car did belong to the man Lucas had sent for Jaime. He was a typical operative, a completely unassuming guy who could probably win an Ultimate Fighting title with one hand tied behind his back. We checked his ID—Lucas had texted Mom his details. He'd also sent us a code phrase, which the guy repeated.

The operative didn't ask our names. Didn't display an iota of curiosity, except when he noticed the glowing sword on Mom's back. Even then, all he did was blink. Mom said, "We're ditching our friend to go to a Dungeons and Dragons convention." He didn't even smile. Jaime was going to love this guy. And love us all the more, not only for deserting her, but for forcing his company on her.

He left. We waited until he reached the motel door, then took off before the fireworks began.

JAIME

Jaime stood under the shower, eyes closed, letting the steaming water massage her neck and back. It might be a cheap motel, but apparently, midday, no one was using the water and she got all the hot water she wanted. And she wanted a lot. Even after twenty minutes of scalding, she swore she could still feel blood and filth in every pore.

She was not, as she always admitted, cut out for a life of adventure. Not unless it came with rich food and soft beds and perfumed baths. And Jeremy. After four years together, he was the key ingredient in her life, even if it did mean the occasional morning spent, drugged and sick, on a dirt-and-pest-encrusted prison cot.

Thinking of that cot, Jaime emptied the rest of the mini shampoo bottle on her head. As she lowered her hands, she noticed dried blood deep under her long nails. With a shudder, she scraped it out and tried not to think of where it came from. When that failed, she played the "what I'll do when all this is over" game, which had gotten her through many an ordeal in the past. Jeremy had made her play it just last evening when she had been feeling helpless sitting around Cortez headquarters as everyone else raced off to action.

Italy, Jeremy suggested. A week in an Italian villa, just the two of them. Maybe more than a week, if they could both swing it. That was usually the sticking point—their own schedules and responsibilities, Jaime's career and Jeremy's Alphahood. But they never complained or wished things could be different. They weren't kids. They'd built their own lives before they'd met and they still led them, taking advantage of any time when those lives could intersect—which made them feel like kids sometimes, ducking out on their responsibilities to play hooky together. Those interludes would grow more frequent when he stepped down as Alpha, and someday maybe they'd even live together, grow old together. But for now, this worked, and you don't mess with what works.

A distant knock startled her. She turned off the water and listened. It must be housekeeping or pizza delivery—hell-beasts and evil sorcerers don't knock—but she wasn't taking any chances.

The knock came again.

"Is that our door?" she called.

No one answered. Jaime wrapped a towel around herself, stepped out of the tub, and cracked open the door.

The beds were empty. She pushed the door. The whole room was empty. She heard a muffled man's voice outside. As she strained to listen, the phone by the bed rang.

She looked around. Weapon. She needed a . . . She grabbed a glass from the sink and went to break it, then realized it was plastic. "Goddamn cheap motel," she cursed.

She looked down at her clothing, left in a puddle on the floor. She tugged out her belt and held it in one hand. As she eased from the bathroom, she clutched her weapon and prayed that Eve *wasn't* out there or she'd never live this one down. Eve still liked to remind her of the "sock puppet" incident, when Jaime had used a sock to hold on to a glass shard in case she needed to fight off a cult of crazed humans who'd discovered magic. Jaime had considered the make-shift weapon rather ingenious, but admittedly, it did pale next to Eve's sword.

The phone was still ringing.

"Ms. Vegas?" the man outside the door called. "Could you please answer that?"

Jaime looked at the phone. She'd never heard of them being used as a method of instant death, so she crept toward the nightstand, gaze fixed to the door. Then, still holding the belt, she lifted the receiver with the same hand.

"Jaime?"

Just that one word and she dropped to the bed, sighing in relief, weapons falling. It was Jeremy.

"Jaime? Are you there?"

"Yes. Alone. In a motel room. With a stranger knocking at the door. Care to tell me what's going on?"

She tried to put a little edge in her voice, but she wasn't very good at edge. She was mostly just relieved to discover she wasn't going to need to defend herself, dressed in a towel, armed with a belt.

When Jeremy explained that she'd been abandoned by her friends, and that Lucas had sent a baby-sitter, she did feel a spark of righteous indignation, but only a spark. Yes, it pricked her ego to be left behind, but she knew she was better off out of it. What did annoy her—really annoy her— was that Eve hadn't given her the opportunity to make that decision herself.

"I know," Jeremy said when she complained. "She felt this was better."

"Not better. Easier. She's quick to wield that damned sword, but not nearly so brave when it comes to personal confrontations. All those messy emotions. Blood is so much easier to clean up."

Jeremy chuckled—that rich, deep chuckle that made her insides flip, and she yearned to just stretch out on the bed and talk to him. Forget everything that was going on. But there was still a man standing outside her door and she should probably get dressed before she let him in.

"Yes, I would prefer that," Jeremy said when she said as much to him. "He might not, but I would."

She laughed. "All right, then. My adventure is over, thank God." She paused. "But if you hear from Eve . . ."

"You're mortally offended at being left behind."

"Exactly."

The poor guy had been waiting long enough. So, wrapped in her towel, Jaime opened the door an inch, told the man she was just popping into the bathroom to dress, then scampered off. At least a minute passed before she heard the motel door close. Anyone smart enough to be assigned as her escort would have the sense to realize that a sneak peek at Jaime Vegas in a towel wasn't worth the risk of offending the werewolf Alpha.

She was almost finished dressing in her hastily wiped clothing when she heard another knock at the outside door. She frowned. The guard had come in—she was sure she'd heard him moving around the bedroom.

A high-pitched voice. "Mommy? Why's the door locked?"

A sigh from the bedroom. The guard called back, "You've got the wrong room."

"Mommy?" Louder pounding. "Is that you, Mommy?"

Jaime threaded her belt through her slacks, then opened the bathroom door. The guard—a dark-haired guy in a suit—was staring out the window, his lips pursed.

"It sounded like a little girl," Jaime said.

He glanced her way. "It is. I'll get rid of her. But I'll ask you to step back in there until I do."

Jaime nodded and retreated. He waited until she'd shut the door. She heard him undo the chain.

"Who're you?" a girl asked.

"Not your mommy. Now, if you've forgotten your room number, go down to the office—"

"What did you do with my mommy? I heard her in here."

Jaime sighed. The girl sounded old enough to know better, but she kept insisting that her "mother" was in there and the more the guard argued, the more distressed she got.

Jaime stopped fussing with her wet hair and reached for the door handle. She could clear up this "mommy's voice" problem by just sticking her head out.

As she twisted the knob, the guard yelled, "Hey! What do you think you're—"

"I'm looking for my mommy. You've got her in here. I know you do."

"Get back here, you little—"

A growl. Then a gasp of pain.

"What the—?"

A crash. Then the patter of footsteps on carpet. The guard's cry, muffled, then garbled. Jaime yanked off her belt, wrapped it around her hand, and turned the knob slowly, her bare foot braced against the bottom. She eased it open, just enough to peer through and see—

Something flew at the door. It hit with a patter, like rain, some of it falling to the carpet. Bright red drops of blood sprayed across the wall and carpet.

Jaime shut the door fast and locked it. Then she looked around frantically for real weapons.

Weapons? Against something that was killing a trained Cabal operative? Her gaze rose to the window.

Was it big enough? It better be. She wrenched the towel bar, stumbling back in surprise when it actually came free in her hand. Thank God for shoddy construction. She wrapped the bar in a towel to muffle the noise, then smashed out the window. She managed to get most of the glass cleared, then someone—or something—began yanking on the door.

A quick sweep of the remaining glass and out she went, ignoring the slivers that bit into her stomach as she wriggled through. Had she been thinking, she'd have gone feet first. She didn't, and tumbled headfirst to the ground, managing to land in an awkward somersault and bounce back onto her feet. It wasn't exactly martial arts, but sometimes decades of yoga paid off.

The motel backed onto a field, with boggy forest about fifty feet away. To either side, the building stretched out at least half the distance. The forest was really Jeremy's domain, not hers. She took a few running steps along the back wall, then saw a shadow stretching out from the far end. Another joined it. She spun, her back going to the wall. Through the broken window, she heard the bathroom door give way with a crack.

She looked out across the weed-choked field to the forest. She took a deep breath, then she started to run.

CHAPTER 9

We walked along the road, with Mom casting blur spells every time a car passed.

"Maybe a cello case," I murmured, eyeing the sword as she reappeared.

"Will I look like a cello player? Or an assassin hiding an automatic rifle?"

Valid point. My mother didn't look like an assassin, but she looked even less likely to set foot in a symphony hall.

"A hockey bag would work," Mom said as we continued on. "Once, just after I got the angel gig, I had to deliver a message to your dad at his hockey game, and we weren't exactly eager to share my new occupation with his teammates yet, so I hid it in his bag."

"My father plays hockey?"

"*Plays* might be an exaggeration. More like watches from the penalty box."

I laughed. "That I can see. But, um . . ." I looked at the sword. "It's an angel sword, Mom. Stuffing it in a hockey bag just doesn't seem right."

"It's a tool, baby. One that come with some serious . . ." Her face clouded for a moment, then she shook her head. "Let's just say that while I've grown fond of wielding a four-foot hunk of metal, I don't have a problem with stuffing the damned thing in whatever does the job. Irreverent, yes, but the Fates expect no less of me."

"Okay. Well, a hockey bag might work, but your chances of finding one in New Orleans . . . ?"

"Mmm, you're right. A sports store is still our best bet, though."

It was. I left her outside, went in and returned with a bow case. We still weren't getting through any metal detectors, but Mom could walk around like a normal person, which meant—as Jaime warned—that she did bump into a few people before she got the hang of being corporeal again. I'd also bought myself a mock turtleneck tank top, which covered the cut on my throat.

We took a cab to the dead sorcerer's place, which we got from his ID, along with his name. Shawn Roberts. He lived in the French Quarter, in an apartment over a shop selling high-end masks.

He didn't live alone either. He had a wife. And a Rottweiler. Both figured prominently in his wallet photos. Both were home, as a quick call from a pay phone confirmed. No, I hadn't asked to speak to the dog, but I heard it barking. And barking. And barking.

"Who the hell keeps a Rottweiler in an apartment?" Mom fumed as we stood beside the building. "And it's two in the afternoon. Shouldn't she be at work?"

We stepped back for a couple of drunken tourists with pink drinks in plastic cups. Mom stared after them then grabbed my wrist to check my watch.

"Little early, isn't it?"

"We're a block from Bourbon Street."

Her face screwed up, as if she didn't know what difference that made. Then she winced. "Damn, I really have been dead too long. Also been away from New Orleans too long. I kept wondering what that smell was."

"The faint traces of rotting garbage, urine and vomit, mingled with street cleaner. Eau de la French Quarter.

And four things you probably don't smell in the afterlife."

"True." She took a deep breath. "As disgusting as it is, it does bring back pleasant memories. I did a lot of business here in the old days. I loved New Orleans, almost as much as I loved Savannah, Georgia."

I smiled. "I remember. As for why Roberts's wife is home . . ." I pulled a couple of business cards from Roberts's wallet. His wife's. Being a considerate husband, he must have handed them out for her. She was a baker. The work address matched their apartment.

"Damn," Mom said.

"We're going to have to lure them out. Question is, what would get both the woman and the dog—"

A whistle. Followed by a happy bark. I leaned out from our hiding place to see the woman in the photos walking from the building, the dog on its leash.

"Our timing is excellent," I said.

I'd grabbed break-in supplies from the sporting-goods store. Amazing what you can get there. Not exactly regulation cat burglar tools, but they'd do the job.

I had rods that approximated picks, but Mom's unlock spell handled that. Then, as she stood watch, I rammed a pencil into the keyhole and broke off the tip.

"Adam's trick," I said. "Makes it hard to open. It'll give us enough advance warning so we can escape."

"I have a perimeter spell for that."

"Which you can use. Never hurts to have backup."

Inside, the place reeked of dog—the smell of fur and canned food and the faint odor from a time or two when Rover must not have been let outside fast enough. Which made me think . . .

"We need to work fast," I whispered. "She might just be taking the dog for a pee break."

I took the computers. There were two—both laptops—on desk shelves. The first started up fine, no password required. It was hers. The second was protected. I didn't have time to crack it. As it was a laptop, I couldn't easily snag the hard drive. I could take the whole thing, but that would be noticed a lot faster than a missing hard drive.

So I joined Mom in her search. She'd hit pay dirt. A cell phone. Roberts didn't have one on him when I checked, and I figured he'd left it in his car. This was an older model that he must not have been quite ready to ditch. The SIM card had been removed, but he had plenty of contact information saved on the phone itself. Enough for us to track down whomever he'd been working with.

We took the phone and left.

We headed for a coffee shop. Easy enough to find in the French Quarter. I'd withdrawn cash near the sports store— Lucas had deemed it safe enough, as long as I promptly left the immediate area after I used the machine. I'd given some to my mother so she wouldn't be wandering around with empty pockets.

"Remember I used to do that?" she'd said. "Always made sure you had a few dollars in your pocket?"

"I thought that was for emergency phone calls."

"You'd only need a quarter for that. I just . . . I remember when I was little, I liked having some money on me. Made me feel safer."

I'd never thought of it that way. Even now, I wasn't really sure what she meant. I guess we'd had very different childhoods. I didn't know much about hers. Just that when she'd left it behind, she left behind everyone in it.

We picked a narrow shop that advertised slow-drip coffee. I had no idea what that was, but it sounded promising.

As we went in, Mom pulled out a five and said, "My treat."

"Not with that."

She looked at the menu board and stared at it a moment. Swore. Then took out a ten.

"You go sit down," she said. "I've got this."

"Okay, I'd like—"

"Mocha with whipped cream and sprinkles." She grinned. "Right?"

I wanted to say yes. Damn it, I really wanted to, but my expression gave me away.

"So what you drank at twelve is not what you drink at twenty-one, right?" she said.

"Mmm, no. Sorry. But if you get a chance to meet Adam, you can buy *him* a mocha. He loves the sweet stuff."

Her smile softened. "I hope I do get a chance to meet Adam, baby."

I blushed, and remembered our kiss after the bomb blast. Did he mean it *that* way? God, I hoped he meant it that way, even though it was a completely inappropriate concern under the circumstances.

I took a deep breath and started to say I'd have an espresso, then remembered where we were and changed it to café au lait. Not my usual drink, but there's something about New Orleans that makes it the only choice for caffeine.

I went out the side door and found a table in the alley. Mom arrived a few minutes later, with two café au laits and an assortment of baked goods.

"I figured you must be hungry. I know I am." She sat down. "Which feels really strange. Took me a minute to figure out what it was."

"You don't get hungry, I take it."

"Nope. Never tired either." She took a long drink of her coffee, then closed her eyes and shivered. "Damn, that feels good. I've spent ten years drinking coffee in the afterlife, feeling like there's something missing."

She took a cranberry-studded cookie from the selection, and I bit into a red velvet cupcake. She waved at my choice. "Some things don't change."

I smiled. "Yes, I still have a sweet tooth. Just not for coffee. Okay, let's check out this cell phone."

She took it from her pocket. I held out my hand. She hesitated then put it back into her pocket.

"Not yet," she said. "Jaime's safe. We're safe." She took a sip of hers. "So tell me about Adam."

I blushed again and shook my head. "Nothing to tell."

"Oh, there's plenty to tell." She tilted her head, studying my face, then gave a wistful smile. "I've missed so much, haven't I?"

I wanted to say no, she hadn't, not really. But that was silly. Nearly half my lifetime had passed since her death. I imagined what it would have been like if she'd been there. What would I have told her about Adam? Would I have sought her advice? Or would I have been terrified of it? Worried she'd say he was too old for me? That she might tease me and tip him off?

Except, if she had been there, the point would have been moot, because there would be no Adam in my life. No Paige. No Lucas. No werewolf Pack. No interracial council. No Cabals, except maybe the Nasts, and only because we'd be hiding from them, my mother trying to keep me safe, which meant keeping me away from the Nasts.

No Adam for me. No Kristof for her. A completely different life for both of us.

A better life?

It felt disloyal to admit that this life *was* better for me. Painful to admit it was also better for her. But it was. I'd said earlier that I wanted to ask if she was happy. Now, looking over at her, I didn't need to. I'd always thought of my mother as a free spirit, loving to wander, needing to see everything, do everything, be everything. But now, as I looked back, I didn't see wanderlust. I saw an anxious restlessness that had kept her up at night, when I'd sneak in and find her staring out the window, only to turn and announce we had to leave again. There wasn't anticipation in her voice on those nights—there was regret.

She was different now. Grounded. Centered. She was still constantly in motion, fingers rubbing her coffee cup, gaze surveying the alley. But it wasn't anxiety, just my mother's usual watchfulness.

"Tell me about you," I said. "About your new job. Being an angel. That's gotta be cool." I grinned. "Considering the size of that sword, I'm guessing angelhood isn't about playing harps and listening to prayers."

"It's not. Glorified bounty hunter is more like it. We go after anyone and anything raising hell where they shouldn't be. Imps and demi-demons, hell-dimension escapees, general afterlife shit disturbers."

"Which explains why you were hot on Leah O'Donnell's trail. So that happens a lot? Souls escaping hell?"

"Not like that. If they do escape, it's from a minor, temporary hell dimension. More like a holding cell for folks who need a time out before they're ready to join—or rejoin—afterlife society. And they'd escape into the afterlife or some other realm on our side of the veil. It takes serious mojo to come here, which is why the Fates should have guessed Leah's escape wasn't an isolated incident."

"But you like the job?" I said. "You seem to be okay with it."

"The job's fine. It's the deployment I could live without."

"Deployment?"

"Ascended angels are celestial soldiers. Career soldiers. We live in the angel realm, like a soldier lives in barracks. Every now and then we get leave, but otherwise, it's a calling, not a nine-to-five job."

"But Kristof . . . ? You don't live with . . . ?" I paused. "No, wait. That's why Jaime says you're on walkabout—when you're deployed. She can't contact you and he can't contact you."

She nodded. "Three months on, three months off. They started with six and six, but I've renegotiated."

"And that's the part you're not okay with. Being separated from him."

"We've learned to deal with it. I've learned to stop bitching about it. I like the job. Love it, though I hope the Fates aren't eavesdropping on me admitting that. As for your father . . . Let's just say I go AWOL more than any other ascended. Fortunately, my partner and I have the best soul-skewering record around, so as long as I don't flaunt it, the Fates look the other way."

I leaned forward. "Tell me a story."

She stopped sipping her coffee. "Hmm?"

"You used to tell me bedtime stories. Wild adventures of yours—suitably cleaned up, I'm sure. Tell me one now. From the afterlife. You don't have to clean it up anymore."

She laughed. "Actually, I might, since the one I have in mind involves your father. All right, then. An afterlife story. Once upon a time, your dad was in court, defending a half-demon who . . ."

As she told me the story, I leaned back in my chair, coffee in one hand, cupcake in the other, and the rest of the world seemed to swirl away. The details of what she was telling me didn't matter. I was ten again, curled up in bed, listening to my mother's voice. Whatever happened after this didn't matter either. For these few minutes, I had her back. Not Eve Levine, notorious dark witch. Not Eve Levine, daughter of Balaam. Not even Eve Levine, ascended angel. Just my mother. Me and my mom.

After that, we got down to business. I wasn't familiar with Roberts's older-model smartphone, but figured it out easily enough. Contacts, recent calls, e-mails, and calendar. Those were the things we wanted. Sadly, none of his contacts were marked "evil confederates in a plot to destroy life as we know it."

"There are a few possibilities in the calendar," I said. "Seems he put in a lot of gym time. He didn't look like a body builder to you, did he?"

"Nope. Just your garden variety office drone, makes a pit stop at the gym once or twice a week to keep his spare tire at bay."

"He seems to have been meeting people at the gym. Which would be more helpful if he didn't refer to them by a single initial. And if he wasn't a salesman."

"Huge contact list?"

"Bigger than mine."

She smiled. "If yours is anything like mine, that's big. Okay"—another slug of coffee. Another blissful shiver— "let's start going through that list. We'll—"

My cell phone—well, Jaime's phone—rang. Some god-awful eighties tune.

Mom winced. "I can change that, right? After three years of listening to it, please tell me I can finally change it."

"You can. Right after this call. It's Lucas."

I answered with, "So how angry is Jaime?"

"Has she called you?"

There was a tightness to his tone that told me this wasn't a casual question.

"She's okay, right?" I said quickly. "We checked the guy's ID, got the passcode, watched him knock on the door. I mean, we didn't stick around to make sure he went in, but—"

Mom was leaning forward, frowning. I pulled the phone away a bit and turned up the volume so she could hear.

Lucas said, "Jeremy had to speak to Jaime to get her to open up, but she did. The operative was supposed to take her to a hotel and call for further instructions. After an hour, Jeremy grew concerned. I'd told the operative to make sure Jaime got everything she needed, though, so I presumed they were . . ."

"Shopping."

"Yes. After another thirty minutes, Jeremy insisted I call our man. Jaime may like to shop, but under the circumstances, she'd only pick up what she needed for a brief hotel stay. So I called. The operative didn't answer. I left a message. It's been twenty minutes since."

Not exactly time to call in the National Guard. I suspected Jeremy was applying pressure, in his quiet but inescapable way.

"Give me the hotel address," I said. "We can pop by and see . . . No, you'd have already called. She hasn't checked in."

"Correct. Paige is running Jaime's credit cards now. I'm having the security department pull GPS records for the operative's vehicle. In the meantime, Jeremy would like you to return to the motel."

CHAPTER 10

Lucas had us pick up a rental car. All the paperwork was filled out in the Cortez Corporation name, so I just had to flash ID. I drove. We really didn't want anyone pulling over my mother and asking for her license.

"Shit," she whispered as we pulled into the motel lot.

A dark blue Toyota was parked in front of our room. The same dark blue Toyota that the operative had been driving.

Mom was out of the car before I stopped. She left her sword in the trunk and raced inside. The motel room door was unlocked.

I was getting out when the car lurched, the back end rising. It thumped down so hard my teeth rattled. I hit the trunk release before the damned thing ripped through the metal. The sword flew—case and all—through the motel room door.

I tore after it. When I got inside—

Blood. Oh, God, there was so much blood.

The operative lay on his back, arms raised to ward off something. His clothing was shredded, exposed skin mangled and torn, like he'd been attacked by . . .

I had no idea what he'd been attacked by.

I dropped to look under the bed.

"Already checked," Mom said. She stood in the middle of the room now, turning slowly.

I ran into the bathroom.

"Checked there, too," Mom called.

I still looked. There was nowhere else to search. The bathroom was empty, but there were bloody footprints on the floor.

Small sneaker prints.

"Mom . . . ?"

She came in. I pointed at the prints.

"Jaime must have put those sneakers back on," she said.

I moved my foot alongside one of the prints. Mine was nearly twice the size.

As Mom crouched for a better look, I followed the prints into the bedroom and noticed as I did that the bathroom door knob was crooked. Broken.

"Jaime locked herself in there," I said. "Whoever killed the operative broke in and—"

I stopped. There was a handprint on the outside of the bathroom door. It was two-thirds the size of mine.

"There's a kid's handprint here," I said. "How could a child—?"

"Child*ren*," Mom said. "The prints are from more than one person. And—"

She stopped and turned to the bathroom window as the curtain billowed. She yanked it up. The window was broken out, jagged glass like shark's teeth in the frame. Blood-tipped shark's teeth.

"She went out here," Mom said.

I pointed to a small shoe print on the toilet seat. "And they followed."

So did we.

Directly behind the motel was a strip of scrubland that bordered a patch of forest. There was no sign of which way Jaime or her pursuers had gone. Jaime was smart enough to head for the road. Had they let her? Or had they herded her into the forest? I was betting on the latter.

I was right. There was a single overgrown path leading in. Fresh footprints in the soft earth. Vines and undergrowth trampled.

We moved quickly and quietly, ears attuned. I picked up the occasional bird cry. That was it.

How long ago had Jaime run? I didn't want to think about that. Of course, I still did. We'd been gone about two hours. Two hours of running through the forest, fleeing her pursuers.

If she'd escaped, she would have found a phone and called Jeremy. If she hadn't called . . .

I jogged faster.

When the path branched, we couldn't tell which way they'd gone. The denser forest meant less undergrowth to break through and drier ground, which didn't hold prints. We split up.

I'd gone about a quarter mile when a figure burst from the forest. It was a girl. Really a girl, no more than eleven. I knew we were looking for children, but I hadn't really believed it, certain there was another explanation.

It was a child, snarling and snapping like a rabid dog, saliva dripping from her mouth, blue eyes flashing, her ponytail spiked with twigs and laced with dirt. Dirt crusted her skin and clothing. Dirt and blood. Some of the blood had to be hers—her face and bare arms were crosshatched with cuts and scrapes. But there was too much to all be hers.

I thought of that body in the motel room. The operative.

The girl ran at me, and I instinctively started casting. I didn't consider my choice of spells. I just thought of that body and I cast from my gut. A demon-reveal spell.

The girl let out a horrible scream of agony that would have made me stop if it hadn't confirmed my suspicion. As I finished the incantation, I slammed into her. Her tiny body folded like a rag doll and crashed onto the ground. I winced, but I still dropped, straddling her, pinning her hands over her head as she writhed, eyes squeezed shut.

"Keeping your eyes closed won't help," I said. "That scream told me I was right, demon."

She opened her eyes. The blue had brightened to an orange-tinged red. She spat and howled and writhed.

"Savannah!" Mom's voice. I heard her feet pounding along the path.

"Over here," I called. "I got one."

I kept my gaze on the girl as Mom came to stand beside me.

"It *is* a child," she whispered.

"Not exactly. Check out the eyes. Never quite seen that color, but it's definitely demonic."

"No, baby, it can't be. She's just a child. The Berithian Treaty—" She stared as the girl's eyes flashed. "That's a demon."

"Um, yeah. I—"

The girl reared up, teeth bared and on a collision course with my arm. Mom caught her in a binding spell.

"Thanks," I said. "I cast a demon reveal, which means my spells won't work on her for a while."

"Which is why you really shouldn't cast it if you suspect a demon."

"I knew what I was doing, Mom."

I'd made the right choice—reveal the demon before risking harm to the girl. Just because I couldn't use spells on it afterward didn't mean I was defenseless.

Mom crouched beside the girl. "I don't understand. The Berithian Treaty . . ." She moved behind the girl and pinned her shoulders. "Okay, I'm going to release the spell so we can talk to her. Oh, and the eye color? That means it's not really a demon. More of a demonic entity. You won't have had any experience with these guys. Strictly hell-dimension dwellers. At least until now."

She snapped the binding spell and the girl started gnashing her teeth and kicking. We had her securely pinned, and when she realized she wasn't going anywhere, she settled for hissing, eyes pulsating between red and orange.

"Where's Jaime Vegas?" Mom said.

The girl spat. Mom pinned one shoulder with her knee instead, and lifted the sword over the girl's head.

"You know what this is?"

The girl chortled. "Yes, but you cannot use it, angel, or you will kill the child."

"How did you get inside her? The Berithian Treaty forbids demonic possession of children—"

"Treaties are for cowards. The Tengu are not cowards."

"How did you possess humans at all?" I said. "Only full demons can possess living—"

"Nothing is as it was. Everything is as it should be. Or soon will be."

"Forget the how," Mom said. "We want Jaime Vegas. The woman you were chasing."

"We know who we chase. Tengu are not fools. While the others pursue chances, we wait and we watch for opportunity. Then we strike."

She lunged, teeth sinking into my arm. Mom hit her with an energy bolt. She let go and fell back, screaming.

"You hurt the child," the girl whispered. "You hurt the child."

"Yeah, well, you know what would really hurt the child?" Mom put her other knee on the girl's shoulder, then wrapped both hands around the sword and leveled it over the girl's chest.

"You will not," the girl chortled. "I know you will not. It is forbidden for your kind to kill an innocent."

"Who said anything about killing?" Mom lowered the sword to the stomach and used the tip to pluck up her shirt.

Then she lowered it within an inch of the girl's bare skin. "All I need to do is cut a hole big enough to rip you out of there. Skewer you on my sword and you're trapped."

The girl closed her eyes. When she reopened them, they were blue again. She looked up at Mom.

"Wha—what? Wh-who are you?" She saw the sword and screamed.

"Nice try," Mom said.

She lowered the tip until it brushed the girl's skin. The girl let out a howl of pain and terror as the skin blistered.

"Pl-please," she sobbed, looking at me. "Don't let her hurt me."

I hesitated and my grip loosened. The girl pulled one hand free and I lunged to grab it, but she only clasped my arm, fingers shaking as tears streamed down her thin face.

"Please," she said. "I don't know what I did wrong, but I'm sorry. I'll be good. Just don't let her hurt me anymore."

"Mom?" I said. "What if—?"

"Cast your spell again, baby."

I did. The girl squeezed her eyes shut and tried to hold in her shriek as the reveal burned through her.

"Like I said," Mom muttered, "nice try, demon."

She touched the sword to the girl's stomach. It blistered on contact, a fiery red splotch that made my stomach churn. Yes, blisters, a burn, maybe a cut—it would all heal. I'd think nothing of doing it to an adult. Only this wasn't an adult, and even if the child couldn't feel it now, she would once the demon left.

Mom caught my attention and cast a privacy spell, so the demon wouldn't overhear.

"That's why they possessed children. I know this isn't easy, baby. It's not supposed to be. That's the point."

I nodded. My mother dragged the sword tip along the girl's stomach. No pressure applied, but the skin broke anyway, blood oozing up.

"You hurt the child!" the demon shrieked. "You must not hurt the child!"

"No, I hurt you. And I'm about to hurt you a whole lot more if you don't—"

"She got away. The necromancer. She did escape us."

"Then why are you still here?"

Silence. Mom drew the sword back along the shallow cut. The demon writhed, then spat, "She is here. The Tengu can smell her. But we cannot find her. She hides."

Mom's exhale of relief was so deep the sword shuddered, making the demon yowl. She raised it off the girl's skin.

"Okay," I said. "So we need to find—"

"In a moment," Mom said. "Jaime's safe. She's found a place to hole up. We need to ask a few more questions."

"But—"

She lowered the sword again. As the demon squirmed, so did I. Yes, we had questions, but the main one had been answered. The rest we could figure out on our own.

"Who sent you?" Mom asked.

"Nobody sent us. We saw opportunity. We acted. The Tengu are not slaves."

"No, but they are boot-licking toads. You saw an opportunity to grab Jaime. And do what? Who wants her? You were going to turn her over to someone. Who?"

"Mom?"

She lifted a finger from the sword, telling me to wait.

"Mom, they don't want Jaime. That's not the opportunity they saw. It's you. They came for you. Jaime's just a means to an end."

Mom turned back to the demon. "Is that right? You saw me materialize and you came for me. You went after Jaime to get me. Who—?"

The demon let out a wail so high pitched it made my ears hurt. Then the girl's body went slack, head lolling back. Eyes closing.

"Here we go again," Mom muttered. "Tengu do love drama."

The girl's eyelids fluttered. Then they slowly opened. She blinked. Frowned. Looked around at the treetops. Then at the sword.

"What the hell?" the girl said.

She followed the sword up to my mother's arm, then to my mother, still kneeling on her shoulders.

"What the hell!"

The girl struggled, kicking and hitting and swearing a blue streak. Not exactly the language you'd use if you were trying to impersonate an eleven-year-old. One look at the girl's ragged clothing, though, and you knew she wasn't just some random child plucked from the schoolyard. She was a street kid.

This time it was Mom who cast the reveal spell. The girl didn't flinch, just keep struggling and shouting obscenities.

Mom eased off the girl's shoulders, lowering her sword and holding the girl by the arm instead. The girl let Mom help her up, then took a swing. Mom lifted her sword and said, "Uh-uh, sweetie."

"I'm not your sweetie," the girl snarled. "If you brought me here for some perv, you'll be sorry. I've got friends, you know. They have blades and—"

As she twisted to talk to my mother, she winced. She pulled up her shirt. "What the hell? You cut me! And burned me! You can't do that. I've got rights."

"Yes, you do," Mom said, keeping her grip tight on the girl's arm. "I'm sorry you got hurt. We didn't mean it. But someone gave you something—drugs or something. You attacked a friend of ours."

"I didn't attack any goddamned—"

The girl stopped. She stared down at her blood-speckled shirt. Then she lifted her hands. Her nails were crusted in blood. Her eyes widened and the tough little girl fell away, horror filling her face.

"It wasn't your fault," I said quickly. "Whoever gave you the drugs is to blame. And our friend is fine. But there are other kids out here. Your friends maybe. They got the same drugs. I'm going to take you someplace safe and—"

The forest erupted as five kids swarmed in, surrounding us. I grabbed the girl and pulled her against me. My fingers flew up in a knockback, but the girl yelped and flung herself away, disrupting my spell.

"Leave me alone," she said. "These are my—"

One of the kids let out a banshee howl and flew at the girl, his hands curved into claws. I pulled her out of the way just in time and kicked, catching him in the thigh. He crumpled, gnashing his teeth, lips drawn back in a grotesque, inhuman snarl.

The others hovered there, circling us, growling and eyeing the fallen boy, uncertain.

"Mickie," the girl said. "It's me, Sara."

He pushed to his feet, lips still drawn back. His dark eyes flickered, then flashed orange. Sara stumbled back against me. I put my arm around her and held her there.

"It's okay," I murmured. "It's the drugs." I glanced over at Mom. "Can we dispel them?"

"Not without the ritual." She hefted her sword. "Or this."

"You kill the children if you use that," the boy—Mickie— said. He was no more than fourteen, with a scarred lip and uneven cornrows. The oldest of them. The others watched him, waiting for a signal.

"Okay," Mom said to the boy. "So I can't use the sword. I saw what you did to that guy in the motel. I'm not stupid enough to fight the lot of you. So, if you let my daughter and the little girl go—"

Mickie cut her off with a sneering laugh. "You think the Tengu are fools? You would not give yourself to us so easily.

We will not let your daughter go. They say she is valuable, too. You will wait here with us until the necromancer is found. Then you will come with us or we kill all the children. One by one, we kill them."

The girl started to scream. It took me a moment to realize why. I guess that's what comes from living my life—I hear a threat and it rolls off me until there's a good reason to suspect it may be serious.

I put my arm around the girl as Mom pretended to negotiate with the leader.

"He—he said—" Sara's thin body shook so much she could barely get the words out. "He's going to kill us. Mickie's going to kill us."

"He doesn't mean it. It's the drugs. We won't let anyone hurt you."

"I want to go," she whispered. "Please, can you make them let me go?"

"Just hold on."

"I know how to . . ." She whispered something I couldn't catch, her voice too clogged with tears and snuffles.

I bent down. "What's that?"

"I said I know a way we can . . ."

She motioned me down so she could whisper in my ear. I leaned over.

"We can—"

She grabbed my hair and sank her teeth into my neck, just above the bandage. I flung her away. She stumbled back. A flap of my skin hung from her teeth. Blood dripped down her chin. Her eyes flashed orange.

I lunged, grabbed her by the scruff of the neck, and threw her toward the others just as the boy behind me charged. Mom slammed him with a knockback that sent him flying sideways. I grabbed his arm and yanked him aside, giving us a clear path out.

When a girl tried to run in front of us, Mom hit her with

an energy bolt that dropped her, howling and clasping her stomach. Another raced forward. Mom brandished her sword.

"You don't think I'll use this to protect my daughter?" she said. "Try me."

They stopped. The one behind her crept forward. My hand shot out. A knockback spell hit the kid so hard he sailed into a tree.

"Go, Savannah," Mom said, her gaze on the kids. "Use your sensing spell to find Jaime, then get out of here."

"I—"

"Savannah . . ." She didn't look over at me, but I felt like I was ten again, when we'd been walking back from dinner, and a group of supernatural thugs stepped into our path. She'd been right to send me away then. But I wasn't ten now and even with my sporadic spells, I could fight. Hadn't I just proven that?

"We can take them," I whispered. "Two are already injured."

The children shuffled forward.

"Stay where you are!" Mom said, her sword cutting through the air.

The children hissed and snarled, but their gazes followed the sword, and they stopped moving.

"You saw that operative," Mom whispered back. "That was a supernatural. A trained guard. We're not—"

One of the boys charged. I launched a knockback. It failed and I was about to jump forward when Mom swung her sword. The boy was still at least five feet away. A warning strike, I thought, but then the tip sliced through his shirt and an orange glow oozed through. Mom deftly skewered the demon and yanked the sword back. The boy collapsed. The Tengu was impaled on Mom's sword, a glowing miasma of red and orange, rolling on itself, a glimpse of eyes and teeth and claws appearing, then vanishing so fast they seemed a trick of the mind.

The sword sliced the orange and red cloud in two, a shriek rending the air, then fading as the two halves evaporated.

I looked down at the boy, still on the ground. His chest rose and fell. Unconscious. There was a line of blood on his shirt, but a thin one, a flesh wound.

"Anyone else doubt I'll use the sword?" Mom said.

The children had gone still.

"I need you to get Jaime," Mom said to me. "There might be more of them out there. She needs help. I'll be fine."

She was right. The first Tengu's scream had brought others running, but that didn't mean there weren't more still searching for Jaime.

"Okay," I murmured.

"Thank you, baby."

I backed away until I was sure Mom had the mob of demon children under control. Then I loped down the path.

CHAPTER 11

One advantage to being in the forest? I knew my sensing spell was working. In the police station, a negative result could mean either the place was empty or my spell failed. The forest is never empty. I got back plenty of small blips.

It didn't work every time. In fact, it fizzled more often than it sparked. But as I searched, I stopped casting it every few feet and used the spell judiciously.

I picked up one ping that was larger than a rabbit, but not big enough for Jaime. It could be a deer, but I hadn't seen any signs of them, so I guessed it was another child. I steered clear. No sense fighting if I didn't have to.

The Tengu inside Sara said it could detect Jaime's scent in the woods. That could mean she'd buried herself under leaves, as we'd tried with the sword. But diving into rotting vegetation would definitely be Jaime's last choice. I had a good idea what she'd done. It was a simple ruse that wouldn't fool most humans, but the Tengu weren't accustomed to tracking anyone in our world.

So I walked with my gaze on the treetops. Sure enough, I caught a glimpse of something burnt orange. Jaime's blouse. I squinted harder. Her face peered out between leafy branches twenty feet up. She didn't say anything, just eyed me and reached for the branch above, as if ready to climb higher.

"I'm not possessed," I said. "Paige had me take an extra dose of anti-possession tea when I was in Miami."

She came down about halfway, then settled into a Y. "They're still around. One passed by just a minute ago."

"Mom's holding most of them at bay. I can handle the stragglers. She's the one they really want anyway. As usual."

"Tell me about it," Jaime muttered as she lowered herself another branch. "We don't need anti-possession brews. We need anti-Eve brews." She paused, sighed, then said, "She's okay, right?"

"She was last time I saw her, but I'd like to get you someplace safe and go back to help her."

"Right. Sorry."

"You're lucky that ruse worked," I said. "From what I recall of Tengu folklore, they're supposed to be avian spirits. Like birds of prey."

"Which would mean they'd be accustomed to looking for victims on the ground."

I wasn't sure how true that was, but it had worked, so I wasn't arguing.

As she slid down, a nearby shriek sent her tumbling to the ground. I backed her to safety between me and the tree. A ragged girl about thirteen stood on the path. Her mouth opened so wide her jaw cracked as she shrieked again.

"She's calling the others," I said. "We need to get out—"

Another girl joined the shriek-fest from the opposite end of the path. I grabbed Jaime, pushed her into the forest, and we ran.

Not my best idea ever, as I realized about ten seconds later. It was boggy ground and we slipped and slid. The Tengu ran as fast and surefooted as antelope. I herded Jaime left and circled back to the path.

We'd just hit it when the thunder of footsteps had me pushing Jaime into the forest again.

"Wait!" she said.

She gestured and I followed her finger to see the blue glow of my mother's sword. A second later, Mom appeared . . . mere steps ahead of three Tengu-possessed children.

One of our pursuers burst from the forest. My hand flew out, hitting her with a knockback before the first incantation word left my mouth.

"Head back to the motel," Mom shouted. "I'll be right behind you."

"Is it this way?"

"I sure as hell hope so."

It wasn't. Not exactly anyway. After about five minutes, we could see a road ahead. We ran to it and found ourselves about a quarter mile up from the motel. One car passed us as we ran and it didn't even slow down.

A guy in the motel parking lot did notice us. He was halfway out of his car when we roared around the corner, raced to our rental, and hopped inside—Jaime and me in the front, Mom in the back. He stared at the kids pursuing us, took in their blood-flecked clothing and scratched, bloody faces, hopped back into his pickup, and went in search of more amenable lodgings.

I put the car in reverse just as two kids launched themselves onto the trunk. Another flew onto the hood. The others went for the side windows.

"You know, I think I've had this nightmare," Jaime said as they banged and howled and plastered their bloodied faces against the glass. "Except with zombies."

"Close enough," I muttered. "Hold on."

I gunned it in reverse. I guess I should have paid more attention in physics class. The one climbing onto the roof shot over the car, but Sara, still on the trunk, flew backward.

I hit the brakes before I ran her over. I knocked the gearshift into drive, hoping I had enough room to turn. The kid who'd flown from the roof leaped up right in my path. I checked the rearview mirror. Sara had wobbled to her feet, holding on to the trunk for balance. Another boy climbed onto the roof.

"Son of a bitch!" I said. "Why do they have to be children?"

"For the same reason you aren't hitting reverse and saying to hell with it," Mom said.

"The kid in front is bigger," Jaime said. "He can handle the impact better."

"Great," I said. "We've gone from 'don't hurt the kids' to 'which one will get hurt the least.'"

"Ease forward," Jaime said. "Knock him down carefully."

"Run him over. But gently," I muttered and gently pressed the gas.

The kid on the roof started jumping up and down. A girl took a running leap onto the roof and did the same, setting the car rocking.

"Just keep—" Mom began.

Jaime screamed as her window shattered. A boy reached in and grabbed a handful of her hair. Mom caught the kid's arm and twisted until he howled and let go, but another was already reaching through.

A crash. Something struck the side of my head so hard I saw stars. A brick dropped beside me. Hands reached through the broken driver's window.

I hit the gas. The hands grabbed the wheel and yanked, and the car shot up over the sidewalk and crashed into the motel. I turned to launch a knockback—or anything else— but the kid suddenly sailed backward. He landed on the asphalt and lay there, not moving.

I looked over at my mother, but she was helping Jaime fight off the kids. One of them went flying. This time, I saw him hover in the air, thrashing, as if something was holding him up. Then his head shot back and he screamed. The scream died midnote and the boy collapsed to the pavement, unconscious.

"Ah, a little deus ex machina," Mom said as the boy who'd grabbed Jaime's hair also went flying. "Or angel ex machina."

"It's Trsiel," Jaime said. "Or I think so. Can never tell with the full-bloods. All I see is a glowing silhouette."

"It's him," Mom said. "No other full-blood would bother." She leaned out the window and yelled, "Better late than never."

"I think he just gave you the finger," Jaime said.

Mom laughed. "Put it in gear, baby. He can handle this and we don't want to be around when the desk clerk realizes he's got unconscious street kids in his parking lot."

I put the car in reverse—Sara was gone now, running across the lot to escape her fate. We passed her and peeled out of the parking lot.

"So those were Tengu," I said as I drove. "I've heard of them, but not much. Like you said, they don't cross over."

"No," Mom murmured. "Not usually. They can, though, under special circumstances."

"A ritual?"

She shook her head. "War. The Tengu are harbingers of war."

When we were far enough from the motel to be sure we'd lost the Tengu, Jaime called Lucas and put us on speakerphone. I explained what had happened.

For the second time that day, I rendered Lucas speechless.

"So the Tengu do not appear to be directly connected to the sorcerer who invoked the hell-beast," he finally said.

"Right. They apparently saw Mom cross over and they came for her, but it's a completely separate shit storm. I don't know if you wanted us to do anything with the poor guy in the motel room . . ."

"No. If we have unconscious children in the parking lot, you need to stay away. I've already sent a message to divert part of the security team from the police station, but under the circumstances, I'm not sure they'll make it before someone discovers the operative's body."

Another voice came on. "We can still handle this. Two more teams are on their way to New Orleans, one security detail and one media cleanup team."

"Hey, Benicio," Mom said. "It's been a while."

"It has," he said. "I'd say it's good to hear you, Eve, but . . ."

"I'm back and causing trouble already. I know."

"So what do you guys want us to do?" I asked. "Hole up? Come to Miami?"

"I'm not going to Miami," Mom said before they could answer. "We've identified the sorcerer and we have a list of potential contacts. I've got a contact of my own here who can go through that list and pick out the supernaturals. That's my next stop."

Lucas and Benicio wanted her in Miami. Preferably in an impregnable cell, I think. Mom argued that her contact wouldn't speak to anyone else. Take Jaime to Miami. Take me to Miami. Leave Mom to face any potential kidnappers alone. If she wasn't putting anyone else at risk, that was her choice.

They agreed on the last part. I didn't. Mom needed someone to watch her back.

That didn't sit well with either Mom or Lucas, but they eventually agreed to a compromise. Jaime would leave. I'd stay, but only until they sent in someone with no personal connection to my mother—maybe Clay and Elena—to take over.

I agreed to that, and we headed to the regional airport where the Cortez jet was about to land.

Before Jaime left, I gave her a few minutes alone with Mom. They both said they didn't need it—joked that they "saw" each other too often as it was. But I insisted. In all those years that they'd worked together—that they'd been friends, as I now realized—they'd never actually inhabited the physical plane together. They hadn't met until Mom was long dead.

To say my mother was not the hugging type is an understatement. Growing up, I don't think I ever saw her make affectionate physical contact with anyone except me. But now, when I stepped away to give them that moment alone and they embraced, I saw how much it meant, and not just to Jaime.

Mom stayed until the jet lifted off. Then we took my new cell phone and left the damaged rental car at the airfield for Benicio to deal with. He'd rented us another—a small Mercedes, which was probably his idea of an economy vehicle—expendable, should we destroy it, too.

CHAPTER 12

Mom's old contact lived in a trailer park just off I-10. I figured he'd been displaced by Katrina and still didn't have a home, but Mom said no, Toby had always lived in a trailer.

If I hadn't known this area had been spared by the hurricane, I'd have been sure this particular trailer had been swept away by the floods and dragged back. It certainly looked that way. It even seemed to have mud spatter, until I got close enough to see it was rust. A lot of rust. One window was boarded up. The roof sagged at two corners. A single hinge held the screen door in place. Where other trailers had nice grass front "yards" and even flower beds, this one had mud, with beer cans piled as statuary.

Otherwise it was a decent trailer park. Respectable enough that we felt comfortable leaving the Mercedes in the visitors lot, though Mom did cast a security spell on it.

We didn't worry about sneaking up on the derelict trailer— the remaining windows were dark with blackout blinds.

"What's his type?" I asked as we approached.

"Blondes, I think. You're safe."

I gave her a look.

"He's an Aduro," she said. Midgrade fire half-demon. "You know how to handle that, I take it?"

"I do."

"Good."

She walked up to the side of the trailer, put her fingers to the aluminum and rubbed, as if clearing a peephole through dirty glass. That's exactly what she was doing, except as an Aspicio half-demon, she could see through more than just glass.

She shaded her eyes and peered through. Then she repeated the process further along.

"He's home," she murmured. "Watching TV. I'm going to have you head around the back. If I'm right, another boarded-up window doubles as an escape hatch."

"Got it."

I found the boarded window and waited while Mom knocked at the door. A minute passed. Then the wood over the window opened. A bald guy with glasses poked his head out.

"Hello," I said.

Toby stopped. Blinked. Glanced back toward the front of the trailer.

"No, you're not seeing double," I said. "My mother is still at the front door."

"You're . . ." His eyes widened, magnified by his thick glasses. "Shit!"

He swung at me, fingers blazing. Those glowing hands would have worked better if I hadn't grown up around Adam. A sharp sideswipe to his forearms knocked them down and knocked him off-balance. As he tumbled from the window, I grabbed him by the collar and hauled him upright.

"Got him!" I called.

Mom rounded the corner. Toby had been struggling, but he went still when he saw her.

"E-Eve," he said. "I thought it was . . ." He glanced at me. "I didn't get a good look, and I know your daughter is supposed to resemble you, so I figured that's who was at my door. You know I don't talk to anyone without an introduction. That's why I bolted. If I knew it was you—"

"You'd have bolted faster."

"I—"

"You thought you got off easy," she said as she set her sword case down. "I died right after you buggered up our deal with the St. Clouds. You got to keep the money, and I was dead and couldn't object. Surprise."

"I—I didn't renege on the deal. I was going to give you the money—"

"Which is why I hear you already had your truck hitched to your trailer, ready to skitter off for parts unknown. Until I disappeared and you figured you were safe to wait it out."

"Okay, so you—you're back. I don't know how . . . Wait, you were never dead, were you? It was all a ruse because the Nasts finally caught up with you. Damn it! I mean, it's good to see you, Eve."

"I'm sure it is. Now get your ass inside before you finally give the neighbors an excuse to get your shit-box evicted."

Like many things in the supernatural world, appearances were deceiving. Open the door to Toby's crappy trailer and you walked into a little mudroom that looked as decrepit as the outside. Close the external door to prying eyes, open the inside one, and it was as if you'd been transported to a luxury SoHo loft.

The place must have been professionally decorated. Postmodern high-tech, which is probably not a design category, but that's what it looked like to me. Paige would be in heaven. The decor wasn't her style, but the hardware would set her drooling. Even I felt a little dampness in the corners of my mouth.

It was as if Toby had walked into the top electronics store in the country, plopped down a no-limit credit card, and said, "Give me the best of everything." Soft music drifted from every corner of the trailer. Lights clicked on as we walked through. A desktop TV-sized computer screen tickered stock prices while a printer noiselessly spit out pages in a growing pile. The lights seemed to lead us in, illuminating our path, then lowering as we sat on the sofa. The TV volume turned up automatically. Toby tapped one button on the side of the sofa and the TV flicked off, the music died and the lights came on full. I tried not to be impressed.

"Okay," he said as he turned to my mother. "I—"

He looked down at the bow case, which she'd tucked into the shadow of the sofa. Blue light emanated through the zipper.

"Ever seen those crime-scene shows?" I said. "Where they use glowing devices to detect blood? Makes cleanup a whole lot easier."

He tried to laugh. Didn't really manage it.

"Okay, Eve, I owe you money. It was ten grand, right?"

"Twenty. Plus interest."

He nodded and hit another button. A laptop rose from the coffee table. "So, if we calculate interest based on the past decade's rates."

"We calculate it based on my rates. Remember what those were?"

"Th-that's ridiculous. No one would ever borrow money at that cost."

"Which is why I never had to lend any. You can go ahead and do the calculations if you like, but I can probably save you some time with an alternate offer. I'll waive the debt for information."

He hesitated, clearly trying to figure out what could possibly be worth that much.

"Did you know you have a group kidnapping supernaturals in New Orleans?" Mom said. "Shipping them off to be lab rats?"

"Wh-what?" His eyes bugged. "No. Seriously? I—"

"I know you've made a deal to keep them from dragging your sorry ass down there, too. Not like they'd want it anyway. Over the years, you've shot yourself full of too many drugs to be a viable subject. But you are useful as another kind of rat. The sort that will turn over any supernatural he owes money to."

Toby's jaw worked. Then he said, "I haven't turned anyone over. They came to discuss the local wildlife and I suggested a few names of black-market entrepreneurs."

"Who could reasonably be arrested and disappear quietly, and if they owed you money or had invested with you . . . Well, then you'll look after their money until they return. Nice scheme. Too bad it went all to hell."

"Wh-what?"

"Lab blew up this morning." I waved at his laptop. "Check the news."

He did, tapping away as Mom talked.

"So the lab's gone," Mom said. "Not like they would have been getting more subjects anyway. You know Officer Medina? Nice lady. Not too bright. Someone switched the sedatives for stimulants or hallucinogens. One of the first supernaturals to get the new batch was a werewolf. Wanna guess how that worked out?"

Toby's expression said he'd rather not.

"Medina's dead. So's the rest of the staff, plus the inmates. Now, I don't know how long it'll take for folks to realize an outpost cop shop has been destroyed, but it's going to happen soon. The question is whether a Cortez Cabal cleanup crew can get done first."

"Cortez . . ."

"Oh, you love the Cortezes, don't you? And they love you right back. Imagine how happy they'll be finally having an excuse to haul your ass to Miami. It's a beautiful city. Not sure you'll get in much sunbathing, but I hear they have skylights in their cells."

"Actually, they don't," I said.

"No?"

"They're underground. Which is never a good place to be in Miami. Benicio swears they take every precaution, but if there's hurricane flooding, what do you think they're going to save down there? The archives or the prisoners?"

"True," Mom said.

"Look," Toby said. "I supplied Jackie with names, not drugs."

"Jackie Medina," I asked, to be clear, and he nodded.

"The Cortezes aren't going to care," my mother said. "Not if it gives them a chance to get you off the street. You're screwed, Toby. Or you are without my help. Because the guy who gave Medina the drugs also cast a very special spell."

She reached down and cracked open her case. Light flooded out. "You see, Toby, you were wrong. I haven't been hiding out. I've been dead. Until a sorcerer crossed me over, I was walking around the afterlife. And I was carrying this."

She pulled out her sword. Toby jumped back, knees knocking his laptop and sending it toppling as he scuttled onto the sofa.

Mom swirled the sword, the blue steel leaving a swath of light.

"Do you know what this is, Toby? One hint—it's not a light saber."

"I—I don't—"

"Take a guess." She grabbed it by the blade and held it out to him. "Better yet, take a hold. Try it out."

He reached for the pommel. When his fingers touched it, he let out a shriek and fell back, his hand raised. Blisters popped up on every fingertip.

"Holy Mother of God," he whispered.

"So you're a religious man? That's good. Makes this easier. If this sword just burned a fire demon, I'm sure you can guess what it is. And that this"—she grasped it by the pommel, then tossed it up and caught it by the blade—"is not a party trick. All this is to say that I can protect you from the Cortezes. And that you might be wise to help the cause by giving me the information I need."

Toby took one more look at the sword and decided he was feeling chatty. Mom settled back onto the sofa, leaving the sword glowing on the coffee table as a reminder.

"I know Roberts," he muttered when Mom finished explaining and identifying the culprit. "Should have turned his name over to Jackie. I would have, too, except that he has a wife and an ex-wife and a kid, so someone would miss him."

"You had contact with him?"

"Me and Roberts don't travel in the same circles. He was one of those guys who pretends he's too good for us. Squeaky clean. Only he wasn't, was he? Damn it. If only I'd known. He cost me a sweet income stream. Jackie paid a grand for every name."

"He cost her a lot, too," I said. "Her life. I'm sure you're upset about that."

It took him a moment to find the right expression of regret. Then he gave us everything he knew about Roberts, which wasn't much. It wasn't until we handed over Roberts's contacts list that we started getting somewhere.

"Oh, yeah, I know a few of these guys." He rattled off names and supernatural types for a half dozen of Roberts's entries. Two were in the business of providing basic services for fellow supernaturals.

"This guy's a doctor." Toby pointed to a name on the list I was writing. "Charges more than a frigging private clinic, but he's good. Discreet, too. So's she." He pointed to the only woman's name on the list. Amanda Griffin.

"What's she do?"

"Hooker. For guys who don't want to worry about hiding their powers. Amanda's a real sweetie. Says most supernaturals want to do more talking then screwing. They just like being able to talk freely. Which is a shame. She's a good talker, but she's even better at screwing."

"Uh-huh. Well, Roberts seemed to need a lot of talking. If she's the A in his calendar, they were chatting a few times a week."

"Son of a bitch," Toby muttered. "Amanda never even told me she was seeing him. She knows I would have liked some dirt on the guy. Would have paid well for it, too."

"You did say she was discreet."

"Sure, but we could have blackmailed the bastard real good."

I looked at Roberts's calendar. "I don't have a lot of experience hiring hookers, but I'm going to guess three times a week is a bit excessive."

"Bit expensive, too," Toby said. "Amanda ain't cheap."

We continued down the list. There was another possibility or two, but none whose initials matched appointments in the calendar. Amanda it was then. When we were done, Mom picked up her sword.

"Find some rope, Savannah," she said.

"Wh-what?" Toby said, starting to rise. "Why do you need rope—?"

Mom pointed the sword at his throat and he fell back into the cushions. "I've told you my secret, Toby. You know that I'm back and what I am. That's very valuable information. After you double-crossed me the last time, I don't trust you."

"But—but you didn't need to tell me! I'd have listened to your offer without knowing you're an angel."

"Huh. My mistake then. But, since you do know, I can't have you running around. You'll need to wait here for the Cortezes."

His voice went shrill. "You promised to protect me from the Cortezes."

"No, I said I could. Not that I would."

"You bitch!" He started to leap up. One wrist-flick of the sword and he sat back down. "You set me up."

"Just returning the favor. Savannah?"

"I'll get some rope."

We had to settle for extension cords and electrical tape, but they did the job. Then I called Lucas and told him where Toby was. They'd have a lot of questions for him, questions better answered in Cortez custody. That's why Mom played the angel card—an excuse to have the Cortezes take him even after he'd fulfilled the bargain. Of course, since she had the big, glowing sword, she didn't need an excuse, but that wouldn't have been fair. In my mother's world, playing fair is important, even if her definition of it is a little malleable.

When we got back into the car, I said, "We need a disguise."

Mom looked over, brows lifting.

"Either we disguise ourselves or we have to leave a trail of bound and gagged supernaturals in our wake," I said. "Which could be appropriate, considering half the supernatural population of New Orleans seems to be eyeball deep in this shit. But the next person who recognizes you might escape before they're in our sights."

"Not in my sights," she said. "I have superhuman vision, remember."

I gave her a look.

"Yes, I take your point," she said. "I don't disguise easily and I suspect you don't either, but I may have a solution. I've picked up a few tricks on the other side. Let's just hope they work."

The trick was a modified glamour spell. The normal one allows the caster to take on the appearance of another person, but it only works if the target expects to see that other person.

Mom's "modification" was actually an older version,

predating the spell we used, and didn't require expectation to work. I'd heard of it before. Even seen it in a grimoire—an old spellbook—at Cortez headquarters. But it required that most troubling of special ingredients: human sacrifice. It took an average of a hundred iterations for a witch to master the spell. Even the Cortezes hadn't taught anyone to use it since before Benicio's time. The cost-benefit ratio was just too high.

Fortunately, Mom had learned the spell to help her celestial bounty-hunting duties, which meant no body count—there's no way of killing someone in the afterlife. So Mom could cast the spell without a corpse. Or she could in the afterlife. Here? She wasn't sure. Also, it was difficult to test, because even after she cast the spell, she looked the same to me. So we accosted a few unsuspecting passersby, which left some people in New Orleans wondering about the crazy women asking what color their hair was.

But the spell had worked. We'd glamoured ourselves based on two photos from *Glamour*, appropriately enough. We picked the two most average looking young women in its pages, which still meant we were well above average. As for clothing, we outfitted ourselves in jerseys, sneakers and jeans. Two students, pretty but nonthreatening.

We almost missed Amanda. When we arrived, she was leaving, gym bag in hand. She looked to be in her early thirties, with soft features and sleek, shoulder-length, ash-blond hair. She was dressed stylishly and conservatively, in slacks, boots and an Oxford shirt. Put a crop in her hand and she'd look ready for a day of riding. Horses, I mean. Not the kind of riding she apparently did for a living.

I strode up behind her and said, "Um, Amanda? Amanda Griffin?"

She turned. Looked me up and down, expressionless. "Yes?"

"Um . . ." I wiped my hands on my jeans. "Sorry, I—I'm just a little nervous. I'm Brianne White. I go to Delgado with my friend here, Sami. Someone gave us your name and, uh . . ."

Her brows arched. Amused. "If you're looking for a little college experimentation, honey, I can give you some names. That's not my thing."

"Experiment—?" I let out a high-pitched giggle. "Oh, no. Not that. I mean . . ."

Mom leaned over and whispered to me.

"Oh, right. Okay." I cast a nervous look around, then lit a light ball in my palm.

"Ah, I see," Amanda said.

"Right. So, we're new to town and we heard about this . . . stuff going on, and this guy we met, Shawn Roberts, he said you could—"

"Don't lie, Bri," Mom whispered. When I looked over, she leaned in and mock-whispered. "She can check on that. Tell the truth."

"Okay. Right." I wiped my hands again. "So Roberts wouldn't tell us where to find you, but he sent us to this guy named Toby. He didn't want to help us either. But then Sami . . ." I cast a knowing look at Mom. "She kinda . . . convinced him."

"I'm sure she did," Amanda said. "And I'm sure it wasn't hard. Look, girls, whatever you heard—"

"We know about the Supernatural Freedom—"

"Liberation," Mom whispered.

"Right. Supernatural Liberation Movement. They recruited a couple of our friends who go to UCLA. Our friends want us to join, but we're not sure if it's a good idea."

"It's not," Amanda said.

I exhaled. "Whatever you're doing, we can help. Sami here, they say she's a Conspicio, but we think she's an Aspicio. She can do the X-ray vision thing."

That stopped Amanda in her tracks. She waved to the wall of the building. "That's the super's apartment. Look inside and tell me what she's doing."

Mom walked over and cleared a peephole. "I don't know where 'she' is, but there's a guy inside. About three hundred pounds, surfing porn, wearing only his—no, I don't think he's wearing anything."

"That's good, right?" I said. "I mean, not about the naked guy, but Sami's power. It would be useful, right?"

Amanda shrugged, but her eyes glittered. "And the blinding power?"

"I can cause temporary blindness," she said. "It only lasts a few minutes, but it's handy."

"I bet it is."

"I can help, too," I said. "I know witch and sorcerer magic up to the third level, and it usually works."

A dismissive nod my way. Amanda laid a hand on Mom's arm. "How about I skip the workout today and treat you girls to a drink. There's a nice little place down the road. Very private."

CHAPTER 13

I got a text from Elena while we were still walking to the bar. Their plane had landed and they were ready to take over as Mom's bodyguards. I texted back to say we'd made contact, and I needed to play this through.

Amanda led us to a neighborhood pub, already dark inside and reeking of hops. We took a booth in the back and Amanda explained the situation. If I were her I'd have gone with a whole lot less detail for potential recruits. But that's what happens when you launch a revolution with no previous revolutionary experience. It all seems like a grand, adventurous game. You'll be cagey, of course, because it's top-secret stuff. But when you have a reason to spill—like trying to woo an Aspicio half-demon to the cause—you're happy for the opportunity to prove how terribly clever you all are.

Amanda's group was anti-SLAM. I'd suspected that because Roberts had switched the drugs, but to be honest, I couldn't see the advantage of feeding stimulants to werewolves—for either side.

Now, as Amanda explained it, I understood . . . they were idiots. Their scheme only proved I was right about their lack of experience with this whole revolt business. I'm sure the plan made sense to them, but to anyone who's seen the dark side of supernatural life, it was a very, very stupid idea, guaranteed to go horribly awry.

See, the plan was this . . .

"Controlled outbursts of supernatural activity," Amanda explained. "This SLM group is trying to persuade supernaturals that coming out of the closet is a good idea. But it's not. We know that, don't we?"

Mom and I nodded.

"The problem is that a lot of supernaturals aren't so sure. They think of how much simpler and better life would be if they didn't have to hide their nature, and they tell themselves humans wouldn't react that badly. I mean, the Inquisition is over."

We nodded again.

"But our argument is that humans wouldn't be less frightened of witches and half-demons than they were in the past. As it stands, they simply don't believe we exist. If they knew otherwise, it would be just as bad as the witch-hunts. Telling supernaturals that doesn't do any good, though. They need demonstrations."

"Controlled outbursts of supernatural activity," Mom said.

"Exactly. You may not be aware of this, but SLM is operating in New Orleans. Heavily operating. We heard they've been using supernaturals in law enforcement to arrest and sedate other supernaturals. Then they take them to a facility where they brainwash them."

Not exactly . . .

"We need to find that facility," she said. "We've located an office they're using for local recruitment, but it's not the laboratory."

"So they do have an office in New Orleans," Mom said. "That's what our friends said. It's on Gray Street, isn't it?"

She shook her head. "McNally. But that's just for training. We need the lab. We're getting close, though. In the meantime, we managed to get one of our people to replace the drug courier. He has provided an officer with drugs that will lower inhibitions instead."

"Making supernaturals more likely to use their powers," Mom said.

Amanda beamed. "You catch on quick, honey. So, as we speak, there are a few imprisoned supernaturals who are going to decide they really don't want to be imprisoned and forget that they shouldn't use their powers to escape. We're about to see some serious fireworks."

Oh, they'd gotten fireworks. And when they realized it, they'd understand just how stupid it was to "plan" a supernatural outburst.

Next Amanda asked about us. We expanded on our fake bios, chattering away until her cell phone rang.

"Hey," she said as she answered. "I was just thinking of you. I've got two new recruits here and I wanted to swing by and intro—"

She paused. Her face screwed up, like she'd heard wrong. "What?"

Another pause. Then, "Holy shit. You—" She swallowed. "You're joking, right?" A pause. "No, of course you wouldn't. But are you sure? Maybe Roberts—"

She blinked. Sucked in breath. Then she listened, just listened, her gaze blank, head nodding, and murmuring "okay, okay" under her breath.

"Toby?" she swallowed. "Are you—?" She caught herself this time. "Sorry, sorry. So Roberts is dead and Toby was seen being loaded into—" She caught herself again as she looked up at us, feigning shock as we listened in. "I'll be right there."

She stood, pawing through her purse for cash, murmuring, "I have to leave."

"Is something wrong?" I said, rising, too. "Maybe we should—"

Mom caught my hand under the table, and squeezed tight enough to stop me midsentence. I stood my ground, giving her a look. Amanda was too flustered to notice. Mom shook her head. I glowered at her, but didn't trust a privacy spell. So I sat waiting until Amanda was out of earshot.

"We should go with her," I said. "I can talk her into taking us along. They'll be distracted by this. It'll be easy to get information."

"Yes, but we don't need it. This chapter of their movement is about to implode and they'll be too busy picking up the pieces to escort recruits to a new chapter."

"But—"

"She told us where to find these SLAM people. That's what I need to do right now. Infiltrate them while they're busy cleaning up a big mess of their own. And find out exactly what they've given Bryce."

I swallowed. "Bryce. Right." I nodded and stood. "Let's go."

She caught my hand again. "I'd like you to go to Miami. Elena and Clayton are here now. They can watch my back."

I stiffened at that. As my mother, she wanted to shuttle me off to safety, even if it meant she might be taken back to the afterlife before we could see each other again. And yet, from her expression, so carefully blank, I knew she was hoping I'd refuse. That I'd give her a reason why I should stay.

So I said, "I know these people. They took me captive. I've met the leader and all the key players. You need me with you."

She shook her head. "I can manage, baby. You'd be safe in Miami. It's what they'd want. Paige, Lucas, Adam . . ."

"I'll call them from the car," I said. "I won't fight them to stay, but I'm not leaving unless they insist."

She hesitated, then nodded.

As we walked to the rental, I checked my phone and found a message waiting from Adam. Just one line: *Would love to talk.*

I stared at that message. Just four words that could mean only "Hey, I'm bored, give me an update!" Except that when Adam did mean that, it's exactly what he wrote. This was different. This was . . . "MORE personal" isn't the right phrase. Adam has been part of my life since my mother died. He's been my friend for years. I've told him things I've never told anyone else and I think he's done the same with me. It's always been personal. But this . . . it seemed different.

I wanted it to be different. That's a given. I've been waiting all these years for it to become something different, but nothing ever changed between us until this morning.

Had it really been just this morning? It seemed like a week ago.

But this morning, Adam had kissed me and it hadn't been just a peck on the cheek. Not a "I'm happy to see you didn't perish under a pile of rubble" kind of kiss. It'd been a real one, the kind I'd been dreaming of since I was twelve and he walked into my cell to set me free, and burned my name in a heart on my prison wall. Burned his name on my heart, too.

It figures, doesn't it? Finally get to kiss the guy, and before you can find out if he really means it, you're whisked away. Thrown in jail. Escape jail. Escape a hell-beast. See your mother resurrected from the dead. Escape demon-possessed children. Terrorize an informant. Have drinks with a hooker. Rush off to infiltrate enemy ranks before they skip town. It's like the universe is conspiring to keep us apart, even if it had only been—I checked my watch—less than ten hours.

I thought of calling him instead of Lucas. But this was work and Lucas was in charge, and passing along a message through Adam wasn't just cowardly—it was unfair, asking him to make a decision about my safety.

So I just texted him back: *Will call as soon as I can.*

As soon as I hit send, I realized that wasn't enough. So I sent a second one: *Can't wait to see you.*

I hit the button. My fingers were trembling, heart thumping, as if I'd just texted a declaration of undying love. I flexed my fingers and swallowed, and stared at that damned screen, waiting for the bleep of a return message, telling myself he probably wouldn't even get it until he had a spare minute and—

The phone blipped. The message appeared: *Ditto.*

"Ditto?" I whispered, a laugh caught in my throat. "Seriously? *Ditto?*"

A second blip. A smiley face.

I muttered under my breath, calling him a few names, even as I couldn't wipe the smile from my own face.

"Adam?"

I nodded as my cheeks flamed. Mom smiled at me, then steered us into the parking lot.

I called Lucas. While he wasn't thrilled with me staying, he understood that this operation had a better chance of success if one of the infiltrators actually knew the parties involved.

Proceed with caution, but proceed.

We were in another coffee shop, sitting in the window, watching a couple approach. They weren't walking hand-in-hand. He didn't have his arm around her waist. No outward sign that they were indeed a couple, unless you looked closer and noticed their hands brushing as they walked.

Mom leaned over the table. "Gotta admit, as good as Clayton Danvers looks from the other side, he looks even better in person." She paused. "Just don't tell Elena I said that." Another pause. "Or your father."

I smiled. "Nothing wrong with window shopping when you aren't looking to buy. Elena's used to it. Clay's the one you don't want noticing you checking him out. He does not take that well. Just ask Cassandra."

Mom made a face. "Vampires."

Clay and Elena walked in. Both are blond with blue eyes. Both were dressed in jeans, sneakers, and T-shirts, none of it less than five years old. It didn't matter. They still looked like they'd stepped out of a magazine spread for *Outdoor Living,* fresh-scrubbed, athletic and attractive. Both were on the far side of forty, but blessed with a werewolf's slow aging and fast metabolism.

I stood and waved. Clay noticed first. He gave me a blank look. When I smiled and beckoned him over, he scowled and looked away and I had a moment of consternation before I remembered we were still in disguise.

Across the table, Mom chuckled. "You're so right. There's a man who does not appreciate attention, even from cute girls."

Elena looked over at us, and after only a moment's pause, smiled and whispered to Clay. His scowl vanished. I moved over beside Mom and let them take the booth seat across from us.

"Good disguises," Elena said.

"Thank you," I said. "And, as a bonus, I got to see how Clay acts toward the rest of the population. That scowl? Really not attractive."

Elena laughed. "I think that's the point."

Clay snorted and took the biscotti from my plate.

"Hey," I said. "Can we go back to being rude and dismissive? At least I get to eat my food, then."

He broke off half. I reached for it. He handed it to Elena.

"I'll go get us more," Mom said, waving me out. "Coffee for you guys?"

"Yes, but let Savannah grab it," Elena said. "She knows what we like."

Elena handed me a twenty, but that was the extent of her "asking." I didn't take offense. I'm pleased that she treats me as part of the Pack. I'd grown up spending summers at

Stonehaven with the Pack and I understood the mentality. Children are pampered and cosseted, which is wonderfully safe and cozy, until you hit the age where you balk at that coddling. That's when you begin the transition to an adult Pack member, which means—since it's a hierarchical structure—you start at the bottom. As Alpha-elect, Elena could order anyone except Jeremy to get her coffee.

As I left for the counter, I heard Elena introducing herself and Clay, and I kicked myself for forgetting that they'd never met my mom. Mom must have said hi through Jaime before, but that wasn't the same thing.

When I came back, Elena's face was grave, her eyes troubled. Even Clay—sitting back, taking the beta position—looked concerned. Mom's voice held an odd note of uncertainty.

"What's up?" I said.

They looked up, as if startled. I set the coffee and biscotti down.

"Seemed like an intense conversation." I looked at Elena. "You didn't just send me away to get coffee, did you?"

She met my gaze. "No. I wanted to get your mother's opinion of this mission."

"Elena doesn't like it," Clay said. "I agree. This psycho de Rais wants you for his collection, Savannah. You've already escaped him once. Now you're going back?"

"So you think Giles really is de Rais?"

"Does it matter? Even if it's not the guy who slaughtered children a few hundred years ago, it's still the guy who's been slaughtering supernaturals today—"

Elena cut in. "I've told Benicio and Lucas my concerns, and they've assured me that the risk is minimal. They trust that your glamour spell will hold, and if anything goes wrong, we'll be ready to go in. You'll also have Eve there, with her sword. I'm still not happy, but your mother has explained why you need to be there."

She took a sip of her coffee, then set the mug down. "I'm going to ask that you keep this mission brief, though. We'll find the building. You'll infiltrate it. You'll get a few details. And then you'll exit, pronto."

"We will," I said.

We only had the street name of the meeting place, which would have been a lot more useful if it was a short street. We split up, and started at opposite ends, searching for an office-front that screamed "activist cell inside." None did. It was just a boring street of boring low-rise office buildings.

As we walked, Mom used her Aspicio powers as discreetly as possible to peer into buildings, but saw nothing. Then a van turned into a lane a block away. A plain white-panel van. Just like the one SLAM had used to transport me from their meeting hall.

I told Mom this as I propelled her along the sidewalk. We broke into a jog. When we reached the lane, we heard a man's and a woman's voice, and the hair on my neck rose before I even consciously recognized them.

"Severin and Sierra," I muttered.

The twins were Giles's enforcers. I'd first encountered their work at the home of a supernatural named Walter Alston. Giles had wanted Alston to summon Lucifer. He couldn't. Severin and Sierra had made sure he was really certain of that by torturing him to death. Fire is an amazing power, but for sheer nastiness, there's nothing like an ice demon.

"So these are the two who are working with Balaam?" Mom said. The bow case glowed blue, the light seeping out. She looked perfectly calm, but that sword was better than any mood ring.

"Yes," I said. "If we can grab them, I say screw infiltration."

"Agreed."

I motioned to the narrow lane where they'd driven the

van. We took another step. Then, from down the lane came a gasp of pain. An oath. Sierra snarling, "Get her!"

A young woman raced out in her bare feet, a cord dangling from one wrist. She veered our way, almost crashing into us. She stopped. Our eyes met. Mascara ran down her cheeks. One of them was marred by a white line where the skin had been frozen.

When running footsteps sounded behind her, I knew what I should do. Grab the girl. She wasn't going to escape the twins—they were too close behind. Stop her and hand her over and win ourselves an introduction. But I thought about what had remained of Walter Aston, eyes gouged out, fingers and teeth lined up on the desktop. I froze.

Mom yanked the young woman off her feet as someone came barreling around the corner. It was a nondescript guy a few years older than me. Severin. He skidded to a halt when he saw Mom holding his target.

"This yours?" Mom said.

I'd never seen anything faze Severin—the guy really did seem to have ice water in his veins, but when he saw Mom holding the girl, he blinked. Then he stared.

Her glamour's gone, I thought. *Oh, shit. If mine is, too . . .*

Sierra rounded the corner. She looked straight at me and my gut clenched, ready to launch a spell. Annoyance flickered over her features, then she turned to Mom.

"That's ours, blondie," she said.

I exhaled in relief.

"I know," Mom said. "I was holding it for you." She looked at Severin. "Where do you want it?"

"We came to see Giles," I said. "We have information for him."

"No one sees Giles," Sierra said.

"Skip that part," Mom said, her gaze still on Severin. "Where do you want your captive? Preferably before she has the sense to scream and draw a crowd."

The girl's eyes widened. Before she could utter a sound, Mom clapped her free hand over her mouth. Severin grinned. Sierra scowled.

"Take her over there," Sierra said, waving toward the van, "with the others."

As we stepped into the lane, we saw two guys helping other captives out of the van. A third man headed our way. I glanced at Mom. Back to plan A.

"So you came to see Giles," Severin said as he followed Mom.

The third guy backed up to the door and helped the other two herd the captives into the building. As we walked, Severin made no effort to help Mom with her charge, just followed along behind her, seeming to enjoy watching her maneuver the struggling young woman as casually as if she were carrying a bag of trash. As they walked, his gaze dropped to her ass.

Sierra's eyes narrowed and she sent ice daggers into Mom's back. I'd suspected her relationship with her brother broke the oldest taboo, and that look pretty much confirmed it.

I cleared my throat. "That's right. We—"

"What's your name?" Severin asked Mom.

"Sami," Mom said. "And my friend there is Bri. We're students at Delgado. Some friends from UCLA told us about you. When we got some information you might find useful, we decided it was time to meet Giles."

"If you have information, you'll tell *us*," Sierra said. "No one talks to—"

"What's your power?" Severin cut in, still addressing Mom. "Half-demon, I'm guessing. Fire? Ice?"

"Vision."

He laughed. "Right."

"I'm an Aspicio."

Now Sierra laughed. "A daughter of Balaam? Bullshit."

I tensed and looked at Mom.

Mom tossed me the young woman. "Hold this."

She strode to the van, peered through the metal side and described what she saw. Then she walked to the door the others had gone through. She waved aside the guy at the door, looked through the steel and described what she saw.

Then she turned on Severin and Sierra, and waited.

"Holy shit," Severin said.

"Not possible," Sierra said. "There are exactly three Aspicios living and we know where they all are."

"Do you?" Mom said. "Seems Lord Balaam doesn't track his conquests as carefully as he should."

Now even Sierra stopped scowling. I'm sure she was thinking of how delighted Balaam would be if she presented him with this gift. A long-lost child. Ready to join the fight when his granddaughter was being such a bitch and refusing him.

Sierra waved for the guy at the door to take the girl from me. He did, then radioed inside for someone to come get her.

"So what's this news you need to tell Giles?" Sierra asked.

"Do you know Toby White?" Mom asked.

Their expressions said they did.

"Shawn Roberts?" she said.

Same reaction.

"What about them?" Severin said.

"I'm not sure if you've been listening to the news, but there was a problem at a cop shop just outside the city. A problem involving a whole lotta dead bodies. One of them was Shawn Roberts."

"And White?" Sierra asked.

"A different but connected issue."

Severin swore under his breath.

"We'll take you inside," Sierra said. "If Giles is there, he might talk to you. He might not. Either way, remember that he's a very busy man."

CHAPTER 14

As they led us through the side door I surreptitiously texted Elena to let her know where we were. Mom was busy explaining the bow case—she'd put it down to deal with the girl and only now did Severin and Sierra notice. Mom said it was exactly what it looked like—a bow. We'd been on the way to her archery class when we'd decided to swing past the meeting house and scope it out, and just happened to catch the escapee and win an introduction Was it a good excuse? No. But if we were trying to smuggle in weapons, we'd do something a little less obtrusive—and a little more deadly—than a bow.

When we got inside, I looked around. The last time I'd been in a SLAM meeting house, what struck me most was how serene it was. Like what I'd imagine from a cult or a commune.

Throw a bomb in the mix and that serenity gets blown to hell.

People darted from one door to another. I heard voices raised in irritation, in anger, in anxiety. Somewhere someone was shouting that he didn't give a shit if it wasn't possible to clear out in two hours—*make* it possible.

When Sierra and Severin came through, people slowed down and lowered their voices, clearly trying not to get noticed. As soon as we passed, the chaos rose in their wake. Finally we reached the one silent door in the hall. Sierra knocked. A woman cracked it open from inside. She was about my age, and so mousy she made the twins look like supermodels. Veronica Tucker, better known as Roni.

Roni had been my first introduction to SLAM, back when I'd been solving the murders Leah had committed. She'd been a witch hunter who just "happened" to be in town at the same time. There were no such coincidences, of course. She'd hunted me, then pretended she'd been set up, to lure me in and hand me over to Giles.

"He's not seeing anyone," Roni whispered. "You'll need to—"

Severin slammed his open hand into the door, sending her stumbling back. Sierra pushed through and shoved Roni aside when she squawked.

The room was small and empty. Sierra headed to a second door. She rapped on it, and waited for a "yes?" then blocked the opening so I couldn't see inside.

"There are a couple of new girls here. They—"

"Recruits?" a woman said. "In this mess, you bring us recruits?"

"No," Sierra said, her voice chilly. "I bring you information. Potentially important information. Giles? The girls say that trouble at the police station has something to do with Shawn Roberts and Toby White. Do you want to speak to them?"

"Yes, yes." Giles's voice. "Of course."

He murmured something, presumably to whoever else was in the room. A moment later, three people came out. I recognized two from when I'd been held captive. The third—a dapper man in his fifties—was a stranger. He stopped and gave us the once-over.

"My dears," he said, extending a hand. "May I be the first to welcome you to the cause." He turned to the doorway. "Giles? If you need someone to show these lovely young ladies around . . ."

"I have better uses for your time, Gord," Giles said dryly, still from the next room. "I'll see you as soon as I'm done here."

They left. Severin held the door and waved Mom inside. I followed. The door closed behind us, Severin and Sierra staying in the hall.

At first I didn't see Giles. Then I spotted him at a table, papers strewn before him. He rose and stepped toward us, hand extended, a welcoming smile on his lips.

Giles Reyes. Or, if the stories were correct, Gilles de Rais—a French nobleman who'd ridden with Joan of Arc. That military service was not, however, what put de Rais in the history books. He was tried and convicted in the deaths of at least forty children. I knew the stories of what he did to those children. I won't repeat them. It is enough to say that now, seeing him for the first time since I'd heard whom he claimed to be, the first thought to enter my mind was *I could kill him.* If I could manage to touch him without throwing up. And that's if I could kill him at all. He claimed to be immortal, and we had Cassandra DuCharme's eyewitness account of him seventy years ago to support that claim.

All I could do was try to see him as the man I remembered—Giles, leader of SLAM, nothing more. Just a well-dressed guy in his thirties, bearded, dark haired and dark-eyed.

"You're clearing out?" Mom said. "Can't say I blame you. I heard about the lab."

His eyes darkened, annoyance creasing the corners of his mouth. "Well, we're making some changes at least. You say you have information for me?"

His gaze moved back to his papers, as if he'd already decided that nothing we could tell him would be worth his undivided attention.

I answered before Mom could. I'd spent enough time with Giles to understand the man a little. He could play the friendly, unflappable leader, but poking him, as Mom had, was like prodding a resting cobra.

"We do, sir. I'm sorry we've come at such a bad time, but we do think this is important. Do you know Toby White and Shawn Roberts?"

"I have . . . worked with Mr. White. My sources suggest Mr. Roberts is a supernatural who doesn't believe in my cause. I suspect you're here to confirm that?"

"Roberts was part of a group who hijacked your arrangement with Jackie Medina. They planned to teach supernaturals that revealing themselves is a very bad idea."

Now I had his full attention. He motioned for us to sit. I told him a little more about the anti-reveal movement. No additional names or details—I didn't care if they were idiots, I wasn't siccing this psycho on them.

"Sierra mentioned something about a police station?" he said when I finished. "I'm afraid I haven't heard anything about this incident. What can you tell me?"

I reiterated pretty much exactly what Lucas had said was on the news. Then I said, "One of the bodies found was Shawn Roberts. He hasn't been identified yet, but he was there. So was Jackie Medina."

"It was *that* station?" He pushed to his feet. "Sierra!"

She opened the door.

"Why wasn't I told that Jacquelyn Medina's police station was in the news?"

"Jacquelyn . . . ? Officer Medina? We weren't aware it was *hers*, sir. That's not an excuse, I know. We'll get someone investigating immediately."

"Yes, you will."

She closed the door.

Giles turned back to us. "What more can you tell me?"

"We also thought you should know about Toby White. He's been picked up by a Cabal."

Giles's mouth closed in a firm line, as if he was fighting to keep from venting his frustration on us. First members of the interracial council blow up his lab. Then this anti-reveal movement takes out a police station under his control. Now the Cabals were in town, snatching up supernaturals. It had to feel like he was getting it from all sides. I knew how he felt.

"Which Cabal is responsible?" he asked.

"I only heard that he was picked up before the police station incident even hit the news, meaning one of the Cabals knew about it, and may have been responsible for making sure it wasn't even bigger news."

"Sierra!" he called again, bellowing now.

She opened the door. "Sir?"

"These young women have been very helpful. Please have Severin escort them to Odele. They'll join her team in Atlanta." He abruptly murmured his thanks to us, a duty his manners wouldn't let him avoid. Then he stood, telling Sierra, "Get Gordon and the others back here immediately and bring everything we've got on this police station business."

We were dismissed.

Severin led us deep into the building to a tiny lounge where he said Odele would be meeting us. He seemed inclined to just hang out with us there, asking Mom what she was studying in school, how she liked New Orleans. For a minute there, I could almost forget he wasn't just a normal guy . . . until Sierra came and hauled his ass off to "discipline" the van-load of captives they'd brought in.

I was really hoping they'd just leave us there, unguarded and alone. They did—but not before Sierra warned us that the door was about to be locked and couldn't be opened by spell-power. If I tried, we'd find *ourselves* in for a little discipline.

A young couple was passing in the hall as Sierra led her brother away. Holding the door open, Severin called them over.

Neither was much older than me, the guy light-haired,

broad-faced and smiling, the girl tiny, with dark hair and a noticeable baby bump. Their hands were clasped, fingers entwined.

"You guys are with Odele's team, right?" he said.

"Sure are," the guy said. "Just waiting to ship out. Anything we can do for you?"

"Actually, yes. We've got a couple of recruits who'll be joining you. Stay with them until Odele gets here."

"Will do," the guy said.

"I heard you caught the traitors," the girl said as she joined us. "Good job. I can't believe they turned on us like that. Two of them were members of our team. I never suspected a thing."

"No one ever does," Sierra said. "That's why we have to be vigilant."

The young couple nodded. Severin and Sierra left, closing the door behind them. The guy told us his name was Jake; his pregnant girlfriend was Lori. Mom and I introduced ourselves, then we all settled into chairs to wait.

"Did you say something about traitors?" Mom said after a few minutes of silence. "Were those the ones we saw Severin and Sierra bringing in?"

"Uh-huh," Lori said. "They were members of the movement. Or so we thought. Then after the lab blew up, they tried to make a run for it. It didn't take long to figure out why. They set the bomb. Apparently, they were Cabal plants."

So SLAM was blaming its own members for the bombing? Technically true—one of their own had set it off, but she was only following protocol to avoid exposure and had died herself. Would Giles really blame innocent members to keep his group from knowing what really happened? Or were they not so innocent? Had that blast made them rethink their commitment and try to break from the group?

"This place is hopping," Mom said. "Did they bring you all in because of the bomb?"

"Oh, no," Jake said. "We were already here, training and getting ready to deploy. That bomb just means we've bumped up the schedule. The mission begins tonight. Lori and I were two of the first to join and, I'll be honest, there were times when we weren't sure it would happen. But Giles has done it. He's perfected the serum and he's about to usher in a new age of supernaturals." Jake patted Lori's stomach. "Just in time, too."

Lori blushed. "By the time our baby comes, things will be different. That's why we joined. To give our child a better life. One where he won't need to hide his powers."

I looked at them, their fresh-scrubbed faces glowing, and I didn't see brainwashed kids. I saw two normal young supernaturals, in love, having a baby, genuinely doing what they thought was right for their child. If I told them to run, they'd think I was the deluded one.

"You said the serum is perfected?" Mom said. "That's the immortality serum, right?"

"Right," Jake said.

Lori leaned forward. "Can you believe it? Immortality?" She laughed softly. "When Giles first told us how old he is, we *didn't* believe him. We figured it was a recruiting gimmick. But then when we saw how hard he was working on this serum, we started realizing he was serious."

"But he discovered the cure for mortality centuries ago, didn't he?" I said. "If he's immortal himself . . ."

"But it wasn't something he could duplicate. Not on a large scale anyway."

That's what we'd figured. I was going to bet his own immortality had something to do with the kids he'd killed in the fifteenth century. Not something easily repeated, but he must have had ideas how it could be done by other means and had been trying for centuries. When Cassandra met him during World War II, he'd seemed to be experimenting with some kind of zombie and vampire hybrid.

"So this plan," Mom said. "Tell us about it."

"And I think that's all our new recruits need to know right now," said a voice from the doorway.

In walked a tall, dark-skinned woman. Jake and Lori rose. We followed their lead.

"Hey, Odele," Lori said, her smile unsteady. "Severin said Bri and Sami are joining us in Atlanta, so I figured it was okay to explain . . ."

"It is." Odele clapped a hand on the younger woman's shoulder. "But I think we can save the rest for the trip. It's going to be a long drive to Atlanta and we really do need to be going." She moved closer to Lori and lowered her voice. "Are you sure you're up to it, honey?"

Lori nodded. "I want to be part of it."

"Her job keeps her on the sidelines, which means I'm fine with it, too," Jake said, putting his arm around her waist.

Odele turned to us. "Okay, girls. I know we're moving fast here, but we're going to need to hold off on the chitchat until we're in the car." She turned to Mom. "Sami, is it?" Then to me. "Bri?"

We both nodded.

Odele patted our backs, one with each hand, and propelled us to the door. "Welcome to the team, girls. We're about to make history."

CHAPTER 15

On the way outside, Odele explained step one of the plan: getting to the van that would take us to Atlanta. Unfortunately, it wasn't as simple as walking out the door and climbing in.

"For one thing, as you may have noticed, we're a little short on parking space here," she explained. "We have cars in a public lot a block over, but these vans? Let's just say they aren't something we want to leave in a public lot."

"They're rolling command posts for the first wave of missions," Jake said. "All our gear, our communication equipment, everything we'll need in Atlanta."

"Including the serum?" I said.

Odele shook her head. "That's too valuable. It will be delivered separately, by Giles himself."

"So where is the van?" Mom asked.

"In a warehouse here in New Orleans."

Mom looked at me. That didn't exactly narrow it down. All I could do was try to send a quick update text and trust that Elena and Clay could follow.

The five of us squeezed into a midsize car. I was in the back with Mom and Jake. I'd hoped to get a chance to text some details to Elena and Lucas, but Jake gallantly offered to take the middle spot and nothing we could say would sway him. Texting was out. Instead, we spent the ride retelling our story to Odele. In turn, she told us her background—a high-school teacher from Atlanta—and her supernatural type. She was a Tempestras, a storm demon, like Adam's stepfather. Jake and Lori were both shamans. In a fight, then, Odele would be the one to watch.

I hoped for more details on the mission. Mom and I had no intention of actually going to Atlanta, but we were so close to hearing their plans that we couldn't back out until we did. Yet we arrived at the warehouse without learning more.

I expected to go to the edge of town. Instead, we ended up just north of the French Quarter, in the Bywater district by the Press Street railroad tracks. There were warehouses here, very old ones, dating back at least a century or two, probably from when the wharf had been busier. A lot of them had been remodeled, replaced by lofts and funky galleries. But there were still sections of old warehouses. And that's where we headed, taking a narrow road into a nest of warehouses that looked as if they might have been slated for demolition pre-Katrina. Now, since they'd been spared, they were left standing until the city could better support more lofts and galleries.

Another car was already there. The other half of the team. As we pulled over, Odele pointed to the three people waiting beside it. Will, a dark-haired guy in a leather jacket, was an Adtendo half-demon, which meant he had the power of enhanced hearing. Andi, a heavyset woman in her early thirties, was a necromancer. Peter, maybe a few years older than me, but already balding, was a magician. The only one with real offensive powers was still Odele. That realization helped me relax a little.

We parked and got out.

"New recruits?" Will said, striding forward. "What the hell is Giles doing giving us new recruits now?"

"We needed to replace Lance and Marg," Odele said.

A few of the group shifted uneasily at the names. I was guessing those were the two who'd supposedly turned out to be Cabal plants.

"So replace them," Will said, "with proven members of the group."

"Sami here is an Aspicio. Giles feels she will be an invaluable addition to the team."

"Her supersight plus your superhearing," Jake said with a grin. "Gotta admit, that's a great combo. And Bri is a witch. That adds something we didn't have either." He put his arm around Lori and turned to the warehouse. "There it is, folks. The first big step. Who's ready? I know I am."

It was a nice try, but Will wouldn't be deterred. He demanded to know more about who we were and where we came from and what on God's earth made anyone think we could be trusted. All perfectly valid questions, since no one had dug very deeply into our cover stories. Giles hadn't even asked where we'd gotten our facts. Will had a right to be concerned. But one look at the faces of the others told me no one else cared. Giles said we were in, so we were in. When Will kept pressing for details, Odele shut him down. This was her mission. Giles put us on her team. That was all he needed to know.

We started toward the warehouse.

"I have the keys, so I'm driving, right?" Jake said. "And Lori rides shotgun?"

"Of course," Odele said. "That will be much more comfortable for her, I'm sure."

"Oh, that's not why he's asking," Lori said, grinning Jake's way. "He needs his navigator or we'll end up in the Gulf. The guy has absolutely no sense of direction."

Mom laughed. "I know someone like that."

Lori looked back at her. "Has he ever gone for ice cream at the corner store and come back two hours later with a melted mess in a bag?"

"Hey, I wasn't lost," Jake said. "I knew the corner store didn't have your favorite—"

I felt a spray of something on my face. Then Andi screamed, and something hit the back of my legs. I went down face first. As I fell, I tried to twist, but Mom landed beside me, her hand smacking the back of my head as she yelled, "Down!"

Peter had dropped right in front of me. I looked over at him and for a second my brain didn't register what I was seeing. There was something covering his face.

No, there was nothing covering his face. He didn't have a face.

I touched my cheek and pulled back my finger. Blood. I'd been sprayed with blood. What kind of spell could—?

Lori fell to her knees, screaming and clutching her shoulder. Blood oozed from between her fingers. Jake dropped beside her.

"Get—!" Mom began.

Lori jerked forward, hands flying out. Red blossomed on her chest.

Not a spell. A gun. I looked around, but saw nothing, just us and the cars and a few buildings at least fifty yards—

"Sniper," Mom whispered. "Stay down, baby. Please stay down. I cast a cover spell."

"We need to get inside," I said. "We can inch toward the warehouse."

"Okay. Just stay on your belly. I'll cast blur spells as we go."

We started backing up. Jake was dragging Lori, screaming for someone to get help, call 911, anything. Mom's hand tightened on my arm.

"You can't help them," she said.

I looked around. Andi stood there, looking dazed, even as another bullet whizzed by her. Only Will lay on his stomach, a few feet away, partially hidden by a rusted oil drum.

"We need to tell them to get inside," I whispered.

"No, they'll draw fire."

I could pretend she meant if I tried to help, they could draw fire to us. She didn't. It was like back in the jail, when Jaime and I let the witch—Keiran—leave, knowing she'd clear the way.

"Get inside!" I shouted. "It's a sniper. You need to get in the warehouse."

"No!" Will yelled. "In the cars. Get in the cars. We'll be trapped in the warehouse."

"A sniper can see you in the cars. You need to—"

"The cars!" he cut in. "Everyone in the cars." He drowned me out and sure enough Odele and Andi started for the cars, Odele in the lead. Then a bullet took her out. Andi froze and looked both ways. She took one shaky step toward the warehouse.

"No!" Will yelled. "Andi, run for the cars!"

Damn it, he was going to get them killed. No time to argue. I didn't see which direction Andi chose. We reached the warehouse door and Mom yanked me inside and slammed it shut.

CHAPTER 16

Jake was already inside the warehouse, bent over Lori. I knelt beside her and felt for a pulse. There wasn't one. I crouched there, staring down at her lifeless body, her swollen stomach. Jake was sobbing that we needed to call for help, someone had to call for help, his voice barely audible now, just repeating the same loop.

A car door slammed. Then I heard a shout, so hoarse I couldn't tell if it was Andi or Will. A moment later, someone hit the warehouse door, as if falling against it.

"Let me in," Will croaked. "I've been shot."

Mom cut me off, shoving me behind the door. "Stay there."

Will pounded now. "Open up! Damn you, open the door!"

I stumbled to the wall and plastered myself against it. I checked my cell phone. No service. Of course. Blocked, I was guessing. If you're going to launch an ambush, you're going to be smart enough to keep anyone from calling for help.

Staying behind the door, Mom opened it. She didn't help Will in, just waited until he staggered through, then slammed it shut.

"I've been shot, you bitch," he muttered, cradling his arm.

"That's no reason to let the rest of us die with you. Not when you were the idiot who told them to get in the cars. I don't hear an engine running. Can I presume Andi won't be joining us?"

"They got her."

"Shot through the car window, right?" I said as I cast a light ball.

He glowered. "Are you going to help me or do you want me to grovel first?"

"Neither," Mom said. "Savannah? Get in deeper. I'm putting a perimeter spell on the door. Then we'll need to scout for more entry points."

"Savannah?" Will said. "I thought her name was—"

Mom snapped our glamour spells. Or I presume she did, because Will's expression went from "what the hell?" to "what the *hell*?" in an eye blink.

"I know you," Will said, staring at me. "You're Lucas Cortez's kid."

Mom's eyebrows shot up at that, but she only said, "Go deeper, Savannah. Now."

I crawled back to Jake, ignoring Mom's protests. I touched his arm. "She's gone," I said.

He shook his head, tears falling on Lori's body. "Sh-she can't be."

"You know she is," I whispered. "And you know she wouldn't want you to sit here, waiting to get shot."

"I don't care," he whispered.

I looked down at Lori and I thought of her in the meeting house, talking about a new life for their child. That's all they'd wanted. All any new parents want, I suppose. Lori and Jake weren't stupid. They weren't evil. They were just two kids, not much older than me, in love, having a baby. They'd joined to secure the future of that baby, no matter how misguided that was, and now that child would never be born, and I think, of everything that happened, all the tragedies I'd seen since I met Giles, this was the worst. The one that made me want to run outside and scream, "I don't care what all of you want—look at what you're doing!"

Instead I took a deep breath and told Jake, "*She'd* care. She'd want you to live. You know that."

I took his arm. He let me lead him away.

If you've seen one warehouse, you've seen them all. Well, not exactly, but when you run with the crowd I do, you see a lot of abandoned or little-used warehouses. They're the hideout of choice for supernaturals up to no good. This one looked like all the rest—a huge cavernous space filled with crap.

"You're Savannah Levine," Will said, following us as I pushed aside a box to clear a path. "You work for Lucas Cortez. He's your guardian."

"Savannah Levine," Jake whispered, as if to himself. "Your dad is—was—Kristof Nast."

"It's bullshit," Will said. "Your mom tried to scam the Nasts by claiming you were Kristof's daughter."

"Excuse me?" Mom walked out of the darkness, bow case in hand, the glow seeping through. "I didn't *ever* claim Kristof was her father."

Will gaped as she strode past him and Jake to catch up with me. "You're . . . You're Eve Levine?"

I looked at Mom. "I think that's the first time you've ever been identified *after* me."

"I've been dead too long." She waved at a pile of refuse. "You boys crawl in there and hide, since you seem to be pretty much useless otherwise. Savannah and I will secure the building. They must be surrounding it now. Taking their time because we're trapped."

When Will opened his mouth, I expected him to say that's why he'd advised against coming in here. Instead, he said, "So she's *not* a Nast, right?"

"That isn't exactly important right now, but because I hate being called a gold-digging slut, I'll confirm it. She's a Nast. Now hide."

Will looked like someone had hit him in the gut. Mom waved for me to join her as we circled the perimeter. There weren't any windows, which made it safer for us. We walked quickly along the walls, taking turns casting sensing spells. There was no one out there. Not yet. As Mom said, we were trapped, so they were taking their time closing the net.

Mom took her sword from the case and slung it on her back. "It won't help against guns, but it's easier than lugging it around." She left the case on a crate. "Now, we need to figure out how to get a message to—" She stopped. "Cell phones. Have you called—?"

"No service. That's the first thing I tried."

"Right." She shook her head. "I really have been dead too long."

"I'm sure Elena saw what happened. I only hope they didn't get grabbed by whoever's out there."

"Oh, we know who's out there. Benicio Cortez decided not to let us handle this after all."

"Lucas would never—"

"Benicio would. And he'd go behind Lucas's back to do it."

I'd like to think Benicio would never order a team to open fire while I'm in the vicinity, but it's never wise to presume on your importance to him. But I could presume on the importance of someone else.

"If he puts me in danger, he loses Lucas as heir," I said. "*That* he can't risk. With Hector and William dead, he's only got Carlos, who'd find a way to overthrow him then run the Cabal into the ground."

My mother made a noncommittal noise in response.

We continued our rounds. There were two more exits— one small door and one set of big, drive-in ones. Both locked. Both guarded, according to Mom's sensing spell.

"Okay," I said as we came around to the front of the warehouse again. "I say we use the van. Break out the doors and keep going. I'll drive—"

"I'll drive. You'll be in the back."

"With the others."

"I don't give a rat's ass about—"

"I do. Not enough to risk my life, but enough to take the time to tell them to get in the van." I looked at her. "I know that's not what you'd do."

She patted my back. "Like I said, you're not me and I don't want you to be. We'll spare the extra minute to get them to the van. Jake's got the keys anyway. Now—"

Mom yanked me behind a pile of planks. We peeked out just as light seeped through the darkness ahead, the door opening. Two figures entered. When the door shut again, everything went dark. I could hear the faint shuffle of their footsteps.

How could they see? Without Mom's sword, we'd be blind. There weren't any night-vision spells—

Night-vision goggles. First sniper rifles, now high-tech surveillance gear. There was no way the anti-reveal folks were that well equipped.

A Cabal would be. The Cortezes certainly were.

Was I wrong about Benicio? No. Lucas says never underestimate his father's capacity for duplicity, but nothing was as important to Benicio as his Cabal, shortly followed by his youngest son. I may doubt Benicio's affection for me, however much that stings, but I don't doubt Lucas and Paige's.

Betray Lucas and Paige's trust by sending in snipers without warning me, and Benicio would lose Lucas and ultimately his Cabal.

Could Carlos be behind this? He was pretty inept, but he had his supporters, those who'd rather have a guy in charge that they could control. They might do this for him. Then blame Benicio, and drive a wedge between him and Lucas.

For now, it didn't matter who these guys were, only that they could be from a Cabal, meaning very well armed and very well organized.

To the van, then. First, though, to Will and Jake. We weren't getting far without those keys. We also weren't getting far with that big-ass sword glowing like a neon sign on Mom's back.

"I can do that," she said when I suggested a blur spell. "But it's still going to show in the dark. I should go back for the case . . ."

She squinted into the gloom of the warehouse.

"The glow doesn't penetrate far," I said. "Just use the blur."

She shook her head. "You go. I'll distract and slow them down."

"No—"

"Yes." Her tone changed to one I remembered well, the one that said I wasn't having cookies before dinner and if I kept bugging her I wasn't having cookies at all. "I'll be right behind you, baby. Remember, the worst thing they can do to me is send me back where I came from." She touched my cheek. "As much as I love being here with you . . ."

"You want to go back."

She blinked. "I didn't mean that. Only that—"

"Yes, Mom. You want to go back. Not this second, but eventually." I managed a wry smile. "I'm a big girl. I can handle that. Your life is there. He—Dad's there."

She paused. "I don't think I've ever heard you call him that."

I hadn't. But from the look on her face, I should have. Even if Kristof wasn't "Dad" to me, that is what he was to her—father of her child, love of her life. She loved me, too, but he was there and her life was there, and she knew I was fine without her. We were fine without each other.

"This is my fault," she said. "I should have made you leave with Jaime. I was being selfish. I wanted more time with you."

I hugged her.

"I'm sorry, baby," she whispered. "I shouldn't have let you stay when it wasn't safe."

"I wouldn't have gone." I pulled back and kissed her cheek. "Try not to get killed too quickly, okay? I could do with a little more Mom time." I paused to clear my clogged throat. "But I'll understand if I don't get it."

She squeezed me. "I'll always find a way to stay in touch, no matter what happens."

"Good."

Another moment, lingering there, hugging each other. Then she sent me on my way.

CHAPTER 17

We should have left a trail of bread crumbs. All I had to see by was a light ball the size of a spark. I didn't want to risk a bigger one.

As for how Mom would distract our attackers, I expected a whole lot of banging and shouting and maybe some shooting. I heard nothing. Not even the sound of footsteps, which meant they weren't coming after me. Whatever she was doing, it was working.

I found Jake and Will after only checking two refuse piles. I motioned for silence, then whispered our plan.

"You can stay here if you want," I said. "When that van leaves, they'll figure we're all in it."

"I need a doctor," Will said. "You're going to get me out of here, then you're going to take me to a clinic for half-demons over on—"

"You're not giving orders—"

"Did you forget about these?" He dangled the keys he must have taken from Jake.

I snatched them from his hand. "Thank you. Now come with us or stay behind. Your choice."

He came. So did Jake, who was still too lost in grief to question anything.

As we crept along, I felt a tingle vibrate down my spine. It felt oddly like a perimeter spell being triggered. Except I hadn't set any. Mom had, along with—

A howl reverberated through the warehouse.

"A werewolf?" Will spun on me. "Did you bring a werewolf—"

I slammed him face first to the floor. "No, it's not a werewolf," I whispered in his ear. "Now zip it."

A werewolf would have been nice, especially if it was one of the two lurking outside. But the howl was coming from the trigger hallucination Mom had set up at the rear entrances. An apparition of a hellhound.

"Stay here," I whispered.

I crawled forward with my light spark. Both guys followed. I considered locking them in binding spells, but that would zap too much of my limited power.

I didn't need to go far anyway. We were closer to the back than I'd thought, and within a few feet I could make out the very dim outline of shapes moving in the near dark. I looked around, then ducked behind the closest piece of whatever and extinguished my spark. The guys stayed close.

The "whatever" that we'd taken refuge behind seemed to be broken crates. I leaned out and tried to get a better look at the intruders. If they were from the Cabal, they'd be in uniforms. Intra-Cabal regulations. Each had to wear a distinguishable uniform so they could be identified by another Cabal if they bumped into each other on a mission. Presumably, it was to keep them from killing each other, but I suspect the Cabals only agreed to it so they wouldn't accidentally slaughter their own men.

These guys were shapeless black wraiths against a dark gray landscape.

I needed light.

I calculated angles and trajectories and potential outcomes. Then I launched a small light ball in the invaders' path, but drew it toward me instead of whipping it away. They saw it. And I saw them.

I pulled back behind the crates.

"It's a Cabal."

"The Cortezes?" Jake whispered. "They came after you, right?"

I nodded.

"What?" Will said. "No, it can't—"

"Can't what?" I said. "Can't be the Cortezes?"

"I just mean, you might be making a mistake. It might not even be a Cabal."

"I know the uniforms. Those are the Cortezes."

Will struggled to keep his breathing steady. Sweat trickled down his face, glistening in the dim light of my spark.

"It's okay," I said. "I can handle this. It's a mistake—they didn't know I was here. I just need to tell them it's me and you'll be safe—"

Will leaped up to run. I grabbed the back of his shirt and slammed him to the concrete floor. Then I straddled his back and pressed my palm against his shoulder—the one that had been shot. He started to yelp, but I stifled it.

"Keep your mouth shut or I press again," I whispered. "The Cortezes will come running. You really don't want them to come running, do you?"

"They won't hurt us, right?" Jake said. "We're with you."

"*You're* okay. Will? He's not so okay, considering he's the one who set you up."

"What?" Jake said.

"He cut a deal with the Nasts. That's who he thought was out there. That's why he wanted you running for the cars instead of into the warehouse. To make it easier for them to pick you off. Then he came in here after us so he could keep an eye on us. That's why he got so worried when he found out I was a Nast. They might not be so willing to pay the big bucks if they find out one of the dead is Thomas Nast's granddaughter."

"So you knew?" Jake said.

"I figured it out when he didn't like the idea that it's the Cortezes out there."

But Will's plan hadn't failed. Not entirely. The security team combing the warehouse? It *was* the Nasts. I just didn't want him yelling for help. I could tell him the Nasts would never let him walk out of here alive, but he wouldn't believe me.

"What do we do?" Jake whispered.

"Find me something to bind him with. I saw a spool of wire to the left. If you can't find it, I'll use your shirt."

He nodded and took off. I winced at the patter of his sneakers, but everything else around us was silent, the security team long gone. Just bind Will and—

The crack of a rifle. Then a thump, off to the left. Where I'd sent Jake. As I rolled off Will, I strained to hear. Will did, too. With his superhearing, if there'd been anything, even the rasp of Jake writhing on the floor, he'd have heard it. Instead he gave a satisfied little grunt. Jake was dead.

I shouldn't have let him go. Goddamn it, I shouldn't have let him go.

Focus. Don't think about Jake. Think about myself and how the hell I was going to get to that van—

Will stiffened. He tracked a noise. As I lifted my head, I saw something moving across the floor. A red spot. My tiny light ball? No, that—

I lunged out of the way just as the dot from the rifle sight began to creep across me. A crack, so close it made my ears ring. The shot hit Will in the side and sent him smacking into the crate, the box tumbling, the crash drowning out everything else as I leaped up, hunched over, ready to run—

"Stay where you are!" a voice barked.

A gun barrel rose from the darkness. I turned to run. A figure stepped from the shadows behind me. Another to the other side. A fourth. Four masked and armed gunmen, their weapons trained on me.

"I'm Savannah Levine," I said, the words spilling out so fast they were barely intelligible. "The Cortezes know I'm here. Sean will know I'm here. My brother. Sean Nast."

Please, please let one of you be on Sean's side. Let one of you at least believe he'll be your next CEO. I don't care whether you think I'm his sister or not. He thinks I am. That means something.

Silence. Then one gun dropped. Two more inched down, uncertain. The fourth didn't budge, but the gunman shifted his weight, his face mask turning toward his comrades.

The squeak of another pair of booted feet approaching. The officer who'd lowered his gun turned toward the newcomer.

"Sir, it's—"

"Shit." The newly arrived officer muttered the word under his breath. Then he pulled off his mask. "Miss Nast."

The one who hadn't lowered his gun made a noise deep in his throat and shifted again. The senior officer's glare shut him down. I recognized the officer. His name was . . . Damn it, I couldn't remember. Lucas always said it was important to know the names of everyone in a Cabal. It was a lesson he'd learned from his father, and one Sean emulated. Treat your employees with respect, starting with learning their names.

As sweat dripped down my face, I really, really wished I'd listened. When four armed security officers surround you, knowing the name of the guy in charge made a big difference.

"H-hello," I said. "We met in San Francisco."

He nodded. Not rude. Not friendly either. Just polite. A couple of years ago, there'd been some security threat against the inner family, so Sean had to bring two extra guards on our weekend riding trip. This guy had been one of them, which made him Sean's man. He had to be, if he'd called me Miss Nast. God, I hoped he was.

He motioned for the others to lower their guns.

"We're on the same side," I said quickly. "This guy—" I pointed to Will, dead on the floor. "He was your contact. I'd infiltrated the group. The Cortezes know about it—"

He lifted his hand, cutting me off, then turned to the others. "This is level-four security, boys. I'm going to need to take Miss Nast outside. I want you to continue combing the building."

As he waved them off, he took my elbow and whispered, "Hurry."

We got about five paces before a voice said, "Captain Kaufman. Who do you have there?"

Kaufman froze. He started to tell me to run, then snapped his mouth shut. I couldn't run with armed men behind me. Kaufman's gaze dropped in unspoken apology as he took hold of my arm.

"Sir," he said. "It's Savannah . . . Levine."

The man standing ten feet away didn't wear a uniform. Didn't carry a gun. He didn't need to. It was Josef Nast.

CHAPTER 18

Josef Nast. My father's brother. My uncle, though he'd never admitted as much. We'd only glimpsed each other in passing, his look always freezing any greeting—friendly or sarcastic—in my throat.

I got that same look now, a slow once-over of distaste and contempt.

"Savannah," he said. "Can't stay out of trouble, I see."

"I—"

"You've put yourself in a very dangerous position. Consorting with known terrorists. Running through a dark warehouse, where no one can be expected to see who you are."

"I—"

"You've caused enough trouble for my family, Savannah. Your paternity claims sully my brother's reputation. The fact that Sean believes them makes my father's chosen heir look gullible and weak. Now turn around."

"No."

"I said—"

"If you're going to shoot me, you'll do it looking into my eyes, which tell you exactly who my father is, as much as you might hate to believe it."

He *didn't* look me in the eyes. He couldn't because I was right—my eyes were his eyes, Nast eyes, that unmistakable bright blue.

"Get on your knees, Savannah."

"Sir—" Kaufman stepped forward. "You can't—"

"You and you." Josef pointed at two of the others. "Take Captain Kaufman outside. Hand him over to Anderson. He's being charged with insubordination."

"No." Kaufman moved to my side as his two comrades stepped forward. "I won't stand by—"

Josef's energy bolt knocked Kaufman off his feet. "Then you *won't* stand by. You two, take him outside."

"But he's right," said a voice in the darkness. "You can't do this, Josef. And you won't." Mom stepped up behind Josef and put her sword tip to the back of his neck. "Can you feel that?" To his men, she said, "I'll have his head by his feet before anyone can pull the trigger. Lower your weapons."

"Don't you dare—" Josef shut up as the sword dug deeper.

"Lower your weapons!"

When one raised his rifle, Mom kicked Josef in the back of the legs, then lunged and cleaved the officer's arm off at midbicep. It happened so fast that he just stood there, watching the gun tumble to the ground in his severed hand. Then he started to scream.

I hit Josef with a knockback before he could rise. Mom planted a foot on his back and nudged the sword-tip along his spine, positioning it between his ribs. Then she nodded toward the injured officer, his screams now reduced to shocked heaves as he frantically tried to staunch the bleeding.

"Someone might want to help him before he bleeds out."

Kaufman was the one who went to his aid. The others just stood there, gazes fixed on the glowing sword. One crossed himself and whispered under his breath.

"Yes, the sword is what it looks like," she said. "And I'm who I look like." She leaned over Josef, who twisted to stare up at her, as shocked as the injured officer. "Hey, Josef. I'd say Kris sends his regards, but he won't be happy about this. He *really* won't be happy. Now, Savannah and I are going to walk away and—"

"I can't let you do that, ma'am," said a voice behind us.

Floodlights flicked on and we saw another half dozen armed men surrounding us. The officer in charge stepped forward.

"I'm going to ask you to remove that sword and let Mr. Nast up. I'm only going to ask you once."

"I'm not—"

"Mom?"

She glanced over. A half dozen rifle scopes dotted my chest. She cast a quick blur spell, and I cast a cover spell as I hit the floor.

"Don't you *dare* threaten her," Mom said. "Do you know what this is?" She lifted the sword, her foot still planted on Josef. As half the men flinched, she said, "Yes, you do. You've sure as hell never seen one, but you know exactly what it is, and you know that if you touch my daughter, you won't just lose an arm. I will cast your soul into the deepest, darkest hell dimension, and no one on the other side will stop me, because if you fuck with me, you are damned. Eternally damned."

A few of the rifles dropped. The rest wavered.

"Lower your guns," Josef said. "Savannah Levine is under the protection of my nephew, Sean, and I cannot allow her to be harmed."

The officers who'd heard a very different story two minutes ago shifted uncomfortably but kept their mouths shut.

"However," Josef continued. "Miss Levine is also under the protection of the Cortezes, which makes her presence here—interfering with a Nast operation—in contravention of intra-Cabal law. Both Savannah and her mother will be taken into custody—"

"Like hell," Mom said.

Josef looked her right in the eye. Whatever she read in that stare made her swallow.

Before she could speak, there was a commotion to the

side. Two more officers walked toward the circle of light, staggering slightly as they dragged in a man in a T-shirt and jeans, unconscious, head slumped over. In the dim light, all I could make out were muscular biceps and light hair and I thought, *Clay.* Then they took two more steps, coming closer to the light, and my heart rammed into my throat.

I jumped up, breaking the cover spell, ignoring my mother's shout. The two men dropped their captive. He hit the floor hard, a dead weight, forehead cracking against the cement.

I grabbed Adam by the shoulders and flipped him over. His face was battered, bruises purpling, eyes swollen shut, his nose now bleeding from hitting the floor.

"We found him sneaking around," one said. "Seems he burned a hole in the wall to get in. He resisted arrest."

"You bastards," I snarled.

When one grinned at me, I leaped up. Mom started for me, but Kaufman got there first, catching my arm and whispering, "Don't."

I glowered at the officers and knelt beside Adam again. He'd been beaten unconscious, but he was breathing. Thank God, he was breathing.

Josef walked over to stare down at Adam. "I don't recognize this man. He must be one of the terrorists. Take him outside and shoot—"

"It's Adam Vasic," I said. "He's a council delegate and under protection of the Cortez Cabal."

He frowned. "I've met Adam Vasic. It's hard to tell with all that bruising, but I'm quite certain that isn't him."

"It's Adam, you son of a bitch," I said, getting to my feet. "He disintegrated a wall to get in. How many Exustio half-demons are there?"

"Are we sure that's what happened?" Josef turned to the officers who brought Adam in. "Did you *see* him disintegrate it?"

One officer smirked. "No, sir."

I bent, rolled Adam onto his side, and yanked out his wallet. I shook out three pieces of ID.

"Here," I said. "You want proof? Take this."

He ignored my outstretched hand and looked at my mother. "Would you like me to take that ID from her, Eve? To confirm this really is Adam Vasic?"

"Kris is right," she said through clenched teeth. "You are a heartless bastard."

Josef's blue eyes chilled. "My brother would never say—"

"No? Really?"

They faced off. Josef looked away first.

"Eve, if you want me to confirm this young man's identity, you'll lay down your sword and come along willingly. I'll take all three of you into custody. Otherwise . . ."

Mom laid down her sword. Josef took the ID cards and gave them a cursory glance.

"Yes, it appears this is Adam Vasic. Put all three of them in the van. You there—" He pointed to an officer. "Take that sword."

"You don't want to do that," Mom said as the officer walked over to it.

The officer hesitated. He wasn't much older than me, and I could tell by his expression that he didn't know exactly what it was, only that a glowing sword capable of slicing off a man's arm wasn't natural.

"The Sword of Judgment," Mom said. "Take a good look, because if you ever see one in this dimension, it's time for last rites. Very, very fast last rites. The only person who can touch it? An angel."

The kid looked at Josef.

"Do you really think Eve Levine is an angel?" Josef said. "She's the daughter of Balaam. Lord demon Balaam. That thing comes from his world. From hell. Now pick it up."

When no one moved, Mom laughed. "You're not reassuring them, Josef. Heaven or hell, it's clearly no toy." She bent, slid her hands under the blade and lifted it like an offering. She walked over to Josef. "If you're so sure it's safe, take it."

"Don't test me, Eve," he said, so low I barely heard him.

"I'll take it, sir."

One of the officers stepped forward. He grabbed the hilt and then let out a shriek so loud everyone jumped. He staggered back. Josef strode over and grabbed the officer's hand. The man's palm was covered in blisters and he trembled with pain.

"Sword lesson number two," Mom said. "Don't touch."

"Set it down," Josef said. "We'll leave it behind."

"Uh, that won't work either."

I'd been crouched beside Adam again, trying to wake him. Now I stood and stepped between them.

"Please don't do this," I said to Josef. "Two men have already been hurt. Just let Mom put the sword on her back and have the officers walk us out. She won't reach for it. You can figure out what to do with it later."

"Put the sword on the ground, Eve," Josef said.

"If she does that, it'll—"

"Enough."

"But the sword will—"

"*Enough.*"

"Don't bother, baby," Mom said. "He's as stubborn as your father. Unfortunately, not as bright. Why do you think Thomas passed him over for Sean?"

"Mom, please," I whispered.

She met my gaze and nodded. Then she bent and laid the sword on the ground.

"Everyone stay back as I walk away," she said. "Savannah's right. Two people have been hurt already. Let's not make this lesson a fatal one."

She straightened and started walking away. Josef waved for the nearest officers to fall in.

"Beside her, please," I said. "Or in front."

The sword started to quiver, rattling against the concrete. As everyone stared at it, my mother kept walking. Josef barked for two more officers to take Adam and two to escort me. Kaufman came toward me and waved over the youngest officer. My gaze was still fixed on the rattling sword.

The kid started to cut across to me. Right between Mom and her sword.

"Don't—!" I began.

The sword flew into the air. I leaped forward and yanked the kid toward me. He spun. The sword flew past. The kid let out a yelp. We hit the floor. As I scrambled up, he lay there, staring at his hand. The last joint of his pinkie finger was gone, blood flowing.

"Oh my God," he whispered. His gaze went to my mother. The sword was on her back, attached to its mysterious holster. "Oh my God."

I grabbed the kid's hand, yanked a tissue from my pocket and wrapped it around the bleeding finger.

"Be glad that's all you lost," I muttered. "She told you to stay clear."

He looked up at me, eyes wide with shock, and managed a nod.

CHAPTER 19

I awoke smelling blood.

Even before I could get my eyes open, panic shot through me, those scenes of blood-soaked devastation—the police station, the motel room—flooding back. I jolted up, limbs flailing, eyes opening to find myself . . .

A cell. I was in a cell.

I swallowed, flashing back nine years to another cell. The one where my mother had died.

I shook off the memory and lifted my hands. No blood. What I smelled was copper. I heard the distant plinking of water against metal. Copper pipes?

I sat up. There were bars in front of me. Thick, rusting metal bars. Concrete under my feet. Dim light from the corridor beyond. None in here. A stone box with metal bars. Not like any prison cell I'd ever seen. Definitely not the Nast cells.

I'd seen those once when Sean snuck me in to speak to a prisoner I needed to question for a case. They were so similar to the Cortez cells that they could have been made by the same designer. There were variations on the type— from utilitarian holding cells to the long-term, ultra-secure cells—but all resembled a hotel room more than a prison. No bars. No cement. No dark corners. No dripping water. This one needed only chains on the walls to make it a proper dungeon.

I pressed my face between the bars, trying to see down the hall. When my heart stopped pounding, I could hear breathing. Raspy, labored breathing. Only it didn't come from the hall. It came . . .

I turned slowly, then let out a gasp. Adam lay on the floor in the dark back corner. I ran to him and dropped to my knees. He was breathing—obviously—but still unconscious.

The blood had been cleaned from his face and there was tape over a cut on his cheek, but that was the extent of the medical care. Bastards. There are very strict rules for dealing with prisoners affiliated with another Cabal. Rules that do not allow beating them and dumping them in a dark cell.

So what did this mean? Would Lucas even be able to find us? Would Sean? And where was my mother? I squinted in the darkness, but there was no sign of her.

"Mom?" I called. "Are you here?"

A cough from somewhere outside. A hacking male cough. Nothing else.

I shook Adam's shoulder. After a moment, he groaned.

"Adam?" I said. "Can you wake up?"

Another groan. He winced. Coughed. Winced again, hand going to his chest. I pulled open his shirt to see that they'd bound his ribs. He was hurt, seriously hurt, and they just dumped him here without even a cot to get him off the cold floor.

"Adam?"

His eyes stayed shut, but his lips cracked open. "Water."

I looked around frantically. I could hear water, but it wasn't anywhere—

Wait. There was a pile of stuff just inside the bars.

"Hold on," I said.

I hurried over and found blankets, energy bars, bottles of water and a pail. What was the pail . . . ?

Then I realized.

I carried everything except the pail back to Adam. I

uncapped the water and let him have a sip, telling him to go slow. Then I wet a corner of a blanket and wiped the crust from his swollen eyes. He opened one.

"Hey," he said, his voice weak. "I feel like shit."

"You look like it, too."

A soft laugh, followed by a wince. "You should see the other guy."

"I did."

"Damn."

I smiled and gave him more water.

"They had guns," he said. "Very unfair. They got one at my head before I could put up much of a fight. So I surrendered. Apparently, *that* wasn't any fun for them."

"Bastards."

"Hmm." His other eye opened. "Elena and Clay?"

"I didn't see them."

"Good. Means they weren't caught." He swallowed and I gave him more water. "Your mom?"

"I don't know. She was with us. Now she's not. So you came with Elena and Clay?"

"Yeah. Joined up in New Orleans. Keep an eye on you. Didn't go so well. Elena's smart. Knew we were outnumbered. Phone was blocked. Wanted us hanging back. I didn't listen. Had to play the hero. Paid the price."

I leaned over him and smiled. "I'd kiss you, but I suspect that would be painful."

He looked at me. Tilted his head, and made my heart hammer. I told myself that I'd said it casually enough, if he wanted to think I was just kidding, he could and—

He put his hand on the back of my head, pulled me down and kissed me. It was a light kiss, our lips barely touching, but it was sweet and sexy and slow, and when it finally broke, I was the one pulling back, worried that I was leaning on him, and hurting his ribs, but he kept me there, hand still in my hair, holding my face close to his.

"I guess that answers the question," he said.

"Was there ever a question?"

"Sure."

I lifted my brows. "I've had a crush on you since I was twelve. I'm sure you noticed."

"I did when you were twelve. And fourteen. And sixteen. But eventually . . ." He shrugged. "You grew up. We became friends."

"So you figured the rest just went away?"

"Faded, I guess. Changed into something else."

"No, I just learned to hide it better."

I leaned over and kissed him again. Just a quick one. "That hurts, doesn't it?"

"Not necessarily a bad hurt."

I laughed and unfolded the blankets. I got one under him and one over him. Then he pulled me against him.

There was so much I wanted to say. So much I wanted to ask. So much that was completely and utterly inappropriate and unimportant under the circumstances.

We talked about what *was* important, filling each other in. That meant I did most of the talking. When we'd finished, I went over to the bars again and craned to see what was out there.

"Really could use Jaime's mirror right now," I said. "I heard someone coughing earlier. But I have no idea where we are or what we're doing here."

"You've been misplaced," a man's voice said. It was smooth and strong, too close to be the coughing man from earlier.

"Who's there?" I said.

"You've been misplaced," the voice repeated. "That's more important than who I am. You wouldn't know my name anyway. You're too young."

"How do you know that?"

A chuckle. It sounded vaguely familiar, but I couldn't

place it. "I'm sorry if I offend you, my dear, but you sound young. That's not a bad thing. Better than sounding old."

Adam appeared beside me, grabbing the bars for support.

"You said we've been misplaced," Adam said. "What does that mean?"

A pause. Then, "You've been hurt."

"How—?"

"I can hear it in your voice. I've been in enough fights to recognize the sound of broken ribs. Go lie down, boy. You'll need your strength in here."

Adam's mouth tightened. He didn't like being called "boy," but the voice didn't sound sarcastic. Adam pulled the blankets over to the bars and lay down, then tugged my pant leg until I sat beside him.

"Misplaced is exactly what it sounds like," the man said. "When the Nasts want to hide someone, they put them here. The paperwork, I presume, will say that you are in the usual prison cells. Then someone will go to find you and . . ."

"We aren't there," I said.

Adam whispered, "It's just a game. Lucas will tell Sean what happened, and he'll find us. They can't hide us from Sean. Not for long anyway."

The man heard us—a half-demon with auditory powers, I was guessing.

"The young Nast? Now that is a fortunate connection. Yes, if you know him, then this would appear to be a simple power play. An uncomfortable one, but you won't rot down here."

That cough again, from farther away, as if reinforcing our neighbor's point.

"How many people are in here?" I asked.

"Hard to say," the man mused. "You're the first new ones in a few years. The rest . . . They aren't what I'd call sociable. Sick. Crazy. A combination of the two, mostly. Locked away and forgotten."

"You—you've been here for years?"

He chuckled. "No, my dear. Mere months in this place would drive anyone mad. I'm a regular but temporary visitor. A special case. I work for the Nasts. Not voluntary labor, but they keep me in reasonable comfort if I behave myself." He paused. "I don't always behave myself."

"So they lock you up down here."

"Yes, and it's my own fault, as they're quick to remind me. But I don't do well with authority. Or with cages, however pretty. I won't be here long. I hear they have a mission for me. If not, they'll still take me out after a few days and put me on ice."

"Kill you?"

A laugh now. "No, my dear. I'm too valuable for that. I mean put me on ice quite literally. I believe there are human laws against the use of prisoners for scientific experimentation. That doesn't apply with Cabals. They make use of us. Cryogenics, in my case. Six months a year seems to be the safe limit. In my case, it has the dual advantages of keeping me under control for six months, and ensuring I don't outage my usefulness too soon."

I'd have been shocked if I hadn't already known all the Cabals were working on cryogenics, one of many scientific races they engaged in. The Cortezes had also managed to freeze subjects for up to six months.

So this wasn't news. But it did spark a memory. Cassandra had been talking about cryogenic science a few years ago. No, she wasn't interested in freezing herself to extend her shrinking lifespan. But she'd heard a rumor that the Cortez Cabal had captured two vampires and was using them for cryogenics experiments. Since vampires don't age, something in their DNA might help perfect the freezing.

Benicio hadn't admitted to kidnapping vampires, of course. He simply said that if such a thing ever happened, it would be off North American soil, that the subjects would be well treated and released without permanent damage.

A few days ago, I'd learned that the liberation movement planned to free Jasper Haig from Cortez custody. It was Jasper—Jaz as he was known—who'd killed Benicio's two eldest sons. He was being allowed to live while they studied his unique chameleon-like power. When we confronted Jaz about this plot to free him, he'd hinted it was the Cabal scientists who'd approached him with an offer. Now the movement claimed to have developed a mortality vaccine using vampire DNA. Could it be the same DNA used in those cryogenics experiments? An offshoot of those experiments? Probably. So what else were they working on?

CHAPTER 20

Our prison-mate didn't talk much after that. He'd made contact. That seemed to be his only goal. Establish himself as a potential source of aid because we had connections. If it was me, I'd have done the same.

Hours passed. Adam and I talked a little, but I wanted him to rest. We had no idea what was happening, and dwelling on it would just lead to panic. Wait and see. It was all we could do.

A guard came by eventually with more water and energy bars. He gestured for us to stand in the back corner, unlocked a tiny grate and pushed the supplies through.

The whole time the guard was there, Adam talked. No threats. Not even questions. Just trying to talk to the guy. Making an impression. Getting him to see us as people, not anonymous prisoners. The guy didn't respond.

"Nice try," said our neighbor when the guard was gone. "But you can save your breath, boy. Deaf and dumb. They all are. Not too bright either, I suspect."

I walked over to the grate. I hadn't noticed it earlier—it looked just like part of the bars. I bent and jiggled it. Then I cast an unlock spell.

"If that keeps you occupied, have at it," the man said. "If you look closer, though, you'll see that you wouldn't get more than your head out."

He was right.

"Relax and wait," he said. "If you're right, someone's

looking for you. If not, use the boy's injuries. Make them worse and he'll get medical attention. That would be a chance to escape."

Adam dozed again. I was sitting, arms around my knees, staring into nothing, when he sat up beside me, hand snaking around my waist.

"It's going to be okay," he whispered.

I nodded.

He shifted closer. "Worrying about your mom?"

"Trying not to. At worst, she dies and goes back where she was. It's only a matter of time before the Fates figure out how to recall her anyway."

"That'll be hard," he said. "Losing her again."

"At least I got to spend some time with her," I said. "Not exactly quality time. But she belongs over there. That's her life now." I gave him a rueful smile. "Do I sound all calm and mature?"

"You do." He kissed me. "Even if it's not how you really feel."

"I will. Eventually."

I leaned against him and closed my eyes.

"The rest will be okay, too," he said. "They'll come for us. Elena and Clay would have followed us to the airport. They'd take the Cortez jet. They'd have arrived at the same time and figured out where Josef took us. From there, it's just a matter of following their noses."

Still . . . so many connections to be missed.

"What if Elena and Clay are down here, too?" I said. "Somewhere."

"All the better, because that kitsune mojo of Jeremy's will find them faster than any werewolf nose."

A throat-clearing from our neighbor. "Excuse me? I don't mean to eavesdrop, but it's difficult for me not to. Did you say werewolf?"

I glanced at Adam.

"We aren't werewolves," Adam said. "If that's what you're worried about."

That chuckle again. "I know you aren't. Clay would be Clayton, yes? Danvers. And . . . the other one."

"Jeremy."

"Yes. You know them?"

"We do."

"Then my name might not be meaningless to you after all. My family name, at least. So I'll introduce myself, in hopes that you will let Clayton know I'm here. Perhaps, as Alpha, he can negotiate my release."

"Clay's not Alpha. Jeremy is."

A pause, then, "Still? I thought he would have stepped down by now."

"He will be. Soon. But Clay won't be Alpha. Elena will."

His silence told me he had no idea who that was. How long had this guy been locked up?

"Elena is Clay's wife," I said. "Mate. Whatever. She's a werewolf, and the Alpha-elect."

"I . . . see. I suppose Jeremy thinks that's clever, leaving Clayton as de facto Alpha while not antagonizing those who wouldn't want him leading the Pack."

I opened my mouth to say that wasn't the case, but Adam shook his head. If this guy knew so much about the Pack—and had superhearing—that meant he was a werewolf. An old-school mutt. Meaning it was best to keep issues of equality out of the conversation.

"And your name?" I said.

"Miguel Santos," he said.

"I thought—" I began.

Then I stopped myself as I struggled to recall the names of the Santos family who'd been Pack members. I had a decent knowledge of Pack history. After so many summers at Jeremy's estate—Stonehaven—I'd been permitted to read the Legacy.

Jeremy had been challenged for the Alpha position by his father, Malcolm, a brutal son of a bitch who'd been backed primarily by the Santos family. There were two Santos brothers, one of whom had three sons. Two of those sons and their uncle had been killed in the fight for Ascension. The father and youngest son left. That son—Daniel—had led an uprising against the Pack years later. Daniel had been killed, meaning the only living Santos from those days would be his father. The age seemed about right, but his name was Raymond, and I was sure I'd heard that Raymond—like Malcolm—had died years before Daniel.

Our neighbor didn't jump in with an explanation, just quietly waited as I worked it through.

"You weren't Pack, were you?" I said.

"Only as a child. I left at sixteen. After that, I was on the cusp of membership twice. Malcolm Danvers wanted me back in, but I was . . . undecided. I spent a few weekends with my brothers—Wally and Raymond—many years ago, when I was considering joining. So I know Clayton and the current Alpha."

"Jeremy."

"Yes. Not the woman, though. That was after my time. I do recall hearing a rumor that Clayton had bitten a mate." He chuckled. "I should have known it was true. Where other wolves whine about being lonely, he solves the problem. Not what I'd want—I never understood the whining myself—but I take it he's happy?"

"Very."

"Children?"

"Twins."

"A mate, children, an Alpha-hood to come, if unofficially. Yes, he must be happy. I'm glad to hear it. I was always fond of the boy. I've heard rumors through the years. He has quite a reputation, which I was glad to hear, too. I always worried, with the influence of . . ." He paused.

"I wasn't as fond of the current Alpha. I mean no disrespect, as he seems to be a friend of yours. He just wasn't . . . my sort of man or my sort of werewolf. Not like Clayton."

I bristled at the insult to Jeremy, but I couldn't hold it against the guy. He seemed a typical werewolf—all muscle and testosterone. To them, someone like Clayton was a *real* werewolf, if they overlooked his PhD and cozy domestic life. Jeremy was too cerebral. But even those types would have to grudgingly agree that the Pack was thriving. Growing now, having overcome internal division and external attacks. A solid and unified force, undivided since Jeremy's Ascension.

Naysayers would credit Clayton as the true power in the Pack, a claim that made him laugh. This mutt Miguel might not like Jeremy much, but he'd like him a whole lot more when Jeremy used his influence to get him out.

Cabals weren't allowed to hold American werewolves captive. If they committed a crime, they had to be turned over to the Pack for punishment. Which, all things considered, might not have been in Miguel's best interests. But whatever he'd done, it must have been at least twenty years ago if he didn't know Elena. Jeremy would probably decide he'd been punished enough. Either way, he'd get Miguel out.

I slept a little after that, curled up against Adam, with his arm over me. When we woke up, new bottles of water had been pushed through the opening, along with extra blankets, as if they'd just realized there were two of us. They'd replaced the bucket, too.

In the faint light from the corridor, I could see that some of Adam's bruises were already fading. His ribs ached, but he insisted they were cracked not broken. Our neighbor wasn't the only one with enough fighting experience to recognize the signs.

Miguel noticed we were awake and chatted with us for a while. It was an oddly normal conversation, like being on an overseas flight, occasionally talking to the guy beside you, but mostly just doing your own thing.

He'd heard rumors that something was going on. I gave him the basics. If he had an opinion about supernaturals revealing themselves, he didn't give it.

Adam and I also played games. When we'd unfolded the extra blankets, we'd found a pack of cards tucked inside. Did they give them to all prisoners? Or did we have a sympathetic guard out there? Someone who knew who I was and liked Sean? We hoped so.

There were other things I wanted to talk about. Personal things. I got the sense Adam felt the same, from the looks he'd slant my way when he thought I wouldn't notice. But neither of us said anything. It wasn't the time. Or the place. Especially with our neighbor listening.

So we played cards. And chatted. And curled up under the blankets together to rest.

CHAPTER 21

When a guard came again, hours later, it wasn't the same one. He wasn't even wearing the same uniform, just standard-issue Nast security garb. When he approached our cell, he lifted a finger to his lips before we could speak, then waved us over close to the bars.

"Sean sent me," he whispered. "He doesn't dare come himself—his uncle has men watching for him. He's in Miami with Bryce. I'm going to take you to him."

When we hesitated, he said, "Sean says you both owe him now and that means he's never riding Trixie again."

Adam laughed. Trixie was an old nag at a ranch we liked in Colorado. The last time we were there, they'd sold the horse Sean usually rode, and he'd wanted to flip coins to see who had to ride Trixie. We'd refused. It wasn't something anyone else would know about.

The guard unlocked the door. "Hurry. Captain Kaufman is waiting for you."

As we stepped out, a voice floated from the next cell. "You'll remember me, won't you?"

"I will," I said and stopped at his cell. "I'll tell Jeremy you're in here. He'll do something about it."

Miguel had moved back into the shadows. But as dark as this place was, my eyes had grown accustomed to the dim light, and I could see him plainly. Judging the age of a were-wolf is a tricky thing. The man in the cell looked about the guard's age—late forties, early fifties. His dark hair was barely shot with silver. He was an inch or so shorter than me, broad-shouldered with a muscular build. Blue eyes, but an average blue, nothing outstanding. I supposed he would be considered good-looking for his age, but I found it hard to see that, because I knew who this man was. Not Miguel Santos.

"Did I mention I used to spend summers at Stonehaven?" I said.

His lips twisted in a sardonic smile. "I find that hard to believe, my dear. The Pack does not—"

"They don't like outsiders. A twelve-year-old friend of the family isn't so bad, though, as long as she knows her place and treats them with respect. That's one thing Clay made sure I knew. Treat Stonehaven and everyone in it with respect. I screwed that up once."

"We need to *move*," the guard whispered.

I continued, "There's this bedroom, see. A locked bedroom. It's the twins' room now, but when I was growing up, it was always locked and when I asked what was in it, everyone changed the subject. So one day I used an unlock spell and broke in. Clay caught me. Gave me proper hell. But he did tell me whose room it was. He didn't really need to, because I saw photos in that room and I figured it out. Do you know who I saw in those photos?"

The man said nothing, but his gaze settled on me and in that gaze I saw something colder than any glower from Josef Nast. It took me a second to find my voice. When I did, I leaned against the bars and whispered, "I saw *you*. And no, Malcolm, I will not tell Jeremy you are here."

I asked the guard—Curry, as he introduced himself—if my mother was down here. He said no, and he didn't know where she was, but that Sean's men were searching for her.

He led us down the corridor into an empty room with chairs and desks and an ancient refrigerator and microwave.

"The guards?" I whispered.

"Only one on duty. He was called from his post."

I arched my brows. "It's that easy?"

"To call him from his post, yes, because even if a prisoner does manage to get out, there's no place to go except up—straight into Nast headquarters."

"Seriously? We're in the basement? How do they hide this?"

"It's not just a basement." Curry opened a door and ushered us into a long hall with rusty pipes overhead. "Do you smell the water? Best construction in the world can't make this place any drier. Ninety-five percent of folks up top don't know these cells exist. Another four percent were told it was closed down twenty years ago. That's what Sean heard, too."

"He never checked?" Adam said. That seemed odd for Sean. At one time, yes, he preferred to bury his head in the sand. That had changed, though.

"He probably did," Curry said. "I know I did. But the old doors are all sealed. They made a new one. A hidden door from the processing room. Prisoners go in to be processed and sent to one of the prison complexes and then . . ."

"They're misplaced," I muttered. "Through a chute in the floor."

"Something like that. Point is—" He opened another door and led us into what looked like a storage room. "The only way out is right through the middle of security central. And there's no way to bribe or disable that many guards."

"So how will we—?"

As we walked into the room, Captain Kaufman stepped from behind a wire rack stacked with boxes. He extended his hand. I shook it and introduced him to Adam.

"You did meet," I said. "But you were unconscious at the time."

"My apologies for that," Kaufman said. "Those men

weren't part of my team. That isn't how we do things." He waved toward the cells. "*This* isn't how we do things."

"It's how Josef Nast does things. And I'm betting Thomas knows this place is down here, too."

Kaufman shifted uncomfortably. Even if he was loyal to my brother, he wouldn't disparage the man who was still in charge.

"Just get us out of here," Adam said.

Kaufman and Curry led us into more storage. No metal racks and neat wooden boxes here. This was a hole in the ground, stuffed with rotting crates and stinking of dead rats.

"Let me guess," I said. "There's a secret passage in here, right through the sewers."

Kaufman flicked on his vest light. Curry did the same. I started to cast a light-ball spell then stopped. I could see fine by their lights.

Kaufman stopped in front of a door. A big, metal door, right there, plain as day. Beside it, a security scanner was set into the concrete wall.

"That's a lousy secret hatch," I said.

"It's not a secret. Not to anyone who works down here."

"Then how—?"

Kaufman took my hand and pulled it toward the box. "Fingers outstretched please, Miss Nast."

My hand went into the box. A mechanical whir. Something tapped my thumb. Then—

"Yow!" I yanked my hand out. My fingertip was bleeding. "If it requires virgin blood, you've got the wrong girl."

Kaufman just stood there, ramrod straight, watching the door. I glanced at Curry. He was puffing softly, anxiety building to panic as we waited for . . .

Another whir. Then a clank. A green light flashed over the door. Kaufman grabbed the handle. As he glanced back at me, his gaze went to Curry, who looked ready to piss his pants with relief.

"I'm sorry, sir." Curry looked at me. "I'm sorry, miss. I didn't mean . . . I'm sorry."

Kaufman pulled open the door as Adam murmured, "Nast blood."

I shot him a puzzled glance as we walked through.

"The door lock," Adam said. "It's some kind of DNA reader."

"It's an escape route for the family," Kaufman said as he prodded us along.

A door that would only open to those with Nast DNA. That's why Curry had been worried. He hadn't been certain I really was Sean's sister, only that Sean himself believed it.

Speaking of which, "So there's an escape route for the family that my brothers don't know about? That doesn't help them, does it?"

"They'd be told if the situation required it," Kaufman said.

Yes, but it proved where Thomas Nast's priorities lay. Better to keep the top-secret jail a top secret from anyone who might argue against it, even if that meant possibly denying his grandsons access to an emergency escape.

On the other side of the door, lights flicked on automatically as we walked. God forbid a Nast should need to carry a flashlight. Or learn a witch's light-ball spell.

There was no stench of dead rat here. No dripping concrete walls or mud floor either. It wasn't exactly a state-of-the-art jetway, but it was clean, sterile even, a long metal tube with railings on either side as the floor gradually sloped upward.

We walked quickly, footsteps echoing, lights flashing off in our wake.

"Where does it come out?" I asked.

Kaufman didn't answer.

"You don't know, do you?"

"I knew nothing about the lower prison cells, let alone this escape route. Curry had been to the cells, but he didn't know about this either. Your brother had to . . . persuade a retired architect to part with the plans. He didn't have a hard copy, of course, but his memory was good."

Or Sean made it good. Bribery or threats. Sean's a carrot guy, but you can't rise to his position without learning to use the stick, too.

Curry had said that Sean was in Miami, with Bryce. When he'd learned of our arrest, he would have called Thomas right away. There would have been some back-and-forth as Thomas claimed to know nothing about the operation, until finally he'd have said, "Oh, right, *that* operation. I haven't heard back from Josef yet." A few hours would pass, then Thomas would confirm that we'd been taken. A lawful arrest. We were being brought to Nast headquarters, where the Cortezes could meet the Nasts to discuss the matter.

But before Sean or any Cortez got on the plane . . . Hmm, there seems to have been a processing problem. We weren't where we were supposed to be. We'd be found, of course, in time. You can't misplace prisoners. Not for long anyway.

The growing rasp of Adam's breathing told me he was finding this long uphill trek tough. By the time we made it to the top, he looked ready to keel over.

"Give us a sec," I said.

"I'm fine," Adam said. "I can rest when we're safe."

The exit door had another blood tester. It opened for me, too, and we came out in a room that looked so much like the entry point that I almost wondered if this was yet another diabolical twist of engineering—make it seem like you're climbing to freedom, only to put you back where you began. Even Kaufman stood there, gaping around, until Adam tried to push past and the officer resumed the lead with a gruff, "Allow me, sir."

As we stepped from the secured passage, Kaufman and Curry took out their guns. It seemed odd, seeing weapons in the hands of supernaturals, but I suppose it was our way that was truly odd—the archaic refusal to use anything but supernatural powers. Guns would stop an attacker faster. More permanently, too, which may be why most of us clung to the old ways.

We crossed the room, expecting to find an exit. There wasn't one, and we kept circling, only to end up right back where we began.

"Um, sir . . ." Curry said.

"There *is* an exit," I said. "We just need to find it. Since the room is obviously empty, I say it's safe to split up. Adam? Sit."

He lifted his eyebrows. I took his arm, led him to a sturdy crate and whispered, "Please. Before you fall over."

He listened. Playing tough guy was fine if it kept us on the move. It wouldn't be so fine if we had to make a difficult escape and he collapsed.

As the officers scoured the walls for hidden doors, I turned my gaze upward. The ceiling was at least twelve feet from the floor. I cast a light ball and scanned the darkness overhead. Sure enough, there was a trapdoor.

"They aren't making this easy, are they?" Adam said as he peered up at it.

Curry shook his head. "It can't be that difficult. Thomas Nast isn't a young man."

I walked over and cleared the old crates and boxes obviously left to make this look like a storage room. Only when I moved my light ball right to the wall did I see rungs.

Kaufman wanted to go up first, but this was where supernatural power trumped firepower. I could cast my sensing spell at the top and make sure all was clear. Or I could if the spell worked. I didn't tell him that part.

I climbed. Then I cast. I could pick up the faint pulse of life. Faint meant distant. No one was right above us.

I tested the trap door. Below, Kaufman reached up to tap my ankle—he wanted to go first. I was only making sure the door didn't need an unlock spell. It didn't, so I let the guy with the gun go ahead of me.

Once Kaufman reached the top, he cracked the hatch open, then slowly lifted it. Curry had his gun raised with one hand, the other flexing beside it, ready to activate some half-demon power—ice, fire, maybe telekinesis. He didn't need to. The room above us was clear. Kaufman climbed through, then waved for Curry to come next so he could stand guard while Kaufman helped us out.

I went last—I wanted to be beneath Adam, in case he lost his footing. He didn't. He went up and through, and so did I, coming out in . . .

Another storage room—of some kind of fast-food restaurant, the wire racks around us stocked with boxes of cups and napkins.

Adam pulled a bag from an open box. "After thirty-six hours without caffeine, I'm thinking maybe I'll take this along."

It was coffee beans, marked with the logo of a California chain. Reading the label on another box, I ripped it open and tossed him a tiny bag.

"Try those."

"Chocolate-covered coffee beans. Even better."

We let Kaufman and Curry case the room. We didn't quite see the point. It was roughly twelve feet square. The hatch had been under a section of tile that lifted when we came out, then seamlessly settled back in place. There was only one door.

That was all just a little too simple for the security guys, who apparently had to make sure there weren't booby traps waiting to blow up a hapless barista.

"It's a coffee shop, guys," I said. "I can sense people outside. Patrons. Drinking coffee. If I listen carefully, I can even hear them talking. As for why the Nast top-secret executive escape hatch exits into a coffee shop . . ."

"They own the chain," Kaufman said.

"Seriously? No wonder Sean always takes me to these. Cheapskate."

Kaufman shushed me politely, then listened at the door.

"Lot of patrons for this hour," Kaufman said.

"There's a show gets out at midnight around the corner," Curry said. "They come here for coffee and dessert. I had to wait twenty minutes for a coffee on my midnight break last week."

Kaufman nodded and whispered back to me, "I'm going to need to keep my gun holstered as we leave."

"Okay."

"Once we're out, we're getting in a cab. There's a car waiting, but it's a few blocks away. Farther from headquarters."

"Got it."

Kaufman eased open the door and stepped out. Adam followed, then me, with an energy bolt at the ready. Curry whispered in my ear, "It's going to be okay, miss. Everything will be okay."

Did I look nervous? Maybe I was. Silly, considering we were sneaking into a coffee shop. A little surreal, too.

In front of us, Kaufman straightened. We did the same. Just four people walking out of the hall marked Staff Only. Two of them in security uniforms and two wearing blood-flecked clothing that looked like they'd slept in it on a filthy floor. We could only hope everyone was too busy talking about the play to notice us.

As we approached the swinging door into the café, the buzz of conversation grew louder. Men and women talking and laughing, forks tinkling against china, mugs clanking against tabletops.

"It's going to be okay, miss," Curry whispered again. "Just stay calm and don't panic, whatever happens."

From the tremor in his voice, I wasn't the one who needed the reassurance. Kaufman waved me up beside him.

Adam put his arm around my waist. Casual. Just act casual.

Kaufman pushed open the door. We stepped out. And twenty "patrons" leaped to their feet, guns pointed at us.

CHAPTER 22

"You bastard," I snarled as I spun on Curry. "You set us up."

"I've got kids, miss. I—"

I sent him flying with a knockback spell. As I turned to confront our ambushers, Adam grabbed my arm and whispered, "No."

He was right. Kaufman had his hands raised and he looked two seconds from throwing up. He was a dead man. If he'd thought he had a hope in hell of fighting his way out of this, he would have, but he raised his hands and said, "I want to speak to Sean Nast. This is his sister—"

"You bought that line of bull, Captain?" An officer stepped forward. "I thought you were smarter than that."

"No, she is his sister," Curry said. "Her blood opened the security gate. She's a Nast—"

A rap at the front door. The shades were all drawn, including the one over the door. A louder knock.

The lead officer waved for his people to move out of the way, walked over, pulled the shade back a few inches and yelled, "We're closed."

An ID badge slapped against the glass. The lead officer winced and mouthed a curse.

"An intra-Cabal security team," he said. "Everyone maintain position, but lower your weapons."

He opened the door to admit a grizzled, thickset man.

Two others followed. All wore suits and looked more like FBI agents than security.

Curry whispered, "That's what I meant, miss. I told the Nasts. I had to. I've got kids. Helping you escape—it's treason. But I made sure you'd be safe. That's why I called the intra-Cabal office. I sent Sean a message, too. He'll know what happened. You won't go back to the cells. They'll have to do this fairly. You're okay."

I glowered at him. "I'd be a lot more okay if I was in a cab right now."

"I—I've got kids, miss."

"Stop whining," Kaufman hissed. "Sean trusted you, Frank, and you screwed him over. Do you think you'll get your golden handshake now? Both sides will consider you a traitor."

Curry paled. I turned away from him. The grizzled man in the suit walked over to us.

"Miss Levine? Mr. Vasic? Bo Stein. I'm going to accompany you back to Nast headquarters for a proper hearing into these allegations."

"That's funny," Adam said. "I could swear that was where we were headed twenty-four hours ago. Before we got locked in a filthy cell with no bed and a pail to piss in."

Stein's lips tightened. "Those allegations will be heard as well, sir. I've been told the Cortezes have also been notified and they are on the way with their legal team. This will be handled properly from now on."

"We're not going back into a cell of *any* kind," I said.

"You won't. We'll be with you until—"

"And I want my mother."

Stein stared at me, as if the shock of my incarceration had scrambled my brain.

"Eve Levine was with us," Adam said. "Captain Kaufman can attest to that. She was brought over from the afterlife. Manifested."

Kaufman nodded. "It's true, sir."

I said, "I haven't seen her since we were put on the plane in New Orleans. I want her found. If they try to say she passed over again, I want Jaime Vegas of the interracial council brought here to make contact."

"We'll begin investigating—"

"Before we take one more step we also want to speak to Lucas Cortez," Adam said. "You say you're with intra-Cabal security, but I don't know you."

Stein handed Adam his cell phone. Adam passed it to me. I called Lucas. He answered on the second ring.

"Hey, it's me," I said.

A pause. Then a sigh, so soft it was more a whisper. "Savannah. Since you're calling on Agent Stein's line, I presume the extrication attempt was thwarted."

"It was."

"We'd hoped otherwise. Sean only learned of Frank Curry's intentions thirty minutes ago, making it too late to warn Captain Kaufman. Are you all right?"

"I'm fine. So's Adam, though they beat the crap out of him when we were arrested. Mom's missing, but they say they'll look into that. Stein's okay, then? We can go with him?"

"You'll have to, I'm afraid. But yes, he is a legitimate representative of the intra-Cabal agency. We'll have this mess sorted soon. Sean is already on his way. He was staying near the airport, so I had him take the jet. I'm following with the legal team on a commercial flight. We'll be there as soon as we can."

And that was that. Nothing more to be done except submit to Nast custody and trust that this time we'd get our due process.

They took us back to headquarters. To the executive boardroom, no less, where Stein said we'd rest—under his guard—until everyone arrived for the hearing.

While we waited, we were allowed to take showers in

the executive wing. Then a Cabal doctor tended to Adam's injuries and confirmed that, yes, his ribs were cracked, but already healing nicely. We were back in the boardroom, getting ready to eat, when the guards brought Mom in.

She walked in with her usual confident stride, her hair sleekly brushed, the sword on her back, gaze fixed on me, her smile genuine. When I hurried over and hugged her, she didn't wince, gave no sign she was hiding injuries.

"Hey, baby, you okay?"

I nodded. "You?"

"Better than you, I bet." She kissed my cheek, then checked out my rumpled clothing and shot a glare around the room. "Seems the company advisers decided that while they weren't convinced of my angel-hood, it was best not to take any chances by mistreating me. They locked me up in a lead-lined cell, but I was comfortable enough. I think they were hoping the Fates would spirit me back and they could wash their hands of the matter."

"They let you keep the sword."

"Mmm." She twisted around. It was bound by a sparking red wire. "Major mojo. Cost a prisoner his life. It seems to be holding, though. Unfortunately. How's Adam?"

I'd thought he was right beside me, but now I realized he'd stayed across the room.

"Are you going to introduce us?" Mom said.

"Intro—?"

Adam and my mother had never met. Even as I realized that, there was a moment where I thought I must be wrong. They'd each been such a huge part of my life, but of opposite halves of it. Although I'd had some contact with my mother for years—and Adam had been there when she'd been "around" in ghostly form, with Jaime mediating—they'd never met face to face.

I glanced over at him, now pouring soda into cups for both of us. I shoved my trembling hands into my pockets.

"It's okay, baby," Mom said, tugging one hand out and squeezing it. "I know."

That's all she said—"I know." But when I looked at him, I knew she knew what Adam meant to me. My cheeks heated.

"Something's changed, hasn't it?" she said.

I started to nod, then shrugged, feeling like I was eleven years old again, when I'd told her about a boy at school who wanted me to come to the dance and I thought he might like me, but I wasn't sure.

"Maybe," I said. "I think so."

"It has," she murmured. "I can see it in the way he looks at you."

I went bright red at that. As we approached, Adam set down the cups and turned to greet us. He smiled, but it wasn't his usual grin. Not nervous, either. Guarded maybe? It wasn't what I expected and it threw me a little.

"Adam, this, uh, is my mom," I said.

"Are you sure?" His grin peeked out now. "Because I don't see a resemblance."

Mom laughed and she embraced him, catching him off-guard. As I said, Mom isn't the hugging type, so it startled me a bit, too.

As she pulled back, she whispered in his ear, probably thinking I couldn't hear, "I should have sent her back to Miami. I'm sorry."

"No, that's all—" he began.

"It's not all right," she whispered. "I'm sorry."

When she stepped back, that guarded look had disappeared, and I understood that Adam had been angry with her for taking me along in New Orleans. He didn't want to be angry—and he sure as hell didn't want me knowing he was angry—but he had been.

"Will you eat now?" he whispered as he came over with my drink.

I nodded, took a plate and loaded it up. Fast food—not much else open at this hour—but it's not like I don't eat the stuff by choice anyway.

We ate without saying much. Not much we could say, surrounded by guards. It was just past three in the morning. Sean would be here soon, Lucas and Paige shortly after. Would Thomas insist on waiting for a more reasonable hour, letting us all stew? No one knew. Or if they did, no one told us.

An hour later, there was a commotion in the hall. I hoped it was Sean, but the door stayed closed. Mom had wandered from the table. She'd seemed distracted, and I thought she was just restless, but when I glanced up she was standing in the corner, her back to me.

I walked over to her.

"—so it's a mess," she was saying. To no one.

"Mom?"

She turned. A faint flush rose on her cheeks and she led me back to the table.

"Who were you talking to?" I asked.

"Oh. Um, no one. Probably. Just . . ." A shrug, then she put an arm around my shoulders and gave me a squeeze. "I'm tired, baby. Haven't *been* tired in ten years. I think it's affecting my brain. So what's going on?"

"No idea," Adam said as she sat.

I looked back at the corner. My father. She sensed him here. Was he?

Another commotion in the hall. The door flew open. In walked two massive bodyguards followed by two guys in suits that screamed "lawyer." With the pomp normally reserved for rulers of despotic nations, they ushered in Thomas Nast.

I'd seen my grandfather before. Met him several times . . . if you can call it a "meeting" when you're in the same room and he's studiously pretending you don't exist. But my first thought on seeing him today was *My God, he's gotten old*. Thomas has always been old—to me, anyway. I remember the first time I saw him, tall, white haired, slightly stooped, and thinking, "This is the guy? The one everyone's so scared of? He doesn't seem so bad." He'd looked . . . grandfatherly.

Yes, I hate to admit it, but the first time I saw Thomas Nast, I'd felt a buzz of hope, because he looked like someone I could imagine as a grandfather. Proud and stern, but soft-hearted. Um, no. The only person who softened Thomas Nast's heart was Sean.

As Thomas walked in, though, it was my other brother I thought about. I'd seen the way Thomas acted when Bryce was around—the same way he acted with everyone except Sean. Short-tempered. Overbearing. Irritated, as if they were all incompetents hell-bent on making his life difficult. The same way he treated the man who had followed him into the room. *His* younger son. Josef.

I'd never met Thomas while my father was alive, but I bet he'd treated Kristof the way he did Sean. The favored child. The heir. The only one who mattered.

I'd seen what such favoritism had done to Bryce. The choices he'd made. How miserable and angry he was. In thirty years, would he become another Josef Nast? Willing to kill me, not because I was any threat to him, but because it might have pleased Thomas. He might finally have pleased his father.

Neither Thomas nor Josef looked my way. I didn't expect them to. Their people fanned out around them, getting their chairs just right, pouring them coffee and ice water, bending over to whisper and point out items on papers and digital displays. Shielding them from any need to acknowledge our presence.

The moment Thomas had settled, Mom stood. She stayed standing for at least three minutes. Daring him to look at her. When he didn't, she started forward, chin up, sword glowing stronger, as if it fed off her resolve. Or her rage.

Thomas still didn't look up. Others did. Until now, they'd struggled to pretend there was nothing unusual about having the long-dead alleged mistress of their former heir in their midst, a woman now whispered to be an angel. They turned. They stared. A few stepped closer, protecting their leader. More stepped back.

"Tho—" Mom began.

The door opened. Voices drifted in.

"I'm sorry, sir," someone in the hall said. "But they aren't permitted to join the proceedings."

"They aren't joining." Sean's voice. I exhaled in relief. "They're here as observers. Ms. Michaels is a delegate—"

"I understand, sir, but we don't allow her . . . kind—"

"The word is werewolf." Clay's southern drawl. "It's okay. You can say it. It won't bite."

"There is a council delegate on trial," Sean said. "Ms. Michaels is here to represent Adam Vasic and the council—"

The door closed, muting their voices. I caught just enough to realize they weren't going to permit a werewolf in the hearing, and there were no provisions that required a council delegate to be present when another one was on trial.

Finally, Elena cut in, her voice raised enough for me to hear it. "We'll wait out here, Sean. There's no rule against that, right?"

The agent agreed that there wasn't.

"Then we'll stay here," she said. "Where we can hear everything."

I smiled. The agent sputtered, but there was nothing he could do. His own fault for not bothering to know enough about werewolves to realize they'd be able to hear from the hall.

I sat back and waited. Sean was here. Elena and Clay were here. Lucas was coming. It would be fine. It had to be.

CHAPTER 23

When Sean came in, Thomas got to his feet. His gaze was wary, but there was no mistaking the sudden spark of warmth.

"Sean," he said. "How was your flight? I'm sorry you had—"

"Bryce isn't doing so well, Granddad. Thanks for asking. And thanks for calling to check on him. He appreciates that."

"I—"

"You've been busy." Sean walked toward his grandfather. "The supernatural world is going to hell. Demonic spirits are breaking through everywhere. A hell-beast materialized in the New York subway. Supernaturals are racking up body counts faster than the demons and hell-beasts combined. Of course you're too busy to check on Bryce. Yet somehow, with all this, you've decided you can take a break to put my sister on trial for treason."

Treason? What? How?

"Miss Levine is not your sis—"

"She *is*!" Sean roared, making everyone draw back. Most had probably never even heard him raise his voice. "I'm told there's a special escape route from this building secured by locks requiring Nast blood. *Her* blood opened them."

"Don't bother, Sean," Mom said. "He can't hear you. Won't hear you."

Sean turned. He saw my mother and blinked. "Eve."

She walked over and put her arm around him, leaning in to whisper, "Your dad sends his love. Always." Then she turned to Thomas. "Are you going to look at me now?"

He sat first, then slowly lifted his gaze. When his eyes reached hers, his face stayed immobile.

"Been a long time, hasn't it?" she said. "Twenty-two years since our little chat."

"We've never met—"

"Oh, cut the crap." She stepped up to his table. His bodyguards kept their positions, but everyone else inched back as she swept aside the pages in front of him and planted her hands on the surface. "You remember that chat. You threatened to—" She stopped. Almost imperceptibly, she turned toward Sean.

"You scared me off," she said after a moment. "I let you scare me off. I was young and I was stupid, and I let you screw up my life and Kristof's life and our daughter's life, and I've never forgiven you for that. I don't care if you acknowledge Savannah or not. She doesn't need you. But you are going to let her leave. Savannah and Adam will walk out that door, and you can keep me in their place and—"

A soft, metallic tinkle. The wire binding her sword had fallen to the floor. "About time, ladies," Mom muttered as she reached back for her sword. "Strike that. Maybe I won't stick around, Thomas. You'll let me go and—"

She shimmered. Not just the sword, but her whole body. "No," she whispered. She looked up. "No!"

She shimmered again, almost fading completely before coming back, midsentence. "Give me five minutes—" Her gaze shot to mine, and I ran to her, ignoring the shouts of the guards.

Then she was gone.

Just gone.

I knew it had been coming, but it felt as if someone had slammed me in the gut. It was like every time I'd pictured her death. I'd never known what happened, but I'd imagined it, in all the ways a daughter could torture herself with thoughts of her mother's murder. Yet nothing I'd imagined had felt as horrible as this moment. This moment when she was here. And then she wasn't.

Adam got to me first, pulling me into his shoulder. I let myself collapse against him, not sobbing, not even crying, but wishing I could, the grief just building.

"Let Savannah go," Sean said to Thomas, his voice low. "Please, Granddad, just let her go. Eve said she's not going to fight you about recognizing Savannah. I'm not either. Not anymore. Eve was right. You don't want to see it, so you won't see it. Just let her go. Let it all go."

I lifted my head. Thomas wasn't looking at me. Wasn't looking at Sean. He was staring straight ahead at the spot where my mother had stood. He looked tired. Old and tired and frail, and I knew he didn't want to do this anymore either.

Sean stepped in front of him. "I'm going to take her out of here, Granddad." As he turned toward me, Josef broke the silence.

"She can't just walk away. She participated in a terrorist act against the Cabal and she must face those charges—"

"Oh for God's sake." Sean spun on his uncle. "Nobody believes that but you, Josef, and you're just trying to screw me over by putting Savannah on trial—"

"Mr. Nast is right." It was one of the men in suits. The lawyer from the intra-Cabal agency. "The charges have been laid. Unless Mr. Nast wishes to formally withdraw them . . ." Everyone looked at Thomas. Finally he looked at me, and it was as if he'd looked into the eyes of a basilisk. He slowly but irrevocably turned to stone. "No," he said. "I do not wish to withdraw the charges."

Sean slumped a little, then recovered. "Fine. But we can't begin until Lucas gets here. As the representative of the Cortez Cabal, under whose protection Savannah falls, Lucas

Cortez must be here to witness the proceedings. As her lawyer, he absolutely needs to be here, to represent her."

Josef glowered at Agent Stein, who stood, tugging at his tie.

"Yes, under normal circumstances, that would be true," Stein finally said. "However, your family has protested his involvement on the grounds that as her former legal guardian and current employer, Mr. Cortez cannot be expected to be impartial in this proceeding."

"He's not meant to be impartial," Sean said. "He's her lawyer."

"Yes, well, the intra-Cabal agency has ruled in your family's favor on this matter. Miss Levine will be represented by Mr. Turin, one of the agency's legal team. As for the Cortez Cabal's interests, we are attempting to video-link in Benicio Cortez, but we've encountered technical difficulties."

"Technical difficulties, my ass," Sean muttered. "All right then, we at least need to wait until those difficulties are resolved before we begin."

"No, we have decided that Mr. Cortez can be updated as soon as the link is established."

Sean stood there, staring at Stein, who wouldn't meet his gaze. Then he dropped into his chair so hard the clunk reverberated through the room.

The intra-Cabal agency—or key members of it—had been bribed, and there was nothing we could do about it. My heart started to thud harder. This was real. I was on trial for treason.

The Nasts' head lawyer stood, cleared his throat and began. "It is alleged that Miss Levine was in charge of a detachment of the reveal movement, having joined the cause to aid her grandsire, Lord Demon Balaam . . ."

"What?" I whispered to Sean as the lawyer continued reading the allegation.

Sean glanced over, his jaw tight. Adam reached for my hand, but pulled back, and when I tried to take his anyway, his fingers were so hot I had to bite back a yelp. He shot me an apologetic look, flexed them and whispered, "We'll get this sorted."

The lawyer droned on. The upshot of the charge? I was secretly a member of SLM and had been getting information for them from the Cortez and Nast cabals—hence the treason charge. Together with my mother—whom Balaam obviously freed from the afterlife—I'd joined up with SLM in New Orleans and had been leading a terrorist cell to Atlanta. At that point, the Nasts swooped in, saved the day and arrested my mother, me and Adam, whom they suspected I'd duped with my version of the events.

"My version?" I said. "My version is that my mother was brought over by Shawn Roberts, to aid the *anti*-reveal movement, which Jaime Vegas will confirm. Lucas Cortez will likewise confirm that I was *infiltrating* the reveal movement when you ambushed—"

"Lucas is your former guardian. Ms. Vegas is your friend and his," Josef said, ignoring the lawyers' attempts to quiet us both. "She will say exactly what he tells her."

"And your version?" I said. "Where did you get this supposed proof that I'm part of SLM? You killed everyone at that warehouse."

"There was a survivor. A necromancer named Andrea Patterson. She's told us everything."

"Please," Stein said. "You'll both be allowed to speak."

He motioned to the Nast lawyer, who continued. "Now, as this witness testified, Miss Levine and her mother . . ."

I didn't catch the rest of what he said. Someone was speaking behind me. I glanced over my shoulder, but saw no one.

"—damned well better figure it out," the voice snapped. "You owe us . . ."

The voice faded again, but beside me, Sean had turned too and was staring at the empty space. The expression on his face . . .

I must have had the same expression on mine yesterday, when Shawn Roberts made my mother manifest.

"Dad?" Sean whispered. His gaze shot to me. "Did you hear . . . ?"

"It sounded like—" I swallowed. "It sounded like him."

The air behind us flickered like tiny lightbulbs flashing, so bright I had to look away.

"—either you'll make this work or—"

The room went silent. Sean's chair screeched as he got to his feet. I looked up.

A man stood there. Late forties. A few inches over six feet. Broad shoulders and a thickening waist, both held in check by a perfectly tailored suit. Thinning blond hair. Bright blue eyes. Sean's eyes. My eyes.

Kristof Nast.

Our father.

CHAPTER 24

He looked exactly as I remembered him. Exactly as he had the day he died. The day I accidentally threw him against a wall and killed him.

His gaze went to Sean, and his stern face lit up in a smile so big it made my insides ache.

He reached for his son, but his hands passed right through him.

"Hmm," he said. "Not quite what I was hoping for, but I suppose I should be glad they pulled it off at all."

"Dad," Sean said, his voice choked.

Kristof murmured something too low for me to hear. Sean responded. Then Kristof reached out again, as if to pat him on the back, and said, "I'm hoping we get a moment later, but I don't know how long the Fates can hold this for. I need to—"

"I know."

Sean stepped aside. Kristof—my father—looked at me and gave me the same smile he'd given Sean and I stumbled to my feet, my heart hammering, thinking *I killed you. You know I did.*

It didn't matter. He'd told me that before, through Jaime, but I hadn't believed it. Couldn't believe it until now, seeing it in his face as he came toward me.

"Savannah."

He leaned toward my ear to whisper, "Your mom's fine.

Furious, but fine. I'm going to fix this for you. Okay?" He pulled back and met my gaze. "Okay?"

I nodded. He bent forward, air-kissing my cheek. Then he straightened, and strode across the room.

No one had spoken since he appeared. I think most of them hadn't breathed.

He walked straight to his father's table.

Thomas's face was completely drained of color. He was shaking. One hand slid across the table top, slowly, tentatively, reaching for his son's. "Kristof . . ."

"That's not Kristof," Josef said. "It's an illusion. A demon's trick. One of *her* tricks. Eve's."

His voice was like a mallet shattering glass, jolting everyone from a dream, lawyers and guards blinking, rolling their shoulders, whispering that Josef was right, it couldn't be Kristof because that wasn't possible, ghosts couldn't just appear like this.

Thomas jerked back as if he'd been slapped, and when he did, it took all my willpower not to march over and slap someone myself. Slap Josef.

I didn't like Thomas Nast. After what he'd done to his family and what he'd done to my mother and to me, I could never forgive the man. But to see that look on his face, that hope and joy crushed with a few words, was more than I would wish on anyone.

My father turned to Josef. "You don't believe it's me? Name your proof."

"I'm not playing this game."

"Then I will. When you were eight, you set fire to a batch of scrolls Dad brought home from a trip. Priceless scrolls that he'd gotten while in Egypt over your birthday—when he hadn't even bothered to call you. You set them on fire. Deliberately. I told Dad I did it accidentally, practicing my energy bolt spell. I thought I was helping you, but I wasn't, because you only hated me all the more when I didn't get in trouble."

He waved at Sean. "When Bryce was five, he was angry with me because I was late for a school play. The next time he was in my office, he shredded all the files on my desk. Sean tried to take the blame. I wouldn't let him because I knew it wouldn't help. Bryce was angry because he thought I cared more about work than about him. He got in trouble for the files, but I made sure I was never late for him again, however angry Dad got about my 'misplaced priorities.'"

"Kristof . . ." Thomas reached out again, his eyes glistening with tears.

"Yes, Dad, it's me. It's been me before, too. Three times I had your necromancer pass along a message. Three times I told you Savannah was my daughter. Three times you ignored me."

"I didn't think it was really—"

"You thought what you wanted. You always did. You still do. And as Eve and Sean both said, the time for that is past. Believe what you want about Savannah. I'm not here over that. I'm here to tell you to let her go. I know what your end game is, yours and Josef's, and I'm warning you not to make my son and daughter a part of that."

"Son?" Thomas looked over at Sean. "I would never threaten Sean—"

"I have two sons, Dad, a fact you tend to overlook. Bryce is sick. He needs help. He needs you to work with the Cortezes to stop these people and find a cure for what they've done to him, because what they've done is terrible, and it's only going to get worse."

"The Nasts don't work with the Cortezes," Josef said.

"Fine. Pursue these people on your own. But do not put on this farce of a trial to blackmail Benicio Cortez. Do not endanger my son's life so you can take advantage of this chaos to overthrow the Cortezes."

"We would never—"

"I know you, Josef. And I know you, too, Dad. I see

what's happening here and—" He stopped short and glanced up. He scowled at the ceiling, then looked back at his father. "They can't hold the spell much longer. When is the last time you've heard of a ghost appearing to anyone but a necromancer, Dad?"

"I . . ."

"Ask Adam over there. It has happened, but the magic requires a thinning of the veil between the worlds. That veil has never been thinner than it is now. It is chaos over there. You cannot let it become chaos here, too, or that veil will rip and the world risks finding more than werewolves and witches in its midst."

He leaned over the table again. "Let Savannah go. Help Bryce. Fix this problem with or without the Cortezes, but do not add to the chaos. Whatever you do, do not add to it."

He cast another annoyed glance upward, and muttered, "I know, I know."

He walked back to Sean, bent and whispered to him. I sat down so I wouldn't eavesdrop. Then he came to me and knelt beside my chair.

"I wish I could stay and really fix this for you, Savannah."

"I know."

"It *will* be fixed. I'm giving them the chance to back down, but if they don't . . . I have information. Blackmail material. They will back down, one way or another."

I nodded.

"I love you. I hope you know that. I was wrong to ever try to take custody of you from Paige, and anything that happened as a result of that is my fault. Completely my fault." He gave me a kiss on the cheek that I swore I could feel. "You set me free, Savannah. As much as I wish I could be here for you and your brothers, you helped me leave all this and find your mother again. I will never regret that."

He stood and turned to Adam. "Take care of her."

Adam nodded. "I will."

He walked back to the place where he'd arrived. As he started to fade, he frowned suddenly, sharply looking over at the wall and saying, "What's that? Hold on. Something's coming—"

He disappeared.

Did the trial end after that? Of course not. But the tone changed. As the lawyers droned on, Thomas's attention turned inward, as if he wasn't listening at all.

Josef didn't give in so easily. Whatever grand scheme they'd cooked up, he wasn't surrendering it just because his dead brother asked. Or maybe he wasn't surrendering it precisely *because* Kristof had asked.

I'd seen what the family dynamics had done to my own brothers. Everything I'd heard about my father supported what I'd just seen—that he'd never favored either son. But maybe because of Thomas's obvious favoritism—or maybe because Sean was more likable—Bryce had suffered. He'd grown up resenting his brother, even though he loved him. That was the push–pull that tore at Bryce. He genuinely loved the brother he wanted to hate.

Josef had no such conflict. Any love he'd felt for his brother had withered since his death. Now Kristof was simply an obstacle to Josef's happiness, much the same as he might have been when they were boys.

So the trial proceeded. But it didn't proceed for long before there was yet another commotion in the hall.

"Good God," my inter-Cabal agency lawyer muttered. "Now what? Angel? Ghost? Hellhound?"

A scream cut him off. It came from the rear door. Before anyone could move, a familiar figure strode through the door.

"Severin," I whispered.

Sierra followed him into the room, and in each hand she held the decapitated head of a young man.

"Are these yours?" she said.

She tossed them. One hit a lawyer, and he stumbled back, clawing at his suit. The other rolled to my feet. I stepped forward, fingertips sparking.

"Oooh, Savannah, getting your powers back? Maybe you'll be useful to us after all."

"Thomas Nast," Severin said. "Lord Balaam has sent us to pass along a message. You ignored your son's pleas on his daughter's behalf. Maybe you'll listen to her *other* grandfather. Lord Balaam demands that you set Savannah free. Immediately."

Josef sprang to his feet. "All right. This goes too far." He turned on his father. "Do you really expect us to think a lord demon cares about this girl? His grandchild?"

"Fine, don't believe me," Sierra said. Then she grinned. "It'll be much more fun that way."

"We came to warn you," Severin said. "While I agree with my sister that it'll be more fun if you refuse, it's my job to strongly recommend you don't."

"We have to get Savannah out of here," Adam whispered across me to Sean. "Balaam is up to something."

I could see the internal struggle on Sean's face. Then a flash of something like grief, his gaze dropping as he nodded. He pushed back his chair and motioned me up.

As I stood, he took my elbow and started for the door. Adam fell in on my other side. It took a moment for anyone to notice. Then Agent Stein stood. "Where are you going?"

"I'm taking my sister out of here," Sean said. "An angel tried to stop this sham of a trial. My father tried to stop it. Now a lord demon is trying to stop it. By allowing this to proceed without the Cortezes' involvement, the intra-Cabal agency has forfeited its role as an impartial arbiter. We do not recognize its authority. We are leaving."

"You are part of this Cabal," Josef said. "You will not—"

"I will. Or I will no longer be part of this Cabal." His gaze was fixed on his grandfather. "That's your choice."

"Don't you threaten us," Josef said.

Sean turned toward the door. Two of the three guards in our path stepped aside. The third hesitated, but made no move to stop us.

"Arrest him." Josef jabbed a finger at his bodyguards. "Go."

Thomas pushed to his feet. "No. This has gone too far. Sean—"

"He's giving you one last chance," Severin cut in. "Will you let Savannah go?"

"Never," Josef said.

Severin smiled. "I'll take that as your final word on the matter."

He walked to the middle of the room, Sierra at his side. Two of the guards pulled their guns, as if finally realizing they should do something. Then they fell to their knees, screaming, hands to their faces. Their shrieks died midnote as they collapsed, blood streaming from their eyes, their ears, their noses and mouths.

Severin's head shot back, eyes rolling back. I knew what was happening, but I told myself it couldn't be—they hadn't made the proper preparations. The last time, they'd had to draw a ritual circle and recite the incantations, and without that, they couldn't—

Severin's chin shot down. His eyes glowed bright green.

Balaam.

CHAPTER 25

The lord demon stopped right in front of me, and stroked warm fingers across my cheek. When Adam yanked me back, Balaam spun on him.

"Don't give me an excuse, brat. I've no love for your sire these days."

I moved between them and lifted my chin, meeting Balaam's gaze.

"This has nothing to do with you," I said. "I appreciate the interest, but I can handle it."

"You shouldn't need to, my child. I'll do it for you." He smiled. "Happily."

"No—" I said, but he was already bearing down on Thomas.

Bodyguards leaped around the table. Balaam fluttered his fingers and the men's eyes . . . popped. Just popped, blood streaming down their faces as they screamed. Balaam snapped his fingers and they stopped screaming. They were still alive, still writhing on the floor, mouths still open, but they made no sound.

"Do you know me, sorcerer?" Balaam said to Thomas.

"I—"

"I sent a messenger to spare us both this visit. You ignored him."

"I—"

"Say my name, sorcerer."

Thomas sat there. An old man. Such an old man, his rheumy blue eyes watery, his face little more than a death mask, skin tight over bone. No one went to him. No one could. Beside me, Sean kept rocking forward, but now it was my hand on *his* arm. A binding spell waited on my lips. I didn't need it. He knew there was nothing anyone could do.

Thomas pulled himself up. He blinked and gained back a decade of his lost years, remembering who he was. His voice was steady when he said, "You are Lord Balaam, and I apologize for the misunderstanding. I meant no disrespect—"

"But disrespect me you did."

"Not intentionally, sir. This hearing is at an end. The girl is free to go. I was saying that when you arrived—"

"It is too late. You mistreated my granddaughter. You mistreated my daughter. You have mistreated me. There is no apology that can be made."

He lifted his fingers. Thomas's eyes bulged and I screamed, "No!" But Balaam didn't blind Thomas. The old man's eyes simply bulged in pain and shock. He wavered there a moment and I thought *good, that's it, just a warning.* Then he fell forward, clutching his chest.

Sean ran to our grandfather. I tried to stop him, but he caught me off-guard. My binding spell failed. I raced after him, Adam at my heels.

Thomas Nast had dropped to his knees. Balaam grabbed the table between them and threw it, hitting several of the lawyers before they could get out of the way.

The only person left near Thomas was Josef. And he just stood there. In shock, maybe. In cowardice, probably. Only Sean ran to his grandfather, shouting for him over the commotion as everyone headed for the exits, the thunder of feet accompanied by Sierra's laughter as she waltzed through the stampede, fingers tapping left and right, freezing as they went, her victims yelping in shock, then spinning out of the way before continuing to the doors.

Balaam stood in front of Thomas, now on his knees, one hand on the floor to brace himself, the other over his heart as he panted, eyes rolling.

Balaam put out his hand.

"No!" I screamed, Sean's cry joining mine.

Thomas's head shot back. His torso shot forward. His shirt split. His chest cracked open, ribs popping. His heart ripped free and sailed into Balaam's hand.

Sean was at his grandfather's side now, dropping to his knees and grabbing him as the old man's eyes closed. I skidded to a stop behind Balaam, who stood there, holding Thomas's heart. He looked down at it. He smiled. Then he crushed it, threw it aside and turned. He stopped short, seeing me there.

"You bastard," I said. "You sick bastard."

His brows arched. "I did it for you, my child."

"No, you did not. This isn't about me. None of this is about me. You used me. You used this."

He reached out and touched my chin, his fingers hot and slick with Thomas's blood.

"You are angry now, but you will reap the benefits, my child. You've seen what I can do. Reconsider my offer." His lips curled in a smile that wasn't a smile at all. "Think on this and reconsider my offer."

He passed me and continued walking, cutting through the chaos, lawyers and guards tripping out of his path, Sierra falling in behind him as they left by the rear door.

I looked over at Sean, kneeling on the floor with his grandfather's—our grandfather's—body. I took a step toward them. A hand caught my arm. Startled, I turned to see Adam, as if he'd been there all along, right behind me.

"You can't," he whispered. "I know you want to go to him, but you need to get out of here. Now."

I looked at the door. As soon as I did, Josef's voice boomed through the room. "Arrest her. She brought Balaam here. She did this."

There were only three uninjured guards left in the room. They seemed to have stayed put out of shock, not loyalty, but Josef's words snapped them out of it. All three turned to me. And in all three pairs of eyes I saw fresh purpose—something they could do, an action they could take, a punishment that could be inflicted.

I glanced at Sean, but he hadn't heard, too wrapped up in his grief. Adam took my arm. I shook him off and started for the door myself. The guards closed in. I slammed one with a knockback. Another dove at me. Adam grabbed him and the guy screamed in pain. Adam tossed him aside and we broke into a run for the door.

I was reaching for the handle when the door flew open. There stood one of the intra-Cabal guards, his gun rising.

"By order of the—"

A blur of motion behind the guard. Hands lifted him and threw him into the room, Adam and I ducking out of the way. Then hands grabbed me so fast I didn't see who it was and I lifted my fingers for a knockback.

"Hit me with that spell and it'll be the last time I save you," Clay growled.

He yanked me into the hall. Elena pulled Adam through, then they slammed the door and Lucas spell-locked it.

I stood there, panting like I'd just run ten miles. A half dozen bodies littered the corridor. Some unconscious. A couple dead. One of the dead men looked as if he'd been trampled. Elena's hair was half yanked from her ponytail and a scratch bisected her cheek. Clay had bruises rising on his face and was wincing as he stretched his bad arm. Lucas's suit jacket lay on the floor and his white shirt was smattered with blood, more dripping from his nose.

I imagined the scene out here when the screaming started inside—Elena, Clay, and Lucas fighting to get in as everyone else fought to get out.

"Thomas," I said. "Balaam killed—"

"Explain later," Elena said. "From those footsteps I hear, we're about to get hit by the second wave."

The first guard rounded the corner before she even finished speaking. He leveled his gun. Lucas hit him with a knockback and Clay dove in to take him out. I stopped the second guy with a binding spell. It snapped before I released it, but there was enough time for Elena to send the guy flying. She threw me his gun. Clay kicked the other one our way.

I caught the first gun and stared at it a second before turning it around, finger going to the trigger—

Adam plucked it out of my hands.

"Close quarters," he said.

In other words, not the place to learn how to shoot. He threw open the nearest door. Office storage. Now gun storage.

I was kicking in the second gun when two guards came running from the other end of the hall.

"Adam!" Elena shouted.

"See 'em!" he called back. "Lucas, can you—"

"I have this side. Savannah, cover Ad—" He stopped and turned to look at me. "Sorry, I forgot—"

"My knockback works."

"Best thing anyway. Conserve your power."

How many times had I heard that? If I was fighting alongside Adam, I should throw our assailants off balance with knockbacks while Adam launched the frontal attacks, as Lucas had done with Clay.

Had I ever actually done it? Of course not. I had to be on the front line. Even if it meant I probably made the fight tougher for Adam.

Spell-casters were ranged attack experts. I'd played enough video games to know that. This was the first time I actually did it in real life.

I hit one guard with a knockback. Adam slammed him in the chest with both hands, scorching through his shirt and leaving the man screaming. The second guy lifted his gun. I hit him with an energy bolt, but I wasn't trusting it to work, so I backed it up with a kick. The guy went down. I grabbed the guns—plus another one that Lucas had kicked my way—and got them in the storage room.

Our end was clear now, but I didn't need werewolf hearing to pick up the clomp of boots running toward us.

I looked at Adam. He was breathing deeply—his bruised face red from pain and exertion. I glanced over to where Elena, Clay, and Lucas were taking on three guards.

"I'm okay," Adam said. "I'm using my powers more than my fists. Not sure how long it will last, but I'm good for—"

A guard came flying around the corner. Only one this time. I dispatched him with two knockbacks in succession, letting Adam take him down and disarm him.

As Lucas passed another gun to me, he called, "The ultimate goal, I believe, is to get out of the building. We can't disarm every guard and—" He kicked one who'd begun to rise, his foot striking him in the side of the head and sending him to dreamland.

"These guys won't stay down forever," Elena said. "Retreat it is." She looked both ways, then pointed in our direction. "Go that way and—"

Two shots from inside the meeting room. The door crashed open, falling off its hinges. A guard inside started firing. We dove for cover. A yelp from inside the room. Then a grunt. I couldn't see through the doorway, but Lucas hit someone with a spell. Clay barreled in. I followed and saw Sean getting up off a guard caught in Lucas's binding spell. Clay knocked the guard out.

"We have to go," Sean said, running toward us. "Now."

I looked around. Josef had left, presumably through the rear door. There were medics tending to the blinded guards, and one was bent over Thomas's body. Sean gave one last look at his grandfather, then pulled his gaze away and straightened.

"We *have* to go," he repeated. "Josef will call in every guard in the city to make sure we don't leave this building."

"We need to split up," Elena said. "Clay and I will take Savannah."

"Good," Sean said. "Smaller groups will attract less attention." He took out his key card and handed it to me. "Use this. All-access pass."

"But you need—"

"I can get us out. You're the one they really want to stop."

He quickly told us the safest route. Then we took off through the rear exit.

ELENA

Elena tried to brush a loose lock of hair from her face, only to find that it was plastered there by blood. *Damn it.* She touched her forehead and found the spot. Just a cut. There likely would be a few more war wounds joining it by morning—bumps and bruises and aches—but nothing serious. She glanced back at Clay. He was rubbing his right arm. The old zombie scratch acting up, as it always did after a fight. Otherwise, he seemed fine. Good. Now, to get them all to safety.

Yet another mission gone to hell. That seemed to be par for the course these days. Damn the Cabals. Damn Benicio, too. Especially Benicio. Oh, sure, just walk into Nast headquarters. Tell them she wanted to watch the proceedings. So what if they're a rival Cabal? So what if she is a werewolf? So what if they'd taken Savannah captive on a trumped-up charge of *treason*. There were rules about these things and the Nasts would follow the rules and let her in.

Bullshit.

Why is it when things go to hell, people still expect others to follow the rules? Any werewolf knows better. When it comes down to raw survival, rules are the first thing to go. It's teeth and claws and every wolf for himself and his Pack. The Nasts would protect their own, and they'd made it very clear that Savannah was not one of their own.

Damn Benicio. Damn herself, too, for listening to him.

Hadn't she learned her lesson after that colossal fuck-up at the warehouse? When Savannah and Eve wanted to infiltrate the group, Elena hadn't liked it. But after consulting with Jeremy, she agreed that the risks were acceptable, as long as they got in and out as fast as possible.

Then Savannah texted to say they were joining a mission to Atlanta. When Clay heard that, his reaction eloquently summed up Elena's own. *Hell, no.* It wasn't just a gut reaction this time. It was experience. As Alpha-elect, she knew a few things about leadership, and if this Giles was letting new recruits join a critical mission, he was panicking. A dangerous situation. Lucas had to pull them out now. Adam agreed wholeheartedly.

Elena knew she could have persuaded Lucas . . . if she'd been able to get in touch with him. But she was only able to reach Benicio, and he'd brushed off her concerns and then it was too late to intervene.

And now they were here, running for their lives, as the Nast Cabal imploded around them.

Elena bustled Savannah through the board room to the rear door. She put her ear to it. Booted feet thudded down the main hall. Someone yelled, "The stairs! They're taking the stairs!"

"Are you sure?" someone else called. "Those ones are locked."

"I'm sure. There's a burned hole where the handle used to be."

Savannah whispered, "Decoy damage."

In other words, Adam had burned it intentionally, to make everyone think they'd gone that way. Good.

When the guard's footfalls faded, Elena nudged Savannah through the door, then glanced back at Clay. They'd been together so long that's all it took—a glance. He mouthed, "Go on." She nodded and led Savannah as he hung back to guard the rear.

They rounded the corner. Ahead was a stairwell, the sign warning Authorized Use Only.

"That's it," Savannah murmured.

"Good, we'll—" Elena caught the sound of boots climbing the steps. "Shit!"

She glanced at Clay, thirty feet back, and waved for him to duck into a room as she jogged to the nearest closed door. She put her ear to the door, then slowly twisted the knob. Behind her, Savannah bounced impatiently, those footfalls on the stairs now close enough for her to hear.

"If it's locked, I can probably cast—"

The door opened. Savannah nudged her, whispering to hurry, the guards were coming. Elena turned to tell her to cool it—she had to check the room first—but someone in the stairwell said, "Through here, sir?" and Savannah gave her a shove, knocking her through the doorway.

"Sorry," she whispered, as Elena recovered.

Savannah turned to close the door behind them, and as she did, Elena caught a scent that made her brain short-circuit for just a second, telling her the impossible—that Jeremy was here, when she knew he was two thousand miles away in Miami.

"Don't close that door completely," a voice said. "It locks from the inside."

Elena spun. They were in what looked like a staff lounge. The lights were dim and at first all she saw was a figure rising from a chair. That scent wafted around the room. Not Jeremy—she could tell that now—but smelling like him, that rich sandalwood scent she knew so well. There was another familiar aspect to the scent, too. The distinct musky smell of a werewolf.

The man stepped forward into the dim light as her eyes adjusted. He was a little taller than Elena, with a muscular build. Black, silver-threaded hair. Blue eyes. In the eyes, she saw nothing she recognized. But when her gaze moved back to take in the whole of the man, her heart stopped. Just stopped and she stood there, frozen, as every hair on her body rose.

She knew that face. She saw a version of it almost every day—a longer version, more angular, with dark eyes, slightly slanted, different, yet familiar enough that it was like the scent—that first thing she thought was *Jeremy*. Yet it wasn't just the similarity that made her heart stop. It was *this* face, one she'd seen when Clay first took her into the locked bedroom to try to help her understand Jeremy all those years ago. The face she'd seen again when they'd cleaned out that bedroom to make way for their children, Jeremy finally ready to let go—happy and relieved to let go. She'd seen this face in the photos in that room, and it didn't matter if she'd never met the man himself. She hated the face and she hated the man who wore it and now, looking across the room and seeing it in the flesh, the only thing she felt was hate.

"Hello," Malcolm Danvers said. "You must be Elena."

"He's—" Savannah began.

"Oh, let her guess," the man said. "That'll be so much more fun." He stepped toward Elena, his nostrils flaring, drinking in her scent. "Do you know who I am?"

She forced the words through clenched teeth. "I do."

"Really? Are you sure? I must be much younger than you expected. And much more alive."

"Temporarily," she said, a growl escaping with the word.

He laughed and walked toward her.

Malcolm Danvers. She was looking at Malcolm Danvers. The how, the why—none of that mattered. This was the man who'd made Jeremy's life hell. The father who'd despised him and never let a day pass without letting Jeremy know it. The man who'd found Clay in the bayou and tossed him aside to die. The man who'd later decided, after Jeremy rescued Clay, that Clay was the kind of son he wanted. Clay never told her that, but she'd heard it from

Nick and Antonio, how Malcolm tried to turn Clay against Jeremy. It didn't work, of course. Madness to try. But Clay and Jeremy still suffered for it.

Now Malcolm was back? Not if she could help it. He was going to die in this room, and Jeremy would never be the wiser.

Elena watched him as he came toward her. As he circled her, she pivoted, following him, every muscle tight, gaze locked on his.

"Clayton's chosen mate," Malcolm said. "You're what I would have expected. Pretty. Physically fit. Smart enough to know when to watch and listen. But giving me a look that says you'll rip my spleen out as soon as I give you the chance. Yes, exactly what I would expect from Clayton."

He laughed, and the sound was like claws scraping her spine, a perversely warped version of Jeremy's deep chuckle.

"You'll give my regards to your mate, won't you?" Malcolm said. "Tell him I remember him fondly, despite his every attempt to ensure I wouldn't. I look forward to seeing him again." He glanced at the door and smiled. "Someday soon."

He started toward the door.

Elena swerved into his path. "You're not going anywhere. Jeremy and Clay think you're dead, and I'd hate to disappoint them."

He threw back his head and laughed. Then he dove at her. She slammed a fist into his gut. He doubled over. A good kick would have dropped him to the floor, but when she tried, he grabbed her leg and sent her flying into the wall. As she scrambled up, Savannah hit him with a knockback.

"Savannah?" Elena said. "Stay out of this. Please."

"Good advice, little witch," Malcolm said as he recovered. "The necks of pretty girls break like twigs. Did you know that?"

He *would* know. Elena had heard that mutts weren't the

only prey Malcolm Danvers hunted. No better than a man-killer, they'd said. Yet the Pack never kicked him out. In fact, they'd almost elected him Alpha. That was one of the many injustices that still dogged the Pack thirty years after Jeremy took over. Mutts had long memories.

Malcolm turned toward her. "Do you really think you can kill me?"

"I'm going to try," she said.

He smiled. "Better wolves than you have given it their best, and gone to a shallow grave. You're very valuable to someone I care about. I don't want to hurt you."

"Then sit down in that chair and we'll see if *your* neck snaps like a twig."

He laughed, but there was no humor in it. "You've let this Alpha business go to your head, my dear. It's a sham, you know. Clayton will be Alpha. You're just the pretty fool who thinks she's a big, bad wolf."

"Then it should be easy to take me down."

His smile turned into an ugly scowl. "I won't kill you, she-bitch. I wouldn't do that to Clayton. But it seems he's neglected to teach you to respect your betters."

"Oh, I respect my betters. But a Y chromosome doesn't automatically place you in that category."

"No? Well, maybe I'll show you what it does mean. Teach you the lesson my boy failed to impart."

Two years ago, that threat would have brought back memories of her hellish years as a foster child, and it would have done exactly what he wanted—it would have scared her. But she'd faced down those demons in Alaska and now she heard his words, looked in his eyes and felt nothing but cold rage.

"Go ahead and try," she said.

He charged. Elena stepped aside at the last moment, grabbed him by the back of the shirt and yanked him off his feet. He broke from her grip, and hit her with a blow to the chin that sent her reeling. She blocked his next punch, then landed one of her own.

Earlier, she'd thought of the aches and bruises she'd feel tomorrow from the fight with the guards. But after a few rounds with Malcolm, they started making an early appearance—a shoulder throbbing when she threw a punch, a leg muscle screaming when she kicked, a blow that didn't have the power it should, a dodge that wasn't quite fast enough.

Having superstrength was a lot more useful against a human opponent. It didn't matter how hard Elena worked out, biology dictated that she'd never develop the upper-body strength to compete with a physically fit male werewolf. Instead, she had to rely on speed and experience. Today neither seemed to be enough.

As Elena fought, she kept reminding herself that Malcolm had to be at least eighty. But he didn't look like he was eighty, and he sure as hell didn't fight like he was eighty, and she had no idea how that could be possible, but it was.

When she sparred with Clay, he held back a little. Even with his bad arm, he was still an experienced werewolf in his prime. If he gave it his all, she couldn't beat him. Her brain insisted that Malcolm was an old man and she was Alpha-elect, damn it—she should be able to beat him. But she couldn't. It was like fighting Clay full out . . . after she'd gone two days without sleep and fought off a battalion of trained Cabal guards.

Soon Malcolm was landing more blows than she was. Even with Savannah discreetly casting knockbacks to push him off balance, Elena was barely holding her own. Then a solid blow to the jaw sent her down. Before she could scramble up, Malcolm was straddling her, pinning her on her back. Savannah started forward, but Elena lifted her fingers, telling her to wait. She looked up at Malcolm, widened her eyes, and poured in every ounce of that old fear she could dredge up.

He smiled. His hand moved to her side, then slid up toward her breast as he bent over. "Is this what you wanted, my dear? I think it—"

She head-butted his jaw, catching his tongue between his teeth. As he snarled, she yanked one arm free and smashed it into his nose. Blood spurted. Elena shoved him off and sprang to her feet. Out of the corner of her eye, she saw Savannah rushing in. Elena waved her back, but the move caught Malcolm's attention and with one last rage-filled glance at her, he charged Savannah. Elena sprang at him just as the door flew open.

Clay came in, muttering, "Easy to find you two. Savannah left the damned door ajar—"

He stopped. So did Malcolm. Elena was already in flight and hit him square in the back. She pinned him this time, face down on the floor.

Then Elena looked up and saw Clay's face. Saw the shock on it. Utter, stomach-dropping shock. She'd wanted to spare him this. If she couldn't spare him, at least she wanted to warn him. But it was too late. It took only a split second for that shock to harden, his eyes going colder than she'd ever seen them. And in another split second, that look vanished, too.

Clay strolled over to them. "Well, if I ever had to see you again, Malcolm, I suppose this is the way I'd choose." He crouched. "Taken down by a woman, huh? Probably rather just let everyone go on thinking you were already dead."

Malcolm bucked and snarled, but Elena had him pinned by the shoulders. She moved her knee up his spine and pushed down. As he hissed, she grabbed a handful of his hair and ground his broken nose against the hardwood.

"You better call off your bitch," Malcolm said, his breathing ragged with pain. "She already threatened to snap my neck."

Clay rested on his haunches and looked at Elena. "Did you say that, darling?"

"I did. Of course, I was hoping to do it before you realized he was alive. But now's a good time, too."

He laughed, and when he did, his blue eyes glittered, all traces of hatred and rage consumed by something else. Anticipation. And when Elena saw that, she was glad she *hadn't* snapped Malcolm's neck.

"You're not going to let her kill me, Clayton."

"Oh, Elena pretty much does as she pleases."

Malcolm snorted, as if to say that was where Clay had failed as a husband. "Perhaps, but if you wanted me dead, you'd have done it years ago."

"Would I?"

"Yes. And you didn't, because as much as you pretended otherwise, there was a bond between us. You were loyal to Jeremy, but I was the one who understood you."

"Huh. Well, I'd disagree, but I know one person who *does* understand me." He looked up as Elena climbed off Malcolm. "Thank you, darling."

"Anytime."

Malcolm smirked and started getting to his feet. A left hook from Clay knocked him back off them. Clay grabbed Malcolm before he could regain his footing.

"Do you know why he didn't kill you all those years ago?" Elena said. "Because Jeremy would know Clay did it for him and he'd feel guilty. But Jeremy's not here now. And he already thinks you're dead. Which means I should thank you. Because today I get to give my husband a gift that'll last me through a whole lotta anniversaries."

Clay grinned. "And he appreciates it."

"Good, but as much as I'd love to let you savor the moment, we are mid-escape here."

"Don't worry. This will be quick."

He ducked Malcolm's swing and threw him across the room. Malcolm bounced back fast, but now *he* was the one who was winded and battered from fighting. One look at Malcolm had given Clay all the energy he needed.

"Maybe quicker than I thought," Clay said as he waited for Malcolm to recover from the next two blows. "This isn't the fight I always imagined."

"He's old," Elena said.

Malcolm snarled and ran at her. Clay tripped him, but Malcolm managed to keep his balance and get out of the way as Clay charged.

"If you want a proper fight, Clayton, let me go," Malcolm said. "Challenge me later. Neither of us is in top form right now. You won't get any glory from this bout if no one knows I'm still alive."

"Glory?" Clay shook his head. "I don't give a shit about glory, Malcolm. Have you forgotten that?"

"You care about your reputation. I know what you did—"

"Everyone knows what I did. That was the point. I only care about my reputation if it keeps my Alpha and my family safe. I won't be keeping them safe if you walk away. I let you do that twenty-five years ago. I'm not doing it again."

He charged. Malcolm feinted, but Clay managed to land a blow that sent him to the floor. As Clay bore down on him, the door burst open and two guards ran in, guns drawn.

Savannah lifted her hands in a spell.

"Don't do that, miss," the man in front said. "We're not going to stop you from leaving, but we do need that werewolf."

Elena glanced over at Clay. She wanted to tell him not to listen, just go ahead, finish Malcolm off. For Jeremy's sake, they had to kill Malcolm and never let Jeremy know he'd been alive. But when Clay glanced toward Malcolm, the guns swung his way.

"Please," the guard said. "I don't have any quarrel with the Pack, but I was sent to get this one. I need you to walk away."

"Do you?" Elena said, meeting the man's gaze. "What if you came in and he was already dead?"

"Then I'd have to explain why I didn't stop you. And the men who left him here would have to explain why he wasn't better secured. He's valuable Cabal property, ma'am. I'm going to insist on this."

When she looked over at Clay, he shook his head. He was right, of course. As leader of this mission, her priority was keeping him and Savannah safe.

"Later," Clay murmured. "We'll handle this later."

He walked over to where Malcolm still lay on the ground. "Now that I know you're alive? I won't rest until you're not. Remember that."

CHAPTER 26

Only two guards tried to stop us as we made our way out of Nast headquarters. The rest pretended not to notice us. One even distracted his comrades so we could sneak past.

In the immediate aftermath of Thomas's death, the staff had turned to Josef, the senior high-ranking Nast. But as the shock passed and news of what happened spread, many must have been reconsidering that. Sean was heir, meaning he was now CEO, meaning it might not be wise to stop his sister from fleeing the building. Especially now, when word had spread that I really was his sister.

The moment we'd cleared the building and any cell blockers, Elena's phone started vibrating. It was Lucas. We ducked between two vans in a nearby lot and she passed it to me while we caught our breath.

"We're out," I said. "And you?"

"Twenty minutes ago," I heard Adam say in the background. "Where the hell were you?"

"Adam was concerned," Lucas said.

"So I hear. We ran into . . . a werewolf Clay knew from years ago. There was a fight."

Lucas didn't ask for details. He knew that any mutt we bumped into would take advantage of the opportunity to fight Clay, and he'd have no choice but to stop and defend himself.

"Can you put Elena on?" Lucas said. "They have a car, and we all need to get to it."

I handed over the phone. Elena gave Lucas directions as Clay started moving us along.

"We're not telling Jeremy about Malcolm," he said when Elena hung up.

Elena didn't answer. When I glanced over, she was just walking, carefully scanning the road.

"I'm talking to *you*, Savannah," Clay said. "Elena doesn't need to be told that."

"We aren't telling Karl either," she said. "Malcolm's resurrection is staying between us."

"Why not Karl, though?" I asked.

"Because I don't want competition over who gets to kill the bastard," Clay said.

"Malcolm killed Karl's dad when he was about fifteen," Elena explained. "Not a fair fight, if the rumors are true."

"Mutt hunt," Clay said as he checked around the next corner, then waved us onto the sidewalk. "Malcolm and the Santos men used to track down and kill mutts, even if they were staying out of trouble, minding their own business. Karl's lucky he got away."

"I think Karl blames himself for what happened," Elena said. "But it's not the kind of thing you can ask him about. He doesn't need this now, though."

We got to the car just before the others showed up, then we drove to Bryce's condo. I'd never been there, not surprisingly given that until two days ago, Bryce and I hadn't been on speaking terms. Sean had keys, also not surprisingly. He figured it wouldn't be under surveillance, since the Nasts knew Bryce was in Miami, too sick to move. We could hole up for a bit and decide our next move.

From the outside, the building was exactly what I would have expected from Bryce. Very Nast. Ultramodern, with

BMWs and Mercedes filling the lot, and probably more MBAs in the halls than in the Harvard School of Business. Not one of those professionals, bustling to or from work, said a word to us.

Walking through the door to Bryce's place, though, was like walking into an entirely different building. It was painted in greens and rusts and oranges, oddly natural shades for a guy who snarked about the camping and hiking trips Sean took with Adam and me. The furniture was all chosen for comfort, big chairs and deep sofas. There were books, too, shelves stuffed with them. Along with stacks of music. Stacks covered in dust. Bryce had been a music student before our dad died. It was hard to remember that now.

Sean and I settled onto a couch in the living room. Clay and Elena had gone into Bryce's home office to call Jeremy, and then the twins. Lucas was on the phone to Paige. Adam was hanging back, pretending to check out the artwork on the walls in the hall, giving me a moment with Sean.

The kitchen—which I could see through the living room door—was the only place that seemed to have escaped Bryce's redecorating. It was all spotless white and gleaming black and glistening stainless steel, like something off the cooking shows Paige watched.

"Kitchen doesn't get a lot of use, I see," I said. "Seems all three of us got the take-out gene."

My voice startled Sean. He looked at the kitchen, as if replaying what I'd said. Then he shook his head.

"Bryce cooks. He's really good at it. He used to say he was going to be a chef one day. Dad took us over to France when Bryce was twelve so he could go to a cooking school there for our vacation. Granddad . . ." He paused. Cleared his throat. "Granddad gave him shit for it. Said Dad was filling Bryce's head with nonsense, but you know Dad. Anything we—" His voice cracked. "Anything we wanted. As long as we were happy."

I put my hand on his arm and leaned against him. He hesitated a moment, then hugged me, his face pressed against my hair, and I could feel him shaking.

"I'm sorry," I whispered. "I'm really, really sorry."

He took a deep breath and spoke to the top of my head. "I hated what Granddad did to you and I hated how he treated Bryce, but he was still . . ." Another deep breath. "I saw other sides of him. Better sides."

I sat up and met his eyes.

"I hope he went someplace . . ." He shook off the thought and cleared his throat. "It was good seeing Dad. Really good. I wish Bryce could have been there."

I nodded, and leaned against him again, as he seemed to struggle to be happy about that part, to find some good in this hellish day. He couldn't quite manage it. Seeing our father, only to lose him again, had hurt, like me with Mom.

Sean straightened suddenly. "Bryce." He got to his feet and started for the hall. Lucas came in, Adam behind him. Sean said, "I need to be the one who tells Bryce about Granddad."

Lucas nodded. "I thought you'd want to. I already told my father that, though I believe he'd presume the same. Bryce woke up about an hour ago, but they've put him back under."

"Put him under?" I said.

"Medically induced coma," Sean said. He drew in a deep, ragged breath. "He's not doing so well, Savannah. I need to get back to him."

"Me too. I mean, not that he wants to see me—"

"He does. But I should go now, even if only for a day." He needed to stake his leadership claim with the Cabal. But his brother came first. He always would.

"We'll go to Miami right away," Adam said. "Is the jet here?"

"It is," Lucas said. "You should go soon."

"You aren't coming back?" I said.

"Not yet. I need Adam to stay here, too."

"What? No." Adam stopped as he'd been about to sit beside me. "Sorry, Lucas, but whatever's going on, I need to sit this one out. I'm in rough shape."

"He is," I said. "Those bruises aren't all from today. The guards who arrested him beat the crap—"

Adam cleared his throat.

"Sorry. There was a fight. His ribs are cracked. He needs a break."

Adam nodded.

"Never thought I'd hear that," Sean said, managing a smile.

Adam looked abashed, muttering that he'd be fine in a day or two.

There was a moment of silence. Adam squirmed. I did, too. We both wanted to go back to Miami so we could have some time alone together. Under the circumstances, it was selfish, and we knew it. Finally, with an apologetic look my way, Adam said, "Lucas, if you really need me . . ."

"I do. I'm sorry. I don't need you to fight, just to get us into some difficult places."

Adam looked up. "If you need me to disintegrate doors when you've got werewolf strength and unlock spells, we're talking heavy fortifications."

"We are. Also multiple points of entry and multiple security systems." He turned to Sean. "When Bryce woke up, he told us where he thinks they're holding the Dahl boy."

Larsen Dahl was the clairvoyant toddler whom Bryce had helped the liberation movement kidnap. Bryce been trying to infiltrate the group by giving them something they wanted so he'd be able to gather information. He'd been planning to take Larsen back and then give the info to the Cabal. Giles had seen through the ploy, though, and Bryce's "reward" had been that shot they'd injected him with.

Getting the boy—and his parents—back was a priority. Equally important was the chance to take their captors hostage—they might be able to answer some questions about the movement. I offered to help, too, but Lucas said no, that I really had been through enough. They needed me back at headquarters to explain everything. And for another reason: they needed me there to keep me safe, because as far as a faction of the Nasts was concerned, I'd just murdered their CEO.

Thomas and Josef had hoped to somehow overthrow the Cortezes by putting me on trial with false evidence. How? As Sean said, it was likely just a step in a long plan. It didn't matter now, because Balaam had twisted their plot to his own advantage.

The murder of Thomas Nast would drive the Nast Cabal into chaos when it could least afford it. Since Balaam had pretended he'd done it to save me, I became the scapegoat. Make me—Lucas Cortez's ward—the scapegoat and you ensured there would be no alliance between Cabals to fight the liberation movement. Put Sean on the run with me, and you further divided the Nasts, rendering the biggest Cabal impotent in the face of this threat.

Such an elegant play. A move truly worthy of a lord demon. I'd be whole lot more impressed if I wasn't at the heart of it.

We left shortly after that. The Cortezes had moved the jet to another regional airport, not yet being monitored by the Nasts.

Sean and I spent the flight talking. I was worried about him. Really worried. He'd just lost his grandfather. He might be losing his Cabal. He'd severed any relationship with Josef, and I knew that stung, because while they hadn't been on good terms lately, they had been close once. Josef's son had died shortly after our dad, and they had bonded over their shared loss.

Now Bryce was sick. Very sick. If he died, what would

Sean have left? Me? He loved me, I knew, but I was still the outsider who didn't really understand where he came from, what it meant to be a Nast.

So I was worried. And I had no idea what to do about it except sit there and listen, and offer words of hope about Bryce and the future. So that's what I did.

Paige

Troy pulled the SUV into a tiny lot near the private airstrip.

"We'll sit out here and wait for the jet," he said.

Paige nodded. If she got out, the guards in the SUV behind them would need to get out in order to watch over her. Then she'd need to make conversation with them. Maybe not "need," but "should." Any other time, that wouldn't be a problem. But she'd passed the point days ago of being able to make small talk. She just wanted to curl up in the backseat and disappear for a few minutes.

When her cell rang, she was about to ignore it. Then she realized it was Lucas.

"Is this a bad time?" he asked when she answered.

"Never."

She bit back her next words. The usual words she'd say when they weren't together. *I miss you*. Now it would only remind him that this wasn't one of their usual little separations, off chasing cases, hating being apart, but still loving what they were doing. There was nothing to love here, and with each passing day that weighed on him a little more.

"Is Savannah's flight on schedule?" he asked.

"It is. She'll be here any minute."

"Good." A long pause. Then his voice dropped. "I miss you."

Paige gripped the phone tighter. "Miss you, too."

More silence.

She cleared her throat. "So . . . how's the weather?"

A bubble of a laugh burst across the line. "The weather in L.A. is perfect, as always. And there?"

"Crappy, as always."

A chuckle now. "I had a call from Mitchell DeLong. Do you remember Mitchell?"

"Vaguely. Necromancer. Lives in Seattle."

"Correct. Except that last night, apparently, he was near Portland, heading to a cemetery to perform a summoning for a client. It was late, and he was tired and driving errati-cally. An officer pulled him over and discovered that Mitchell had forgotten to properly stow his summoning materials, including three desiccated human fingers."

"Never good."

"Particularly when dealing with a small-town police force that doesn't appear to understand that desiccated flesh indicates extreme age. They're quite certain the rest of Mitch's victim is nearby and they're holding him until they find it. He'd like me to come in and clear the matter up."

"Uh-huh. Did you tell him we're a little busy?"

"I did. He hadn't heard anything about the situation. No matter, though. He understands that we are other-wise engaged and therefore has offered to pay double our usual fee."

Paige smiled. "Has he?"

"In light of that, I suggest we consider the offer. I'll tell my father that while we realize that this end-of-the-world business is important, we do have a detective agency to run, bills to pay, a reputation to uphold, and so on. We'll simply pop up to Portland for a couple of days."

"Me too?"

"Of course."

"Thanks." She smiled and settled into her seat, curling her legs up under her.

A moment of silence, then he said, "We are going back, Paige. I know that's the elephant in the room, the topic we are both trying so hard to avoid—whether all this will mean we can't go back to Portland, to the agency, to our regular life. Whether my responsibilities at the Cabal will at last prove too great to ignore. They won't, I promise. My father is healthy. The Cabal is healthy. This tragedy at the Nasts will ripple through all the Cabals, and will require some additional work from me, but once this is over, we're going home."

"Okay . . ." She said the word carefully, uncertainly. *Go home. It sounded so simple. So obvious. Why wouldn't we go home? We had a house, an agency, a life there.*

But they had a life here, too. Even a home, having finally accepted a condo from Benicio a few years ago. They had work here, too. She used to think that only applied to Lucas. But, although she had no job title, no official responsibilities, her inbox and voice mail were always filled with messages from Cabal employees asking this or that, needing this or that. If they couldn't get to Lucas, they came to her.

Did that make her his assistant? He'd say no. Emphatically. She was his partner. And yet to the rest of the Cabal, "assistant" was closer to the truth.

God, how she would have bristled at that ten years ago. Playing helpmate to her husband? Never. She was Paige Winterbourne, former Coven leader, leader of the interracial council. But life changes. Perspective changes. She'd come to understand that Benicio wasn't going to award her a VP title anytime soon, and if he did, it would only be to please Lucas. She'd come to understand, too, that Lucas needed her help. He needed her support—her wholehearted support, untainted by envy or ego. He needed her to be there, at his side, the one person he could count on to keep him on the right path, call him on the bullshit and have his best interests at heart—always. As long as he thought of her as his partner and treated her as such, that was all the validation she needed.

"I mean it, Paige," Lucas said after a moment. "I know my father will require our assistance once this is over. There is work to be done. But we're going home first. He'll get a few days of our time to deal with the aftermath. Then we go home. We rest. We take care of business at the agency. And when that's done, we come back to do more . . . until we can leave again." A pause. "Sound like a plan?"

She smiled. "It does. A good plan."

"Then that's what we'll—Hold on." He covered the receiver and murmured a few words, then came back. "That was Adam. I need to go. Tell Savannah he says hello."

"I will. I think that's her ride coming down right now."

"Good. I'll call when I can."

Paige stood at the edge of the tarmac, as close as they'd let her get to Savannah's plane. Closer than any regular person would ever get, even to a private flight. There are, admittedly, advantages to being Benicio Cortez's daughter-in-law.

She found herself straining for that first glimpse of Savannah. She'd spoken to her on the phone earlier, but only for a moment or two, both of them surrounded by others, unable to really talk.

Was Savannah upset that Paige hadn't gone to L.A. with Lucas? She couldn't—he'd needed her to stay in Miami. Paige was sure Lucas told Savannah that. Even if it slipped his mind, Savannah would have understood there was no place for Paige at that hearing. But logically understanding wasn't the same as emotionally understanding. Savannah had been arrested for treason by her father's own Cabal. She'd watched her mother disappear from her life again. She'd seen one grandfather killed by the other. And Paige hadn't been there for her.

But she was here now, eagerly waiting for Savannah to step off that jet. Was it enough? She hoped so. God, she hoped so.

When Savannah first appeared, there was a moment where Paige thought Eve had somehow stayed in their world after all. It was just that fleeting first glimpse, a tall woman with long, dark hair, her arm hooked through Sean Nast's. Of course, it was Savannah. But somehow—chalk it up to exhaustion—Paige expected to see a girl get off that jet. The girl she remembered, the one who always needed her, as hard as she tried to pretend otherwise.

Paige didn't think of Savannah as her daughter. She'd never tried to take Eve's place. Being only a decade older than Savannah had always made that easy. Savannah was like a little sister and, eventually, as probably happens with most little sisters, she became a friend. When Paige watched her step from that jet, she realized the "little" part was gone now. Savannah didn't need Paige to hold her hand and tend to her bumps and bruises. She could look after herself. Paige was happy about that. Proud of that. But maybe, just maybe, a little sad, too.

Paige turned her attention to Sean. He was coming down those steps, looking neither left nor right. He was the one who needed them both now. She watched him flinch when an engine roared off to the left, then shake his head as if embarrassed by how jumpy he was.

She hurried over to them. Her first smile was for Savannah, but she barely seemed to notice it, her attention focused on her brother. Paige gave him a hug and murmured that the car was near, that someone else would get his luggage. Savannah had let go of his arm and stepped back, as if relinquishing him to Paige's care. Savannah met her gaze then, passing her a small, tired smile and mouthing "thanks" as Paige bustled Sean to the car.

Paige got him seated inside, with a glass of ice water and a shot of brandy. He picked up the brandy, stared into the amber for a moment and downed it in one gulp. Then his lips twisted in a ghost of a smile.

"That's better."

Paige took out the bottle.

He held up his hand. "No, I shouldn't . . ." A pause. "Maybe one more. Thank you."

As she poured, she realized Savannah wasn't getting into the SUV. She turned to see her still standing there.

Paige gave the brandy to Sean, then stepped back and closed the door. She barely had time to put her arms out before Savannah fell into them.

"I'm sorry for what happened," Paige whispered. "And I'm sorry I wasn't there."

Savannah shook her head. "I'm glad you weren't there. You're lousy in a fight."

Paige sputtered a laugh. "Thank you." She pulled back to look up at her. "How are you doing?"

"Fine." She tried for a smile, then swallowed and shook her head. "Not fine."

She collapsed against Paige again and she hugged her as tightly as she could. Yes, the little girl was all grown up, but she still needed her. At least, for a while longer.

CHAPTER 27

I would gladly have stayed asleep for a few hours. But it felt as if I'd barely drifted off on the ride from the airport before Paige was shaking my shoulder.

We were already parked and she and I were the only ones left in the vehicle. Outside, Benicio was telling Sean how sorry he was to hear of Thomas's passing.

"We didn't often see eye-to-eye," Benicio was saying, his voice low. "But I've known him since I was a boy. He'll leave a hole in our world that won't soon be filled."

I got my bearings and climbed out after Paige. Benicio left Sean and came over to me.

"We'll get this sorted, Savannah," he said. "You'll be vindicated and avenged. You have my word on that."

Vindicated and avenged. A couple of weeks ago, I'd have been burning for just that. Now the words seemed empty. I didn't want justice with a flaming sword. I wanted peace and resolution. Fix this crisis. Fix our world.

We headed for the doors, Benicio's longtime bodyguards, Troy and Griffin, moving in to flank us, Paige and Sean staying behind with the other guards.

"Troy will be with you for a few days, Savannah," Benicio said. "Until we get this matter sorted."

I glanced over at Troy, who mouthed, "Lucky you."

"As much as I'm sure Troy would love to baby-sit me," I

said, rolling my eyes at him behind Benicio's back, "he should stay with you. You could be targeted—"

"I'll have Griffin and two of my backup men. I *could* be a target—you *will* be a target."

"You're twenty-one now, aren't you?" Troy said.

"I am."

"Good, then I can take you drinking."

"Only if you can do it in the executive lounge," Benicio said. "You're going to be on lockdown for a while."

Troy leaned behind Benicio to motion that we'd discuss it later and I had to laugh. Benicio sighed and shook his head. Griffin glanced back for Paige and Sean, but they hadn't caught up yet, so we got on the elevator and he punched the button.

"Paige tells me your spells are coming back," Benicio said as the doors closed.

"On and off. I'm dealing with it."

I'm dealing with it. Shocking how casual that sounded. Even more shocking how casual it felt. My powers blew hot and cold, completely beyond my control, but I *was* learning to work with it. Maybe learning to live with it.

"I'd like you to reconsider that ritual Adam found," Benicio said.

I almost asked "What ritual?" Then I remembered: the one Adam had dug up to restore my powers.

"He says there's a time limit," Benicio said. "I don't want you getting so caught up in this crisis that you lose sight of that."

"I'll put it in my calendar."

"I'm serious, Savannah. Adam said you're holding off because you think your powers were taken to help you control them. But given what just happened, you need to consider the possibility that's a lie. A trick. The demons have spies. They could have known Adam was on the verge of finding that ritual and made sure you wouldn't use it."

I looked over at him. "I *am* taking it seriously. I just . . . I'm fine for now. We'll watch this space, okay?"

He nodded. Then he reached into his pocket. "It seems Adam is quite concerned that you'll suffer separation anxiety, being away from your cell phone for too long. I've replaced it—again."

"Thanks. I'll try not to fall into a sewer or get kidnapped again."

I opened the phone. There was already a text from Adam, checking in. I was about to text back when the elevator reached its destination. We stepped out onto the floor that housed the medical ward.

Sean arrived a moment later and caught up with us. "Is Bryce still unconscious?" he asked Benicio.

"Yes, but I can have them wake him if you'd like."

Sean shook his head. "I'll just sit with him."

When we got to the room, though, the doctors were busy with Bryce and asked us to wait outside. I ducked into a nearby office to call Adam.

"Hey," I said when he answered. "Did I catch you in the middle of a top-secret break-and-enter?"

"I wish. Everything's moving slowly here. Very slowly. I'm getting plenty of rest. So what's up there?"

"I have a six-foot-four shadow. I'm just glad it's Troy. I like Griffin well enough but . . . you know."

"Not exactly a sociable guy." He hesitated. "But I'm glad you have someone. It makes me feel better."

I could tell it didn't really make him feel better. If Lucas was Benicio's right-hand man, Troy was his left. To give me his most trusted guard when trouble was brewing? It said I was in more danger than I thought.

"I just hope he's not going to follow me too closely after you get back," I said.

"We'll make sure he doesn't."

"About that. Us. The others . . . I don't know how you

want to . . . handle it. Should I talk to Paige? You talk to Lucas? Or are we going to see how things go first . . . ?"

"I should be the one to tell them. If they have a problem with it, they'll want to talk to me. Their biggest concern will be you—that you'll get hurt . . ." He trailed off and my heart started to thump.

"Adam?"

"Still here. Just thinking that maybe we should hold off telling them."

It thumped harder.

"Just for now," he continued. "Until we've had a chance to talk."

Really thumping now. "Okay."

Sean popped his head in the door. "Anytime you're ready."

I said good-bye to Adam, and tried to push the call from my mind as I followed Sean into the hospital room.

When I saw Bryce, my gaze shot to Sean to gauge his reaction. All I saw was relief, meaning Bryce must not look any worse than he did last night.

Dead. He looked dead.

I've only been to a few funerals in my life. I avoided them growing up. It brought back too much; not just my mother's death, but the thought that she'd never had one, that she didn't even have a grave, that I had no idea where her body was.

As I got older, I went when my presence meant something to someone else. Like when Adam's grandmother passed on. Or when Paige lost a childhood friend to cancer. Or when a cousin of Lucas's died in a car crash.

This was like seeing my brother laid out in a casket. His tanned skin was sallow. His blond hair was combed wrong. His hands were folded on his stomach. His lips were unnaturally red, as if a mortician had applied lipstick.

Was he breathing? It didn't look like it.

The first thing Sean did was fix Bryce's hair.

"Hey, Bryce," he said. "I'm back. I brought Savannah with me."

I moved up alongside him and said hello. Sean talked a bit more to him, somehow managing to relate the last twenty-four hours with no mention of dungeons and sham trials, the death of our grandfather and the utter devastation that had befallen the Nast Cabal.

When Sean stopped talking, we sat with Bryce for a minute. Then the doctor poked his head through the door, and instead of waving him in, Sean motioned him out of the room.

"But I'd like to hear—" I began.

"Out there," he said.

We followed the doctor to the office where I'd called Adam. Sean explained to me that he'd insisted no one discuss Bryce's condition in the room. Comatose patients sometimes could hear what was going on around them, and he wasn't taking that chance.

"His condition is stable," the doctor said. "At this point—"

"That's all we can hope for," Sean cut in, uncharacteristically impatient. "Yes, yes. I know. Until you know what it is, you can't treat it."

"We are making inroads," the doctor said. "We've finally been able to analyze his DNA and pinpoint the modifications that were made."

"Modifications?" I said. "To his DNA?"

Sean's nod to me was curt, just short of "shut up and listen." Then he caught himself and squeezed my arm. "Sorry. This is all new to you, isn't it? Bryce's genetic code has been altered. It sounds scary—it *is* scary—but we presume the changes are supernatural in nature. That's what happens, for example, when a vampire is reborn or a werewolf is bitten. A makeover at the genetic level."

"That's what it is, isn't it?" I said. "Vampire."

"In part," the doctor said. "It's a hybrid, which is why it was so difficult to analyze. There's also werewolf."

"Werewolf *and* vampire?" Sean said.

"Yes, and a third strand, too. We're . . . we're still running tests on that. We have preliminary results, but I'm reluctant to say anything yet. Even if we are correct, we've seen no signs that it's had any negative effect, despite what one might think—"

"Zombie," I said. "That's the third type, isn't it?"

He hesitated, then nodded.

It wasn't a lucky guess. We had known from Cassandra's WWII run-in with Giles that his immortality experiments combined vampires with zombies.

The doctor hurried on, "But we've seen no signs of deterioration. The Boyd Cabal has been experimenting with zombie DNA for years, in hopes that it might unlock the secrets to immortality, and they've made some advances. We think some of their researchers were involved in this. It seems—"

He stopped and cleared his throat. "Mr. Cortez will want to explain all that. It isn't my place. But I can assure you that your brother's condition is stable. We are, however, going to keep him in the coma, while the DNA transformation continues. That seems . . . best."

"What happened?" I asked.

The doctor looked over sharply. "I didn't say—"

"Something happened when he woke up, didn't it?"

The doctor looked at Sean with anxious eyes.

"Please answer my sister," Sean said.

He hesitated, then said, "We are unfamiliar with the transformation process of a bitten werewolf. Fortunately we have someone here who has taken one through the Change successfully."

"Jeremy Danvers," I said. "With Elena."

He hesitated. "Yes, sorry, I forgot you are acquainted with them. We are also fortunate that Mr. Danvers was in the building when your brother woke and with his assistance—"

"What happened?" Sean said.

"He began, uh . . ."

"Changing," I said. "Into a wolf."

"Not exact—" He cleared his throat again. "Mr. Danvers has only witnessed one initial transformation of a bitten werewolf, and that's hardly a sample large enough for generalization—"

"It wasn't a normal Change," I said. "Something's wrong."

"I—I believe you should speak to Mr. Cortez about this. And to Mr. Danvers, who should still be available—"

"He is," said a voice from the doorway. Jeremy stepped in. "I heard you were back. I need to speak to you both about Bryce."

The doctor got out of there as fast as he could. Jeremy told us that Bryce had woken and started what looked like a partial Change. That was normal. As were the screams of agony that went with it, though Jeremy downplayed those for Sean's sake. Bryce had been fevered to the point of delirium, also normal from Jeremy's experience with Elena. What concerned him was the rate at which the Change came on.

"It's happening faster than I saw with Elena," he said. "It appears to be a mutated form of werewolf, as well. More similar to the Shifters the Pack encountered in Alaska."

The Shifters were a small group of what appeared to be an evolutionary precursor to modern werewolves. Jeremy and the others Changed into wolves—real wolves. Those guys had been closer to the beastlike Hollywood wolfman.

"We were concerned about the damage the Change might be doing to his body," Jeremy said. "I had them administer a sedative. It was then that he was able to tell us what he knew about Larsen Dahl."

"So the moment he recovers from nearly changing into a wolfman, Benicio grills him about that?" I said.

Jeremy gave me a look. "I would not have allowed that, Savannah. Bryce offered the information. He didn't seem to realize he'd started to Change."

"Is that normal?"

"No. But none of this is normal."

My cell phone bleeped that I had a message. Jeremy's buzzed at the same time.

I checked mine, then looked at him. "Benicio?"

Jeremy nodded.

"He wants me to come up as soon as we're done here, so I can debrief them and be debriefed." I glanced at Sean. "He'd like you to join us, if you can."

"I'll come."

CHAPTER 28

Paige met us heading into the meeting and gave me a rundown on everyone's whereabouts. Lucas was still in L.A., of course, with Adam, Clay and Elena. He'd be joining us by phone when he could. Aaron and Cassandra were dealing with trouble in Washington, where some moron had tried to expose a vampire. Jaime was here, but waiting for my parents to contact her, and wouldn't be joining us. Hope was present, with Karl, who was worried sick, probably because Hope was still having disturbing visions while heavily pregnant. There were also assorted Cabal executives on hand. When I walked in, though, I noticed one conspicuous absence.

"Where's Carlos?" I whispered.

"Putting out fires in New York," Paige whispered back as we found seats.

"Really?"

"Benicio suggested it. Carlos's men agreed. They're convinced this is his opportunity to show his leadership skills."

"What leadership skills?"

"Exactly. But they went along to prop up their straw man, and Benicio says together they're competent enough." She pulled out her chair. "So Carlos is out of everyone's hair and may actually be doing something useful."

That was one potential problem resolved. At the meeting, though, I realized it was only a drop in the bucket.

I thought I knew how bad things were getting. But I'd only seen what was right in front of me, a narrow slice of the chaos rolling over the supernatural world.

Benicio played us footage of some of the attacks made by the anti-reveal movement. A hell-beast had manifested in the New York subway system. Blurry video showed a subway train arriving at a crowded station. The beast appears. Only a few see it, but panic whips through the crowd. Someone says it's a bomb. People are trampled. People fall onto the tracks in front of the oncoming train. *Too* many people fall onto the tracks, meaning magic is at play.

Hundreds of people claimed to have been there. Most, it turned out, hadn't been within five miles. Reputable news sources were already writing it off as mass hysteria, at most some large animal loose in the subway. The exposure threat? Minimal . . . so far.

Then, in Nashville, during a rooftop wedding reception, two uninvited guests appear: a werewolf and a vampire. Not just any werewolf and vampire, but ones that— judging by the blurry cell phone images on the Internet— had been locked up and starved long enough to tip them into madness.

Neither the Pack nor the council recognized the wretches. From the babble caught on those tapes, they seemed to be speaking foreign languages. Caught outside the U.S. or lured in, held captive, starved, driven mad . . . and released on a rooftop filled with half-drunk wedding revelers with the exit doors barred behind them, a cell phone blocker cutting off all hopes of aid.

Bodies began hitting the pavement, party-goers so desperate to escape that they leaped to their deaths. By the time authorities reached the roof, all the guests and event staff were dead. The werewolf and vampire were gone, too, leaving only cell phone videos of two disheveled and crazed "humans" ripping people apart.

"The group responsible hasn't launched an attack in twelve hours now," Benicio said after the cases had been presented. "We've captured three key members and they are undergoing interrogation. Another half dozen members have been detained. Still more have been stopped."

He meant killed. No one needed the clarification.

"As most of you are aware, the Boyd Cabal has been working with us on this. They disabled one branch before it could act. The St. Clouds handled another, but after the death of Thomas Nast, they have cut off contact with us. We can trust, however, that they will continue their efforts."

Sean added. "As for the Nasts, I've been in touch with a few senior executives. We'll be joining your efforts, together with a contingent of staff loyal to me."

Benicio nodded. "I believe we'll see more help from your organization as the shock passes and they realize this is not, sadly, the time for grief. Nor is it the time for a battle over succession."

"I hope so," Paige murmured beside me.

She didn't sound too optimistic, and based on what I'd seen, I wasn't either. We could get men apparently loyal to Sean onside, but they couldn't be given any access to Cortez information or positions of authority, in case they were spies for Josef. By the time the average Nast Cabal employee decided to throw in his lot with Sean, it might be too late to help.

"Speaking of these attacks, I have some good news," Benicio said. "We managed to avert situations in Boston and Denver, based on Hope's visions."

"There," Karl said. He was sitting on a sofa at the back of the room, with Hope curled up beside him. He turned to her. "You were helpful. You've been thanked. Now you can go back to bed—"

"I need to—"

"You need to rest."

Hope had looked run down the last time I'd seen her. Now she looked as if she'd *been* run down, hit by the same steamroller that had squashed me. Her dark curls were lank. Her face was thinner, bones even more defined. The bags under her eyes had graduated to full-size luggage. But her eyes were bright, alert, and determined. Very determined.

"I need to listen to everything, so I can put my visions in context," she said. "And I am resting." She curled up under Karl's arm, resting her head on his chest, her hand on his leg. "Resting and safe, as long as you're here."

Karl rolled his eyes at such an obvious play. But it worked, too. He shifted to make her more comfortable and settled in with a sigh.

Sean and I were up next. Everyone had questions, and there seemed to be some dispute over whether the demon who'd killed Thomas was actually Balaam. No one liked to believe the lord demons were taking such an active role in this.

"This is the second time Balaam has come to me," I said. "Everything we've learned so far tells us that this fight goes right to the top of the demon hierarchy. They all think they have something to gain or lose if supernaturals are exposed. Balaam is for it. Asmondai is against it. Those seem to be the two factions. I don't know about the other lords, but the one they all want on their side is the one who's gone AWOL."

"Lucifer," Hope murmured. "He's MIA and I'm getting all his voice mail."

"Or he's the one sending you the visions," I said. "Trying to help without taking sides."

"Then I wish he'd damned well man up and take one," Karl growled.

I turned to the Cabal execs. "According to my mother, it's not just the demons who are choosing sides. We're getting celestial interference, too. Whether you believe any of that or not doesn't really matter. Anything you thought you knew about our world? Forget it. Someone has tossed out the rule book. Ghosts can cross the divide. Hellhounds can manifest. Demi-demons can possess living children. Lord demons are taking a hand in Cabal politics."

I looked at Benicio. "What about the original bad guys? What have Giles and his liberation movement been doing since I left them?"

"We're trying to find out," Benicio said.

He explained that he'd dedicated his best resources to finding Giles and his crew, who'd vacated their New Orleans meeting house before the Cabal could invade.

I said I wanted to go back in the field. I knew Giles and his people. They all knew me. Presumably I was still useful to them. So at the very least, I'd make good bait to draw them out.

Benicio said no. Lucas said no. Paige said no. Even Sean—who's never played the overbearing big brother—said he'd really rather I didn't. They all insisted there was plenty I could do at headquarters. Only, there wasn't. I wasn't a researcher or a strategist. I belonged on the front lines. Here, I was no more useful than any admin assistant.

Yet as long as I was a spell-free target, I was ordered to stay under twenty-four-hour guard. I couldn't even go back to Paige and Lucas's condo for the night. Several offices had been cleared and transformed into bedrooms. Benicio was staying on site. While Lucas was away, so was Paige. Only the werewolves got to take their significant others and leave, and even they had to agree to stay in secured condos and accept armored cars, along with a small army of guards.

So I got a futon in an empty office. Troy got a cot outside the door.

Adam called before I went to sleep. Larsen Dahl had been at the location Bryce had given us, but he'd been moved. They were trying to find out where. Or Lucas was. Adam had been sidelined to rest, like me. If only we were "resting" in the same place, it would have been a lot more tolerable.

I woke up early, feeling as if I had to be somewhere. Then I remembered I wasn't going anywhere, and lay back on the futon, staring up at the ceiling.

Eventually, I realized sulking wasn't going to do anyone any good. I might as well get up and figure out how I could make myself useful.

There was a suitcase of my stuff in the corner. I dressed and eased open the door. Troy was sitting on the edge of his cot in a T-shirt and boxers, running his hand through his sleep-rumpled hair.

"You don't have to get up," I whispered.

"Yep, I kinda do." He yawned and shook himself. "Compared to Benicio's schedule, this was actually sleeping in. Just give me a sec to dress."

I withdrew into the office to wait. I felt bad making Troy get up, but he *was* used to it. Normally, bodyguards would alternate night shifts, but Griffin was a single parent—his youngest not yet in college—so Troy spent most nights in a bedroom outside Benicio's.

Troy didn't have kids. Or a wife. I'm sure he had company when he wanted it—he was decent-looking for a guy in his forties and a big, brawny bodyguard is going to have his appeal at any age.

I'm not the type who thinks people can only be happy with a family, but . . . Well, maybe I am. A family of some sort. I guess Troy has that with Benicio and the Cabal. He nearly died a few years ago, protecting his boss from Jaz and his brother Sonny. Afterward, Benicio had given him a huge bonus and beefed up his pension, which was his way of saying "If you want to retire, I understand." Troy hadn't, of course. I supposed he wouldn't, not as long as Benicio was alive.

Troy tapped the door when he was ready. He was not only dressed, but looked a helluva lot more awake than I felt.

"Coffee," I said.

He grinned. "That I can do."

"I don't suppose there's any chance of going out to get it."

The smile faltered.

I lifted my hand. "Sorry. Not your rules, I know. As long as I can get caffeine, followed by a shower, I'm good."

CHAPTER 29

C affeinated and clean, I was walking through the executive suites, Troy trailing me, when Karl swung out of a doorway behind us.

"You," he said. "Come here."

"I have places to be, Karl," I said. "And you'd get a better response if you actually bothered to learn my name."

"Savannah," he said. "Please. It's Hope."

That *please* got my ass moving. Karl was already back in the room by the time I got to the door. Hope lay on a sofa. She just lay there. Eyes open. Unblinking.

"I'll get help," Troy said behind me.

"Please get Paige," I said. "And Jeremy."

"I've already called him," Karl said. "He's on his way. She just collapsed."

I leaned over her and checked her pulse.

"She's alive," he growled, as if he wouldn't be just standing around if the situation was that dire. "Breathing fine. Pulse rate fine. But she's locked in a vision and I can't snap her out of it."

"A vision? How—?"

"Her eyes," he said.

They were jittering back and forth, as if she was watching something moving very fast.

"It's like REM sleep," he said. "Only her eyes are usually closed and I can always bring her out of it."

Then Hope convulsed. Her hands went to her swollen stomach as her back arched, teeth grinding so hard I could hear them. Karl shoved me out of the way and caught her by the shoulders. He lifted her and sat on the couch, stretching her across him, massaging her back with one hand and stroking her cheek with the other, murmuring under his breath.

Just as she seemed to relax, her stomach moved and I jumped.

"It's just the baby kicking," Karl said. He laid a palm on her abdomen as the baby continued to kick hard enough to make his hand move.

"Feisty little guy," I said.

"Girl."

I looked at him.

"It's a girl. Hope wanted to know." He paused. "No, she knew *I* wanted to know."

"Because a boy means a werewolf. You were hoping . . ."

"For a girl," he said firmly. "I would have been fine with a son, but I would prefer a daughter."

"Oh."

He kept rubbing her belly. Any trace of the sophisticated, debonair guy I knew as Karl Marsten was long gone. His clothing looked like he'd slept in it. His cheeks were stubbled. There were lines around his mouth and eyes. From the looks of his hair, I doubted he'd showered since his last shave.

"I'm sorry she's going through this," I said. "But I'm sure the baby will be fine."

"It's not the baby I'm worried about." He rubbed a hand down his face. I could hear the scratch of his stubble. "Of course I don't want anything to happen to our daughter, but . . . It's not her I'm most worried about."

"I know."

"I just wish . . ." His jaw worked. "I wish Hope didn't have to go through this. Any of it. The chaos hunger and the visions keep getting worse and she tries so hard—so damned hard—to cope with it, and nothing seems to make it better, and . . ." He looked at me. "You said you met Balaam. Well, if I ever meet Lucifer . . ."

The old Karl flared for a moment in his eyes. Then he looked away, because there was no way to finish that threat. What could he do to Lucifer? Give him a piece of his mind?

The children of Lucifer were rare. Blessedly rare, most would say, though not in front of Hope. Just like no one would remind her that, at thirty, she was the oldest known Expisco. The oldest survivor, Adam said once, before catching himself. But it was the right word. The curse of Lucifer was something his children had to survive. Most didn't. Not for long. Certainly not long enough to bear their own children.

Karl's gaze stayed on Hope, lips tight, almost angry, as if annoyed with himself for confiding in me. But when he looked up, the anger was gone, his expression neutral. "You can go if you like. They should be here soon."

"I'll stay."

A nod. "Thank you."

Silence for a minute, and I wasn't sure if I should say anything to distract him or if I should just keep my mouth shut. I was about to risk speaking when Hope shot upright. Karl grabbed her by the shoulders. I leaped forward, but he stopped me with a curt "No," then a more conciliatory "She's fine. It's just more of the same."

She sat there, eyes open, pupils jittering, as Karl rubbed her back, telling her it was okay, she was fine, wake up, she should just wake up.

She said something. I didn't catch it and leaned forward, but stopped at Karl's glare.

She spat a rapid-fire line of . . . something.

"Is that . . . Hindi?" I asked.

"She doesn't know Hindi. Not more than a few words."

Karl knows more languages than Jeremy, which is a feat since Jeremy used to work as a translator. Karl's knowledge is conversational, though, picked up on his travels.

"I don't recognize—" he began.

She spoke again, the words coming out so fast they could have been English for all I knew, until—

"Latin!" I said. "And . . . Greek, I think. I don't know them, really, just in spells, but there were a couple of words . . . Damn it, we should—" I stopped and tugged my new cell phone from my pocket. "I can record it."

Hope started again, her voice rising, the words coming ever faster, nearly shouted, like a revival speaker on speed. I fumbled with the damned phone and finally got it recording. Her eyes were starting to water, her voice going hoarse. She heaved for breath, talking too fast to catch it.

"Hope! Wake up!" Karl shook her as hard as he dared, his own voice spiked with panic. "Please, you need to—" He turned on me. "Go get—"

I was already going, my phone on the floor. I threw the door open. A few helpful staff members were clustered around it.

"Move!" I said.

They started to, then were nearly bowled over by Jeremy, who was coming at a run, Troy behind him.

"She's—" I began.

"I hear her," he said, his tone grim.

He ran to Hope's side. She was still shouting, red-faced, coughing now as she struggled to breathe.

"Get the doctor," Jeremy said to me. "She needs to be sedated."

"If it's a message, presumably she'll stop once it's imparted," Benicio said as he stepped in. "We should let—"

"Get the damned doctor," Jeremy said in a rare snarl.

Troy and I were already running for him—and found him stepping off the elevator. He had the sedative in his bag. By the time we got back to the room, Hope was hyper-ventilating and her skin was turning blue, and Benicio had stopped arguing that we should let the message play out.

It kept coming even after the needle went in. Her voice dropped as the sedative took effect, then slowed to a mumble, then finally stopped, and she drifted off into silent sleep.

I left as soon as Hope was okay. The room was crowded enough—Paige had arrived, and was helping Jeremy and Karl cool Hope with damp cloths. I was just in the way. So I gave Benicio my phone and told him that I'd managed to record Hope's outburst. He said he'd get a linguist to analyze the recording.

CHAPTER 30

The job of a bodyguard, apparently, is to look after his charge's body in every way. Well, most ways. Keeping me fed was a priority, it seemed. After the harrowing experience with Hope, Troy decided I needed a proper breakfast. So as we walked, he gave me options. I picked something. Couldn't remember what it was a minute after agreeing. He must have stopped to flag down someone to go get it and I must have kept walking. The next thing I knew, I didn't have a hulking bodyguard at my side.

Hands caught me around the waist. My fists flew up.

Adam caught them. "Please don't hit me. I've barely recovered from the last beating. Though I am glad to see you leading with your fists instead of your spells."

"If you don't want to get hit, don't sneak up behind me," I said as he bustled me into an empty office. "And you'd better be careful. Troy is going to come looking for me at any second."

"No, he won't." Adam kicked the door shut. "I just texted him and asked for a minute alone."

He caught me up in a kiss. I barely had time to start enjoying it before I remembered that he'd said we needed to talk and little alarm bells started going off. The moment I started worrying, I stopped reciprocating. He pulled back.

"Savannah?"

As I wriggled from his grasp, he looked alarmed. "What's

wrong? Did you talk to Paige? Did she say something?" He exhaled. "I know she's not going to be happy about this. The age gap is—"

"I didn't tell Paige. But when we talked about telling them . . ." I rolled my shoulders. Eased onto the desktop and tried to get comfortable. "Damn it. I'm no good at this. I'd rather just stick to the kissing part."

A chuckle. "We could do that."

"I wish," I muttered. "Okay, I'm going to sound like a total nervous girlfriend here but . . . you said we needed to talk. It sounded ominous."

"It did?"

"Well, no, I guess not, but . . ." I looked at him. "I've been worrying."

"Shit." He moved in between my knees as I perched on the desk. He put his hands on my hips and met my eyes. "It wasn't supposed to worry you. It's just . . . something we need to discuss."

"Okay, so let's discuss."

He glanced at the closed door.

"Yes, we're wasting valuable private time," I said. I hesitated. How honest was I ready to be? There was part of me that wanted to play it cool. Casual. But it wasn't casual.

So I continued. "Truth is, normally I wouldn't have thought anything about it. Guy wants to talk? Sure. Whatever. But . . . I'm a little anxious here. A lot anxious."

"All right then. But I'll warn you this is the kind of conversation I've never initiated. And when a girl does? My cell miraculously starts vibrating, with an emergency call from the agency."

I smiled. "I've pulled that a few times myself."

"Which is why we get along so well. But this isn't . . . It's not the usual thing. Meet a girl. *Hey you wanna grab a drink sometime?* Hook up, break up, delete her number. Fun while it lasted. You're . . ." He exhaled again. Shifted his weight. "I've known you forever. We work together. We hang out together. We share friends. We *are* friends. You know me better than anyone."

"So you don't want to start something and risk that."

He gave me a look. "Obviously I'm trying to start something. We've already started something. The big question is: What? Yeah, I know, you say you've been wanting this for a long time but . . . this might not be what you expected."

"Okay."

He hesitated, as if that wasn't the answer he expected. Or wanted.

I said, "I think, if I'm reading this right, you're not sure about rushing to tell Lucas and Paige because you're thinking maybe, after a few days, I'm going to say 'Huh, not really what I hoped for' and break it off. I can't imagine I would. But I'm thinking the same thing—about you. Maybe you're going to decide this isn't what you want. We already have something good, right?"

"We do."

"And we risk mucking it up entirely if we try to make it something better. There's no satisfaction guaranteed or your old relationship refunded. But if you're asking if I'm serious enough to give this a shot, I am. Are you?"

He held my eyes for a long second before saying, "Absolutely."

"Good. Now can we get back to the kissing part?"

As good as our earlier kisses had been, he'd been holding something back. Now I got the full deal, the deep, god-I-can't-breathe, god-I-don't-care version. Arms around him. Legs around him, too, heat scorching my thighs and everywhere in between and thinking it was just me until heat shot down my throat, like a sudden lick of flame, and I gasped.

"Shit," he muttered. "That's new. Sorry. Give me a sec."

He closed his eyes, concentrating on squelching the fire, but I pulled him back into the kiss whispering, "Don't."

Licks of fire shot through me, from the heat of his hands, the heat of his skin—delicious pulses of flame. It wasn't long before I was tugging his shirt up, hands seeking bare skin, scorching hot skin and—

A throat cleared behind us. I broke away and caught my breath.

"Er, Troy," I said. "Sorry. Could we . . . get a few more minutes?"

Adam glanced over his shoulder. "Please. I promise, her body is well guarded."

"So I see," Troy said drily.

Which wasn't Troy's style at all. My gaze shot to his eyes. Bright green eyes.

"Bal—" I started as I disentangled from Adam.

Then I stopped. The tone hadn't sounded like Balaam's. And the expression fixed on me—annoyance mingled with displeasure—wasn't Balaam's either.

"I'm not your grandsire, girl," he said as Adam moved between us. "And you don't need to protect her from me, Adam. I have no love for Balaam, but I have no issue with the girl." A hard look at me. "Though I would prefer not to find her in your embrace. May I have a moment with my son?"

Silence as we figured out what he meant . . . and who he was.

"Asmondai," Adam said, in a tone more suited to the inconvenient appearance of a drunken uncle than the father he'd never met.

"I'm sorry." The lord demon's voice dripped sarcasm. "Is this a bad time?"

"Any time would be a bad time, actually. Whatever you're selling, I'm not buying."

"I am not *selling*—"

"So you popped by to say hi? Make my acquaintance? I've got a dad, thanks. You're just the jerk who knocked up my mom and left her to figure out what to do with a son who likes setting things on fire."

When a demon lord deigns to visit his offspring, this is probably not the reception he usually gets. Asmondai was speechless for a second, then said, slowly, "I understand that you're angry."

"No, I'm not. Hint?" Adam lifted his hands. "Not even warm."

He was right. When he rested his hand on my leg, it was cool.

"What if I've come to help you?" Asmondai asked.

"Oh, I'm sure you have. Just like Balaam came to help Savannah. Offer her power, glory, queen of the universe, if she helps him in return. She refused. Now she's under lock and key in this place, with a Nast bounty on her head. Because Balaam tried to 'help' her. So how about we skip that stage and go straight to *no*. Not interested. Piss off."

"Piss off?" Asmondai lifted one brow. "You may have inherited my talent for politics, but you've not yet mastered the art of rhetoric, have you?"

"I'm sure I'm a huge disappointment, so why don't you just write me off and go."

"I have no intention of writing you off, Adam. Of all my children, I've chosen you because you're different. You're—"

"Special?" Adam said. Now I felt heat flare through his hand. "Does that sound familiar, Savannah?"

"Pretty much exactly what Balaam said to me," I said. "He chose me—a mere granddaughter—because I'm special, and it has nothing to do with the fact that I'm connected to the interracial council, the Nast Cabal, the Cortez Cabal . . ."

"I can't claim quite that many connections," Adam said.

"But I'm the only child of yours who's actually on the front line of this battle."

Asmondai said, "But how did you get on the front line, Adam? When you were her age"—he waved at me—"you were a college dropout. Living at home. Taking the easiest jobs you could find, just enough to pay for your toys. You were an interracial council delegate because of Robert Vasic, and the only reason you showed up at meetings was because occasionally they led to an adventure. Now you're a key delegate on that council. You're a renowned private investigator. You're an expert on demons and supernatural lore. And you're a valuable frontline warrior, an Exustio half-demon who has fully mastered his powers. You've earned your place."

"I don't—"

"You don't care about my approval. I understand. But I'm here to help you because we're on the same side."

"No, we're not. You have your own agenda. It may overlap with ours, but that doesn't mean you're on our side."

"You are indeed growing into your birthright, my son. Agreed, then. But our agendas do overlap, and to that end, I'm bringing you information, no strings attached. You want to know what these people are doing with that virus, do you not?"

Adam straightened.

The lord demon smiled. "Good. Then I will tell you."

Troy was not impressed when he finally got his body back. He took anti-possession brews—you can't have a demon taking over a CEO's bodyguard—but those didn't help against a lord.

He muttered about Adam's relatives and mine, popping up all over the place, causing trouble. Trying to make light of what was, as we all knew, a very serious situation. No supernatural really worries about being possessed by a lord demon because the only time they take human form is to procreate. They don't answer our summons, and they sure as hell don't drop in to say hello.

Most supernaturals knew better than to try to contact a lord demon to ask for a favor. A friend of mine lost the use of her legs summoning Asmondai—and still never actually met the guy. But now they were taking human form to ask *us* for favors. That told us just how desperate the situation had become.

Benicio was meeting us in the boardroom. As we hurried there, we bumped into Elena and Clay, intently heading someplace of their own. They'd been recalled with Lucas and Adam, pending more news on Larsen Dahl.

I asked if they'd seen Hope.

"She's awake and recuperating," Elena said. "Karl wants to eat, so we're hunting down breakfast. We'll join you in the boardroom. Benicio's still working on getting that message translated. Hope may have more information to add from her vision."

"After she eats," Clay said.

Elena smiled. "Always the top concern. Can we grab you guys something?"

I said we were fine and they continued on.

"I disagree," Lucas was saying to a white-haired man as we walked into the boardroom. "If Lucifer is going to communicate through Hope, why would he speak in languages she doesn't understand?"

"It is possible," the man said. "We have accounts—"

"Minor demons," Adam interjected. "None from lords, right?"

The old man scowled at him. "We have very few accounts of lord demons communicating with anyone at all."

"Eight confirmed cases in the last fifty years," Adam

said. "Aside from the times they hooked up with human women, when I'm sure they did plenty of talking, though not necessarily in Latin . . . unless they were trying to seduce a member of the debating team."

The old man's scowl deepened.

I said hi to Lucas as we sat. He looked tired, but managed a rare smile for me.

"Lucas and I have talked about Hope's earlier visions," Adam said. "I agree that it's not Lucifer attempting contact. More on that later. For now, we need to bump up the number of confirmed lord demon visits. I called this meeting because I have new information, and it came directly from Asmondai, not twenty minutes ago."

Adam waited for everyone to digest that, then said, "From Bryce, we had an idea what the plan was. Take this virus and turn key people into supernaturals. From the test results, we know they're using vampire and werewolf DNA and likely zombie. Presumably, then, they're hoping to not just make these guys regular supernaturals, but to give them the superhero treatment. Semi-immortality and invulnerability from vampires. Heightened senses and physical strength from werewolves. Prolonged youth from both. The best we've got to offer in one package. If it works, those who get it are going to be thinking this supernatural stuff ain't so bad, meaning they aren't going to argue to lock the rest of us up."

Paige nodded. "Because they'll *be* one of us, too. So they're choosing men and women who'd have some say in how revealed supernaturals are treated. Politicians, I presume."

Adam shook his head. "Eventually, but according to Asmondai, their first targets are deeper sources of power. Money men. Guys with deep pockets and lots of clout. Would that work? I have no idea. But I'm thinking we don't want to find out. We need to get to the targets before they do."

"Wonderful," one of the VPs said. "And how do you propose we do that? Determine the most powerful financial leaders in America and hope these terrorists use the same criteria?"

"No. Asmondai gave us names. He wants this stopped and thinks we can do it. There are two initial test cases. Two more will follow immediately after."

"Good," Benicio said, getting to his feet. "We'll get there before they strike and establish round-the-clock surveillance. We'll be ready for them."

"We need to dispatch those teams *now*," I said. "According to Asmondai, they're hitting the first two tonight."

I was heading back into the field. Adam, Elena and Clay were going with me, so I'd be well protected on all sides. Also, we were in serious shit and already overextended. They needed everyone out there.

While Asmondai had been very helpful, there was a lot he couldn't know. How exactly did SLAM plan to do this? How long would they wait after the two test cases before hitting the next two? And, most important, what were the risks of this injection? Bryce said they called it a virus. How did it spread? It wasn't airborne, it seemed, or even spread by close contact—I'd had lots of contact with Bryce when I was getting him out of the lab and I was fine. Did it spread at all? Or was "virus" just a convenient name?

The linguists were still working on Hope's message. They'd deciphered most of it. Now the problem was figuring out what it meant. It seemed to be about a place . . . if the person describing it was a sideshow fortune-teller. A winding road. Fields of gold. A house in ruins. Cows in a meadow. That could describe a million locations in America alone. Really not helpful.

But we had as much as we were getting for now.

Lucas, Paige, Jeremy and Jaime were going after one of the initial test cases in Dallas. Adam, Elena, Clay and I were taking the other in Austin. There would be a security team dispatched to each city with us, but this wasn't a "swoop in with a SWAT team" kind of mission. The bulk of the Cortez and Boyd security forces—along with Cassandra, Aaron, Sean and others—were being sent to track down and begin surveillance on the second wave of targets.

In just over an hour, we were at the airfield, bags in hand. We were going to Austin. Cassandra and Aaron were with us—they were heading to Houston to meet a security team and monitor a second-wave subject. Yep, there's money in Texas.

The leaders of the Austin and Houston contingent were on the jet, too. They kept their distance, though. They obviously weren't comfortable being so close to werewolves.

The easiest way to thwart the Austin attack would be to kidnap the target—Maurice B. Lester, head of Lester Oil. Yet that wouldn't help us catch those who planned to infect him. If he wasn't available, they could move on to Lester's wife and kids—the next best thing to infecting a bigwig is to infect his loved ones, which guarantees he won't be advocating universal imprisonment for supernaturals.

In the end, we were stuck with the simplest and most frustrating plan. Watch and wait.

After half a day of following Maurice Lester, we'd been at BJ's BBQ for an hour now. Lester and his party had only just ordered dinner. We'd almost finished eating in a side room, where we were out of sight, but Elena and Clay could follow the conversation at Lester's table.

"I'm sure the discussion is fascinating," Clay said, "if you give a shit about oil."

"Antonio appreciates it," Elena said as she tapped her phone. "I'm texting him stock tips. Get a few pitchers of beer in these guys and they forget they aren't alone in the place."

"No," Adam said. "They just don't care. Only people they can see are minimum-wage servers and a table of college kids. Their stock tips are safe."

"Can you pass those to me?" I said to Elena. "I wouldn't know a stock tip if someone wrote it on the table, but my investment guy can use them."

"Speaking of writing on the table," Elena said, gesturing at the art unfolding beneath me. "You're going to have to cut that out before you go."

Adam nodded. "It's the best crayon-on-tablecloth work you've ever done."

I laughed and kept sketching. It was nothing really, just a shot of the restaurant interior, more doodling than drawing.

"I haven't seen you draw in a while," Elena said.

I shrugged. "I do. Just . . . not as much these days. But as long as I'm sitting here with a brown paper tablecloth and crayons . . ."

She leaned over to look more closely. "There's a lot more color than your usual stuff."

"Because there aren't any grays and blacks in the crayon cup," I said.

"Ah."

Clay rocked back in his chair, casting bored glances at Lester's table. At first, we'd jumped every time someone walked past him and nearly raced in when a colleague thumped him on the shoulder. By now, even when the server leaned over to ask something, we didn't twitch. Asmondai had said the group would strike tonight. While that wasn't set in stone, it was unlikely they would inject Lester in a restaurant, surrounded by his friends and associates.

"Go scout outside," Elena said as Clay thumped his chair back down.

"That an order?"

She smiled. "It is."

"Thank you."

As he got up to go, his fingers brushed her back. Just a light touch. Making contact. I'm sure that as we'd been sitting there, Clay had his leg against hers under the table.

When Clay zipped back a few minutes later, Elena got up.

"Are they leaving?" she asked him.

"Nope. And they won't be for a while. A car full of Saudis just drove up. I'm guessing they're here for Lester."

They were. Seemed they were supposed to be here an hour ago, but were delayed. Dinner was about to begin in earnest.

"I say we give the kids a break." She looked at us. "I know you've had a rough couple of days, and I already reserved the hotel rooms so—"

"Great," Adam said. Then quickly added, "I mean, great that you reserved them already. But we'd hate to cut out on you guys like that."

"Cut," Clay said. "While you have the chance."

"The Omni up the road," Elena said. "The room is under Vasic. You guys usually share when you're on a case, right? So you can watch each other's backs?"

"Uh, yeah."

"Good," Elena said. "Go on then. Rest. The hotel is a couple blocks from here. We'll call if anything happens."

As we headed out, I whispered to Adam, "Do you think they know?"

"Nah. Elena's just being considerate."

CHAPTER 32

We did not walk. We went out the front door, saw a cab, and decided speed was of the essence.

We tactfully avoided making out in the cab or the elevator. Once we got the room door open, though, all bets were off. Adam had me inside and up against the wall before the door swung shut.

As I started to kiss him back, I caught a glimpse of the room over his shoulder and stopped.

"I don't think we've been nearly as discreet as we thought," I said as I nodded at the king-sized bed.

He turned to look. "Nope, apparently we weren't."

I laughed and pulled him close. Before our lips could touch, he backed up. He looked over his shoulder at the bed, then at me.

"I think we should wait," he said.

"What?"

He put his hands on my shoulders. "Let's not rush into this."

"Rush?" I sputtered.

"I want you to be sure, Savannah."

"Hell, yes, I'm sure. I've never been more sure . . ."

I caught the glitter in his eyes then. The twist of his mouth, like he was biting his cheek to keep from laughing.

"You . . . you . . ."

He let out a whoop of a laugh. "Sorry. I had to. The look

on your face . . ." He was laughing too hard to finish his sentence, hands falling from my shoulders.

I narrowed my eyes and took a step toward him. "May I remind you that my spells are much improved?"

"Sorry." His hand went up as he choked on a laugh. When I glowered, he reached for me, hands going to my hips. "Come here."

"Mmm, maybe not." I backed away.

He moved forward, putting his hands on my hips again, warming me through my jeans as his lips went to my ear. "I'll make it up to you."

I grasped his wrists and pushed his hands away. "No, I think you might have a point. We are rushing things and it's not like we really need to do this now."

"Umm . . ."

"I know *I* don't."

I kept backing up. He started to step forward, then stopped himself. The start of a smile disappeared in a flicker of uncertainty, as if he was pretty sure I was joking—really hoped I was joking—but wasn't completely sure.

I started unbuttoning my shirt. He grinned and tried to grab me again, but I put my hand against his chest.

"Uh-uh."

"But . . ." He gestured at my open shirt buttons.

"We told Elena we were getting some rest. I'm not going to nap in my clothing."

I unbuttoned the shirt halfway, then flicked open the clasp on my jeans and shimmied them down. I took the clip from my hair next and shook it out. Then I finished with the shirt, letting it fall open. Adam let out a soft breath.

I backed up onto the bed. He watched me. Just stood there, watching me. I peeled the bedspread back and slid onto the sheets, pulling my bare legs up under me, shirt opening, swinging my hair over to cover my breasts.

"Do you want to take a nap with me?" I asked.

"Yes," he answered hoarsely.

I shrugged off the shirt. Then I reclined on the pillows, one knee up, hair brushed aside. I hooked my thumbs in the sides of my panties and inched them down my hips.

"Are you sure?" I said. "Because if you aren't sure—"

He was across the room, on the bed, mouth to mine before I could finish.

I leaned over the side of the bed, hair falling in a curtain as I peered at the carpet. Adam tugged me back up.

"What's wrong?" he murmured as he pulled me against him.

"I have rug burns." I rubbed my ass. "I'm trying to figure out how I got rug burns."

"We were on the floor."

"Were we?"

"Briefly, yes."

"Huh." I pushed up in bed. "How'd I miss that?"

He chuckled. "Well, either it was so good you lost track of where we were, or it was so bad you were busy compiling your grocery list."

"I don't buy the groceries. Paige does."

Another chuckle, this one vibrating through me as he pulled me on top of him. "Then I'm going to pick option one. And if I'm wrong, don't tell me."

I stretched out on him, arms folded on his chest, chin propped on them. "No, it *was* option one. You were very good. Of course, I expected it. I'd heard that about you."

He blinked and lifted his head to meet my eyes.

"Purely unsolicited information," I said. "Some of your hookups liked to share."

"*That's* not at all awkward."

"It never bothered me. I always figured since you had to wait for me, you might as well be getting some practice."

He laughed. "Well, you're very good, too. I might remember the floor, but only because I hit my knee on the nightstand. Otherwise, it's all a blur. A nice blur."

"Thank you. I had practice, too."

Another laugh. "And *that* doesn't bother *me*. As long as you don't get any more practice anyplace else."

"Mmm. Maybe. Depends on whether you can keep up."

"Oh, believe me, I can keep up."

He flipped me onto my back, slid onto me, and we "rested" some more.

CHAPTER 33

I woke up first. I stretched and felt Adam's arm over me, his leg across mine, and there was a moment, confused and drowsy, when I forgot what had happened. I was shot back to all the other times we'd shared a bed on a case or a tent on a camping trip, and I'd lain there, knowing he'd only thrown his arm across me in his sleep, and I'd think *I wish* . . .

Now I opened my eyes and saw him there, naked, his arm around my waist, his leg over mine and I thought *Oh*. That's all I could think for a minute. Just *Oh*. Then I squeezed my eyes shut and felt a prickle of tears, emotions cycloning through me, joy and wonder and bliss and a little terror, too, the terror of finally getting the one thing I wanted above all others, and realizing that getting it doesn't mean keeping it. But whatever happened, I would never forget the feeling of waking up and seeing him there, and I'd never regret it.

His eye cracked open and he hesitated, as if, like me, he had to take a moment to clear his head and remember. Then he smiled, slid his other arm under me, and pulled me into a slow, delicious kiss.

A phone buzzed. We both bolted up, blinking and looking around.

"Yours," he said.

"Right. So where . . ."

He stretched over the edge of the bed, reached down, and pulled up my jeans. I tugged the phone from the pocket.

I answered. "Hey, Elena. Are we late?" I checked my watch. We'd been gone just over an hour.

"No, but Lester has decided he needs to leave pronto."

"We'll be right there."

As soon as we were through the hotel front doors, we saw the rental car come flying around the corner two blocks down. Clay gunned it. We met him at the curb and jumped in, not even getting the door closed before he peeled away.

He made a quick right—nearly mowing down people using the crosswalk—and roared past two streets before taking the next corner, circling back the way he'd come. I saw the back of Lester's town car turn a corner ahead of us.

"Keep back about a hundred feet," Elena said. "There's not enough traffic for us to get closer and we're fairly sure we know where he's going."

"Got it."

"So what happened?" I asked as Clay fell into tailing position.

"We'd moved onto the patio to nurse drinks. We overheard Lester excuse himself. He came outside. He seemed to take a call. A very quick one. Then he went back in and said there was a situation at home."

I remembered the conversation Adam and I had earlier that day. About getting called into work at convenient times.

"You said it was a quick call?"

She nodded. "Very quick."

"Did you hear it ring?"

She shook her head. "I figured it was on vibrate. But I see what you mean. It might have just been an excuse."

Lester did head straight home, though not fast enough to suggest there was any situation there. The tactical team confirmed that—they'd been watching the house since we arrived that afternoon and hadn't seen anything out of the ordinary. Just Lester's wife and college-age son for dinner, then the high-school-age son bringing a friend over to play video games.

After Lester went inside, he seemed to call it a night, meaning we were stuck outside, patrolling the perimeter with a squad of tactical guys who really didn't appreciate our intrusion. Especially when their orders now came from someone who was both female *and* a werewolf. Elena acted as if she didn't notice their reservations.

As for the house itself, I'd never seen *Dallas*—before my time—but Elena said she once had a foster family whose idea of family time was to watch the show, whether everyone wanted to or not. She was pretty sure Lester had his place modeled after JR's ranch house. Or maybe it was the other way around. It was big. It was boxy. It was blindingly white and shimmered in the Texas heat.

Since the property was a ranch, there was a lot of acreage to be watched. If anyone was planning to break in, though, they weren't hiding in the hay barn, because that's where the tactical team had set up, on the unused second floor, a spot that gave them a good vantage point on the house.

The size of the property meant that while it was difficult for us to monitor, it was just as difficult for Lester to maintain proper security. His fence would deter deer and little else. Two guards were out on patrol. The rest of the security was on the house itself, much of it electronic. Two Cabal technicians had gotten access to the attic. By the time dusk fell, we'd be able to rappel across the narrow gap between the second floor of the barn and a dormer window.

The sultry June evening was perfect for a few beers on the back deck, which would put them in our sight line—but the Lesters didn't seem to share my opinion. They'd all locked themselves in their monstrous house, and pulled the blinds.

"The teens are playing a video game with the volume jacked up," Elena said. "The older son is complaining because he's trying to do homework. Sounds like our place, after Uncle Nick bought Kate a drum set. She insists on playing Metallica riffs in the same room where Logan is practicing French."

"Or Logan insists on practicing French in the same room where she's practicing Metallica riffs," Clay said.

"True," Elena said. "They always want to be together. Which would be easier if they shared any common interests besides bunny rabbits. Typical kids."

I grinned. "Yes, typical five-year-olds—playing Metallica and learning French for fun. As for the bunnies, I'm not going there."

"Don't. Anyway, sounds like situation normal at the Lester house tonight. The kids fighting, while Mom's telling them to stop bickering before their dad comes down to chew them out."

"Except at our place," Clay said, "it's me saying, 'Cool it before Mom comes down.'"

"Because I'm much scarier than he is," Elena said. "Now if I could just convince every mutt in the country to see it that way."

Adam said, "So Lester's upstairs?"

"Oh, sure, bring the conversation back on track," I said. "Spoilsport."

He smiled. "Sorry. I was just going to say that if he's alone upstairs, someone could get to him without the rest of the family realizing."

"The house is secured," said the head of the tactical team—a guy named Eagle. He'd been working away as if he wasn't listening, but clearly he had been. "We have men watching every angle, and they've been at their posts since we arrived. After they were in place, we went over the house with heat scanners to ensure no one was already there, hiding. No one has entered that house without our knowledge."

"So where *is* Lester?" Elena said.

"We have no visual of the house interior yet, ma'am."

"But you said you have heat scanners and I know you have a floor plan. Which room is Lester in?"

Eagle barked a command to the guy handling the equipment, as if this was his oversight. A few minutes later, the technician was spreading the blueprints on the desk.

He pointed to the master suite. "Before he pulled the blinds, we managed to get a visual. That's the bed, right beside the window. He's lying down."

"I don't like the sounds of that," Elena murmured. "What time is it?"

"Just past nine," I said. "Seems early for bed, especially when he didn't have a very strenuous day."

"Could be reading or watching TV," Adam said, and glanced at Elena. "Why the concern?"

Clay answered for her. "Because there's one very good reason to leave dinner early, come home, and go to bed at nine."

"If he's feeling sick," I said. "Shit. But when was he injected? We've been with him for hours."

"Must have been before we got to him. Took a while to kick in."

"Okay," Elena turned to Eagle. "We need to get in that house. Now."

"We're waiting until dark—"

"Who's in charge of this operation?"

"The Cortez Cabal."

If I'd been on the receiving end of Elena's look, I'd have run for cover. Eagle just stood there, smirking slightly.

After about twenty more seconds of silence, though, Eagle lost his smirk. He started to sweat. Elena let it go another ten seconds, then growled, "Try again."

"You're in charge of this immediate operation, ma'am, but I work for the Cortez Cabal, and I'm the guy with twenty years' experience. Mr. Lester is resting. Or answering his e-mail. Or watching TV. We're not going to blow my operation because you got hysterical—"

"Either we get your men's help to enter the attic now, or we do it ourselves and increase the chances of blowing *your* operation."

He hesitated, then said, "I need to call Mr. Cortez."

"You have thirty seconds. Then I'm going in."

Eagle phoned both Lucas and Benicio. Neither picked up.

"We'll have to wait until they call back," he said.

"We can't." She turned around. "Can anyone here help us get into that house?"

Eagle stepped toward her. "Don't you dare—"

Elena had him by the neck, two feet off the ground, pinned to the wall, before he could get another word out.

There were two other officers plus the tech guy in the hayloft. Tech guy decided his equipment looked very interesting, and busied himself with it. The officers both turned to Clay.

"Don't look at me," he said. "I'm only getting involved if you decide to do the same. But remember, whatever our kids think, I'm definitely the scarier one."

They stayed seated. Elena looked at Eagle, still suspended by his throat.

"I'm a reasonable person, so I let you try to contact the Cortezes. But it is not reasonable of you to expect me to wait for a callback when our target may be infected. Oh, and a word of advice?" She brought him down to eye level. "You may think it's clever to accuse a woman of being hysterical, but it's only going to piss her off."

She dropped him. He landed on his ass, wheezing and clutching his throat. When she turned away, he muttered, "Bitch."

I looked at Elena. "Note that he didn't dare say that until you turned your back."

"They never do." She went over to the technician. "Can you contact the guys over in the attic? Tell them I know they aren't ready, but we need to come in."

"Yes, ma'am."

She turned to the two officers and didn't even get a chance to open her mouth before one said, "We'll get the rappel system in place and have some men watch for the patrolling guards. You should be able to get over there quickly and safely."

"Thank you."

CHAPTER 34

We did get over quickly and safely. At least Adam and I did. Clay took one look at the flimsy rig and decided to stay behind and handle radio contact. Elena was game—she'd done some rock climbing with us—but quickly realized she wouldn't be fast enough on the traverse to avoid being spotted if my blur spell failed. She decided to stay with Clay.

Adam and I crossed and crawled through the dormer window into the attic, which was dusty and as hot as hell. I suppose no matter how wealthy you are, you don't clean or air-condition your attic. It was also full of crap. Boxes of old clothing. Stacks of LPs and VHS tapes. Piles of toys and baby furniture. I had to wonder at the last. Were they planning to drag this old stuff down when they had grandkids? I think their sons—and certainly future daughters-in-law— would expect them to buy new, considering they were billionaires and all.

The technicians met us at the window and led us over to where they'd tapped into the security system. One showed us the laptop screen displaying the view of all six cameras. They were all aimed outside the house.

"Do we have any interior views?"

"We've been drilling holes and threading cams through. I can give you the boys' rooms and the guest rooms."

"What we need is the master suite."

"It's at the far end of the second floor. The attic doesn't extend that far, so we haven't managed to get a line in." He picked up a pair of headphones. "We have sound, though. Just got that snaked through far enough to pick up decent levels."

His partner grunted. "Which would be a lot more useful if that kid would turn off the damned video game."

He was right. We could hear the music blasting even without headphones. One of the Grand Theft Auto titles, it sounded like.

"And here's the upstairs," the tech said, as he flipped a switch.

The music now sounded slightly farther away. Then, as I was about to take the headset off, I heard the muffled click of pumps growing louder.

"Do we have more than one feed on the second floor?" I asked.

He nodded.

"Is this the one closest to the master suite?"

He shook his head and hit a button on the laptop. "We're still in the hall here, but this is a bit closer."

When he switched the feeds, the pump-clicking quieted. Then it grew louder again as the footsteps approached the master suite. A pause. Then a rap on a door.

"Maury?" Mrs. Lester said. "It's me."

No answer. A faint jangle as she tried the handle.

"Maury? Why is the door locked? I told the boys not to bother you. They know you aren't feeling well."

Shit. He *was* sick. Injected? Or just too much barbecue?

She knocked again. Then she muttered, "Lock the door and fall asleep. Wonderful."

As her steps retreated, Adam got Elena on the radio and told her what was happening. Elena thought Mrs. Lester might be going for a key, so she advised us to hang tight.

Mrs. Lester did return. She knocked and called again, though, before using the key. I suppose, in some marriages, not knowing what's happening on the other side might be the only thing that keeps you together.

When Lester still didn't reply, she went in, calling a warning as she did. She closed the door, too, which meant that her voice disappeared under the roar of the music.

"Let me listen," Elena said through the radio.

I pulled off the headset and put it to the radio speaker.

"She's looking for him," Elena said. "He's not in bed."

A moment later, there was an exclamation even I could hear. "Oh! There you are. I—"

Silence. We waited through three more seconds, then Elena said, "Get in there, Savannah, take the lead. Blur spells and cover spells. Have Adam follow at a distance."

"Got it." I turned to the techs. "Show me where to go."

One of them led us to the trap door. We got it open. There was a set of stairs that could be lowered, but we didn't dare use those. I leaned out, making sure the way was clear, then got in position to drop.

Just before I did, the other tech hurried over to exchange my radio for an earpiece. I slapped it in, then lowered myself through the hole. It was still a two-foot drop. No way to muffle the thump of my fall. Adam followed quickly. We waited for someone downstairs to come running, but our thuds must have been drowned out by the game sounds.

The second-floor hall was long and wide and central, with rooms off both sides and a sweeping staircase in the middle. Passing that staircase was the riskiest part—the master suite was at the far end. I moved under a blur spell. Adam kept his distance. I could have covered him, too, but that took extra juice.

When I got to the door of the master suite, I flipped my back to the wall, where I could see partway down the steps. I waved Adam over while I kept watch.

Adam took up position against the wall on the other side of the door. I reached for the door handle and slowly turned it. It wouldn't budge. Mrs. Lester had relocked it. Damn.

I should have brought the picks. A spell was an extra drain wasted on a task I could do manually.

I leaned over and checked the lock. A simple household one. A flip of my credit card did the trick. I cracked open the door and listened. The damn music was still booming from downstairs. I thought I picked up a thump from inside the room, but that was it. I closed the door and whispered to Elena.

"Go in," she said. "Keep a blur spell on and be ready to run if you're spotted."

"Where do we run?" I whispered. "We jumped through the trapdoor."

Adam answered, "Elena? Tell the tech guys to ready the ladder. If we come running, get it down."

I opened the door again, an inch at a time.

I could see the bed, with the covers in a snarl, half on the floor. Otherwise, nothing. I leaned in farther. There were four doors. Two were open, but the angle was wrong to see through either of them. I listened hard, but the rap music below had gone up another notch.

I double-checked my blur spell then eased into the bedroom. It was massive. Wasted space mostly, with nothing except a king-size bed and nightstands, along the far wall by the window.

The first open doorway was to my right. A sliding door to a walk-in closet, it looked like. Dark inside. I turned and gestured for Adam to be ready in case anyone came flying out of it when I passed. Communicating while in blur-form wasn't easy, but he understood.

A sour smell rose from the sheets. I reached out and touched one. Soaked with sweat. No other signs of trauma, though. No signs of the Lesters either.

A crunch behind me. I spun. Nothing there. The music downstairs rose another notch.

"Can we kill the tunes?" I whispered. "Cut the power or something?"

"I wish," Elena muttered. "If we cut the power that would definitely bring the boys running."

"Right."

I sidestepped toward the open door. It led into a narrow hall with a sitting room at the end, and a doorway to the right, partly open, showing a shower stall. The hall was decorated with some kind of funky art or wallpaper, a radiating pattern of black, like a sunburst.

I took another step and saw the lines weren't black. They were red. More red drops below on the wood floor. Arterial spray.

I backed up. "Adam?"

I heard a sound from down the hall. This time it was an unmistakable crunch.

"Uh . . ."

"I heard that," Elena said.

A smacking sound, then a guttural snarl.

"And that," she said. "I'm going out on a limb here and saying Lester's infected, and the virus is working a helluva lot faster than it did with Bryce. We've got a werewolf."

"Eating," I said.

"Hmm." I heard Clay's voice in the background, then Elena murmured, "I know." She came back clearer. "You know what happened with Bryce, right? The type of Change?"

"Wolfman not wolf."

"Yes. We don't know exactly what we're dealing with and—" Clay's voice in the background again. Then Elena said to us, "You're not hearing any signs that she . . . Mrs. Lester . . . that she's still alive?"

I looked up at the blood spray. "No."

"Okay, then I hate to say this but . . ."

"Let him keep eating."

"Yes."

She sounded relieved that I wasn't horrified by the thought. While Lester was feeding, Lester was occupied. We couldn't take down a werewolf without a fight that would bring three boys racing up the stairs to their deaths.

Elena told us to stay in the bedroom and monitor the situation. Clay was readying a sedative and they'd brave the rappel system and bring it over themselves. They didn't trust a team member to do it, not with a werewolf involved.

So we waited. One problem with knowing exactly what was happening in the bathroom? As loud as the music was, it wasn't enough to cover the sounds of bones crunching and teeth clicking. A werewolf devouring his meal. We just tried to think of it that way. Werewolf and meal. Not a man eating his wife.

Less than two minutes later, though, we heard feet thumping up the stairs.

"Mom!" A voice called. "You gotta do something about Rob. Every time I ask him to turn it down, he jacks it up."

I managed to get the door shut and locked before the kid reached the top of the stairs.

"We've got company," I whispered.

No response through my earpiece.

"Elena?"

The kid's footsteps thudded down the hall. On the other end of the radio I heard nothing.

Shit.

Adam had eased the bathroom hall door closed. Whatever condition Lester was in, any Change would make turning doorknobs very difficult. With any luck, that added barrier meant he wouldn't hear—

The boy pounded on the door.

"Mom! You said you were just coming up to check on Dad!"

A snort from inside the bathroom. Then a thump.

The kid pounded again. "Come on, guys. Locked? Really? I've been able to open this since I was six!"

And at eighteen he should damned well know that a locked bedroom door wasn't to keep him out—it was to tell him not to enter. To give his parents privacy.

Another grunt from inside the bathroom. The scrabble of footsteps. Feet? Claws? I couldn't tell. The more this idiot kid yelled, though, the more he attracted whatever beast his father had become. So I opened the door, grabbed him and yanked him inside. I dragged the kid down. At first he struggled, but once he was on the floor with me straddling him, he just lay there, gaping.

I slapped my hand over his mouth.

I glanced over at Adam. He was poised to help but I waved him back. I was fine. The kid was just lying there. Judging by his build, he wasn't on the football team. From the vacancy of his gaze, not on the chess team either. Or perhaps just in shock.

Over the music, I could hear Lester snuffling in the bathroom hall. He pushed at the door. Just testing it. More snuffling.

The kid started to struggle again. I leaned down.

"If you want out of here alive, you'd better—"

He bit me. As I yanked back, he said, "Do you know who my father is, you thieving bitch?"

I pulled a glove from my pocket and stuffed it into his mouth.

"It's *what* your father is that's the problem," I muttered.

The kid bucked. I slammed him down, again, but he was struggling in earnest now, legs and fists flailing against the floor, grunting against the gag.

Lester growled and pushed at the door.

I locked the kid in a binding spell, then turned to Adam. He was already leaving to find Elena. He looked back. Lester had stopped growling and sounded as if he was just shuffling about, trying to figure a way past the closed door.

"He's not going anywhere," I said. "And neither is this one."

Adam nodded and took off, loping down the hall as silently as he could.

Fingernails scraped the door. Tentative at first. Then harder.

"Come on, Elena," I murmured. "Before he realizes he can break that door down with one—"

Lester hit the door hard. I scrambled off the kid, locking him in a binding spell as I eased toward the bathroom hall door. Lester had resumed his shuffling and snuffling.

"Savannah?" It was Adam on my earpiece.

"He tested the door. I think he's given up but . . . hurry."

"I am. I'm at the trap door and—"

Elena's voice sounded in the background.

"Got 'em," Adam said. "Heading your way in—"

The en suite door flung open, knocking me back. Lester stepped out.

It *was* Lester. Not a wolf. Not a wolfman. Maurice Lester, an overweight, jowly man with dyed black hair, wearing slacks and a dress shirt with the tie loosened and thrown over his shoulder. Only his white shirt wasn't white anymore. It was stained with blood.

I stopped midspell. Shit. He'd shifted back. Now what was I supposed to—

Lester lifted his head and his bloodshot eyes met mine. The pupils were mere dots in reddish brown irises. His nostrils flared as he inhaled. Then his lips curled and he snarled, flashing teeth threaded with bits of flesh. Okay, he hadn't Changed back. He just never physically transformed in the first place.

I hit him with a knockback. Lester shook it off and charged. I tried to jump out of his path as I cast a binding spell, but he slammed his fist into my shoulder. It was like being hit with a lead bat. I sailed off my feet and into the wall with enough force to knock the wind from my lungs. As I hit the floor, I saw Lester's son struggling to his feet.

"Dad?"

Lester lunged. I clambered up. A binding spell was on my lips, but before I could get it out, Lester was on his son. The binding spell failed. I leaped on Lester's back as his teeth sunk into his son's neck. I cast an energy bolt on instinct. He roared and ripped his head back. His son's blood sprayed.

Before I could cast again, Lester hit me with a pile driver to the side of the head. I flew off him. My stomach lurched. Blackness threatened, but I staggered back to my feet.

Adam ran into the room, hypodermic needle raised. He jabbed it into Lester's back. Lester reared up. He swung at Adam. Adam ducked. I caught Lester in a binding spell, but I'd used up too much power and it only stopped him long enough for Adam to get out of the way.

When the binding spell snapped, Lester lurched into the hall. We followed. Elena was standing under the trap door as Clay lowered himself. When they saw Lester, they stopped, thinking the same thing I had—that he was in human form so he must have reverted. Then they saw the look on our faces and Elena started after Lester, Clay jumping down to follow.

Lester was already thundering down the stairs.

"The boys," I said.

"I know," Elena said as she tore past me. "Is the other son—?"

"Hurt. I'm going back for him."

Adam stayed with Elena and Clay. I raced back into the bedroom. The boy lay on the floor, his throat ripped out, open eyes staring. I checked for vital signs anyway. None. He was gone.

CHAPTER 35

I got downstairs to find Lester, snarling and yowling outside a locked door. The two boys were on the other side. They'd caught one glimpse of him and barricaded themselves in. Elena had managed to inject Lester with a second sedative, and he was finally fading. Elena, Clay, and Adam just stood there, watching.

When Lester finally dropped, Elena walked to the door and, with a gloved hand, jammed the knob so the boys couldn't get out.

"What—?" I said.

She lifted a finger to her lips. Then she motioned for Adam and Clay to carry Lester's body and we retreated.

It wasn't until I was outside that I realized what she was doing. We had two survivors. Both had seen Maurice Lester covered in blood. Now they were trapped in there, where they'd remain until the police showed up to free them. All the evidence from the murders would point to Lester as the perpetrator, and he'd be long gone.

Working with a Cabal team might be a pain in the ass, but Elena did agree there was one advantage. She could hand over Lester and walk away. All the associated cleanup belonged to someone else. Which was good, because we had fresh problems to worry about.

While we were hiking to our distant parked rental, Elena

apologized for vanishing when we'd tried to contact her. "I had a call when you were inside. Too urgent to ignore, and I'd been assured you'd stay patched into the line if you needed me."

"Tech fail."

"Typical," Clay muttered.

Elena nodded. "Anyway, you remember Veronica, right?"

"Ver—?" I began. "Oh, Roni. Right."

"She placed a call to Cortez headquarters earlier tonight," Elena continued. "She wanted to speak to you. She left an urgent message with the poor guy on the switchboard, who's probably really wishing he'd called in sick today. He was shuttled into an interrogation room for an hour of grilling before they decided the message was legit. It seems Roni is in Houston with an infection team."

"That's where Cass and Aaron are, isn't it? Monitoring one of the secondary targets?"

Elena nodded. "Which is why I need you and Adam there. Aaron can handle it, but I'm concerned that Cassandra may not take the threat seriously enough."

"She's been doing a lot better lately," I said as we continued through the pasture. "But I agree Aaron could use more reliable backup. The question is whether Roni's telling the truth. Last time she had me come running to her rescue, you got knocked around by guys with guns and I finally tied Jaime's record for most kidnapped supernatural ever."

"I think you've beat it now," Adam said. "Definitely if you include the Nast dungeon."

"That was an arrest, not a kidnapping." I looked at Elena. "What exactly did Roni say?"

"Well, that's the problem, and the cause of the poor operator's angst. Because we've got every Cabal line tied up on these missions, Veronica called the *real* business line and got a guy who's accustomed to dealing with lay-people trying to submit résumés or get corporate contact information. When he realized what was going on, he panicked and forgot to turn on the tape."

"Ouch."

"According to him, she gave her name and said she needed to talk to you. She insisted on leaving a message, which he jotted down. She gave the name and the address of the Houston target and said you needed to get there because, quote, 'It's all gone wrong. He won't listen to anyone.' Then some garbled stuff about the virus and the targets, which he didn't get verbatim. The upshot is that they're striking in Houston tonight and she wants you to stop it."

"Any return number?"

"It was blocked and she hung up before he could ask for it. But the name and address matches the secondary Houston target Asmondai mentioned. I gave Aaron a heads-up. Nothing so far."

Elena sidestepped a pile of horseshit without even a glance down. Her nose kept her shoes clean. Mine hadn't been so lucky.

I walked along in silence for a moment, then said, "And you guys?"

"Lucas needs Clay and me in Dallas. He's had a tip that the target's whole family was infected. They're not showing any symptoms, though, so he doesn't want to act yet but he wants us there for when he does."

CHAPTER 36

When we got to the airport, the jet was waiting, cleared for takeoff. I could tell Elena was debating whether to follow through on Lucas's request for them to continue on to Dallas. Having been a victim of Roni's last cry for help, she didn't like sending us into the breach with only vampires and a skeleton tactical team for backup. But before we could land in Houston, the situation in Dallas changed. At least one family member—a grown daughter—was definitely infected. They'd managed to capture her and were quarantining the others, but a second daughter and her fiancé had been out clubbing and had lost their Cabal tail. Jeremy was on it, but he needed Elena and Clay.

So Adam and I got off the plane in Houston alone. We'd just left the private hangar when we saw Cassandra hurrying toward us. Her boots clicked across the pavement as her long jacket snapped behind her. Sunglasses were perched on her sleek red hair, as if she'd pushed them up there and forgotten them after darkness fell. Cass forgets a lot of things these days. As far as anyone can figure, she's passed the end of her semi-immortal lifespan and is hanging on by her fangs . . . and sheer stubbornness.

"Shit, Cass, you're practically running to see me," I called. "Missed your detecting partner, didn't you?"

"Actually, I was hoping to send you on your way again

before it's too late." She peered toward the runway. "Has the jet left?"

"It has."

"Damn it. Aaron tried calling. He texted, too. Both of you."

I took my cell phone out. "We had them off for landing. What's up?"

"Nothing, which is why I was trying to stop you from getting off the jet." She waved us to a rental car illegally parked along the sidewalk. "After the outbreaks in Austin and Dallas, Benicio decided we should take secondary targets into custody, to be safe. Cabal operatives did that twenty minutes ago."

"Are we sure that solves it?" I said. "The Dallas guy's family was infected, too."

Her arched brows shot up another half inch. "Did you read this man's file? I know Lucas e-mailed it to all of you earlier."

"Details," I said. "I left that to Research Guy here."

When Cassandra handed Adam the keys, he grinned and waggled them at me. "Gotta love the old-fashioned ladies. They know who belongs in the driver's seat."

"No," Cass said. "We know who belongs in the chauffeur's seat."

I laughed and we climbed in, Cass and me in back.

"This guy doesn't have family," Adam said as he started the car. "His ex-wife lives back east. No kids. That's why I think the group put him on the backup list. He's influential and powerful, but there aren't any family ties to exploit."

"Oil?" I asked.

Cassandra fluttered her fingers. "Some kind of politician."

"Lobbyist, actually," Adam said.

"Yes, yes," she said, as if it were the same thing.

Adam shook his head. "Lucas actually put the two of you on a case?"

"We worked quite well together," Cass said. "Or we did, after you two started speaking to each other again. Please don't ever send her to me when you're angry with her, Adam. It's dreadful. All that moping and angst. It's like being partnered with one of those fictional vampires."

I sighed.

Cassandra looked at me. "You aren't even going to glare at me for embarrassing you in front of Adam?"

"Only if you say something embarrassing."

"And that isn't?" She studied my face. "Interesting . . ."

"Moving right along," I said. "I'd better call Lucas and see what he wants us to do."

I didn't need to. The moment I turned my cell back on, Lucas rang. He sounded exhausted—Dallas was not going well. He refused to elaborate, except to say that he really wished Benicio could have gotten in touch with our pilot to take us straight on to Dallas.

"We can be there in three hours," Adam called from the front seat. "We'll swing by and grab Aaron, then hit the highway."

Lucas agreed that was wise. With the jet gone, driving would be fastest.

I'd just started mapping the new coordinates when Cassandra's cell rang.

It was Aaron. I could tell by her tone when she answered. The two of them had met back in the nineteenth century. Lots of time together, followed by lots of time apart. Cass's fault, naturally. They'd been friends for about six years again now, and I was sure they'd been lovers for a while. You could tell by the way she talked to him.

That softer tone didn't last long this time. She quickly said, "I'm going to put you on speaker."

"—rather you didn't," he was saying as she clicked it on.

"Too late," I said.

He sighed. "Yeah. Probably need to, however much I

hate the damned thing. Sounds like everyone's talking in a submarine. You guys are still in town, then? Good. We have a problem."

"Of course we do," Cassandra murmured. "God forbid we might have wanted to relax for the night, have a glass of wine."

"I'll grab you some wine later, Cass," Aaron said. "I saw a carton at a corner store. I'm sure it's a great vintage. Now, the problem. Ten minutes ago, the Cabal tech guys intercepted a 911 call from Jordan's office."

It took me a second to remember that Jordan—Ron Jordan—was the target's name.

Aaron continued. "It was one of his assistants. She said she's working late and she's sick, really sick. So is the guy working with her."

"Damn it," I said. "No family, so infect the staff. How many of them have gone home already?"

"I'm really trying not to think about that," Aaron said. "I'm five minutes from the building, hoping no cops are around to pull me over."

"The Cabal intercepted the call, right?" I said. "So the 911 dispatcher didn't get it?"

"Unfortunately, it went through. The dispatcher sent an ambulance, but the Cabal was able to call 911 back from what seemed to be the same address. The guy said he was the assistant's boyfriend, and he was getting them to the hospital himself."

I told Aaron we'd meet him there.

Anyone who saw Aaron Darnell never wondered why Cassandra had hit on Clay all those years ago. Aaron was also a blond, well-built, good-looking guy. He was bigger and not as drop-dead-gorgeous, but they could have been siblings.

Jordan's office was in the kind of building you'd expect for a wealthy lobbyist. Central location. Tall and modern, with lots of steel and glass. A reception desk staffed by security guards who would know at a glance whether you belonged there. I suspect they would have buzzed Cass in without her even flashing an ID badge, but we didn't have to get past them. The Cabal team had infiltrated the building when they'd first begun monitoring Jordan. We met them in the parking garage and they let us in.

"Status check?" I said when we were on the elevator.

The team leader—Estrada—said, "We've established that the floor is clear. No other late night workers. The door to Jordan's office is closed and locked. We're not hearing anything from—"

He tilted his head, listening through his earpiece. His expression went grim.

"Strike that," he said.

He hit the floor button beneath the one he'd selected. The team had set up earlier in an unoccupied suite over Jordan's office, where they could drill down for sight and sound. They'd left when Jordan had, then hurried back after the call.

When the elevator stopped, he said, "This is Jordan's floor. You folks go on up to 1104. Someone will meet you there."

I started getting off behind him. "We'll—"

Aaron stopped me. "Actually," he said, "I'm going to second the SWAT guy. If Jordan's staff is infected, I don't think someone's stuck them all with needles."

"Viral, you mean."

"Which is what this thing is supposed to be. Better let the SWAT guys and the vamps handle this. I'm not worried about getting a shot of werewolf DNA. I always thought they had more fun anyway."

"You would," Cassandra said.

They got off the elevator. I looked at Adam.

"They have a point but . . . Shit." He glanced at me.

"They're right. Tough as it is to run for cover, I don't want you getting whatever Bryce has. Don't particularly want to get it myself either."

The elevator doors started to close. I reached out to stop them.

"I agree about the not-getting-infected part. But we can watch from here, right? Safe distance?"

"Except the elevator is going to sound an alarm if we keep holding that door." He prodded me off. "We stay here. Where's the nearest stairwell if we need a quick getaway?"

I pointed to the Exit sign over a door beside us.

"Good."

"God, we're getting responsible," I said.

He smiled. "Being careful just means we'll live long enough to have more adventures."

The team broke into Jordan's office. I strained to hear, but only picked up footfalls and hushed instructions from Estrada.

Then a low moan came from the other end of the hall. I glanced around for any of our team, but they'd all disappeared into the office. Adam and I crept toward the sound.

"Help," a voice rasped. "Please help."

A young woman was making her way along the hall, leaning against the wall as she came. She was covered in blood. I started forward. Adam grabbed me.

She saw us, and her head lolled as she struggled to make eye contact.

"Puh-please help me."

She kept shuffling along, leaving a smear of blood along the wall. Her arms and face were covered in deep gouges that oozed blood. Her legs were scratched up, too, her pantyhose in shreds.

Adam clamped a hand on my shoulder and backed me up. "We need to get help for her—"

The woman stopped and started scratching at her arm, her nails digging bloody furrows as she moaned, "It burns. It burns."

I remembered the laboratory. The patient swathed from head to foot, desperately trying to scratch.

"She wasn't attacked," I whispered. "She's infected. I'm getting help."

I raced down the hall to the open office door and burst through. There were two people on the reception floor. One was a man in a suit, his shirt in shreds, torso covered in scratches, the bottom half a sodden bloody mess. The other was a guy barely out of his teens.

Aaron was holding the young man down as a team member bound his throat, the blood pumping so hard I knew he wasn't going to make it. Aaron struggled to keep hold of his hands, both slick with blood. One got free and went straight for his own throat, clawing. Aaron managed to grab it before he did any more damage.

"Stay back, Savannah," Aaron growled without looking up.

Almost everyone was doing that—standing back. The team member binding the young man was gloved and masked. The others stood around, watching.

"There's a woman in the hall," I said. "She's infected."

Estrada sent one of the team out after her.

"A woman called this in," I said. "Where is she?"

"In here," Cassandra called from the next room.

I found Cass prowling around a big office. On the floor lay a woman a few years older than me, blond, dressed in a blouse and skirt. She was lying in a pool of blood.

"Did they shoot . . . ?" Another step and my question was answered. The young woman's face was partially changed, brow and nose misshapen, bloody teeth bared.

"The virus appears to have been more successful with her," Cassandra said.

"Not if they were trying for invulnerability."

"True, but I might suggest you step away. Just in case."

I moved back fast. Cass opened the door to a private washroom, poked her head in, and looked around.

"Looking for clues?" I said.

"I sense someone." Vampires can detect signs of life. "It's very faint, though. Someone not long for this world."

"Still a potential hazard. Or someone who needs help."

"My thoughts precisely. In that order, as well." She left the office, still talking, expecting me to follow. "Is your sensing spell working, Savannah?"

"Let me give it a shot."

I cast. It clicked on the first try. I could pick up the people in the reception area. No one else here, though—the spell doesn't work on those without a heartbeat, like Cass. But there did seem to be something in the other direction. Faint, like she said.

I started walking that way. Cassandra swept in front of me. Halfway down the hall, she stopped and tilted her head. Then she pivoted toward a half-open door.

It was dark inside. She went first. I brought up the rear. As I stepped through, a figure lunged out behind Cass, appearing from the darkness. It stopped abruptly.

"Savannah," a soft voice breathed. "Thank God, you're here."

Roni took one teetering step toward me, then collapsed on the floor.

CHAPTER 37

We stayed with Roni as the Cabal medical team arrived and got busy, sedating the wounded and carrying them down to a waiting van. We brought Roni with us straight to the airport where the backup jet was now waiting. We'd been in touch with Lucas. The situation in Dallas was under control, so he wanted us to take these victims back to Miami.

We loaded the wounded and the dead into the cargo area. All except Roni.

As far as the medic could tell, she wasn't showing any signs of infection. It looked as if the infected woman had started making a meal of her then got distracted, maybe by the tactical team bursting in. Roni was in rough shape. Really rough shape. She'd lost a lot of blood—and a fair bit of flesh—in the attack. For now, all the medic could do was staunch the bleeding, load her up on drugs, and hope she made it back to Miami.

One problem with pain meds is that they have a tendency to put you to sleep. It might have been more humane to let her drift off into drugged oblivion, but we didn't have time for humane. We needed her awake, which meant the medic had to give her a shot to keep her lucid.

"What happened in there?" I said as soon as she was conscious.

Her gaze went from me to Adam, whom she'd met, then

to Cassandra and Aaron. She stared at them, then whispered, "You're the vampires, aren't you?"

Aaron nodded.

Roni squeezed her eyes shut. Tears brimmed along her lashes. "I wish I'd never heard of vampires. I wish I'd never heard of any of it. Vampires, werewolves, demons." She opened her eyes and met mine. "And witches. I especially wish I'd never heard of witches."

How different her attitude had been a week ago. Then she'd been a witch hunter who dreamed of being a witch. A human, who dreamed of being superhuman. She'd been getting blood transfusions that Giles promised would grant her that dream, as she was taught tiny spells to "prove" it worked.

"What happened?" I said again, firmer now.

Her eyes closed, tears squeezing out. "I thought he was going to make everything better. Make the world better. That's what he said and he made it sound so real that we all believed him. We followed him. We did everything he asked us to." She opened her eyes. "Did you find out who he really is?"

"Gilles de Rais," I said. "Slaughtered dozens of children in fifteenth-century France."

"He said that wasn't true. He said he found the secret to immortality and when he wouldn't give it to his enemies, they told those lies about him. They had him executed. Except he didn't die, because he'd found immortality through his research."

"Or through bargains with demons," I said. "That's part of the legend, too."

Her gaze dropped. "He told us he'd found it through research, by accident, and only now perfected it. Everyone believed him. Some believed him so much that they volunteered to be test subjects. Others waited, but then they got tired of waiting. Like Dave."

"Dave?"

She looked toward the back of the jet, where the rest of the wounded were in quarantine.

"The young guy who got infected?" I said. "He did that to himself? How?"

"The water. In the office."

"You poisoned the water cooler?" Adam got to his feet. "That means there will be more employees infected. I need to warn—"

"There aren't any more," Roni said. "That was the idea—put the stuff in after the office closed. Only Mr. Jordan stayed late with two staff. I wanted to wait until they left, but Dave called Giles. I knew what Giles would say."

"Get in there and dose the water."

She nodded. "Dave did it. He pretended—" Her face convulsed with sudden pain.

"Forget how he did it," I said. "So it was just those three, then Jordan left."

"There was another woman from down the hall. She stopped by to talk."

Adam stayed standing. "I'll call the Houston cleanup team and get that water gone."

"So Dave decided to help himself to it," I said to Roni.

She shivered. Aaron pulled the blankets up around her and she whispered her thanks, then said, "That's who's left. The ones who are as crazy as Giles. And some who just keep hoping. Keep telling themselves Giles isn't crazy, he's just . . ."

"Devoted to the cause. Really, really devoted."

She nodded. "It all went wrong so fast that most of us were . . ."

"Blindsided," Aaron said.

She nodded again. "First we heard about the Cabals getting involved, and that made people nervous. Some had worked for the Cabals. They spread stories. Then they disappeared and we told ourselves they'd just left but . . ."

She swallowed. "When the lab blew up, Giles tried to keep it a secret, which was a bad idea because when people found out, they figured he had a reason for hiding it from them, that it meant the whole plan was derailed, the virus gone, Althea dead."

"Althea" was Anita Barrington, a renowned immortality quester and Giles's partner. She'd died escaping the blast.

Roni continued. "Then we heard about the subway and the wedding, and Giles said it was a sign that we needed to act faster. But hearing about people dying because of super-naturals made some members think the *opposite*."

"That revealing ourselves might be a bad idea."

"At least we should slow down. Then Thomas Nast died and people were talking about angels and demons and . . . it just . . ."

"The liberation movement imploded," I said. "Too much pressure from too many sources. Members bailed. Outside support dried up. Giles went ballistic and swore to show them all the error of their ways by launching the first wave of infections. With a virus that still hadn't been proven. Am I close?"

She nodded. "He said it worked. That they'd finished trials and Bryce Nast was an immortal, superhuman warrior. He even showed us pictures. That's why Dave drank the water."

"Photoshop is a marvelous thing," I said. "My brother is lying in a hospital bed in Miami."

Her gaze dropped, and I knew that whatever she'd been telling herself, she'd still hoped she was wrong.

"Are there two strains of the virus?" Adam said. He'd come back partway through the conversation. "The one in Austin seemed different."

She nodded. "That one has to be injected. The other can be spread through water or food, which is easier, but the chances of it working aren't as high."

"So what's the plan now?" I asked.

"I don't know. Giles stopped talking to me. He just gives orders through Severin and Sierra. I know he was trying to contact Lucifer. He says Lucifer holds the key. Lucifer can make this work."

"Where is he?"

"I—I don't know." She started to shake. "I want to help, but I don't know. No one does."

"The place where they were holding me. Where is it?"

"In Indiana."

"Where in Indiana?"

"N-near Indianapolis. B-but not too near. It isn't in a city. I've never gone there by myself. We just get in the van and Severin or Sierra drives."

I tried to get more—landmarks, distance from the airport, anything. I kept the grilling as gentle as I could, reassuring her that it was okay, no pressure, but of course there was pressure and she knew it, and it wasn't long before she began hyperventilating. Then the medic intervened and said he had to sedate her for the rest of the trip. Whatever else she could share, she'd need to do it in Miami.

Veronica Tucker died before we landed. There was no agonizing, dramatic exit. We weren't even sure exactly when she passed. We were sitting there, talking among ourselves as she slept. Then the medic came in to check on her and said she was gone.

Her injuries had been severe. He told me he'd doubted she'd make it through the trip. He kept reassuring me until Adam told him to shut the fuck up. I hadn't asked him if my interrogation led to her death. I understood that it may not have helped, but we needed that information.

I hadn't liked Roni. She'd gotten me kidnapped and could have gotten my friends killed, all because she wanted supernatural powers so she could be "special."

A silly, selfish twit. Not the best epitaph. I hadn't wanted her dead, but I wouldn't lie awake at night thinking of how it could have been different. She'd done us wrong and then she'd helped us. The slate was clean.

The jet landed right after that. We were getting off when I stopped and hurried back on, Adam behind me. The medic popped his head into the main cabin as I headed for Roni's body.

"I need to grab something from her," I said. "Does she have any rings?"

The medic stared at me.

"It's a personal item," Adam snapped. "In case a necromancer needs to contact her spirit to ask more questions."

The medic mumbled something about tending to the living and withdrew. I folded back Roni's covers. She was indeed wearing rings.

I was tugging one off when Roni tugged back, her arm jerking.

Adam yanked me away. "She's infected."

Roni's eyes opened. They stared at the ceiling. Then her lips parted. They stayed like that for a moment, then she whispered, "Child of Asmondai. Is that you?"

"Who are you?" Adam said.

The corpse didn't move. It just stared blankly at the ceiling.

After at least ten seconds, we heard another whisper from the corpse. "Kimerion. I am Kimerion."

"Yeah?" Adam said, stepping forward. "You're no demi-demon if you can't move that body."

"Weak," the voice rasped. "I got too close to de Rais and Balaam's demons found me. Haven't been able to contact you."

That part was true—Kimerion had been out of contact for days.

"Lucifer," Kimerion said. "De Rais needs to summon Lucifer. His only chance."

I sighed. "We know that."

"Like your grandsire, you have no patience," the demi-demon hissed. "Yes, de Rais has long wished to summon Lucifer. That wish is now an obsession. He is desperate. He thinks he knows the key. He no longer waits and plots to obtain it."

"And that key is ∴ . . . ?"

"The blood of Lucifer."

"Hope," I said. "He thinks her blood will open the lines of communication with Lucifer. Let Giles offer his allegiance. Cut a deal."

"No deal. No allegiance. A threat."

"What?"

Adam answered. "He'll threaten to kill Hope and her baby."

"Threatening a lord demon? Is he crazy?"

"I believe we've already established that," Cassandra said, coming up behind me.

"But that won't work. Lucifer may take an interest in his children, but not enough to save her."

"Lucifer is diff—" Kimerion began.

A long, exhaled hiss of breath. Roni's eyes closed.

HOPE

Karl was prowling. From one side of the bed to the other, into the hall, down the hall, up the hall, back to the bedroom, pacing like a caged lion. Or caged wolf, Hope supposed she should say.

She could stop him. Tell him he was making her dizzy and keeping her from getting some rest. But she was enjoying watching him pace. He was wearing only sweat pants and the sight was very nice indeed, muscles rippling under scarred skin. It was not a sight she got to see outside the bedroom—he was too self-conscious about those scars.

He paced back into the room and stopped at the foot of the bed.

"You should be sleeping."

"Mmm. Later. Not tired yet."

Hope gave him a once-over. He chuckled and bent forward, hands on the end of the bed.

"I could help with that," he said.

"You could . . ."

"I will."

He crawled across the bed and tugged down the sheet over her, his hand sliding down her thigh. She considered the offer. Not sex, sadly. That had gotten unwieldy a couple of weeks ago, and they'd switched to backup plans. Karl's backup plan was nice. Very nice. However . . .

"Not tonight," she said, moving his hand away before she changed her mind.

His brows shot up and she sputtered a laugh.

"Never thought you'd hear those words from me? Sorry. But you're distracted and I'd rather wait until you're not. Otherwise . . ." She lowered her voice. "It's less than perfect."

Now it was his turn to laugh. That was the thing about Karl that others didn't understand. His ego might barely fit in a room, but he knew it. It was like that muscular body, developed as a way to deal with his world, so much a part of him that it didn't take much to maintain. Karl knew what he was. A first-rate fighter. A peerless jewel thief. A wealthy, cultured, powerful, handsome man. Not a bad catch, really. If you could get past the ego part.

Hope told him so as he slipped under the sheet and lay down beside her. He only laughed and tugged her against him, head on his arm.

"If you were concerned about my ego, you shouldn't have agreed to marry me," he said. "Or have my baby. Beautiful young wife. Beautiful baby on the way. Two more reasons for me to be very, very pleased with myself."

"She might not be beautiful."

His brows shot up again. "Genetically impossible."

Hope laughed and moved closer, closing her eyes to luxuriate in the heat of his body. His hand moved to her stomach.

"How is she?" he murmured.

"Sleeping, I think. I haven't felt her move in a while."

His hand massaged her stomach.

"Are you trying to wake her up?"

"No, of course—"

The sheet bobbed as the baby kicked. She glared over at him. "Happy?"

"Sorry."

He rubbed the spot. She sighed, but only to be dramatic. These days, she should know better than to tell him when their daughter had gone quiet. It only worried him, and he had enough to worry about.

Hope thought back to the first time she'd met Karl Marsten. At a museum fund-raiser where he'd been determined to steal something and she'd been determined to stop him. Had someone told her that she'd be married to Karl Marsten one day, she'd have laughed herself to tears. She might have grown up as a socialite, but Karl was exactly the kind of man she'd spent her life avoiding. Even after they became friends, the thought of winding up here, in his bed, wearing his ring wouldn't have occurred to her. Okay, maybe the "in his bed" part. But definitely not the ring. And the baby? Unfathomable. Karl Marsten was not the kind of man to be tied down with a wife and child.

On their wedding night Hope had raised the issue of children. She'd done it jokingly—*okay, we're married now, so when do we take the next step?* She could still remember his face when she said it. His expression. Not shock. Not horror. Longing, quickly hidden as he stammered and mumbled. Yes, stammered and mumbled, two things she would have insisted were beyond Karl Marsten's capabilities.

When would they start a family? Well, he wanted one. That is, if she wanted one. He hoped she wanted one. But there was no rush. Not really. She had her career, and of course, when she was ready, he'd take his share of responsibilities. More than his share, if that helped. But it really was up to her. Entirely up to her. So . . . when did she want to start a family?

Now. That's what she'd said. Now. And while there was no way of knowing for sure, no one would ever convince her that their daughter was *not* conceived that night. Their wedding night.

"You should sleep," Karl said, pulling her from her thoughts.

"I know. I'm just . . . I guess you're not the only one who's distracted."

"I'm less distracted now," he murmured, his fingers dropping between her thighs. "Why don't you let me see if I can help with—"

A cell phone rang. Karl leaped up—one second she was resting against him, the next he was standing beside the bed, having somehow managed to not even get tangled in the bedsheets. She rose to say that it was just one of the guard's phones—theirs were on the bedside table, silent. But when she opened her mouth, he motioned her to stay quiet.

She sighed and lay back on the bed. And just when she'd been about to take him up on that offer. The truth was that Karl wasn't going to be any less distracted until every member of the reveal movement was dead or locked in a Cabal prison.

Hope sighed again. She supposed that protective streak was the price you paid for being with a werewolf, but even Clayton seemed positively nonchalant about his family compared to Karl. She didn't even want to think what it would be like when their daughter was old enough to date. It might be wise to fit her for a nun's habit at birth.

Karl was now standing in the hall, leaning over the stair railing, straining to hear the conversation. He didn't need to strain. The guard was one of those guys, usually encountered on public transit, who doesn't quite trust the amplification qualities of modern technology and practically shouts into the receiver.

Even Hope could hear him say "What?" into the phone.

Karl tensed, but the guard's tone didn't give any cause for alarm and she wasn't picking up any chaos waves.

"It's nothing," she said. "Come back to—"

He lifted a finger, still asking her to be quiet.

"Sure," the guard said. "Bring it over."

"What's going on?" Karl called down when the guard rang off.

"Nothing, sir. Peters next door offered to bring over some pizza. He has extra." A pause. "Would you like some?"

The guard seemed relieved when Karl said no. She didn't blame him. While Karl was careful not to eat too much in public—even with those who knew he was a werewolf, he considered it uncouth—the night guards had arrived to find the fridge bare. As high as a normal werewolf's metabolism runs, it has nothing on a stressed-out one.

Karl retreated to the bedroom, closed and locked the door. She pulled back the sheet and he climbed in, pulling her into a kiss that made her decide maybe he wasn't as distracted as she feared and—

The doorbell rang. Karl growled at the interruption. Hope laughed, wrapped her hands in his hair and pulled him back down—

The room swirled into a dark vision. A flash of light. A voice said, "What the hell?" There was the soft whistle of a silenced gunshot. Another flash. A man lying on the floor, eyes open and unseeing, beside his head a pizza box, slices spilling out.

Hope jerked upright. Karl swore and reached for her shoulders, massaging.

"Relax," he murmured. "Just relax. It'll pass—"

"No." She wrenched away from him and scrambled up, words tumbling out. "It's real-time. A chaos vision. Downstairs. The guard. He's—"

Karl was off the bed before she could get out another syllable. A split-second pause while he listened. Then he grabbed her, fingers digging into her arm, hauling her out of the bed even as he murmured apologies. He threw open the sliding closet door and pushed her inside.

"Do not come out," he whispered. "No matter what happens, Hope, do not come out. Do you understand me?"

She wanted to say, *No, don't go. Come with me. Hide in the closet. Lock the door and hide, just hide, please hide.* She knew it would do no good. As she blinked back chaos flashes from downstairs, she knew what was happening. The guard from next door had betrayed them and they were under attack and it didn't matter how many guards were on their side, how well trained they were, Karl had to go down there and he had to fight.

So she nodded and reached up on tiptoes to kiss his cheek, but it was too late, he was already turning away, not noticing. She wanted to call him back. *Just wait. Wait one moment. Please, please, please.*

The closet door closed. His footsteps whispered across the carpet. And he was gone.

She moved to the door, went to press her ear against it. A blast of chaos—light and sound and terror and rage—sent her crashing into it, and she stumbled back as fast as she could, before anyone heard. Another chaos blast. A flash of Karl, grabbing a black-clad man at the top of the stairs and breaking his neck before throwing him over the banister. Hope took a deep breath and forced herself to back into the corner, then lowered herself to the carpet, knees up as far as they would go with her swollen stomach. She huddled there and closed her eyes and let the visions sweep over her.

Chaos. It was food and drink to a demon. It was a drug to her. There's good chaos—happy confusion, joyous celebration—but that was like watered wine to an alcoholic. She needed the stronger stuff. Hate. Rage. Fear. Pain. As the battle raged below, Hope should have been in heaven, drinking it in. But she felt nothing. A blessed defense mechanism—if the chaos threatened her or those she loved, she felt nothing. Nothing more than anyone else would feel, locked in a closet as her husband fought for their lives. Terror. Frustration. Helplessness.

She didn't want to cower here. She wanted to be at his

side. But she knew that even if she had the energy to fight, if she showed her face outside this room, they'd stop what they were doing and refocus everything on getting to her—and her daughter.

Benicio had asked them to stay at headquarters. They'd given in at first. But Karl couldn't rest and she couldn't sleep and neither of them could shake the feeling that they were prisoners and that Benicio only wanted them there so she could be watched for fresh visions. Karl demanded new arrangements. Benicio had taken her aside and begged—*begged*—her to reconsider. She'd refused. Make it safe someplace else, she'd said. They'd be fine there. She'd have Karl, and Jeremy would be right next door. Only Jeremy wasn't next door tonight and they weren't safe and—

The bedroom door opened with a click. Hope stiffened. It wasn't locked? Why wasn't it—?

Of course he hadn't locked it. That would be like sticking up a sign saying "Hope is in here!"

She should have grabbed a weapon. Something, anything, so she wouldn't be cowering there, waiting to be discovered. All she could do now was be still and silent.

Footsteps rounded the bed. They stopped at the closet. She clenched every muscle, ready to leap up, to attack. Another two steps. Going past? Was he really going to—?

The sliding door opened. The one *beside* her. Caught off guard, she staggered to her feet and stumbled, her back to the wall, hands raised. There stood a man with a gun, but seeing her, he turned the gun away.

"It's okay," he whispered. "We're not going to—"

He looked sharply to the left and aimed the gun at her again just as Karl shot into view.

"We aren't going to hurt her," the man said.

"Then lower that gun," Karl growled.

"I will, just as soon as you step back, sir. I don't want to hurt her, but my orders are to bring back the child. We have a doctor outside, ready to deliver the baby if anything goes wrong."

"You son of a—"

"I do *not* want to hurt your wife. Please just step—"

A shot. Hope staggered with the blow, feeling it hit her, pain ripping through the back of her skull.

Back of her skull? No, that wasn't possible. She was facing the . . . She looked at the man's face. The shock on it as he stumbled out of the way. Out of Karl's way. Karl pitching forward. Karl falling.

Another shot. Karl's body jerking. Jerking as the bullet hit him. That was it. The only reaction. No flash of shared pain in her brain. No slamming fist of chaos.

Karl hit the floor. Hope leaped out, screaming, and dropped beside him. She saw the blood on the back of his skull. Saw the bullet hole. She saw it and she searched desperately for the faintest hint of chaos from him. One hint of pain. One hint of fear. One hint of anything. Anything.

But there was nothing.

Nothing.

CHAPTER 38

I called Benicio to tell him about Giles's new target as we left the plane. He told me that Hope and Karl were at their condo, which wasn't surprising, given the hour. There were five bodyguards already there—two on sleep-shift next door—since Jeremy and Jaime were still in Dallas— and three in the condo itself. Benicio would get them all on duty hustling Hope back to headquarters.

"Karl isn't going to like that," I said. "He'll want to take Hope and run. Protect her himself. Is Elena on her way back? Karl listens to Elena."

"The jet just left Dallas. I'm going to try to persuade Karl, but if that fails, I'll have Elena head straight to the condo."

"I'll go over and talk to him."

Silence on the other end of the line. Across from me, Cassandra arched her brows.

"Yes, I know he doesn't respect me the way he does Elena, but I might be able to talk to him. Worst case, we'll hang out on his doorstep until Elena arrives."

We split up. Adam stayed with me, and Cassandra and Aaron went back to headquarters.

The three Cabal-owned condos were part of a gated community, and our driver hadn't brought the access ID, so he dropped us off a block away. To get in, we hopped a four-foot fence. Apparently, around here, they were only worried about trespassers with vans for robbing the places.

When we got to the house, Adam double-checked the number. The place was pitch black.

He rapped on the front door, then rang the bell. No voices answered. No footsteps either.

"Gone," he murmured. "Karl must have been too tired to argue."

"Damn. We're never going to get a cab out here at this hour. Really wish someone had let us know *before* we got out of the car."

A white SUV marked Security turned the corner. Adam and I ducked around the side of the condo as I called Benicio.

When I told him there was no sign of Hope and Karl, he sighed. "Too many pokers in the fire, and too many fires. They must have reported in to the security center. Let me check. Perhaps they're still close enough to come back for you two."

I hung up and we waited. When I heard buzzing, I looked down at the phone still in my hand, then at Adam.

"Not mine," he said.

He edged toward the front of the condo with me right behind him. The security truck had disappeared. We could hear the sound better now. It wasn't a phone vibrating—it was one ringing, set on an annoying buzz tone. We followed the noise to the front door, where we could hear it right on the other side.

I quickly texted Benicio. The phone stopped buzzing. Two seconds later, mine vibrated with Benicio's incoming call.

"That was you," I said. "Shit."

I explained what we'd heard.

"Let's not jump to conclusions," Benicio said. "I'll try the guard again from another phone while I have you on the line." A pause, then, "It's connecting and . . ."

The phone inside the front door began buzzing again.

"We're going in," I said.

The front door was locked, and it wasn't going to open with a credit card. Or an unlock spell. We hadn't brought any tools, so we needed to pull out the big guns—Adam's power. That meant finding another door to tackle: a burned-out front door might alert that security van on its next round.

Benicio had the floor plans on file from when the Cabal had bought the condo. He directed us around to the back, where the glass patio doors had been replaced by solid steel ones. I tried my unlock spell just in case, to save Adam from the energy drain if I could.

When my unlock spell didn't work, Adam spread his hands on the steel, closed his eyes, and concentrated until sweat popped along his forehead. Then another pop, this one from the door, then it crumbled in a shower of metallic dust.

We stepped inside. Back when this had been a patio, I'm sure the door opened into the kitchen or living room. But while Benicio left the exterior alone—to conform with the condo board regulations—he'd had the inside gutted and redone. The back door now opened into a small vestibule with mats and shoes. A code was required to get through the next steel door. Luckily, Benicio had given us that.

Inside, it was completely dark. From the outside, it had looked as if the blinds were drawn. In here, I could see that the blinds were only a cover—the windows had roll-down metal shades, too.

I lit a light ball. It failed the first time. My fault—as hard as I was trying to play it cool, my heart was racing, and I couldn't focus. I tried again and just as the last words left my mouth, I tripped. Adam caught me. The light ball sparked to life and I looked down to see an arm stretched across my path. It was attached to a guy in a suit. One of the security officers. Shot in the head.

To the left was another body: another Cabal guard. Right beside him was the corpse of a young woman dressed in black. One of the attackers.

I cast a sensing spell and picked up signs of life over our heads. I motioned to Adam that someone was up there, and we crept toward the stairs. As we stepped into the hall, I saw that the door to the front controlled-entry room was open. Propped open by the body of the third guard, the one whose phone we'd heard. There was a pizza box on the floor beside him. Ambushed by pizza delivery guys? I couldn't believe Cabal security would be that easily fooled. There must be more to it.

I hurried for the stairs. Adam caught the back of my shirt, slowing me down. I nodded and paused at the bottom, listening. Then I looked up to see the body of another attacker draped over the railing, his eyes open, head wrenched back at an impossible angle.

"Broken neck," Adam whispered. "Karl's work. Good."

I nodded. We climbed to the top of the stairs to find another black-outfitted attacker, neck broken, on his back in the hall. The master bedroom was right across the hall from the stairs. We stopped and listened, but there was no sign of anyone up here. I cast my spell again.

The pulse of life seemed to come from another room, farther down. When we reached the door. I peered through, but could see only darkness. Adam motioned for me to ready a spell. Then, on the count of three, he kicked the door wide open. We swung in, my light ball ahead of us.

The room was empty.

There was blood on the carpet. As I walked to it, I heard a whimper and whirled. No one was there. I shone my light ball around. I glanced from the bed to the closet to another door, presumably to an en-suite bathroom. All decent hiding spots if you'd been wounded. But not so good that your kidnappers would somehow fail to find you.

I strained for another sound.

"Help," a voice whispered. I tracked it to the bed. "Please."

Adam motioned for me to cover him. I readied a knock-back as he made his way toward the bed, fingers glowing. Then he lunged. No one lunged back, and Adam dropped from sight on the other side of the bed.

I ran over to see him pinning a man to the floor.

"They left me," the man whispered. "They just left me."

He hadn't even lifted his hands to ward Adam off. There was a gun right on the floor beside him, but he made no move to get it.

I noticed that his legs and arms were askew, awkward, and as Adam backed off, the man lifted his head to follow us. Nothing else moved. Just his head.

"Neck's broken," Adam whispered. "Karl snapped it and threw him in here."

"They left me," the man whimpered. "They knew I was here. They came in and they saw me. Then they just walked away."

"Where are Hope and Karl?" I asked.

He only stared at me.

"Your targets," I said. "Did they take them?"

"They left me." He met my gaze. "They just left me."

"He's in shock," Adam said. "We'll get him to headquarters and they can question him."

We headed to the hall. Through the partly open master bedroom door, I caught a glimpse of a foot.

I raced in and dropped beside the body of a dark-haired, barefooted man clad only in sweatpants. Lying in a pool of blood. With two bullet wounds in his back. More blood glistening in his dark hair. His face was turned to the side, eyes closed.

Karl.

I bent beside him and swallowed hard. I flashed on him at headquarters, holding Hope, so worried about her, always worried about her. I remembered his expression. Lost. He'd looked lost. A man who always knew exactly what he wanted and exactly how to get it, faced with the knowledge that the woman he loved was hurting and there was nothing he could do about it. That she was in danger, and there was nothing he could do except stay by her side and fight for her.

He'd done everything he could. Gave everything he could. And still it wasn't enough, because it was never enough, could never be enough.

It took me a minute to realize Adam was beside me, touching Karl's neck.

"He's been shot in the head," I murmured. "He's not going to be—"

Adam took my hand and pressed my fingers to Karl's neck. Warm skin. Faint pulse. Oh God, there was a—

I leaped to my feet. "We need a medic. Fast."

Karl was alive. Barely. The medics carried him out to a van. We went with him. I presume a second van took the paralyzed guy. Didn't ask. Didn't care.

The medic warned us that he didn't expect Karl to survive the trip. The head wound was actually only a bullet graze. It was the shots through his back that had done the damage. The medic couldn't tell exactly how much damage, only that his heart hadn't stopped. Not yet.

It didn't stop on the trip, which was surprising, considering how long it seemed to take. When we got there, the medics hurried Karl into the hospital ward, where a surgeon and her team waited.

I overheard the surgeon tell Benicio that it was a miracle Karl had lived this long and maybe they should just keep him comfortable and try to revive him long enough to say good-bye to his Pack. Benicio told her to get Karl into that operating room and make sure he lived long enough to say hello to his daughter. A tall order. One I don't think even Benicio believed could happen, but his tone was the incentive the surgeon needed.

As soon as Karl was rushed into surgery, I went to sit with Bryce. He was still comatose, but I wanted to sit with him. Sean was back in L.A., dealing with the fallout.

When Jaime and the werewolves arrived, Elena took it the hardest—she was the closest to both Hope and Karl.

Clay stayed at her side, but didn't try to calm her down. Calm wasn't what she needed. She took charge, getting all the details on Karl's condition, even if she needed Jeremy to translate the medical lingo. Then she turned her attention to the efforts to track Hope, marching upstairs with Clay to see what was being done.

"You want to be with them?" Adam whispered as they left.

I looked toward the operating room. I wanted to know what happened in there, but sitting with Jaime and Jeremy wasn't going to help Hope. As long as someone was here to speak for Karl, I needed exactly what Elena needed—action.

We got as far as the elevator before Jaime came after us.

"I know this might be the last thing on your mind right now, Savannah," she said. "But your mom figured out who took your spells. It's a long story, but the short version is that she's working to make contact with him. That's not easy. He's . . ."

"Someone who's not supposed to make contact with us," I said. "A deity, right?"

"Er, no. Not exactly. He's a eudemon." She hurried on. "Which means he's not the kind of demon we're used to—" She glanced at Adam. "And why am I telling you this? You're the demonologist. Sorry."

"I know what it is, too," I said. "Cacodemons are the type that make deals and babies. Chaos demons. Eudemons don't have a chaos hunger, which means they have little interest in our world. They're impartial observers. Not demonic, not celestial."

"Yes, well this one has trouble with the impartial part. I think he's been observing for too long, and he's itching to get out of his seat and get involved. It's not the first time he has. Both your mother and I have had run-ins with him."

"Aratron," I said.

"Yep. We don't know why he's done this. He's been helpful before. This is not helpful."

"Actually, he thinks it is. And he may be right."

I told her about Aratron's master plan—take my spells and teach me to learn to fight without them. "Lousy timing, it's true, but I guess if he took away my spells when I was just manning the agency reception desk, I'd have no incentive to learn the lesson. And he hasn't let anything catastrophic happen. When I needed to protect Cassandra in L.A., he gave me full power plus."

I hesitated and glanced at Adam. He nodded.

"Tell Mom to hold off," I said to Jaime. "If I need help, I'll ask for it, but for now, I'm going to trust Aratron to let this play out. If he's a eudemon, he's not going to screw me over for a chaos feast." I looked at Adam again. "Right?"

"Right. Historically, the role of eudemons is said to be one of balance. We've rarely seen them get involved, so they've been considered irrelevant. But in this case, it seems Aratron is fulfilling his role—trying to restore balance. We'll trust him until he shows us that we can't."

Upstairs, we found Elena and Clay with Benicio interrogating the man whose neck Karl had broken. It looked like the guy was going to be paralyzed for the rest of his life, which was likely to be very short anyway—I doubted Benicio planned to fund long-term medical care for him. But no one was telling him that.

When we arrived, a doctor was reporting that they could move the man to the Cabal hospital for "further examination and treatment" as soon as Benicio was done questioning him. The doctor said nothing about his condition or prognosis, but his calm tone would suggest to the panicked man that treatment was possible, and that the sooner he answered Benicio's questions, the sooner he'd get treatment. When you're lying on a gurney, paralyzed, you'll take your optimism wherever you can find it.

Brett—that was his name—started with the whole "it's all gone wrong" lament we'd heard from Roni. At least she'd had the sense to turn stool pigeon and alert us to the attacks. Brett was only experiencing his epiphany now that his life was on the line.

In Brett's case, his loyalty had one advantage. Giles seemed to have shut Roni out because he'd questioned her commitment to the cause. With Brett, he'd been more forthcoming.

"He's going to use Hope Adams to summon Lucifer," Brett said. "I'm not exactly sure how."

"Just tell us what you can," Benicio said.

"People started leaving the movement, but they didn't completely break ties. They just stopped checking in regularly. They made up excuses. They needed to get back to work. Someone in their family was sick. Whatever. They're keeping in touch, though."

"Waiting for something to happen," I murmured.

"Exactly. That's what pissed off a lot of us. We're doing the real work, the dangerous stuff, and they're hanging back, waiting to see if we succeed before they'll commit again. Giles promised he'd get them back. He just needed to do something really big."

"Like kidnap Lucifer's daughter."

Brett nodded. "He was keeping it all hush-hush, so it'd be a big surprise. Once he had her, he'd let everyone know. If they didn't return, they'd be kicked out."

Now, if some guy had said to me "Hey, come watch me summon Lucifer and threaten to kill his daughter and his first grandchild," I'd have caught the next plane heading in the opposite direction. But these were regular supernaturals, and they had no more experience with demons than your average human. They didn't know any better.

"When is this demonstration supposed to take place?" Benicio asked.

"As soon as possible. But he has to give people time to get to the compound. He was talking about doing it tomorrow night if they got her tonight." He paused. "Or I guess it's tomorrow already. Tonight, then. After people have had time to arrive."

"And this compound? Where is it?"

That's where Brett—like Roni—was a lot less helpful. Only select members knew the location. The rest only knew that they flew into the Indianapolis airport, were picked up in a van and were driven out into the countryside for a couple of hours.

"We can try contacting Kimerion again," I said. "Or even Asmondai. A demon will be able to find it."

"No, they won't," Brett said. "Giles knew demons and deities would get involved and interfere. He chose a location they can't find. He can summon them there, but they can't locate it on their own."

There was nothing else he knew that might prove useful, so we left him then, to the ministrations of the Cabal medical team.

When we stepped out with Benicio, I asked Adam. "Do you know what kind of locations he's talking about? Ones that demons can't find?"

"I have some ideas—" He stopped. "Demons and deities. That would cover demons and demi-demons, demi-gods, angels and presumably anything higher up the celestial hierarchy. But there are other entities. Lower spirits."

"Which we have no way of communicating with," I said. "I've summoned elemental spirits by accident, but they don't speak."

"Whether they're even sentient is in question," Adam said. "There are older entities that might try to pass on a message, but don't really know how."

"They would be limited to old languages," Benicio said. "Their knowledge of even those might not be sufficient to communicate coherently."

"Hope's message," I said. "Someone was giving us directions."

"Directions" was pushing it. The spirit had done exactly what you'd expect from a being that doesn't have a lot of experience communicating with humans. He'd given lots of details that were useless until you plugged in the theory that the place was in or near Indianapolis and had magical properties that would keep out trespassing major entities. Then you could start plucking out the geographic references and making sense of them.

Benicio called the entire research department in early, along with a few people from HR, and put them to the task of finding all staff—from janitors to managers—who'd lived in Indiana.

By seven, the research wing was busier than I'd ever seen it. The employees weren't thrilled to be dragged out of bed so early, but they were a bit happier when they found a gourmet breakfast buffet waiting for them, and a lot happier when Benicio promised them all three paid days off for the inconvenience, plus bonuses for anyone bringing him useful information.

I hoped Adam qualified for those bonuses, because he showed up the Cabal's entire team. He focused on sites that supernatural historians called "spirit blocked." In other words, sites that higher order spirits were said to be unable to locate.

Most were on ley lines and other geographic locations that humans think have special powers. They don't. But like ordinary humans, supernaturals hold a mishmash of beliefs, human and otherworldly. So they, too, often seek out these "special" spots to conduct powerful rituals. Maybe out of honest belief or maybe like clutching a rabbit's foot while picking the lottery numbers—you're pretty sure it's not going to help, but it can't hurt.

Now if your average person is asked to locate the nearest ley line, he's going to have some trouble. Same with supernaturals. So there are about a hundred "hot spots" that get passed along among practitioners. When supernaturals flock to these sites and conduct rituals for a century or two, mystical or not, you're going to screw with the mojo of that place. It becomes spirit-blocked, which is great, because then you don't have to worry about unwanted guests. Which means the places become even more popular.

There were six spirit-blocked sites within a four-hour drive of Indianapolis. With that list, and staff familiar with the areas, plus researchers analyzing satellite photos, we soon found our spot.

Karl was out of surgery. He'd survived, but now the surgeon was saying it would be a miracle if he made it to noon.

After she left, Clay said, "Bullshit. You know what she cares about? Same thing everyone else here cares about. One, impressing the boss. Two, not pissing off the boss."

"They do appear to be erring on the side of caution," Jeremy said. "Extreme caution. Before you arrived, I tried to get more details of his injuries. I may not be a doctor, but she knows I understand the terminology. She stayed vague, which suggests his condition wasn't as bad as she feared before she started operating."

"She just doesn't want us to know that," I said. "If she says the bullet wounds weren't critical, and he dies, she's in trouble. If she pretends he's at death's door and she saved him, she gets a big bonus."

"Either way she's motivated." Adam glanced toward the ward. "Is Karl still sedated?"

Jeremy nodded. "He should wake in an hour or two, but I'm considering asking them to keep him under until we have news. Preferably good news."

"Yeah," Clay said. "He wakes up and Hope's gone? He's not staying in that bed. I wouldn't."

"He'll kill himself going after her," Elena said. "I say keep him under."

Jeremy nodded. "Agreed."

Elena drew Clay aside for a moment. She whispered something to him, and he whispered a response, and then she stepped back to us, turning to Jeremy.

"I'm not going to Indiana. Karl should have someone here who knows him, to speak for him if things go wrong. As Alpha, you need to lead the rescue. As Alpha-elect, I should stay with Karl."

"No," Jeremy said. "You're more capable of taking an active role in the field. You'll go in my stead."

Elena shook her head. "I don't bring any skills that Clay doesn't have. You do. If Hope's in an underground compound, your kitsune powers are going to be a lot more useful than my nose."

Jeremy looked uncomfortable, as he always did when someone brought up that side of his heritage. "They didn't help when you were trapped in an underground cell, and I'd really rather—"

"Elena's right," Jaime cut in. "We know the place is warded, and that was the problem when Elena was captured, too. Maybe your powers will work this time; maybe they won't. Point is that it can't hurt to have you there."

"So it's settled," Elena said. "Now, please go. In order to keep Karl calm when he wakes up, I really need good news."

CHAPTER 40

Three hours later, we were in the middle of freaking nowhere.

"It's not nowhere," Adam said as we paced outside the crumbling farm house the Cabal had declared mission headquarters. "It's Indiana."

"It's a cornfield," I said, waving my arms. "Even the people who lived here had the brains to bail."

"The land is owned by a farming conglomerate," Adam said. "The farmers sold their fields—"

"I'm venting," I said. "Not looking for a lesson in modern agriculture."

"Believe me, I feel your pain. And I'm going to do something about it."

He pointed past the tent they'd set up as a base. There was a decrepit shed twenty feet away. I glanced around, then cast a quick blur spell over us. When we were behind the shed, Adam caught me up in a big hug. I hugged him back, and waited for phase two. When it didn't come, I pulled back to look him in the face.

"We're hugging," I said.

"Were you hoping for something else?"

"Um, kinda. Yeah."

He grinned and kissed me. A smack on the lips that lasted about two seconds.

"Better?"

I glowered at him.

He laughed. "Personally, I'm with you on the whole distraction idea, but I have a feeling it's going to be about three minutes before someone notices we're gone and phones us, which really isn't going to help the frustration issue."

"True."

"So this is the best I can offer, as lame as it might be."

"It's not lame," I said and put my arms around him, buried myself in his neck and closed my eyes, listening to the slow beat of his heart, the tension sliding from my back as he rubbed it.

"I was sure I heard them." Paige's voice drifted over.

We disentangled fast, but it was too late. Lucas was right there, with Paige behind him.

Lucas looked from me to Adam. His gaze stayed on Adam.

"We were . . ." Adam began.

"I can see what you were doing." Lucas's voice was so cool I shivered, but it wasn't me he was staring at.

"There's a conference call," Paige said. "Trouble with the Boyds. We'd like Adam to help explain a few things."

"It'll be under the tent," Lucas said. Then to Paige. "I should—"

"Good idea."

They exchanged a look, and he walked away, ramrod straight. I felt like I was fifteen again, caught letting a guy in the house while they were out. From Paige, I'd gotten a long talk about personal safety and the expectations that could be raised by inviting a guy into an empty house. From Lucas? Silence. Disappointment, I think, but confusion, too, as if he really had expected better of me. Smarter of me.

"Shit, I'm sorry," Adam said to Paige when Lucas was gone. "I'm really sorry."

Paige had her arms crossed, but she didn't look angry.

"That was stupid," Adam said. "Really stupid."

"Not arguing," she said.

I stepped forward. "It was just a hug."

"Oh, that's not the issue," Paige said. She jerked her thumb at Adam. "He knows the issue."

Adam glanced at me. "I should have told them about us. Responsibility fail. Big responsibility fail."

"Again, not arguing," Paige said.

"I could have told you guys, too," I said.

Adam shook his head. "This one should have come from me." He looked at Paige. "I *am* sorry. Savannah and I talked, and we agreed you should know. We just . . . with everything . . . we hadn't gotten to it. I know you're not going to be happy about the whole thing—"

"I never said that. He's the one who's not going to be happy." She gestured at Lucas, now disappearing into the tent. "I told him it was coming. He thought I was 'misreading the situation.' *Pfft*. After eight years, you think he'd know enough to trust me on that sort of thing, and to accept that as brilliant as he is, he has absolutely no emotion-reading skills whatsoever."

She smiled at Adam's expression. "What, you didn't think I'd figured it out? How long have I known you? I can even tell you when things changed. Last year. After Savannah saved your butt on that that demi-demon case in Ohio. Am I right?"

"Um, yeah."

"So you knew and didn't tell *me*," I said to Paige.

"Of course I didn't tell you. I figured it would happen when you were both ready. If that took a few years, well, given the age difference, that wouldn't necessarily be a bad thing. This is fine, though. The maturity gap isn't that big."

"Thanks," Adam muttered.

She grinned at him. "You're welcome. You're still in deep shit with Lucas, and I'm not fixing that for you. This isn't the time to fix it, but making a start wouldn't be a bad idea."

"Got it."

He loped off.

Paige put her arm around my waist as we followed. "Happy?"

"Very."

She squeezed me. "Good."

I glanced over. "Lucas is not so happy."

"He's just worried you'll get hurt. Adam doesn't have a good track record—or any track record—at committed relationships. But I know Adam wouldn't start this if he didn't plan to give it his best shot. He wouldn't dare." ·

"Too much to lose. Friendships, his job . . ."

"Sure. But he also knows I have developed a very nice repertoire of spells. All of which I'll use to kick his ass if you get hurt."

I laughed, and we walked toward the tent.

SLAM's compound was some kind of old bomb shelter, surrounded on all sides by a couple of hundred feet of rocky, fallow ground. Beyond that? Cornfields. Thousands of acres of cornfields owned, as Adam said, by some conglomerate that largely seemed content to just let it grow. And had also been content, I guess, to sell or lease the shelter and the surrounding patch of land.

All this meant that we had no obvious way of getting in. There was a road . . . which ended at a twelve-foot electrified fence. The fence had a gate, but since we'd started monitoring, it had only opened twice. Once when a van left the garage, another when one arrived. Young guys with machine guns had met the vehicles, made everyone get out for a search, then let them go inside the garage. Presumably, the bomb shelter entrance was under it, but there was no way of getting close enough to use heat scanners and see how many people were guarding the entrance.

So infiltration was proving problematic for the Cortezes. The fact that the Cortezes insisted on infiltration, rather than attack, was proving problematic for the Boyds. Hence the teleconference when everyone really had better things to do.

I could see the Boyds' point. We'd found ground zero for this movement. The leader was inside, along with presumably everyone capable of disseminating that virus. There were no human observers for miles. So why the hell weren't we storming the place, killing the guards and piping deadly gas into the hole? Oh, right, there was a kidnapped woman down there. One woman. A small price to pay to contain this virus.

Lucas could have played the sympathy card. This wasn't just a woman, she was a valued ally, a friend who'd stuck around to help the cause, knowing she was in danger, a pregnant woman whose husband now lay at death's door.

He could have played the political card. This woman was a member of the werewolf Pack. Mated to a Pack brother. Carrying his child. The Pack had fought at the Cabals' side since the beginning of the crisis and to tell them that this woman was not worth any extra effort would be . . . unwise.

But Lucas knew which arguments would work. Fear and self-interest. This woman? She's the daughter of Lucifer. She's carrying his grandchild, quite possibly the first he's ever had. Did they really want to kill her? Kill her child? Had they already forgotten what Balaam did to Thomas Nast for merely arresting his grandchild? Demons didn't do well with disrespect.

Finally the Boyds agreed it was best to examine all other avenues first. We had the exit road covered by covert ops teams, so it wasn't as if the folks stuck in the bunker could escape.

Nast troops—Sean's men—would be arriving soon. A contingent of St. Cloud security and espionage agents were on their way, too. A rare show of cross-Cabal support. Fat lot of good it would do, as Clay muttered. I silently seconded him.

It didn't matter how many fighters we had. A brute show of force wouldn't get us into the compound. It just meant we'd have a hundred or more armed men milling about, bored and spoiling for a fight. The rival Cabals could start scrapping at any moment.

Lucas and Paige left to consult with the ops guys. Jeremy and Clay went with them. Adam and I didn't. Group strategizing wasn't really our thing. Besides, they didn't invite us.

CHAPTER 41

S o we blew off some steam. No private sessions. We'd learned our lesson on that one. Instead we ran a circuit in the corn.

"I think we could do it with spells," I said. "Cause a distraction, then Lucas, Paige and I go in under blur and cover spells."

"It'd have to be a distraction that didn't scream 'you're surrounded by SWAT teams.'"

"True."

Adam went quiet.

"What's up?" I said as we jogged around the far bend of our improvised track.

"I know you won't appreciate the reminder, but . . . your spells aren't up to it, Savannah. They aren't reliable enough. Lucas and Paige could cover you, but . . ."

"If they have to cover me, they might as well take in someone more useful. Like you or Clay."

"Hey, no, I never said—"

"But it's true. You and Clay have unique talents. Right now, Paige and Lucas are the better spellcasters. I wouldn't bring anything new to the table."

He shook his head. "You said you wanted to let Aratron play this out, but I think we need to try summoning him. Get your powers back."

We jogged past the base. Tactical officers stood in clusters, some checking me out, some glowering at us, as if we were showing them up by making use of our downtime.

I waited until we were in the cornfield again, then said, "Is it even possible to summon a eudemon?"

"I've seen rites in the old books." He paused. "Rites that take a week to prepare, use ingredients I've never heard of and have never actually been proven to work."

I glowered at him. "Helpful."

"I don't think we need that. If Aratron's watching over you, he can't be far. I say we try a basic summoning—"

"It won't work," called a voice behind us.

We stopped and turned to see one of the officers—a dark-haired man in his thirties—gingerly making his way through the corn.

"Eavesdropping?"

He smiled. It wasn't a big smile, barely an expression of amusement at all, but I recognized it.

"Aratron," I said. "Well, that was easy."

"You know who I am then? Good. The cloak of mystery had its charms at first, but it was getting tiresome." He waved for us to follow. "Come, children. We need to talk."

As we headed deeper into the cornfield, I said, "I know you have some master plan for me, and I've gone along with it so far, but I need my spells back. We have to get into that compound. Gilles de Rais is going to—"

"—summon Lucifer using his daughter." He peered over in the direction of the ruined farmhouse. "Jaime Vegas is here, is she not?"

"Yes, but—"

"We met once."

"Yeah, she told us, but—"

"It was when she discovered those humans learning magic. A precursor to this whole debacle. Hope Adams was with her at the time. I'd expressed an interest in meeting Hope. That never came to pass."

"I'm sure Jaime did her best. Now—"

"Oh, that wasn't a complaint. There is no way for Jaime to contact me even if she'd been so inclined. I was merely making an observation. Musing on how things have come full circle it seems. From Hope Adams to Hope Adams. Interesting, don't you think?"

No, I did not. I suspected that Hope—captive in that subterranean vipers' nest, thinking her husband was dead, and that she and their daughter would shortly follow—wouldn't find this delay all that interesting either. I decided I liked Aratron better when his visits were short and cryptic.

"If we can arrange a meeting with Hope later, we'll do that for you," Adam said. "As for getting in, we were thinking—"

"I heard what you were thinking," Aratron said. "Discussing actually. I said it wouldn't work."

"You can't give me back my spells?" I said.

"Of course I can. And I will. When you get inside that compound. But magic will not get you into it. The exterior is warded against them. Once inside, you can cast. But you cannot use spells to get inside."

"Okay, so—"

The sound of someone crashing through the cornstalks cut me short. Troy strode into the field. No—not Troy. I didn't even need to see those blazing green eyes to tell me that.

I shook my head. "You know, Asmondai, Benicio's going to start getting a little pissed if you keep possessing his bodyguard like that."

He ignored me, bearing down on Aratron. "You have interfered once too often, spirit. Did you think I wouldn't learn of your meddling? Taking the girl's powers so she cannot protect my son?"

"Um, I'm not exactly helpless," Adam said.

"You have crossed a line that you should not have crossed," Asmondai said to Aratron.

Aratron only lifted his brows. "Is that a threat, demon? Please, do tell me how you plan to carry it through. Your kind have no dominion over mine. In fact, if I recall correctly, it is the other way around. Not that we have invoked that power in millennia—you do get so resentful—but a reminder might be in order."

"Don't threaten me, spirit."

"Then save the bluster. It suits Balaam better." He turned to us. "There is another way into that pit. Gilles de Rais is waiting for someone. A necromancer whose assistance could make the difference between success and failure. Gordon Scott. Have you heard of him?"

"Oh, yeah," I said. "Class-A dirtbag who fancies himself a zombie master? The council has tangled with him a few times. He seems to think the antislavery laws don't apply to dead people. So he's mixed up in this? Why am I not surprised?"

If we'd had time to compile a list of supernaturals who might be involved, Scott would have been on it. Not only was he an opportunist, but it was rumored he'd been allied with the group that took my mother and me captive all those years ago. Using an underground compound was probably his idea, based on that experience.

"He's been de Rais's best hope of summoning Lucifer," Aratron said. "He's the one who set them on Walter Alston."

"This spirit is misleading you," Asmondai said. "Scott parted ways with de Rais two days ago."

"Yes," Aratron said. "Which is why de Rais waits. He has sent a message telling Scott that he now has Lucifer's child, which is the route the necromancer himself suggested after their failure with Walter Alston. De Rais hopes Scott will return."

"Ah-ha," I said. "So if we can find Scott and hitch a ride in with him . . ."

"Impossible, I fear. He is, at this moment, one of those empty shells he once exploited."

"He's dead? Well, he can't have been dead long, so if you know where his body is, we'll have Jaime give him a taste of his own medicine. Resurrect him—"

"He isn't merely dead. He's quite dead."

"Quite dead?"

"Flayed."

"Oh. What'd he do? Piss off a lord demon?"

"No, it was a group of your garden variety demonic underlings. He thought he might be able to contact Lucifer himself if he summoned enough of his foot soldiers. He was mistaken."

"Well, we can't work with flayed. He'd need skin." I looked at Adam, who confirmed that with a nod.

Asmondai appealed to Adam. "Are you really listening to this spirit, my son? You are brighter than that. You have studied your histories of his kind. Have they ever helped mortals?"

"They've been known to help restore balance," Adam said.

"Tell Balaam's grandchild when they last did that. And how they achieved it."

Adam looked at me. "Eudemons are said to have been responsible for several plagues."

"Which solved serious issues of urban overcrowding," Aratron said. "And led to many of the scientific advances in hygiene, medicine, and disease control that allow you to live such long and healthy lives today."

"The thousands of people who died in agony might have rather you guys found a kinder, gentler way to go about it," I said.

"Kinder and gentler does not inspire fear. Fear inspires innovation."

I turned to Asmondai. "I'm okay with the plagues."

He gave me a sour look. "You won't be, if that's what he's planning now. This virus you're trying so hard to suppress could be another method of establishing balance, as he sees it."

"Then he wouldn't be trying to stop de Rais," I said. "In this case, he's on our team."

"He's handicapped you by taking your spells. He is not on your side, girl."

"No," Adam said. "*You're* the one who's not on our side. You want this thing stopped—the virus, the reveal, all of it. Not for our benefit, but because you think it would be the end of supernaturals, and you'd kind of like to keep us around. We can be useful. De Rais thinks Lucifer will help him; you think Lucifer will destroy de Rais. So you're here to make sure we don't interfere. As for Hope? She's inconsequential."

Aratron laughed. "Your son has indeed inherited your astuteness, Asmondai. You must be very pleased."

The demon glowered.

I turned to Aratron. "What about a glamour spell to make someone look like Scott— Wait. The ward would kill that, wouldn't it?"

"It would. But you are on the right track, child. Gordon Scott can get inside those gates. You cannot use Scott himself, but you could make someone appear to be him. How can that be done without a glamour spell?"

"It can't," Asmondai said. "You're wasting their time, spirit. Perhaps you are also in no hurry to stop the summoning of Lucifer."

Aratron kept his gaze on me. "You know there is another way. A special tool tucked deep in the Cortez security cells."

"Jasper Haig."

"Who loves Lucifer's child. Who would gladly do this to save her."

Asmondai snorted. "Free a man like that? In the midst of all this? I do believe you may have a taste for chaos after all, spirit."

"Asmondai has a point," Adam said slowly. "Jaz isn't a tool we can easily control. What incentive do we offer? He might claim to love Hope, but the way he terrorizes her? That's not love. We could offer to set him free if he does this, but he'll know that's a lie. He's too dangerous. He's never getting out of there."

"Which is why he'll do it," I said. "In order to save Hope, we have to let him out temporarily. It'll be the first real chance he's had to escape. He'll take it. He's arrogant enough to think he can get away. First, though, he'll want Hope. Whether he really loves her or not, he wants her. He won't try to escape until after he's freed her, so he can take her with him. In other words, he won't try escaping until he's done what we want him to do."

Adam nodded. "That might work."

Aratron turned to Asmondai. "Your child is astute; Balaam's is cunning. Do you see how well the two of you could work together?"

Asmondai snarled and stalked off into the cornfield.

Aratron waited until he was gone, then said, "That, children, is his grudging agreement that our plan might just work. Now go. Put the wheels in motion, as they say. Before de Rais tires of waiting for his necromancer."

CHAPTER 42

Both Benicio and Lucas suspected Jasper Haig would want more than a day pass in return for saving the supernatural world. But it turned out I'd been right. He asked for nothing. If Hope was in danger, then by gosh he was going to save her. Or something like that.

So Jaz was coming. Under lock and key. Heavy locks and well-guarded keys.

Lucas had just gotten off the conference call setting this up. We were in the tent—him, me, Adam, Clay and Paige— when Jaime came hurrying over, Jeremy behind her.

"Eve's found a break in the warding against spirits," she said. "It's a small one, but she can get through with Kristof. We'll have eyes on the inside in a few minutes."

"Finally," Paige said, and everyone breathed a sigh of relief.

That relief didn't last long. The first report was certainly positive—Hope was alive. She was being held under a doctor's care. Group members were milling about. There was no sign that the summoning was imminent.

But we had hours to wait until Jaz arrived, and while it was good to have an inside view, it was nerve-racking, too. Every time my mother or father came back to report that something was happening, we were certain Giles was preparing to summon Lucifer. Then it would turn out to just be lunchtime, and we'd grumble and pace and settle back into watching and waiting.

Lucas was off with Paige, endlessly plotting and managing. If word came that the summoning was beginning before Jaz arrived, he needed a backup plan. I'm sure he had several. No one asked what they were. No one really wanted to know. They almost certainly didn't end with Hope's survival.

Finally we got word that the jet was about to land at the regional airport. Adam, Clay and I took off for the landing strip and arrived just as the jet touched down. We stood in the airfield waiting for the door to open.

"Remember that scene in *The Silence of the Lambs*?" Adam said. "Where they bring Hannibal Lecter off the plane in a straitjacket and mask? Kinda feels like that."

"Except Lecter had to kill his guards and wear their faces to impersonate them. With Jaz, we don't have to worry about the face ripping part."

"He's just a psycho with one special power," Clay said. "It means you need to keep an eye on him. Doesn't mean he's any tougher to kill than anyone else."

"Is that what you're going to do when this is over?" I said. "Kill him before he goes back to headquarters?"

"Only if he tries to get away. You don't think he'll do that, do you?"

I smiled. "Of course he won't."

The door of the plane opened. Two guards came off first and walked stone-faced down the ramp, then took up positions flanking it. Jaz appeared.

Twenty-nine years old. Black curls. Long-lashed green eyes. Cast Jasper Haig in a movie, and he wouldn't be the killer. He'd be the hot nice guy, the sweet friend that the heroine finally noticed once she got over her infatuation with the hot jerk guy. Which is probably the movie that ran in Jaz's head every time he thought of Hope.

He wasn't wearing a straitjacket. Or a mask. He wasn't even shuffling out, chains rattling in his wake. It took a second to realize that thin cables ran between his feet and his hands. Modern technology. It really lacks drama.

There was, however, one nice touch that would play well cinematically. The werewolf at his shoulder, prodding him along.

"Shit," Clay said, fumbling for his cell phone and checking for a missed message. "Something must have happened to Karl."

Before we could answer, he loped off to meet Elena. We jogged behind him.

"Is Karl—?" I began.

"Karl's fine." By her tone, it almost sounded as if she wished otherwise.

"Fine?" I said. "But he was at death's door this morning."

"Oh, he still is. Apparently that doesn't matter."

Before I could ask what she meant, she greeted Clay with a quick hand squeeze and a tired smile. He murmured something I didn't catch, and she nodded.

"Quite the welcoming committee," Jaz said. His grin lit on Clay. "Clayton Danvers. This is an honor."

"Want me to take this trash off your hands, darling?" Clay said.

"Please."

Clay took Jaz by the shoulder.

"Good," Jaz said as Clay led him away. "Your mate? Nice lady, I'm sure, but not very talkative. I'm hoping you're the chatty one, because I have a lot to ask—Oww."

I shook my head and walked over to Elena.

"We didn't know you were coming," I said.

"Neither did I. Normally, this is exactly where I'd want to be. But right now, I should be sitting at Karl's bedside."

"Benicio made you come?"

She snorted. "Benicio doesn't make me do anything. Sadly,

I can't say the same for a certain conniving bastard who happens to be a member of my Pack. I'm not at Karl's bedside because Karl is not in his bed."

She turned to the jet door. As if on cue, Karl appeared, leaning heavily on a cane. A young man hovered anxiously behind him with a wheelchair.

"Sit in the damned chair!" Elena said. "Jasper already knows you're in no shape to fight him, so the macho act is only going to ensure you don't live long enough to meet your daughter."

I expected him to snap something back. Or at least glower and ignore her. But he lowered himself into the chair and let the nurse roll him down the ramp.

"Too weak to argue, I see," I said.

"Oh, he argues just fine. He's playing along now because he already got his way."

"Someone told him about Jaz, I take it."

"Damned nurse. I could have wrung her neck. Or his. Manipulative bastard. He knew something was up. When I slipped out to talk to Benicio, Karl charmed her into telling him what was going on. I come back? He's out of bed and getting dressed. I tried to get them to sedate him, but he's on too many other drugs to risk another dose. They worried about an adverse reaction. So I was screwed."

Clayton came back to meet us, Jaz now secured in the van. "I'd have done the same if you'd been taken."

She grumbled something uncomplimentary under her breath.

"So you're saying you'd have stayed in the bed if it was me?"

She sighed and uncrossed her arms. "It's not that I don't understand. It's that I couldn't stop him. He's putting his life in danger by coming here. As Alpha-elect, it's my duty to protect him. As a Pack wolf, he should have obeyed me. When I was kidnapped and taken to that compound,

Jeremy made you stay behind. He *was able to* make you stay behind."

"Different circumstances. I stayed while we planned. Once the attack was launched, Jeremy wouldn't have tried keeping me back. You tried with Karl because he could kill himself. You could have tried harder, I bet, but you knew that the stress of being stuck in that bed could have killed him just as easily."

She sighed again. He put his arm around her waist and steered her toward the car. They murmured together, too low for Adam and me to hear, and we hung back so we wouldn't.

When they caught up to Karl in his wheelchair, we picked up speed to join them.

"I do appreciate this, Elena," Karl said, his voice quiet. "I know it's not what you wanted, but I'm grateful—"

"Stuff it, Karl. You're here because you didn't leave me a choice. Remember all those years of fence-sitting? Trying to decide whether you wanted to be in the Pack? You never really got over that, did you? Well, I'll make it easy for you. If you survive this, you're out."

Karl didn't respond. He just looked from the van to the SUV. "Where do you want me?" he asked Elena. "And, yes, right now I think I know the general answer, but more specifically . . ."

"Up front in the van. Where you will not speak to Jasper. That's the condition you agreed to. Don't forget it. You are here for Hope when we get her out. You will not interfere with the mission. You will have no contact with Jasper Haig. You agreed to all that."

"I did."

Elena pointed at the van and the nurse rolled him off.

"Bastard," Elena muttered as we climbed into the SUV.

"Punish him later," Clay said. "Or really kick his ass out. Your choice. For now, he owes you. Use that to keep him in line."

"That's what I plan to do. Now, fill me in. How exactly are we getting inside?"

Elena was not getting inside. A very limited number of people could be smuggled in with Jaz. I was going in—I knew the players and I'd been in this compound before. For backup, I needed a non-spellcaster, in case the wards extended farther than we thought. Lucas debated sending Clay or Elena with me, then decided, as useful as brute strength was, the ability to disintegrate a door might come in more handy. So, too, might the ability to pick a lock and disarm an alarm. So Adam would be my wingman.

Lucas took us aside after that had been decided.

"Will this still work?" he said. "With the change in your relationship, I'm not altogether comfortable putting you together on this."

"Right," I said. "Because couples shouldn't be trusted on dangerous missions. You should tell that to Elena and Clay. Or to yourself and Paige."

"It's not a matter of trust, Savannah. It will be different now. I know that from my early days of working with Paige."

"If you're asking whether we'll slip off midmission to make out, the answer is no."

"I don't think that's what he means," Adam said. "Being partners off the job could affect our priorities." He looked at Lucas. "I didn't just wake up yesterday and realize I have feelings for Savannah. Even before it was *this* kind of feeling, I cared about her. That hasn't changed. Your situation was different. No offense to Paige, but when you two started working together, she needed someone to watch her back. Savannah can take care of herself."

Lucas paused, then nodded. "All right then. Adam, you go and get ready. Savannah, can you hold on a moment?"

He waited until Adam was out of earshot, then said,

"You're angry with me because I'm not pleased with this new development."

"Um, yeah. No one else seems to have a problem with it."

"Because, it seems, they all foresaw this change in your relationship. I thought Paige was mistaken. Perhaps I hoped she was mistaken. Paige may joke about maturity levels, but there is still a significant age difference. He's a year younger than me, Savannah. I'm not comfortable with that. Not at your age."

"And when would you be comfortable with it. In a year? Two?"

He considered the question. "Ten. I would be more comfortable with it if you were thirty-one. Perhaps thirty."

I glowered at him.

"You asked my opinion."

"You're worried about me," I said. "I get that. I don't think you're the only one concerned about the age difference. I know Adam didn't plan to let me know how he felt yet. He thought I'd died in that blast and he kissed me when it turned out I was still alive. The cat was out of the bag. He couldn't stuff it back in and tell me to wait a few years."

I met Lucas's gaze. "Maybe I am too young. Maybe it won't work. But this isn't some random older guy I met in a bar. I've known Adam half my life. We've been friends—really good friends—for years. I think that counts for something. But however young you think I am, Lucas, I'm old enough to make my own mistakes."

"I know." He steered me toward the tent. "I suppose I'll get used to the idea. But if he hurts you . . ."

"You'll sue for damages."

He smiled. "I will."

CHAPTER 43

The plan was simple enough—get in with Jaz, who would impersonate Gordon Scott, then work backward, eliminating security from the inside out to clear the way for the rest of the team to enter without alerting Giles.

Jaz had the most prep work. He had to become Scott. That wasn't just a matter of adjusting his physiognomy to look like the guy. He had to dress like him, act like him, *become* him. As I realized what we were asking him to do, the sheer magnitude of the task hit me. He could do it in days, maybe. But we were scheduled to infiltrate in less than an hour. Inside, de Rais was getting anxious. He wouldn't wait much longer.

Turned out the task wasn't as huge as it seemed. Not for a guy who'd learned to flip in and out of identities the way Jaz had. Even before the jet left Miami, he'd told Benicio he needed every scrap they had on Scott. Not just information and photographs, but video. He really needed video.

Luckily, Scott was a perennial troublemaker. Our agency had a file on him. The council had a file. The Cortezes and the Boyds and the Nasts all had files. The Nasts—through Sean—supplied the video. They'd bought information off Scott twice and taped both interviews. Jaz had studied those tapes and the files on the flight.

When Jaz walked out of the tent, I kicked myself—hard—for not checking those photos myself. I'd met Scott.

Three days ago. He'd been one of the SLAM members meeting with Giles when Mom and I infiltrated the group. Now Jaz *was* Gordon Scott, exactly as I remembered him from our one brief encounter. He'd mastered his walk and voice and mannerisms. Earlier, I agreed with Clay that the world was better off without Jasper Haig in it. Now, seeing the transformation, I could feel what Benicio must—that this was an incredible power, and incredibly valuable. Still didn't mean I wouldn't kill the bastard if he got in the way of rescuing Hope or stopping de Rais.

Precautions had been taken to ensure Jaz wouldn't go off-plan. De Rais had already made it clear that he'd love Jaz as an ally. So what was to stop Jaz from walking into that compound, revealing himself, and saying "Here I am. Protect me from the Cabals, give me Hope and I'm all yours."

A little device taped to his side—that's what would stop him. It was a modified insulin pump, intended for diabetics. It even contained insulin. So if Jaz was searched, it would seem legit—Scott wasn't the kind of guy who'd have gone around telling people he was diabetic. But this pump was controlled by a remote, which could dump insulin into Jaz, putting him into a coma.

It was a wickedly clever, diabolical idea. Naturally I presumed it was Benicio's. Turned out it came from Lucas. Proof that as morally upright as he may be, Lucas does have Cortez blood running through his veins.

When everything was ready, we got into an old Mercedes the team had bought at the nearest used-car lot. Jaz drove. Adam and I squeezed into the trunk.

Any other time, I'm sure being curled up together in a trunk would have been deliciously tempting. But we were both too stressed to even joke about it. We spent the short trip testing our communication equipment, which fed to each other, to Jaz, and back to Lucas.

It was only about a mile to the compound gates, but it seemed to take an hour, rumbling along the dirt road. Finally, through the mike we heard Jaz power down his window.

"Hello there, boys," he said. "I bet you didn't think you'd be seeing my handsome face again, did you?"

"Mr. Scott," a young man's voice replied. "We didn't know you were coming."

"No one does, and I trust you'll keep my little secret a few minutes longer? I want to see the old boy's face when I show up."

"Yes, sir. Absolutely, sir. He'll be very pleased."

"I'm sure he will," Jaz said in Scott's smug voice. "Now, if you'll open the garage and let me park this beauty . . ."

They did. Through his open window, we heard the outside guards radio the inside ones to say that Gordon Scott had arrived and it was a surprise for Giles. Then Jaz rolled the Mercedes inside.

"Hello, boys," Jaz said, when we were in.

"Hello, sir. You can park right by the van over there."

We knew from my parents' surveillance that one van was parked in the garage, with an open space on the far side. The plan was for Jaz to back the Mercedes into that space so we could hop out, hidden by the van.

"Well, now, boys," Jaz said. "I was hoping I could leave her right here, where you two can keep an eye on her."

I stiffened. Adam clamped a hand over my mouth before I could say anything.

"Um, I'm not sure, sir . . ." one guard said.

"Oh, I'm just joshing you, boy. I'll park her over there by the van."

We waited as he backed it in. Then we cracked open the trunk and confirmed that he'd parked in the right spot.

"Bastard," I whispered.

"Get used to it," Adam said. "He's going to have some fun with us."

As if on cue, we heard Jaz call to the guards. "Hey, boys, do you think you could grab my suitcase out of the trunk?" He waited a beat, then said, "Oh, no, wait. It's here in the backseat."

"Now that he's got us in, we can kill him, right?" I whispered.

"I wish. Just remember, he's hooked up to a death machine. We go down, he goes down."

Which would be a lot more reassuring if we were dealing with a sane man. Knowing Hope was finally within his grasp might be the only thing that kept Jaz from deciding to commit suicide by Cabal and take us along for kicks.

I peeked out of the trunk. Jaz stood there, watching me. I waved for him to look around and give the all clear. He pretended not to understand.

I considered a sensing spell. After all, I was supposed to have my full powers back. Yet I paused before casting, and when I did, I caught the murmur of the guards' voices at a distance. I waved Adam out.

I cast a cover spell on Adam first, to be sure it worked. Aratron said the antimagic ward had only been cast around the perimeter, and Mom's tests supported that, but we needed to be sure. When Adam did disappear, I cast a cover spell on myself.

Then Jaz called, "Actually, I do need help with something in the trunk. Can one of you give me a hand?"

When the guard came, Jaz stuck to the script, leading him to the trunk. "Can you get that for me?"

"Get what?"

The guard leaned into the trunk, squinting to see in the dim light. I cast a binding spell. I was so accustomed to having them fail that I'd already begun a second before I realized the first had worked. Adam injected the guard with a sedative while I held the spell. Then we got him into the trunk. The guy weighed well over two hundred, most of it fat. This was where werewolf strength would have come in handy. Jaz sure as hell wasn't about to help. As we loaded the guard into the trunk, his boot clunked against the side.

"You need help?" the second guard called.

Jaz could have said, no, we were fine. But he just stood there. I zapped the second guard with a binding spell as he came around the car. We sedated him, too. Then we stripped both of their uniforms, bound and gagged them and left them in the trunk, out cold.

Adam walked over to Jaz. He was a few inches taller and about thirty pounds heavier, but Jaz didn't flinch, just stood there, smirking.

"You think it's funny to mess with us?" Adam said.

"Actually, yes."

"Do you know what my power is?"

"Do I care?"

Adam took the car keys from Jaz. He gripped them in his hand. When he opened it, metal dust spilled onto the ground.

"It works with people, too," he said. "Especially useful for body parts. Amputates, cauterizes and destroys the evidence all in one shot. If you screw with us again, Jasper, I'm starting with your fingers." He paused. "Or maybe a small body part that you won't be needing anytime soon."

I made a show of turning off my mike and motioning for Adam to do the same. Then I lowered my voice. "Look. We aren't here to fight you, Jaz. If you do this and you get away, that's not my concern. I'm here because I need a cure for my brother. You had a brother, right?"

For the first time since he'd stepped off the jet, genuine emotion flashed across his face. Grief, rage and pain, quickly reined in.

"Karl killed him, I know," I said. "Believe me, I have no love for that jerk. But I do love my brother. He's all that matters to me here."

Jaz glanced at Adam.

Adam put his arm around my waist. "I want what she wants."

"So cool the games, okay?" I said. "That pump on your side means you're stuck following the script. You might as well make the best of it. Don't blow your chance to get out of here with Hope."

He should have been smart enough to know I was bullshitting about Hope. But she was his blind spot. Or maybe he just found it easy to believe we'd let an acquaintance be taken against her will if it benefited us. He certainly would.

Adam and I put on the guards' uniforms. They were army surplus, with name tags. Then I cast glamour spells on us.

"I don't think that worked," Jaz said when we were done. "You still look the same to me."

"Because you expect to see us," I said. "The others will expect to see the guards."

He rolled his eyes, smirking slightly at such substandard camouflage powers. I pushed him toward the door to the bunker.

Despite what I'd said to Jaz, I wasn't completely convinced that the glamour spell had worked. The test came quickly. The stairs led down to a secured entrance guarded by two more young men. Jaz pulled Scott's cheerful-condescending routine. They barely looked at us, but they *did* look, which proved that we passed.

We expected them to say something about us leaving our posts. But Clay had said that these were just kids. More like hall monitors than trained guards. He was right. They let us through without comment.

We did, however, hit a snag of another kind—the "hall monitor" just inside the secured doors.

"I'm going to have to call Giles," she said. "No one's allowed past without a card." She glowered at us. "You guys know the rules."

"It's a surprise, gorgeous," Jaz said. He gave her his lazy, sexy Jaz smile, which I'm sure would have worked a lot better if he didn't look like Gordon Scott, late fifties, pot belly and jowls.

Adam tried charm, too, but his "guy" was about nineteen, chubby, with acne. My "guy" was much cuter, so I tried a sexy smile, but probably looked like I had indigestion.

Damn it. We'd been so close. Now we needed to take all three out before anyone called for help.

I glanced at Adam. He nodded. We could do this. He motioned for me to focus on the girl while he took the guards behind him. I started whispering a binding—

"Hey, Nina," someone said as the door behind the girl opened. "Do you know—?"

Two guys walked in, a young woman behind them. They stopped when they saw Scott.

"Mr. Scott," one of the guys said. "Damn, Giles is going to be happy to see you. Does he know you're coming?"

"No, it's supposed to be a surprise," Jaz said. "But this young lady seems intent on spoiling it."

"I just passed Giles back there." He turned to the hall monitor. "Want me to take them?"

"I . . ." She sighed and adjusted her name tag. "I guess so."

There was no way we could take down six people before someone raised the alarm. So on to plan B it was. At least we were inside.

As we started to follow the newcomers, one of them turned to Adam and me.

"We can take it from here, guys," he said.

Jaz hesitated, then sighed softly, as if we'd spoiled his fun. "Actually, kids, I kind of like having bodyguards. Got lots of enemies, you know. Some folks might not be too happy to see me back."

They shrugged a "suit yourself." We took one step and an alarm blipped. The hall monitor jumped in front of us.

"You know the rules," she said. "No guns inside."

We surrendered our weapons. Then we went inside.

The smell told me this was definitely the same compound where they'd held me captive. When I'd gone down this hall before, though, I'd been blindfolded. Now I took my first good look.

My parents had reported that the place wasn't that big. Just a large central meeting room and a half dozen small side rooms. Yet I'd remembered a very long walk from my cell to that meeting room. As I looked around, I realized it really was just a meeting room ringed by a corridor. In other words, they'd led me around that perimeter a few times so I'd get the impression I was in a much bigger place.

Giles stepped from a doorway. I froze. But his gaze passed right over me and settled on Jaz. Emotions flickered over his face. Negative, mostly. He might have needed Scott, but Giles didn't like needing anyone, especially not a conceited mortal necromancer who responded to his summons if and when he pleased. The anger lasted only a second, though, before Giles found an appropriate expression of delight.

"Gordon, my friend," he said. "You've come at last."

"You didn't really think I'd miss the big show, did you? Not when I'm going to play such a critical role." Jaz rubbed his hands together. "Summoning Lucifer himself. I cannot wait."

A flash in Giles's eyes suggested he couldn't wait either—for Lucifer to flay Scott for his impertinence. It made his smile turn real as he walked over and clapped Scott on the back.

"We're all eager," Giles said. "And we really do need to get this show on the road."

"Can I see the girl?" Jaz said.

That was not part of the plan, but I knew he'd ask. Giles took us down the hall and unlocked a door. When we got inside, I was surprised to see Hope just lying on a bed, eyes open, no sign of restraints. When Jaz walked over and stroked her hair, she stiffened almost imperceptibly and closed her eyes.

"Yes, she's a beautiful young woman," Giles said. "And I know you like pretty girls, Gordon. But this one is off your list."

Jaz chuckled. "Pregnant women don't really do it for me. Particularly when their daddy could turn me inside out."

Giles paused, as if relishing the image. Jaz continued stroking Hope's hair, his gaze fixed on her.

"Is she sedated?" Jaz asked.

"No, it wore off hours ago, but she just lies there. Her husband was killed when we picked her up. She seems to be taking it badly. One would think the daughter of Lucifer would have a little more fight in her but . . ." Giles shrugged. "I'm not complaining."

"I'd like a few moments alone with her," Jaz said.

"I'm sure you would."

Jaz gave Giles a look. "As I believe I pointed out, she's the daughter of a very powerful lord demon. I'm hardly going to violate her. To contact Lucifer, I need to establish a link with the girl. I can accomplish that better if we have time alone together."

"We can stay," I said.

"I said *alone*."

There wasn't much I could say to that. I hoped Giles would insist on one of us remaining in the room, but he'd had a hard enough time getting Scott here—he wasn't risking a fight now. Besides, Jaz was wired for sound, so we'd hear what he said to Hope, and Adam could incinerate the door if necessary. I also knew Jaz wouldn't hurt her. Not while he still hoped she could be his.

So we stepped outside. Giles told us to stay put. Then he left. Which meant we were free inside the compound. That would be a whole lot more helpful if we hadn't just left Jaz alone with Hope.

"Probably exactly what Jaz hoped for," I muttered. "Now what?"

"You scout, I stand guard; we both listen."

I nodded and took off.

CHAPTER 44

As I headed down the hall, trying doors and popping my head in, I could hear Jaz through my earpiece, impersonating Scott, talking to Hope about how important she was, blah-blah.

"What the hell's he playing at?" I said into my mike.

"No idea."

Then Jaz said, "Sounds like someone at the door," though when I glanced back, I saw only Adam there, leaning against the opposite wall.

"Just a moment," Jaz said. "I'll see who's—"

A thump and a hiss of pain from Jaz. I wheeled. Adam had leaped forward and was poised in front of the door, glowing fingers raised.

Inside, Jaz chuckled. "Seems you aren't paralyzed with grief after all, Hope. Just playing possum. They're fools for thinking otherwise."

The scuffle of stockinged feet against the floor. The squeak of a mattress, as if Hope had retreated to the bed.

"Yes, I'm sorry for spoiling your attack," he said. "You should have known it wouldn't work on me."

"Go to hell, Jaz."

He laughed. "You know me so well that you can see right through—"

Another scuffle, this one louder, then Jaz's voice. "I know you're angry, but in your condition, you're never going to be able to kill me."

"I'm not trying to kill you. Just to shut you up."

He laughed again. "Touché. I know you're upset because of Karl. I think you're better off without him, but that's a discussion for another time."

I muttered, "Bastard."

Adam answered through my earpiece. "Did you really think he'd tell her Karl's still alive?"

Inside the room, Jaz continued. "Right now, the important thing is you. You and the baby. It's his baby. It's all you have left of him."

"You don't give a damn about my baby, Jaz, so shut the hell up before I scream for help. If you're here in disguise, that means they don't know it's you. One shout from me and you'll be in the next cell."

"Where I'd be completely unable to rescue you. You're right. I don't care about Karl's brat. But you do, and I care about you, so if that baby's welfare is going to prod you out of here—"

"Do I look like I need prodding? I've been waiting for my chance. If you're going to get me out, then let's get on with it."

Another laugh, this one punctuated by the smack of a kiss—and the smack of a slap. Then another laugh.

"Guy doesn't take a hint, does he?" I said as I got back to Adam.

"He's just glad she has feelings for him. Hate is a feeling."

"Yeah, he can just keep telling himself that, right up to the point where she successfully strangles him. I'll be helping."

Inside, we heard Jaz try the door. He rattled the knob.

"Locked you in, didn't he?" Hope said.

"A problem easily fixed. Just give me a moment."

He rattled it again, then whispered under his breath. "Open the door, guys."

I clicked on my feed to his earpiece. "Once you tell her who's opening it."

He jiggled the knob again.

"Playing lone white knight isn't going to fly," I said. "She needs to know we're here, so if things go wrong, she knows who she can run to—"

"Is Gordon still in there?" Giles rounded the corner. "He'd better not have touched her."

"He just seems to be talking, sir," Adam said. "I think he needs a few more minutes—"

"Too bad. The show is about to start. You two get back to your posts."

Giles opened the door. "Ah, I see she's up. Good. This will work better if she's feeling more herself." He turned to us. "Still here? Go in and bind her then."

Giles handed us rope as we went in.

"I'm a big fan of yours, ma'am," Adam said as he walked in. He stopped in front of her, his back to Giles, blocking his view. Then he lifted his glowing fingers and grinned. "A really big fan."

It could have been the fingers, but I'll bet anything it was the grin, so unmistakably Adam. Hope nodded quickly and dropped her gaze.

"Thank you," she said.

I went behind her to tie her hands. Adam tried to block Giles, so I could whisper to her, but Giles said, "Her feet, Smith. Get her feet," and Adam had to bend.

Damn it. I'd wanted to tell her Karl was alive. That wasn't possible, though. So I bound her hands. I didn't dare do it too loosely. Sure enough, when we finished, Giles checked. I had left her a little wiggle room. Would it be enough if she needed it? I didn't know.

Giles pulled a wheelchair from the corner and we loaded Hope onto it.

"Good," Jaz said. "She's all set. Now, I just need about twenty minutes to prepare—"

"You've had all the time you're getting. Your audience awaits."

"Er, no, I can't just—"

"You aren't ready?" Giles turned, his face coming close to Jaz's. "Then maybe you should never have left. I don't need your theatrics, Gordon. Just get in there and perform."

Jaz argued. Even I tried, carefully interjecting a suggestion that maybe they could compromise and give him ten minutes.

"I don't believe anyone asked you," Giles snapped at me. "Now get back to your post."

"Sorry, sir, I didn't mean—"

"I've told you to get back to your post twice already, Walker. Now get back there."

"Sir?" Adam said. "I understand you need people on the doors, but I really wanted to watch—"

"Back to your posts!" Giles roared.

A group heading into the meeting room stopped to stare. The oldest was a guy I recognized as one of the leaders from when Giles kidnapped me.

"Is there a problem, Giles?" he asked.

"Nah," Adam said. "Sorry. We just got a little carried away. Hoping we could watch the show from down here. But I guess someone needs to stand guard . . ."

Giles pushed Hope's wheelchair away, taking Jaz and leaving us standing with the other man.

The man waited until Giles was gone, then whispered, "We do need all the guards on the floor, but there's the video feed in the back room. Just wait until Giles has gone."

"The room behind the auditorium, right?" I said, remembering it from my first visit.

"Exactly. But if he catches you . . ."

"It wasn't your idea."

The man smiled and clapped a hand on my shoulder. "Now, if you'll excuse me, I have a show to catch."

One good thing had come of my scouting—I'd found an empty, unlocked room. Once inside, Adam closed the door and I spell-locked it.

"Lucas?" I said. "You're there, right?"

"Yes," he said through my earpiece. "I just didn't want to distract you. I heard everything. We're coming in."

"I'm sorry. We—"

"There was nothing you could have done differently. The main thing is that we have you and Adam inside, and Jasper is with Hope. While I don't trust him to hand her back to us, I do trust him to keep her safe."

"I don't think the guards inside the garage were replaced."

"They weren't, which gives us a buffer. With any luck, we can disable the outside two and get in before anyone notices."

"We can take out the girl at the door."

"No, she's been replaced by two armed guards."

"Damn."

"It doesn't matter. I want you and Adam in there. Go to the room with the video. Watch from there. That's backstage, is it not?"

"It is. We'll be behind Giles and Jaz."

"Good. Once the guards are taken out and our men are in place, you and Adam will go in and take down Giles."

I nodded. "With any luck, once Giles is in custody and the kids in the audience realize they're surrounded by Cabal tactical goons, they'll surrender."

CHAPTER 45

The backstage door wasn't locked. As I pushed it open, I saw the room wasn't empty either. A young man and woman sat on a single chair. Even from the back of their heads, I recognized them.

Sierra turned first. "Private viewing room, chumps. Get back on duty."

I finally remembered the name of the guy we'd just spoken to. "Chris told us to watch from here, in case you two need help."

Sierra grumbled.

"Fine," Sierra said. "Sit down and shut up then."

We eased into the room. Adam closed the door behind us. There were plenty of chairs to choose from. Sierra was on Severin's lap.

They'd pulled their chair right in front of the screen. That meant we had a lousy viewing angle, but it also meant we could sit behind them while whispering to each other.

We didn't do much whispering. We were both too busy listening to the Cabal's progress through our earpieces. It was frustrating as hell, watching Hope on the video feed and knowing we couldn't help. But the cavalry was coming.

Giles's plan was to threaten Hope and bring her daddy running. It was a scene I've watched in plenty of movies. The classic demonic sacrifice. A gorgeous young woman bound to a table, knife poised above, her dark curls spilling artlessly, her amber eyes wide with horror and glistening with tears as she writhed against the ropes. Torture porn with a black magic twist.

Or that's what I imagined.

That wasn't what Giles did at all. Probably because the woman in question wasn't a nubile young virgin. She was a heavily pregnant woman that many of the audience likely felt they knew, the witty *True News* reporter who'd kept them laughing as she kept their secrets safe. Did they really want to watch her writhing on a table, a knife poised over her huge belly? Of course not. So Giles kept her in the wheelchair, wearing a loose dress to make her condition less obvious.

First, he assured his people that no harm would come to Hope.

"Lucifer will not allow it," he said. "This is his oldest surviving child. His first grandchild. We have already seen how the lord demons will interfere to protect their offspring. If a lord demon will kill Thomas Nast for his granddaughter, Lucifer will move heaven and earth to protect his own. He may wear the guise of a demon, but he is an angel. Cast out from heaven, yet pure of soul. Merciful and good."

Really? Did Giles believe that? Did anyone here believe it? Yet I could see the first row of the audience on the screen and I could tell by their faces that they did. They wanted to, so they did.

"Remember who Lucifer is. The fallen angel. The angelic turned demonic. He was cast from heaven because he questioned. Because he does not see black and white, and for that reason, he has bowed out of this fight. He cannot be sure which side he belongs on, nor which side is right. He has been burned before, so he shies away from the fire."

I had to admit the guy was good.

"What we are doing today is not threatening Lucifer. That would be blasphemy. No, what we do is exactly what we have been trying to do for weeks. Invite him to a meeting.

Give us the chance to show him why we are the right choice for all—mortal, demonic, celestial. He has not heeded our invitations, so we must take this regrettable measure. Once he has come, though, there will be no threats. No disrespect. We will explain our position and he will see our truth. Lucifer will join our cause."

A thunderous round of cheers and applause. It was bullshit, of course. No demon or angel would interpret this as anything but blackmail. Yet the lie was enough for them to sit quietly as Jaz took center stage and prepared for the summoning.

Lucas's voice came over my earpiece. "We're in the garage now. We managed to successfully reroute the external video to show images from an hour ago, covering our entrance. The two outside guards have been disabled. We're going to use glamour spells to allow Elena and Clayton to imperson-ate them and attempt to breach the next security point."

Less talk, more action, I wanted to say. But when Lucas is stressed, Lucas explains. So I kept my mouth shut until he finished, then whispered, "Sounds good."

I clicked on the feed into Jaz's earpiece. "Compound breached. Stall."

He said nothing, but I thought I heard a derisive snort. No one needed to tell him to stall. Rushing wouldn't help Hope and it wouldn't help him.

"Before I begin . . ." Jaz said. A rustle of impatience rolled through the audience. "What I am about to attempt is very dangerous, to myself, to Giles and to Ms. Adams. So I will need your complete attention and silence. Also, I know there are fellow necromancers in the room. I must warn you . . ."

Don't try this at home, kids, was the gist of his message. That and making it clear that what he was doing was not a standard necromantic ritual, and therefore would not resemble any they were familiar with. In other words, covering his ass so he could pull off a bullshit fake rite, and drag it out as long as possible.

I hate giving bad guys credits for ingenuity. Hate it more when I find myself mentally taking notes.

As Jaz droned on, Adam and I listened to Lucas's updates. Elena and Clay had made it into the stairwell. They'd disabled the guards without raising the alarm. A twenty-man tactical team had now entered the garage. Elena and Clay were approaching the final security point, where they'd take out the last—

Another voice came in behind Lucas's, muffled, talking fast, urgency bordering on panic.

"What's going—?" I began.

Lucas cut off the comm link. I glanced at Adam.

"It's okay," he murmured. "A minor hiccup. He doesn't want us overhearing and panicking."

Great, but silence only made me panic all the more.

I glanced back at the video screen. Jaz was lighting candles on a table. Lighting them very slowly, reciting gobbledygook about dark and light forces and balance. Giles stepped forward and offered to help with the lighting, but Jaz waved him aside, saying he had to do the ritual alone.

"Lucas?" I whispered. "Anyone? What's going on?"

Sierra glanced back at me. "If you two keep whispering, I'm going to kick your asses out."

"Sorry," Adam said. "Just getting impatient."

"Severin? Sierra?" A voice crackled over a radio left on the table. "We have a breach."

"Shit!" I said, leaping to my feet and forgetting, for a second, to use my guy voice.

Sierra didn't notice. She scrambled up and grabbed the radio. "Sierra over. Repeat."

"They've breached the compound. It's a Cabal. Or all the Cabals. I don't know." The young man's voice rose as he spoke.

I slid up behind her, as if trying to hear better. Adam followed.

"Cool it," Sierra said. "Have you activated the doors?"

"We're doing that now," said the guy on the radio. "The van was driving up, and they saw dozens of them, and they called it in, but then the Cabal guys saw them and opened fire and they're dead. They're all dead!"

"Okay, you need to—"

I grabbed the radio and backpedaled as Adam leaped between me and Sierra.

"Relax," I said, emulating Sierra's bark. "You need to relax. Everything's under control. This is all part of the plan. Do not interrupt Giles."

A screech of pain. I looked up to see Adam grappling with Sierra, his fingers glowing. Severin had jumped from his chair. It crashed to the floor.

"What's—?" the voice on the other end began.

"Hold your fire," I said. "Everything's under control."

I snapped off the radio as Severin ran at Adam. I cast a binding spell. It didn't work. I could feel the power surge, but nothing happened. The room was warded. Our glamours had stayed intact. Apparently we just couldn't cast in a warded area.

I lunged at Severin. His fingers latched onto my arm. I felt a blast of cold. Then agony as my flesh began to freeze. I managed to punch him in the stomach hard enough to make him let go. Then I kicked his feet out from under him and—

A grinding noise across the room stopped me. I looked over to see a steel door sliding over the entrance into the auditorium.

Back at the laboratory in New Orleans, when they sounded the alarm, they'd sealed off the infirmary with a solid steel door, one Jeremy's strength and Adam's fire couldn't breach.

I ran. There was still enough of a gap to get through—

Severin grabbed my leg. He yanked me down. Then he held me there, fingers biting in, the cold so excruciating that I howled.

Adam stopped grappling with Sierra and threw her aside. He dove at Severin and caught his leg.

"Let her go," he said, his voice a rumble, eyes glowing.

Severin gasped. He could feel the fire blazing. He didn't let go, but as Adam wrenched at him, feeling returned to my leg, fire melting ice.

I kicked Severin off and hobbled to the door as Lucas came back on the comm link, telling me they were now in the building.

The steel door was closed. I glanced at the video. Inside, the audience had heard the doors sealing.

"For your protection," Giles said smoothly. "Mr. Scott is just about to begin the ritual."

He must know what had happened, but he wasn't letting it interfere with his summoning. I quickly updated Lucas.

Adam and Severin were on their feet, facing off. Sierra bore down on them. I leaped in her way and let my glamour fall.

Sierra glowered at me. "You stupid little bitch. Haven't you learned your lesson about interfering?"

"Yes," I said. "I learned that I owe Balaam some payback for *his* interfering at the Nasts. Starting by taking out two of his faithful servants before *they* can interfere."

"Do you have any idea how pissed off he's going to be?" Severin said.

"Yeah, we do," Adam said. "But my father's just as pissed off with him, so we'll let the two of them duke it out."

They turned to Adam. His glamour was gone, too, and he lifted his glowing hands.

As Sierra rushed me, I rushed her right back. That caught her off guard, and she checked herself, giving me time to plow into her and knock her flying. As she came back swinging, I remembered her fight with Clay, her pattern, the simplistic moves.

Well, at least you were doing something useful, I imagined Clay drawling.

I ducked her first blow. Dodged her second. Caught her third. Two out of three ain't bad. Of course, it would have been even better if, by that third, she wasn't so furious that it felt like being hit with an ice-blast ray. My shirt absorbed some of the cold. It flash froze, actually, a big chunk at the shoulder shattering. One glance at that hole—and imagining my skin there instead—made me a whole lot more careful. And a whole lot more angry.

I got in a kick followed by an uppercut. That knocked her down. As she scrambled up again, I hit her with a solid kick. She flew back. I jumped on her, grabbing her forearms before she could touch me. Severin saw his sister down and stopped fighting Adam, coming for me instead. A punch stopped him. Adam made sure he stayed stopped. He didn't even bother disarming his ice-powers, just grabbed both his hands. There was a sizzle, like water on a griddle. When he let go, we had one melted ice-demon. His powers would take a while to recharge. A long while, I hoped.

Severin may have been a decent fighter. Maybe even as good as Adam. But he relied too much on his powers and when they were gone, he reacted a lot as I had. He was thrown off his game—distracted and unable to gather himself for a real fight. Adam bound him. Then he melted Sierra's ice and we tied her up with her brother.

"You know Balaam's going to set us free," Sierra said.

"Funny. He hasn't yet," I said. "I think he's given you two enough chances."

"Never," she said. "He'll come for us."

"And your point?" I said as I eased back. "That we should kill you?"

"No, her point is that's it's not too late to fix this, Savannah," Severin said. "Balaam is going to win. Whether you win, too, depends on whether you're on his side. You still have a chance. Join him and—"

I silenced him with a gag.

EVE

Eve strode up the steps to the afterlife courthouse, with Trsiel right behind her. The guards moved in to tell her it was closed. Then they saw the sword—and Trsiel—and knew she wasn't coming to look for her lawyer lover this time. They parted to let them through.

"Ukobach?" she said as they passed.

"Cell 24-D," one of the guards replied. "Is there anything we can—?"

"We've got it."

Trsiel slowed to murmur his thanks. Eve shook her head. Precious time wasted, not just on the civilities, but on what always followed—the guards practically prostrating themselves because a full-blooded angel deigned to speak to them. At least they realized he was a full-blood. Some didn't. It was his own fault really. He wore his sword on his back and dressed in casual, modern clothing. If you missed the faint glow of his skin, there was no sign he was an angel until he spoke and that melodious, compelling voice gave him away.

As Trsiel extricated himself, Eve continued down the hall. Past the courtrooms. Take a left. Down the stairs. A right. Another left. Trsiel caught up. By now they were past all the guards, so Eve snapped the blur spell and Kristof appeared beside them. While they could have insisted he be allowed in, bringing a lawyer would have signaled that they were up to something.

"There's 24-D," she said, gesturing at a cell. "But we really want . . ."

"Thirty-two-B," Kristof said. "They're holding Raim in 32-B."

The guards would never have let them in if they admitted they were here to see Raim. He was an earl in Lucifer's court. Several angels had "rescued" him as he was being interrogated by Balaam's demons, who were certain he knew where his liege was hiding. He was now being held as a prisoner of war, mostly so neither side could use him to find Lucifer. The Fates would prefer that particular lord demon stayed out of this fight.

Kristof leaned over, his hand brushing hers, voice dropping. "We'll get back to Indiana as soon as we can."

She nodded and gave his hand a quick squeeze. They'd been helping Lucas and the others at the compound when the message came. One of Kristof's informants told him that Raim was being held in the afterlife cells. Trsiel had offered to handle it alone, but interrogation really wasn't his thing. Years spent working with Eve meant he was fine with sneaking Kristof into the cells or lying about their destination, but getting information from Raim could require a little more deception than his nature allowed. So they'd zipped off, alerting Jaime to call them back if there was a crisis.

Eve opened the door to 32-B. Inside, it looked like little more than a closet. An empty closet.

"Ready?" she said.

Kristof nodded. "Right behind you."

"I'll wait here," Trsiel said, taking up a position outside the door. "But you call me in if you need help."

"I will."

Eve took a deep breath, then stepped into the cell. Light flashed, stuttering like a broken bulb. Her stomach lurched as the ground disappeared beneath her feet. Then came a jolt as she touched down so fast her knees buckled. Damn dimensional jumps. They were jarring at the best of times, but the ones into the dimensional holding cells were the worst, as if the Fates didn't want to spare decent magic on mere prisoners.

Someone shrieked. Eve gripped her sword and looked around. Everything was still bright white. Another shriek— one of laughter, not terror.

Eve blinked hard as she took a few cautious steps forward. The light dimmed and she could make out what looked like a dining room. Folding tables had been added to extend the seating to twenty. Unmatched tablecloths, but it didn't matter because every inch of them seemed covered with plates or food. Enough food for an army of imps. Turkey, stuffing, sweet potatoes, cranberry sauce . . .

The table was jam-packed with people, too. Residuals— ghosts who weren't really there, just replaying on a loop. At least twenty adults, talking and bickering and laughing, a dozen kids racing around, a dog following them, barking.

"Thanksgiving," she murmured.

"Torture, that's what it is," a voice rumbled.

"Plenty of people would agree with you." Eve stepped forward and pointed to a teen, his face contorted with pained boredom as an elderly aunt peppered him with questions. "I'm sure he would."

"I'm glad you are amused," the voice replied. "Have the Fates forgotten that the torture of war criminals is a serious offense?"

"I'm pretty sure the infliction of Thanksgiving isn't covered under the Geneva convention."

She peered around. The demon was nowhere to be seen. Not surprising, really. On these planes, they rarely took form. But Raim was here. She could feel the hot wind of his presence rushing past.

"The noise never stops," Raim said. "They talk and talk and talk. Except when they're shouting. Or shrieking. Or . . ."

His voice quivered, as if he was shuddering. "Laughing."

"Hey, be glad you didn't get the dimensional holding cell down the block. It's a circus. With mimes." She took another step. "Do you know who I am?"

"Eve, Daughter of Balaam. So your father finally swayed you to his side?"

"Nope, I'm still on *my* side, as usual."

A soft chuckle, cut short as he said, "If you've come to find my liege, I'll tell you what I told your father's minions. I don't know—"

"Yes, you do. And you're going to tell us."

"Or what? You'll make the dog bark louder?"

"No. If you tell us, and we find Lucifer, we'll help you get out of here."

"A prison break? How charming. Will you dig the tunnel? Or is that the Nast's job."

"It's a joint effort. We can't break you out, obviously. But if you tell us where to find Lucifer, Kristof will present and defend your case, free of any chits or charges. I'll speak on your behalf, make up some story about how you helped me on a previous case blah-blah. It's not a guarantee, but it's better than anything else you'll get."

"And in return, I'll hand over my liege lord?" He laughed. "Not likely, mortal."

"Kristof and I only want to speak to him. That will go in the contract. We'll tell no one else where he is. We've come to you and put forward a case that made you decide this meeting was in your liege's best interests, so you agreed, under very strict conditions. You can tell him that we tortured you into confessing."

It took a little more convincing, but Raim was reasonable. He'd help as long as they provided an ironclad contract, which Kristof already had prepared. A few quick amendments, a blood oath, and they were off, with Lucifer's whereabouts in hand.

They left Trsiel behind. That wasn't the plan—at least, not the part he knew about. He'd be furious, but it was the right thing to do. Eve had asked him to do enough already. If there was fallout from this, it would land squarely on her shoulders.

Getting to Lucifer was easier than Eve expected. He wasn't surrounded by his legions. He wasn't even surrounded by his inner court. That made sense, she supposed—it was hard to hide an army, and even the inner court would expect all their attendants to come along. There was none of that. Just Lucifer, alone in the mountains.

"Mount Nebo," Kristof said as they finished climbing from their teleport drop-off. "Fitting, I suppose."

"Is it?"

"From the stories of Moses. The Israelites were still wandering and ran out of water. God told Moses to speak to a rock. In frustration, Moses struck it instead and was, as punishment, forbidden to enter the Promised Land. He could only glimpse it from the top of Mount Nebo."

"A little harsh, don't you think?"

"Lucifer would doubtless agree. The fallen angel. Cast out when he challenged God's will."

"Do you believe that?" Eve asked.

Kristof shrugged and wiped dirt from his hands. "I believe most legends have some basis in fact."

At the top of the mountain, they found an excavated church. If she crossed over to the other side of the veil, she was sure it would be filled with tourists. But on their side it was still and empty, the wind whispering past, bringing a sprinkle of sand with each gust.

They walked inside and found a lone figure hunkered down, staring into a mosaic-lined pool of water.

"Huh," Eve said as they approached. "You know what's a really good way to fight the apocalypse? Meditate."

The figure rose and turned, and Eve's breath caught. From the back, she'd thought it was a demon taking human form, as they often did. But then she saw his face, the faint glow of his skin and his eyes.

An angel, she thought. *He really is an angel.*

An angel with a ruined face. That's what made her breath catch. Lucifer's skin was pitted and scarred, some of them white with age, others angry red. Only the skin around his eyes was untouched.

"Lucifer," she murmured.

He smiled and it was a strange smile, not what she'd expect from either angel or demon. There was no anger in it. No outrage. No arrogance. And that's what really threw her off balance. All lord demons were arrogant, and the same could be said for most angels.

She stood there, gripping her sword, her rehearsed speech flying from her mind.

"She needs you," Eve blurted at last.

"I know."

"Hope, I mean. Your daughter. She—"

"I know."

He glanced back toward the pool. Kristof took a step closer and nodded. Eve followed and saw what he did— that it was a scrying pool, and in its depths was Hope, in a wheelchair, bound and pregnant.

Eve spun on Lucifer. "And you're just watching? Your daughter—and your granddaughter—are being threatened. Threatened with death if you don't come, and you sit on your mountain and *watch*?"

"Yes."

"You—"

"What else would you have me do, Eve?" Lucifer said. "Go down there and give Gilles de Rais what he wants? Do you even know what he wants from me?"

"No idea."

A faint smile. "Then that makes two of us. I suspect, like your father and Asmondai, he only wants me to side with him as a figurehead. A mascot, even. De Rais's people know my name, as they do not know the names of a legion of other demons. If the mighty Lucifer bows to him, it will prove he is all powerful. His followers will fall in line. They'll help him release that virus. Is that what you want?"

"No. I want you to stop him."

"How?"

She stepped toward him, sword glowing as she clenched it. "How?"

"Yes, *how*. You know my daughter. What are her powers?"

"Visions. She's a chaos bloodhound."

The barest hint of a smile. "An apt description. Yes, that's her power. That's mine, too, on a much greater scale, and without the side effects she suffers. When I was cast out, they stripped me of my angel powers and gave me that. So tell me, now that Hope is in serious danger, how can her powers help her?"

When Eve didn't answer, he said, "They can warn her, but it's too late for that, just as it was too late for me to warn her. As for offensive powers, she has none. I have none."

He looked into the pool. "I could go down there and possess Jasper Haig, but he's trying his best, and I couldn't do better. I would possess Gilles de Rais if I could, but it turns out his experimentation with immortality has made him impervious to that. I could possess my daughter, but that would do little good, except to save her from her fear. I would do that—I would gladly do that—but she stands more chance of surviving without me in her head. She's bright and resourceful, as is everyone else trying to help her." He glanced at her. "As is your daughter. Which is your primary concern."

Eve didn't argue. She wanted nothing to happen to Hope—or anyone else—but she wouldn't lie. Savannah was her priority.

"Nothing I can do will help my daughter or yours," he

said. "I can only watch and have faith in my child." He met her gaze. "Do you have faith in yours?"

"Yes."

"Then do not waste time haranguing me. Your place is down there, with your child. Mine is here, watching mine."

He turned back to the pool and crouched again, staring into its depths. Eve turned to Kristof. He dipped his chin. Telling her Lucifer was right. There was no divine intervention here. It was up to them—to Hope, to Savannah, to all of them.

CHAPTER 46

As Adam and I finished securing Severin and Sierra, Elena and Clay burst into the room. They were still dressed in the guard uniforms, but their glamours were gone, snapped by Lucas so they wouldn't be shot by the Cabals.

"There's a door to the auditorium right there," I said, pointing. "But it's sealed. It's made of the same stuff as the doors at the lab. Adam couldn't incinerate it and Jeremy couldn't bust it down."

"But I can burn the walls," Adam said.

"Find a good spot," Elena said, kicking Sierra aside as she crossed the room. "We need to come out in the wings, where Giles won't see us. Or he'll use *that*."

I followed her finger to the screen. Giles stood beside Hope. His right hand gripped a knife, hidden, out of sight of the audience.

"Son of a bitch," I whispered.

"No worries yet," Elena said. "He's playing it cool and—" She stopped and sniffed. "What's that?"

Clay inhaled. "Some kind of chemical."

A clang in the ventilation system. Then a slow hiss.

"Shit!" I said. "What the hell is Lucas doing?"

"Lucas is doing nothing." His voice came over my earpiece. "Like the laboratory the auditorium is engineered to release that. Someone activated it trying to open those doors. You need to get in there. Now."

Adam raced to a spot along the front wall. I kept my gaze fixed on the screen. It didn't take long for someone in the auditorium to smell the fumes. And it took only about two seconds more before that someone ran for the nearest door . . . and found it still sealed shut.

People stumbled from their seats, running for the useless exits.

Giles shouted at them to remain calm, then turned on Jaz. "Finish it."

"I'm trying, but it's a very involved process that cannot be rushed and—"

Giles lifted the knife. "Lucifer! I know you've heard us. I know you're there. Now get your ass out here or I'm going to slice your bitch daughter from throat to belly!"

That's when the audience screaming started for real. I looked at Adam. He was leaning against the wall, fingers splayed.

"I'm trying," he said, as if he could feel me watching him.

"I know."

His power was like mine—if you use a lot, you need to rest and let it recharge. It was low now from the fight with Severin and Sierra.

Clay was trying to bust down the door while Elena rapped along the wall, searching for an another spot to break through.

I turned back to the video screen. Jaz had stepped in front of Hope, blocking her from Giles. Hope was wriggling in her bonds.

"Get out of my way," Giles said.

"You're not touching her."

Giles lunged, knife flashing toward Hope's leg. Jaz wasn't fast enough to block the blow. Hope convulsed with pain and shock as Giles backpedaled, the knife blade slick with blood.

"Lucifer!" He flicked the blade, spattering blood. "Will a lord demon let me kill his child so easily? All you need to do is come out and face me."

I could barely hear him. Pandemonium had erupted in the auditorium—people passing out from the gas and being trampled by others. The fumes stayed at the rear, not affecting the people on stage.

"Lucifer! Do not test me, demon! I have done worse than this to get what I wanted."

No response except more screams from the audience.

"Lucifer!" Giles shouted, veins popping.

He wheeled on Jaz, who stood between him and Hope.

"Get out of my way, mortal," he snarled.

"Not a chance."

"Move now!"

Jaz's face rippled. The wrinkles smoothed out, the angles of his face softened. In less than a minute, he was Jasper Haig.

"Like I said, not a chance."

Giles lunged again, this time aiming straight for Jaz. He didn't move. Barely even flinched as the blade slashed open his arm.

"I told you, I'm not moving," Jaz said.

"Are you crazy?"

"Well, that's the diagnosis, though I've never been happy with it myself." He glanced over his shoulder. "Getting close to untying that rope, my love?"

"It would go faster if I had the knife," Hope said.

Jaz laughed and turned back to Giles. "Women. So demanding. I don't suppose you'd care to indulge her by handing me—"

Giles lunged again, this time slicing Jaz's leg.

"I think that's a no," Jaz said, between clenched teeth. "I'd try to take it from him, Hope, but I'm not good with knives. Apparently, he is."

"Do you think this is a game?" Giles said.

"I think everything's a game. If you mean that I'm not taking you seriously, I beg to differ. I'm sure you will kill me. First, though . . ."

Hope got her hands free and bent to untie her legs.

"Progress," Jaz said. "Now, if you'll just give us another minute . . ."

With a howl of rage, Giles plunged the knife straight at Jaz's chest. Jaz twisted so it caught him in the side.

"Not quite yet . . ." he gasped, blood soaking his shirt.

Hope got her legs free. She pushed up from the chair just as Elena and Clay smashed through the wall and Adam managed to incinerate a hole. I followed him through it.

Hope stumbled our way, with Giles in pursuit. A bleeding Jaz leaped into his path. Giles's blade sank into his chest. I grabbed Hope. Adam got between us and Giles as Elena and Clay circled to the other side, blocking Giles's escape.

"Good timing, huh?" Jaz said. Then his legs gave way and he crumpled to the floor, the knife buried in him.

Giles went for the knife, but Clay had him by the back of the shirt. Chaos raged all around us, but for once, Hope didn't seem to feel it. She just stared at Jaz, lying on the floor, blood pooling around him. When she tried to go to him, I didn't stop her, just kept my hand on her arm to support her. She knelt in the blood and gripped his hand.

Jaz's eyes opened and he managed a lazy grin. "See, you do love me." His eyelids fluttered, then closed, and he exhaled one last time, then his head lolled back on the floor.

Hope laid his hand on his chest. "No one should die alone," she whispered. "Not even you."

"Hope?" A rough voice sounded from the wings.

Karl lurched through, braced on a makeshift crutch, waving aside a guard tripping along after him. Hope looked up and she stared. Just stared. Then she struggled to her feet, sliding in the blood, as I tried to help her.

"They forgot to use silver bullets," Karl said.

She gasped and ran toward him and—

I flew off my feet. I saw Hope fly, too, and grabbed for her, but missed. I hit the floor and for a second, everything went dark. Something echoed in my ears, like a sound I couldn't quite pick up. Then the shouting started. Lights flickered and came on and when I looked around, the door was open and the audience was streaming out, tactical team members streaming in, the two groups struggling with each other and shouting.

"W-was that a bomb?" I said as I staggered to my feet. I felt Adam's warm hands on my waist as he helped me steady myself.

"I don't know," he said. "But it was something."

I hurried to Hope. She was still on the ground, clutching her stomach now, her face contorted in pain as she heaved breaths.

Jeremy ran and dropped beside her as Karl hobbled over.

"She's coming," Hope gasped. "The baby's coming."

"What can I get?" I said.

I looked around as I said it, and saw Elena bent over Clay. Leaving Hope, I hurried over to them, Adam right behind me.

"He's just unconscious," Elena said. "But Giles . . . When I came to, he was gone."

"Shit!" I frantically searched the crowd for sign of him.

Then a voice said, "There. He went through there," and I saw a young woman holding her bloodied nose and pointing backstage.

Adam and I took off.

We came out of the back room only to be swept up in a raid. A couple of hundred young supernaturals were trying to get to the compound's exit while our tactical teams tried to round them up. Every one of those kids was convinced that Cabal capture meant death. So they fought back, and we stepped into a maelstrom of spells and shoves and waving guns.

I tried to get through without using my powers, but ended up resorting to knockback spells to clear the way. We'd gone about five feet when a Cabal goon pointed a gun at us.

"Hands against the wall," he barked.

"Savannah Levine. Adam Vasic," I said. "Now move your ass."

"Better yet," Adam yelled over the din. "Did Gilles de Rais come through here?"

"I saw him," another Cabal officer called.

"Where'd he go?"

The guy pointed to a door. I hurried over and pushed it open. The room was empty. There was an upended table in the middle and a rumpled throw rug under it. I stepped in, fingers raised to zap Giles. Then I heard a now-familiar noise. A steel door closing.

Behind the table, there was a hatch. There was still enough room for me to clamber through it, and as I went I lit a light ball and saw a ladder along the side. I grabbed that and went down. Adam barely made it through behind me.

We scrambled down the ladder to a room at the bottom. A corridor led off to the side.

"Secret escape hatch," I muttered. "Does everyone have them these days?"

"We'll install one at the agency for you."

"Good."

I contacted Lucas and told him where we were. There was no way the Cabal team was getting through that steel hatch door anytime soon, though. So he told us to go ahead and give chase to Giles.

CHAPTER 47

We could hear Giles ahead, feet pounding, breath coming hard. He was panicked and not being careful, his flashlight beam bobbing as he ran. We were careful. We ran as lightly as we could until we spotted him at what looked like the end of the tunnel.

I cast a cover spell. He turned and peered toward us. Maybe he'd heard us, maybe he hadn't, but a wave of his flashlight seemed to reassure him that he was alone, and he let out a sigh of relief before making his way up a ladder.

We crept close as he climbed. At the top, he pushed open the door and looked down again, but the cover spell still hid us. He climbed out. We went after him.

When we reached the top, I cracked the hatch open as little as possible and peered out to see . . .

Corn.

We were in a cornfield, the tall stalks all around us. I closed the hatch again and whispered the news to Adam. Then I gave Lucas one more update before I opened the hatch again and cast blur spells so Adam and I could crawl out.

We found Giles about twenty feet away, doubled over, catching his breath. Adam whispered a game plan.

Still under the blur spells, we split up. Adam circled around to the other side of Giles. The ground was damp and muffled our footsteps. I caught the occasional moving cornstalk marking Adam's progress, but Giles didn't seem to notice. I tracked the swaying corn until I knew Adam was in position. Then I crept forward.

I stopped about five feet from Giles. He looked up sharply, as if he could sense me there. I ended the spell. He saw me and turned to run just as Adam lunged.

Giles managed to twist out of Adam's way, but I jumped into his path. He looked from Adam to me.

"You can't kill me," he said. "I'm immortal. You know that."

"Immortal, yes. But you're not a vampire. I'm guessing you've got some zombie juice swimming in your veins. That means you're not invulnerable."

"Yes, I am."

"Have you tested that theory?" I watched his expression. "Jumped off buildings for fun?"

Giles hesitated, then pulled a vial from his pocket.

"Do you know what this is?" he said.

"I can guess," I said.

"Good. So you know it's not something you want me to uncap." He paused. "How's Bryce?"

I stiffened.

"Not well, I take it. Would you like the antidote?"

I didn't answer.

"In the interest of fair play, I'll give it to you. A gift. I presume you have a radio?"

Again, I said nothing.

"Call Lucas Cortez. Tell him to go to my office. The safe is in the bottom desk drawer. The code is 1429. The year I fought alongside Joan of Arc."

I could tell by his expression he expected me to be impressed. Without reacting, I conveyed the information to Lucas. He was already in Giles's office and had found the safe. The code opened it.

"The antidote is in a pouch with instructions. They're written in code, but it's not a complex one. Benicio Cortez will have someone who can figure it out. Now I'm going to put this down." He bent and laid the vial on the ground. "And you are going to let me walk away."

He straightened up and started walking. I let him get about five feet before I locked him in a binding spell.

I walked over and patted down his pockets.

"Yep, backup vial," I said as I felt it through the fabric. "Let's take this off your hands before we escort you back inside."

As I reached for it, something hit me. It was like a micro version of the blow inside. I stumbled. The spell snapped. Giles jumped me. I went down. Adam lunged, but Giles was already on top of me, pinning me to the dirt, vial in one hand, the other wrapped in my hair.

Giles wrenched my head back. When I gasped, he pushed the vial to my lips. Adam grabbed Giles around the neck and I smelled burning flesh. I struggled to cast a binding spell, but Giles had the vial at my mouth, and I couldn't get the words out.

"You should have let me go while you had the chance," he rasped, his eyes rolling in agony. "All I need to do now is—"

Adam yanked him off me. I scrambled up and hit him with . . . I don't know what. He screamed in agony and clutched his stomach. I could see it ballooning under his shirt, the skin glowing, as if he'd swallowed a fireball. Then it burst. Flames licked out as he dropped to the ground, writhing and howling, blackened intestines tumbling out between his fingers.

Adam stared. Then he knelt and wrapped his hands around Giles's neck again and squeezed until he put him out of his misery.

Just to be sure, I bent and checked for a pulse. Adam checked for breathing. We found neither.

"Yep. Immortality but not invulnerability," I said.

"Good call. Let me carefully get that vial out of his hand in case his death grip snaps it."

He bent over Giles's ruined body. He was peeling back his fingers when Giles's eyes snapped open.

"Watch—!"

Giles reared up, grabbing Adam. I cast a binding spell and it worked—I felt it work—but Giles didn't stop, just picked Adam up like a rag doll and whipped him. As I raced toward Giles, I knew what I'd see.

Bright green glowing eyes.

"Balaam," I said, stopping short.

"Very good, my child."

He reached down and picked up the unbroken vial. Then he took two long strides and scooped up the second one. I cast another binding spell.

"Your magic won't work on me, little one," he said. "You've fought well, but it's time to surrender. Go tend to your lover. He's injured."

I looked over at Adam. He lay crumpled on the ground, but I could see his chest rising and falling.

"He's just unconscious. He'll be fine."

Balaam laughed. "How cold you are. I'm impressed. I suspect Asmondai's son would not be."

"Then you suspect wrong. He wouldn't want me running to his side and letting you walk away with those vials. Give them back."

"Oh, well, in that case . . ." He held them out, then shook his head and laughed. "No, child. You can fight me for them, but there's no point. Even if you managed to get them away from me, I can find more."

"If that was true, you wouldn't have come for these two. The rest of the virus must already be in Cabal custody. Those vials are your last chance for the biggest chaos banquet you've ever had."

"And you're going to stop me, are you?" He smiled. "I do appreciate your tenacity. And your bravery. You are indeed a child of my blood. But you've inherited my recklessness as well, and you don't have thousands of years of experience to temper that impulsive streak."

He came so close I felt the heat of him.

"You cannot fight me. *Cannot*. If you insist on trying, I will need to teach you a lesson. One I'd rather not impart." He nodded to Adam. "Take your lover and leave. You have my word that this"—he lifted the vials—"will not affect you. I will take it far from here before I unleash it."

"I'm not letting you unleash it anywhere."

His green eyes flashed. "I'm being benevolent, child. Do not test me."

He turned to go. I cast a binding spell, then an energy bolt, then in desperation, a knockback. He just kept walking.

I ran at him and jumped on his back. He flung me aside. I hit the ground so hard I left a dent in the dirt. I scrambled up, though, and tore after him.

He turned, caught my arm, and held it in his vice grip. "I have warned you, child. Do not test me."

He snapped my arm. Pain ripped through me. Then he threw me down on my back and towered above me.

"Perhaps it's more than recklessness. Are you dense, child? As stupid as a bull, charging blindly, knowing no good will come of it."

Maybe not, but I could try to distract him long enough for the others to show up. I was careful not to let the thought solidify in my mind. He'd already proven he could read it.

I lay there, panting and cradling my broken arm as he turned. He took two steps, then looked back. I hadn't moved. A satisfied snort. He continued walking.

I slowly got to my feet. Then I charged him again. This time, when he turned, I saw it coming and dodged out of the way. I got behind him, grabbed his hair in my good hand, and swung off my feet, yanking with everything I had.

"Adam did a good job of burning Giles's neck," I said,

through gritted teeth. "I'm sure if I pull hard enough, I can rip your damned head off."

He spun and I lost my grip. Then he nailed me in the chest so hard I heard ribs crack. I went flying and hit the ground again. When I tried to rise, I doubled over, coughing and spitting blood.

"I do not want to hurt you," he growled as he loomed above me again

"Yeah?" I wheezed. "I'd hate to see what would happen if you did."

"I would rip *your* head from your neck and I would keep you alive while I did it." He bent down. "This is a lesson, child. I'm proud of you. Now, accept defeat and back down."

I looked up into his green eyes. "Would you?"

He didn't answer.

"Then I come by it honestly," I said, and grabbed his hair with my good hand again, and wrenched with all I had.

He backhanded me and I went flying. When I hit the ground, I couldn't breathe and lay there, heaving and coughing up blood. Then, slowly, I pushed to my feet.

"You will not accept the lesson, will you, child?" Balaam said. "Your own pain means nothing to you. But I know a lesson that *will* hurt."

He walked toward Adam and put out his hand. Adam convulsed and gasped, his eyes flying open, blind with pain.

"No!" I shouted.

A gust of wind ripped through the corn, stalks breaking and flying aside. Even Balaam stumbled. He glanced at me.

"Interesting. But not enough, child."

He turned back to Adam. I closed my eyes and poured everything I had into the spell, shouting the words. Over my shouts and the roar of the wind, I heard Balaam.

"Dispelling me?" His voice drew closer as he came my way again. "As if I were some minor spirit? You cannot—"

As I finished the incantation, he stopped short and when I opened my eyes, I saw the surprise on his face as Giles's body wobbled.

"Seems like maybe I can," I said.

I closed my eyes and started the spell again. He hit me. I don't know if he physically hit me or sent me flying with a wave of energy, only that I sailed off my feet and landed so hard I blacked out from pain. But when I came to, the words were still on my lips.

I didn't even open my eyes. Just shouted the incantation. When I finished, I looked to see him only a foot away from me, face contorted in rage, but frozen there, as if he was losing his hold on Giles's body.

He drew back his fist to hit me again.

"Hey!" said a voice behind him.

Balaam wheeled to see Adam staggering to his feet.

"She's as stubborn and bullheaded as you are," he said. "No use hurting her . . . unless you're afraid she can really cast you out."

Balaam snarled in reply, too furious to even form words.

"Well, then, if you want to stop her, I'm the one you need to hurt."

"No," I said.

Adam didn't listen. He was distracting Balaam so I could try again. He believed I could do it. He was betting his life I could do it.

I closed my eyes and if I'd thought I'd tried my hardest before, it was nothing compared to how hard I tried now. Everything disappeared as the incantation took over. That was all there was—the words, the power, the will, the desperation.

If I failed—I didn't want to think of what would happen if I failed. But I had to, because that was the only thing that was going to make it damned well certain I'd give this everything I had. Fail, and Balaam would kill Adam. Fail, and Balaam would unleash the virus. Fail, and my world—and everyone in it—could be destroyed.

Do not fail. That was the only option.

I recited the incantation and then I recited it again and then—

A hand on my shoulder. A voice in my ear. "It's over, Savannah. He's gone."

I looked up at Adam. I took his arm and I pulled myself up and only then did I look over at Balaam. Only it wasn't Balaam. It was just Gilles de Rais's ruined body, lying in a cornfield.

I picked up the vials in my good hand, lowered myself to the ground and sat there, cradling them, Adam beside me with his arms around me.

CHAPTER 48

The Cabal team showed up about thirty seconds later. Figures, doesn't it?

I radioed Lucas and Paige to meet us back in the auditorium. According to the team members who'd just arrived, something had happened there. Something I really wanted to see.

When we made it back, I saw Elena and Clay first. Elena noticed the blood on my shirt and rushed over, but I waved her away.

"Is she here?" I asked. "Is she okay?"

Elena smiled and nodded. "She's fine."

With Adam helping me, I crossed the stage to where Hope lay on the floor, Jeremy tending to her, Jaime gripping her hand. And Karl . . . Karl was holding a baby.

"Nita Elena Adams Marsten," Hope said, smiling. "Yes, it's a mouthful, but she'll grow into it."

"She's beautiful," I said. And she was—with black hair and wide blue eyes, staring up at her father.

"She's putting a spell on him," Hope said. "Not that she needs to. Someone already has Daddy wrapped around her little finger."

"Takes after her mother," Karl said.

Everyone laughed. I just sat and stared at Nita. I'm not one for babies, really. But this was different. This was . . . I won't say a miracle, because that's corny. But after everything we'd gone through, this new life just seemed . . . perfect.

"I'm sorry I couldn't come sooner," Karl said.

"What?" Hope blinked. "Um, if you mean when I was taken captive, you were nearly dead at the time, so—"

She stopped. Karl had been looking down at Nita. Now he lifted his head and his eyes shimmered. They weren't orange or green like a demon's. And they didn't just glow like Aratron's. They shimmered iridescent, with points of a thousand colors.

"Oh," Hope said.

She lifted her hands as she struggled to keep her expression calm. He handed the baby back to her and she clutched Nita tight, her gaze never breaking with those eyes.

"I was watching," he said. "But it seemed best not to interfere."

She just nodded and cradled Nita, who started to fuss.

"The grandchildren of demons don't inherit their powers," he said. "But I am not a demon."

"No," Hope whispered. She looked at Nita, and her eyes filled with tears, then she looked back at him and said, fiercely, *"No."*

He pushed the sweaty curls from Hope's forehead. "She will not inherit the hunger for chaos. That is . . ." He tilted his head. "A consequence of living among demons. It is the powers she will inherit—the visions and the rest. That will not be easy, but it will be . . . easier. More important, it will be easier for you. She's taken some of your power. It will dilute it, and dilute the hunger. That will help."

Hope stared at him, still shaking her head. "Please, no. I don't want that. I'll keep it—all of it. Please."

Lucifer didn't answer.

I cleared my throat. "The visions aren't easy to deal with, I'm sure. But you've done a lot of good with them. She'll do a lot of good with them. And if it cuts down on your chaos hunger . . ."

"That's good," Elena said, kneeling and squeezing Hope's arm. "It'll make life easier for you, which will make it easier for her."

Hope looked up at Lucifer, "Do I have a choice?"

"No."

She swallowed. "Then we'll deal with it."

"Of course you will." Lucifer leaned over and kissed her forehead. "You always do."

He leaned back on his haunches and closed his eyes. When they opened, they were blue again, Karl shaking his head.

"What happened?" he said.

Hope just smiled and handed him his daughter.

Back to Miami, where we discovered that after a birth, we now faced the opposite. Bryce was dying. His body couldn't adjust to the virus. He was on life support.

But we had the antidote, right? Except Giles had played one last trick. He gave us the antidote and the coded instructions, which had been deciphered before we returned to Miami. But it wasn't just a simple matter of giving the antidote to Bryce. There was a ritual to be followed, a ritual that required a critical ingredient.

The life of a vampire.

"Oh, stop being dramatic," Cassandra said as she paced the boardroom. "It requires a vampiric life. That a vampire surrender his immortality and return to being human. Offering mine is hardly noble. I'm dying. I have only a few years left at best. Give me the rest of my mortal lifetime and you're doing me a favor."

Aaron shook his head "The ritual doesn't guarantee you a human life, Cass. It theorizes that's what happens if you give up your vampiric one. For all we know, you'll turn into a pile of three-hundred-year-old dust."

"Well, then you've saved the cost of cremation, haven't you?"

He glowered at her. There were only a few of us in the boardroom—me, Adam, Paige, and Lucas. Cassandra thought Sean should be present—his brother's life was at stake—but Sean had demurred. He was staying downstairs with Bryce. This was a decision he didn't dare influence.

Cassandra might pretend she was being selfish, but she knew the risks. She was offering her last years to save Bryce.

Aaron wanted to find another vampire. Surely there was one locked in a Cabal prison somewhere, on a legitimate charge, a vampire whose crimes deserved the death penalty.

"It would take time," Lucas said. "Bryce doesn't have time. However, there may be a larger problem here. Cassandra's vampire life is nearing an end. It . . . may not be enough."

More arguing followed. Aaron retreated to a chair and sat there, staring, until he said, "What if it was two vampiric lives?"

We all turned to him.

"What if we both offered ours?"

Cassandra strode to him. "You are not giving up—"

"I wouldn't be giving up anything," he said quietly. "I never wanted to be a vampire. You know that." He looked up at her. "This is a chance for us both to be human again. I don't want to be a vampire if you're not."

"And if it fails?"

He held her gaze. "Then I don't want to be here if you're not."

Cassandra choked on her reply. She stood there, facing him, back to us, and I could hear her trying to speak, but she couldn't.

Paige reached over and squeezed my hand. "Let's go," she whispered.

We crept out and left them alone.

CHAPTER 49

A few hours later, we were in the Cabal underground ritual chamber. It was another three hours before the rite was completed. It had taken a whole team of spellcasters, including me, Paige, and Lucas to pull it off, and even then, we had a couple of false starts.

When we finished, Benicio dismissed the others. I could tell they wanted to stay and see if it worked, but this next part wasn't for public viewing. This next part could mean that two of our friends gave their lives—mortal and immortal—for my brother.

Cassandra and Aaron lay on mats beside the ritual circle. They were hooked up to heart-rate monitors. They'd been conscious until the final incantation. Then they'd gone still, eyes closed, the machines remaining dark and silent.

"How long will it take?" I murmured to Adam, who'd been supervising the ritual. "Something should be happening, right?"

He rubbed my good arm, but said nothing. What could he say? This ritual wasn't in any of his books. It wasn't in anyone's books.

I knelt beside Cassandra's mat.

"Come on, Cass," I whispered.

As I stared down at her pale, still face, my heart started to hammer. What if she didn't wake up? I hadn't said goodbye. Nobody had, as if not daring to admit that they thought this could fail. If she was gone, we couldn't even contact her through Jaime. When vampires passed, no one knew where they went. No one even knew for sure that they went anywhere, and that vampirehood *wasn't* their afterlife. An eternity as a ghost traded for a few hundred years more on earth.

"Come on, Cass," I whispered. "Please."

The machine blipped. I jumped and looked over. It blipped again. Then again.

Cassandra shot upright, eyes snapping open. She looked around. Then she grabbed her chest, eyes going wide.

"What's—?" I began, leaping to my feet. "Someone—"

Cassandra gasped. She blinked hard as she slowly, almost tentative inhaled and exhaled.

"Forgot that part, huh?" Adam said, grinning. "Yep, you gotta breathe now, Cass."

"That's inconvenient," she said.

She blinked some more, then reached over toward the ritual circle and snatched up a knife.

"Hey!" I said. "What—?"

She ran the blade across her palm before I could stop her. Blood welled up. She studied it, then closed and opened her fist. The wound continued to bleed.

"That's *very* inconvenient." She turned toward Aaron. "I hope you're satisfied. You do realize I'm probably going to die in my sleep from forgetting to breathe. Or from stepping in front of a bullet because I forgot—"

She stopped. Aaron lay there, his machine silent.

She scrambled up and went to him. She shook him by the shoulders.

"Aaron?"

No response. She shook harder, panic lighting her green eyes.

"Aaron!"

She spun to us.

"Don't just stand there. Get him a doctor. Where are the doctors? Goddamn it! He risked his life for you and you can't even provide proper—"

"Are you sure you want her alive?" said a voice behind Cassandra.

Aaron's eyes opened. He yawned. Cassandra's gaze shot to his monitor, still dark and silent.

"It—The ritual didn't work for you?" she said.

Aaron reached up and fussed with the monitor, discreetly pulling at something under it. The machine started up.

"Nope, it worked. The machine just screwed up." He glanced at Benicio. "Better have someone take a look at it."

Cassandra glared at him. "You did that on purpose."

"As long-delayed revenge for leaving me with an angry mob in Romania? That would be petty of me."

He smiled and tugged her over. She sniffed, but sat beside him on the mat.

"Though," he mused, "if I did want to scare you, it was probably because I hoped to hear abject apologies for past mistreatment. Or, at the very least, heartfelt declarations of eternal love. Not cursing out your friends for failing to ensure proper medical surveillance of the procedure."

"That's how Cass says 'I love you,' " I said.

He grinned. "I think it is." He pulled her down in a kiss and, behind her back, waved for us all to leave.

We did.

There *had* been a doctor nearby, waiting to be called in. Why only one? Because the others were all busy rushing the ritual potion to Bryce.

Despite my moment of panic, Cassandra and Aaron's recovery had been near-instantaneous. Not so with Bryce. After they treated him, there was nothing to do except wait. His vital signs remained stable and that was the main thing.

The doctors hung around for the first thirty minutes. Then all but one left. By the two-hour mark, they were all working on other patients, rotating through every ten minutes to check on Bryce.

Sean and I sat with him. Adam stayed, too, at first just sitting with me, then running errands, like getting dinner.

"I'm coming out," Sean said as we ate our Vietnamese take-out. "As soon as I get back to L.A. I suspect the politic thing would be to wait until everything has calmed down and a decision has been reached—whether the split is permanent or Uncle Josef and I can come to some agreement."

"Only if that agreement includes you handing him the CEO crown," I muttered.

"Probably. But I'm not going to be the one to break up the Cabal. I'm willing to negotiate. If he isn't, so be it. I could wait for all that to die down. On a business level, that would be smart. But it's not fair. If the Cabal stays split, Uncle Josef and I will be campaigning for the loyalty of the employees. I need to be upfront with them."

"And if you don't do it now, it'll get harder to do it later," I said.

"I know. Bite the bullet. Take the risk."

"It'll be fine."

He shrugged, and I could tell by his expression that he thought I was being as hopelessly optimistic as he'd been about reaching a settlement with Josef. I disagreed. Sure, he might lose a few employees, but for most his sexual orientation wouldn't matter, and even if it did, they'd be working for him, not marrying him. He'd proven himself as a company leader for years. He'd continue to do so, whether he led the Nast Cabal or half of the Nast Cabal.

His cell phone buzzed. He looked down at it and sighed.

"I really need to take this," he said.

"And I need to run a few errands of my own," Adam said. "I'll be back soon."

"Take your time," I said. "Looks like it'll be a long night."

They left. I picked up my magazine. I was still on the first article when a groan from the bed had me leaping up.

Bryce was grimacing. He tried to lift his hand, but it was tied down.

I clasped his fingers. Before I could speak, he croaked, "Water."

I lifted my water bottle to Bryce's chapped lips. He drank, then opened his eyes. I texted Sean fast, then turned back to Bryce.

"Hey," I said.

He frowned. "Savannah?" He tried again to lift his hand. Then he looked over to see the bindings. "Wha . . . ?"

I undid them. "Sorry. Doesn't look good, does it? Waking up tied to a bed with me here. I didn't kidnap you, if that's what you were wondering. I'm guessing everything's a little fuzzy but—"

"No." He blinked. "Yeah. It's fuzzy. But I remember. The lab. The experiment. The explosion. The pit." He paused. "I owe you."

I shrugged.

His gaze moved to the cast on my arm. "What happened?"

"Not much. I killed Giles. Broke up the reveal movement. Got your antidote. Fought Balaam and sent him back to hell."

A faint smile. "All by yourself?"

"I may have had some help."

The smile grew and he started to say something, but just then Sean ran into the room, out of breath.

"Hey, bro," Bryce said.

Sean walked over and embraced him. I started backing out of the room, but Sean caught my arm and pulled me over.

"Welcome back from the dead," he said to Bryce.

"Actually, it was the undead. But it felt like dead. *Still* feels like dead." He made a face and reached for my water bottle. I handed it to him. He took a drink, then asked, "Did they find Larsen and his parents?"

"They did. We'll discuss that later. I'm sure you'll have to make amends, but I think you've already been punished enough."

"I'll make amends," Bryce said. He turned to me. "Lots of them."

CHAPTER 50

I headed upstairs, looking for Adam. He wasn't in the archives and wasn't answering his cell. I popped my head into the lounge where I'd last seen Lucas. The sofa was back in place. And occupied. Lucas sat at one end, Paige curled up against him. They were both sound asleep.

We'd barely returned from Indiana before Benicio started using the events of the last week to persuade Lucas that it was time for him to take his place in the Cabal. Not as reluctant heir. Not as part-time executive. As CEO. He'd led the charge to avert the biggest threat our world had ever faced. He'd proven to all that Benicio's crusading bastard son could indeed hold the reins of the most powerful Cabal in the country. Now was the time to seize the opportunity for a smooth transition.

To his credit, Lucas didn't laugh. He didn't turn and walk out either, as he would have a few years ago. There was work to be done in the aftermath of this averted disaster. Small fires to be extinguished before they flared up. But he insisted his place was in Portland, running the agency with Paige. He'd do what he could here, then go home with us. Benicio had him for another week. After that, well, the teleconference equipment at the Cabal was top-notch. They'd manage, as they had for the last few years.

Would Lucas ever become CEO of the Cortez Cabal? Maybe. In time. But Benicio was still healthy and there were supernaturals out there who needed Lucas, protector of the underdog, more than they needed Lucas, Cabal CEO.

I looked at them—my friends, my bosses, my foster parents—curled up on that couch. Then I smiled, backed out, and spell-locked the door.

I was calling Adam again when I heard a familiar clicking of stiletto heels and looked up to see Jaime and Jeremy coming my way.

"I thought you guys made your escape already," I said.

"We tried," Jaime said. "I got stopped by a certain demanding master manipulator."

"Benicio."

"No, the Fates. They want me hanging around to act as mouthpiece for your mom while the Cabals clean up this mess. Which reminds me, she wants to talk to you. Your dad does, too. I think they've done some manipulating of their own with the Fates. You might get one last face-to-face before the veil closes completely."

"Ms. Vegas?" a young man hurried along the hall. "Mr. Cortez needs—"

"I know, I know." She turned to me. "Give me an hour."

"Wait, first, have you seen Adam?"

"He was with Elena, I believe," Jeremy said. "They're . . ." He looked down the hall. "I'll take you there."

Jaime smiled, squeezed his arm, then followed the clerk. Jeremy and I headed the opposite way.

"So are you staying in Miami with Hope and Karl?" I asked.

He shook his head. "None of us care to linger longer than we need to. Once Jaime's done we're joining the others in Russia."

That's where Antonio and the rest of the Pack had relocated during the trouble here, taking refuge with the Russian Pack.

Jeremy continued, "Taking a baby on an intercontinental flight doesn't seem wise, especially with one parent still recovering from the birth and the other from near-death. But Karl wants Hope and Nita out of Miami, and Hope wants to go. Benicio will send us in the private jet with a doctor."

Apparently, then, Karl had resolved his issues with Elena. I'd never doubted it. He might like to play lone wolf, but now that he had a family, his first instinct was to take his wife and child to the safety of his Pack.

"Are you going to be in Russia long?"

He shook his head. "We'll head home in a few weeks, if you'd like to spend some time at Stonehaven this summer. You haven't done that in a few years."

"No, I haven't. I think I'll take you up on that." I glanced at him as we turned the corner. "So, I guess with all this turmoil, you won't be stepping down as Alpha anytime soon."

"Actually, I will. Elena's ready. I already knew she was. She wasn't so sure. But now there's no question—she can do this. It's time."

"Have you told her?"

"Not yet. When I get to Russia, I'll break the news. She's ready to be Alpha." His crooked smile grew, eyes sparkling. "And I'm ready to *not* be Alpha. Maybe get in a few adventures while I'm still young enough to enjoy them."

He rapped on a closed door. Elena called, "Come in!"

I pushed open the door to see her with Clay, chairs pulled up to a desk, the twins on a huge monitor.

"Savannah!" Kate yelled. "I see Savannah!"

Kate scrambled closer to the camera, shoving her brother aside. As they bickered, I glanced at Jeremy. He'd stayed behind the door and was now retreating, motioning to Elena that he'd talk to the kids later.

"Smart man," she murmured.

Logan had reclaimed his half of the screen and was leaning forward, frowning. "What's wrong with Savannah's arm?"

I lifted the cast. "Broke it doing something dumb."

"Was it rock climbing?" Kate said. "You promised to teach us."

"I will this summer. I'm coming to visit after you get back."

Kate let out a whoop. "I wanna break my arm so I can get a cast and have everybody sign it."

"That's stupid," Logan said.

She shoved him. "You're stupid."

"Sorry," I whispered to Elena as the twins tumbled out of sight. "I was actually just looking for Adam."

"Oh, he's down the hall making some phone calls. I'll take you."

"Yeah, run while you can," Clay muttered. He leaned toward the screen. "Guys! You've got five minutes before bedtime. Do you want to know when we're coming home?"

"Now!" Kate yelled, popping up. "I want you here right now."

"They can't teleport, dummy," Logan said.

"If you call her that again—" Clay was saying as we closed the door.

"Kids getting bored?" I said as Elena led me away.

"No, the guys are keeping them busy. They just want Mom and Dad to quit this crazy save-the-world nonsense and go camping with them this weekend."

"Gotta have priorities," I said.

We took a few more steps.

"So I take it you're not worried about Malcolm?" I said.

She shook her head. "Another adventure for another day. We need a break and, last we saw, he was safely in Nast custody." She pushed a half-open door. "And there's Adam."

He turned and motioned to his cell phone.

"Thanks," I whispered to Elena. "Oh, and congratulations."

"For what?"

I grinned. "You'll find out."

I stepped into the office and eased the door shut as Adam got off the phone.

"Ah, so that's why you've been ignoring my calls."

"Ignoring . . . ?" He checked his messages. "Shit. I was on hold. Never even heard the beep." He strode toward me. "Is it Bryce? Is he—?"

I held up a hand to stop him. "Awake. The doctors checked him. He seems fine. I'm giving him some time with Sean. He needs to tell him about Thomas."

"Right." He shook his head. "That's a shitty thing to wake up to."

"Which is why I left them alone. So, I know it's getting late, but I was hoping to talk you into a drink, if you're done with work."

"Wasn't working." He walked to the printer, took off a couple of sheets, and handed them to me. "For you. A little 'thanks for saving the world as we know it' present. There's a T-shirt coming, too, but it'll take awhile."

"T-shirt?"

"Yep. It says 'I defeated Lord Demon Balaam and all I got was this lousy T-shirt.' "

I laughed. "I'll count myself lucky if that *is* all I get. I'm still waiting for him to show up and use my *hide* for a shirt."

"He won't. Too humiliating. Better to just blame Gilles de Rais for screwing up everything." He waved at the sheets. "Now read."

I skimmed the first page. "Our ski trip to Switzerland?"

"On my dime. And a very expensive dime it is, too. That place ain't cheap. But you're worth it. Just remember that when I ask you to come heli-skiing with me."

"I'm not doing skiing of any kind." I lifted my cast. "Did you forget something?"

"Did you check the dates on that reservation?"

They were for two months from now.

"Oh."

"Yeah, '*oh*.' I figure that'll give you time to recover."

"Time to find an apartment, too. I'm moving out as soon as we get back to Portland."

"Good. There's a vacancy at my apartment." He lifted a hand before I could speak. "In my apartment *building,* I mean. I know you're not ready for cohabitation. You need to live on your own. At least for a while." He put his arm around my shoulder and led me from the room. "Now, you mentioned buying me a drink?"

"I don't think I said—"

"Yep, pretty sure you did. We might want to make it a double. Have you checked the office e-mail lately? Apparently, the world didn't stop while we were busy saving it. Lots of work waiting."

"Lots of *adventures* waiting."

He grinned over at me. "Always lots of adventures waiting."

And so there would be. Things had happened in the last few weeks. Big things. Maybe even things that would ultimately alter our world. But one thing wouldn't change. There would always be work to do, threats to defeat, adventures to be had.

I wouldn't want it any other way.

A FINAL NOTE
FROM KELLEY . . .

Thus ends the Otherworld, with Savannah looking forward to a lifetime of adventures. It may seem an odd note to finish on, but this is how I've always envisioned the ending. I'm not sending the characters into their rocking chairs, to doze away their retirement years. I haven't created a world where that is even possible. There is no final victory that could let them all live peacefully-ever-after. But as Savannah says, they wouldn't have it any other way. Theirs is a life of threats and challenges and, yes, adventures. This is, for me, their happily-ever-after.

Will readers ever share in those future adventures?

Yes. I do have more stories to tell. And I will tell some of them in three anthologies of short fiction, the first to be published in 2014. I may even, someday, return to share a bigger story, when the time is right. Even now, before we close the book on the Otherworld, I have one more tale to tell. As much as I love Savannah and her world, I can't end this without going back, once more, to where it all began. So, I'm concluding this with a final story, as Elena and Clay return to their Pack after the crisis is over for—what else?— another adventure.

From Russia, with Love

I was dreaming of the ravines, racing through them, feeling . . . lonely. Crushing loneliness—and frustration and self-loathing because I shouldn't have been feeling lonely, damn it. I'd chosen that life. I'd chosen that man. Good choices, both of them. And yet . . . not for me. That's what it came down to in the end. Something can be good and decent and worthy, and still not make you happy because it doesn't fill that pit inside you. And you won't be happy until it is filled, however hard that will be. So that's what I remember. The loneliness, and venting my frustration on the coyotes, and racing through the forest when I was really running from the man who'd bitten me, the man I'd still loved . . . and hated . . . and loved.

"Elena." A voice whispered in my ear as my paws ripped up the soft earth. "We're here."

A hand shook my shoulder. I growled and tried to shrug it off. Then I felt it, the warmth of his touch.

"Clay . . ."

I opened my eyes. He was right there, blue eyes inches from mine. I inhaled the rich scent of him, and for a second, I was back in that forest, back in that time, and I felt my insides crumple, as if I was still only dreaming of him, and hating myself for it.

Then he pulled back and I saw his face, the faint lines around his mouth and his eyes, and I catapulted through time, back to now, back to here. Here. Now. On a plane. Going to see our children.

For a moment, that too seemed like a dream and I felt a prickle of anger for letting myself imagine it.

"Elena?"

I blinked and looked out the window, into the darkness, at the city lights below. I could see my reflection. Not the young woman in the forest. Not anymore. I lifted my hand to the glass and saw the ring on my finger, the same ring he'd given me twenty years ago, before it all went to hell. The ring I'd kept throwing back at him until, finally, I put it back on.

"Till death do us part," I whispered.

"Hmm, that sounds ominous," Clay said. "You planning something I should know about?"

I smiled and leaned against his shoulder as the plane descended into Saint Petersburg.

I travel a lot, both as a freelance journalist and as the Pack's mediator, but I can count on one hand the number of times I've left North America. Landing in a country where I don't know the language is disconcerting. I feel lost, and I hate that. So I was quiet as we disembarked and went through customs, anxiously scanning the signs for international travel icons and trying to remember my very few words of Russian.

"Baggage," I murmured. "Baggage . . ."

Clay steered me through the crowd. He knew even less Russian than I did, but being in a non-English-speaking country doesn't bother him, because he has no interest in communicating with anyone anyway. I let his sixth sense for escape routes guide us as I gawked about, taking it all in.

"We'll come back to Saint Petersburg next week," he said as he prodded me along. "Bring the kids. Check out the museums."

As we walked, Clay rolled his shoulders, stretching.

"How's the arm?" I whispered.

If anyone else had asked, she'd get an abrupt "fine." A festering zombie scratch five years ago nearly cost Clay his arm, and he's been dealing with the fallout ever since. Following the week of hard fighting we'd just been through, he'd been feeling it again.

After a moment's hesitation, he said, "Not more than a twinge or two since yesterday. Guess I've finally learned to compensate."

"I'm sure all the guys you knocked out would agree."

He grinned and waved me toward the baggage claim.

In the arrivals area, I caught sight of Nick Sorrentino almost immediately. He was easy to spot. It was midnight and most of the people around him looked as if they'd been sleeping in the terminal. Nick was bright-eyed, clean shaven, and impeccably dressed. The young man beside him didn't look nearly as chipper. Nineteen-year-old Noah—Nick's ward—was chugging Coke to stay awake. Though they'd been in Russia for a week, he hadn't quite adjusted to the time difference.

As I scanned the crowd around them, Clay whispered, "You better not be looking for the kids."

"Of course not. I—"

"—told Nick not to bring them."

"Right."

"And you weren't just saying that because you thought you should, while secretly hoping Nick would bring them anyway. Right?"

"Er, no. Not really . . ."

He gave me a look. "If you want the kids, you can't tell him not to bring them. You're Alpha-elect. He'd consider that an order."

"Damn." I sighed. "Do you think I should have said he could bring them?"

Clay shrugged. "Tough call. Worrying that they'll get grabbed in the airport is a bit paranoid. On the other hand, we did just stop a crazy supernatural cult from unleashing a killer virus. A cult that was after our kids. So I'd say a little paranoia is warranted."

That's why the kids were here in the first place, under the added protection of the Russian Pack. That cult had been gathering supernatural rarities, because their leader had proclaimed them as signs of the coming supernatural revolution. Twins born to two bitten werewolves was, in our world, an extreme rarity, so Kate and Logan had been high on Gilles de Rais's shopping list.

When we made it over to Nick, he swooped me up in a feet-off-the-ground hug and kiss that earned us a few stares from onlookers. There's a time when I would have squirmed away, worrying what people might think. I've learned not to care. Nick was my Pack brother and my friend. So I hugged him back and kissed him and he told me the twins were fine, sound asleep when he left. He knew that's the first thing I'd want to know, so he told me without being asked, which is the real mark of a friend.

Noah didn't hang back like he used to, as if uncertain he'd get a welcome. But with the instincts of a hereditary werewolf, he knew his place in the Pack, and he waited until I was done with Nick before stepping forward.

"Is Hope okay?" he asked as I hugged him. "How's the baby? Karl isn't being an ass, is he? He'd better not be, after everything she's been through."

I tried not to smile. Noah had developed a bit of a crush on Hope, which meant he had no love for her husband. Which also helped endear Noah to Clay.

"Mother and child are fine," I said as we headed through the terminal exit doors. "A miracle, all things considered. Karl's doing well. Recuperating and taking care of them. Behaving himself."

"He damned well better," Clay said. "He's in shit and he knows it. He ignored a direct order from Elena. He's on probation now."

"Probation?" Noah jogged to catch up as we crossed the road. "What if he leaves the Pack?"

"He won't," I said. "Having a baby means he needs us more than ever."

"He's definitely off the fence now," Clay said. "Tripping over himself to make sure he doesn't get kicked out." He smiled, relishing the memory.

"He'll be here for the Meet," I said. "Jeremy told him he could skip it, but he's coming, with Hope and the baby."

"Good."

There was no fight over who'd drive the rental car. Nick gave Clay the keys as soon as we drew near. There wasn't a fight over the passenger seat either. Nick just opened the door for me. Like Noah, he's a hereditary werewolf and innately understands hierarchy. He might be a year older than Clay, but he falls below us on the ladder, and he's fine with that. A higher position means more responsibility. As far as Nick is concerned, he has the better end of the deal.

He does have his responsibilities now, though. Namely the younger werewolves—Noah, Reese and Morgan. Noah and Reese might live with both Nick and his father, Antonio, but Antonio has stepped back, leaving "the boys" to his son. Morgan hasn't settled yet—he's still too restless for an apartment in the city—but when he's on Pack territory, he stays with the Sorrentinos, which puts him under Nick's jurisdiction. It's a responsibility that suits Nick, fulfilling his wolf's instinct to teach a younger generation, while letting him skip the often chaotic and mystifying baby-and-child stages.

As Clay drove, we talked about what had happened back in the States, and what was happening here. They'd spent the past week with the Russian Pack, Morgan joining them when we'd finally made contact with him. Now, as the danger passed, our Pack had moved to a rented cottage, where we'd relax and recuperate for a few days before Jeremy showed up for the Meet, to discuss any fallout from the mess back home.

Clay and I knew of some fallout that *wouldn't* be discussed. Fighting our way out of Nast headquarters, we'd discovered that Jeremy's father, Malcolm, was not nearly as dead as everyone thought. Jeremy didn't know. If we had our way, he never would. Malcolm was a brutal, murderous bastard, who'd vented his worst on Jeremy.

Right now, Malcolm was still in Nast custody. We'd leave him there until we could negotiate with Sean Nast and get him back. Then we'd kill him. If that was my first act as Alpha, I'd be satisfied.

There was a time when that thought would have horrified me. Perhaps it still should. Politically, I do oppose the death penalty. Does that make me a hypocrite? Maybe. But I oppose it not because it seems unnecessarily cruel but because I think life in prison is a more fitting punishment. And there's always the risk of executing an innocent man. When Clay and I carry out the Pack's death sentence on a man-killing mutt, I know damned well he's guilty, because Jeremy would never order it unless my investigation left no doubt. Obviously locking up the perpetrator isn't an option for us.

Malcolm was already locked up and would presumably stay there for the rest of his life. But as long as there was a chance he could escape and come after Jeremy, I'd rather see him dead. It was that simple. If that makes me a bad human being, so be it. I know it makes me a good Pack wolf, and that's what matters.

The cabin we'd rented was a little over an hour outside Saint Petersburg. We were on a highway for almost that long before Nick told Clay to turn off onto a regional road. After about five minutes, Clay took a sudden right.

"Um," Nick said. "If you heard me say to turn, your ears are still plugged from that flight—"

Clay turned left sharply, then hit the gas, zooming a little ways down a forested road before slamming on the brakes and turning off the engine.

"Piss break?" Noah said.

"We've got a tail."

"What?" I said, craning around to peer behind us into the night.

"A car followed us off the highway. It was hanging back. Lights off."

As I watched, the moonlight illuminated a dark car passing the end of the road. It paused, as if the driver was peering down our way, then continued on.

"How far are we from the cabin?" I asked.

"About five miles," Nick said. "But . . ." He sucked in air. "Okay, you know how I said the kids were sleeping when I left? They weren't. There's no way we were getting them to bed when they knew you guys were coming. We told them Antonio would drive them out to meet you."

"What?"

"You only said not to bring them to the *airport*. I texted Antonio about ten minutes ago to say we were on our way. They were going to meet us on that road back there. As a surprise."

"That's them following us then?" I said.

He shook his head. "We rented a VW van."

Meaning we had someone following us . . . while our kids were on the way to meet us.

"I'm calling Antonio now," Nick said before I could ask.

"I'm calling Reese," Noah added.

Noah couldn't get a signal. Nick could, but there was no reply, suggesting the others were out of range. I cursed under my breath as he tried again. We spent so much time off the grid that it wasn't the first time this had happened.

You'd think we'd wise up and invest in really good two-way radios.

As Nick kept trying, the car reappeared on the road behind us. It stopped and idled there.

"What's he doing?" Clay asked, squinting.

"Nothing, I think. He's just watching us."

We could turn around and go after our pursuer. But that was risky, with Antonio and the kids so close by.

I thought fast. Then I told Clay my plan.

As I made my way through the dark forest, I reflected that a Russian forest did not look, feel or smell that much different from the woods at home. I also reflected that I shouldn't forget that I *wasn't* at home, because I had no idea what was out here in the way of deadly fauna. So far I'd only picked up the familiar scents of squirrel and rabbit. Nothing too worrisome. Not that it mattered. A grizzly could lumber into my path right now and I wouldn't let it deter me. My children were on the other side of these woods.

As I walked, I kept hitting speed dial, cycling through Antonio, Reese, and Morgan. There wasn't really any point in leaving a message every time it rang through to voice mail, and I was probably racking up a four-digit phone bill, but it made me feel better. Every few rounds, I'd ring Nick, too. That was a little more productive, as he reassured Clay that I hadn't yet been devoured by rabid Russian squirrels.

I'd climbed out of the car and slipped off into the forest after our pursuer had carefully backed up, getting all but the nose of his car out of sight. Once I made it to the kids, Clay would go after whoever was in that car.

When I emerged onto the main road, I could see the van parked ahead of me. I kicked into high gear, jogging along the ditch.

I expected the door to fly open, Reese or Morgan tumbling out, wondering what the hell I was doing. But the van remained silent and still. I drew close enough to see through the darkened windshield. The front seats were vacant. I broke into a run, and yanked open the side door to find a pair of empty child seats.

I could smell them all in the van—Antonio, Reese, Morgan and the twins. There was no scent of blood. No scuff marks in the roadside dirt suggesting a struggle. I peered into the dark night, heart hammering.

Maybe one of the twins had to go to the bathroom.

So they all went traipsing into the forest? Not likely.

What, then?

I dropped to a crouch and picked up a trail immediately. Reese had climbed down from the passenger's seat and gotten the twins out. Then Antonio and Morgan had joined them from the driver's side and . . .

I followed the trail around the van, in a complete circle.

What the hell?

It went into the forest about twenty feet, then just . . . ended.

That wasn't possible. I hunkered down for a better sniff. As I did, I thought I caught a stifled giggle. I straightened fast and inhaled, but there were no scents on the breeze. A tree branch creaked. The wind sighed through new leaves.

I bent again. Something dropped from above, hitting me squarely on the back and knocking me down on all fours. Arms went around my neck. Small arms, smelling faintly of soap and candy.

"Mommy!"

Kate somersaulted over my head, landing on her back and wrapping her arms around my neck again as I rose. I hugged her tight and lifted her. Then I looked up. A face peered down from the branches above, teeth glinting in a Cheshire cat grin. Before I could say a word, Logan dropped from the tree, nearly taking us both down with him.

"Hey, Momma," he said as he hugged me.

I gave him a one-armed bear hug back. I didn't get "Momma" very often these days. That's what he used to call me, until he decided he was too old for it.

I kissed their cheeks and boosted them up, one arm under each. That was still easy to do, at least for a werewolf. They were both a bit small for their age, and had lost their baby fat. Kate still had her round cheeks, framed by blond curls, which made her look deceptively angelic. Logan's face had already thinned out, the shape starting to look more like mine, his hair somewhere between the gold of his father and sister and my silver-blond.

"Did we surprise you?" Kate asked.

"Yes. Scared me a little, too."

"Why? We're with Antonio."

A voice sounded from the forest. It was Morgan. "Still, finding an empty van is going to worry your mom. As I tried to tell these guys . . ."

Even before they stepped from the shadows of the forest, it was easy to tell who was who. Morgan was in the lead, the tallest and leanest of the three. Nick's father, Antonio, right behind him, was the shortest in the Pack and the most muscular even now, as he passed sixty. Last came Reese, between the two in height and size.

"Sorry if we worried you," Antonio said. He kissed my cheek. "The kids just wanted to have some fun."

"Where's Daddy?" Kate said, squirming.

I lowered them to the ground. "He's coming. Reese? Can you take them? I need to talk to Antonio for a minute. Let's start heading to the van. Morgan? Bring up the rear, please."

Reese hung back with the kids as I started out with Antonio.

"We were followed," I murmured.

I thought we were far enough from the kids. Unfortunately, I have a tendency to underestimate their hearing, and I barely got the words out before Kate said, "By who?"

I winced. "I don't know. Someone in a car might have been following us, so your dad just wanted to be super careful. The cell phones didn't work, so I came to warn you. It's okay, though. Dad has it under control."

"Course he does," Kate said.

Logan jogged up beside me. "Is it really okay, Mom?"

"She's a little worried," Kate said to her brother.

I have no idea where Kate gets her emotion-reading skills from. Certainly not her father. And not me either. She already has a knack for reading body language or facial expressions or vocal tone that borders on preternatural.

Before we stepped from the forest, I caught the distant sound of a car engine. I waved for them to stay back as I leaned out. A car was coming up the road. With its lights off.

Had our pursuer slipped away without Clay noticing? I found that hard to believe. Clay can handle a car like no one I know. If that vehicle had budged, he'd have whipped around and cut it off before it got anywhere near us.

I squinted into the darkness.

It wasn't the same car. The one following us had been boxier and lighter in color.

The car stopped. It idled there, as if it had just noticed the van. Then it reversed down the road and backed into a lane, out of sight.

"Antonio," I said as calmly as I could, "I want you and Morgan to get in the van. Head down the road as if you just pulled over for a pit stop. Then block that car in the lane and see what we've got."

"Unless that little car is stuffed with werewolves, we could handle it more directly," Antonio said.

I hesitated. Morgan was the Pack's weakest fighter. He was training, but he was a long way from being ready to undertake combat missions. Although he was a hereditary werewolf, his family believed in lying low and staying out of trouble, and had isolated itself in the wilds of Newfoundland for generations. Reese, on the other hand, had been raised by a father on the run from the Australian Pack. While he favored flight over fight, he'd come to us battle-ready, and had actually taken on the role of sparring partner to help train Morgan.

Yet whoever didn't go with Antonio stayed with me, protecting the twins. I couldn't rely on Morgan for that. It wasn't just a matter of his fighting ability—the kids didn't know him well, and wouldn't stay with him if I needed to go scouting.

So I had to rely on Antonio for this one. Even at his age he was as good a fighter as Clay. He also had the experience to know when he could face a challenge, and when he should hold tight and wait for backup.

"Okay," I said. "If you two can handle it, go ahead. Otherwise, just block him in."

Antonio nodded, and he and Morgan headed out.

Reese and I retreated into the woods with the kids. We'd gone a couple of hundred feet when we reached an old hunting cabin, long abandoned. It listed to one side, but seemed intact. A shove on the walls didn't set any boards creaking ominously. The windows were shuttered, leaving a single point of entry at the door. Easily defensible.

"We're going to hide in there?" Kate said as I came back out after scoping out the interior.

"It'll be fine," Reese said. "The spiders here aren't any bigger than house cats. Or so I've heard."

She gave him a look.

"At least they aren't poisonous," he said. "If it was Australia, they'd be poisonous."

"Everything's poisonous in Australia," Logan said.

We tried prodding them inside, but Kate dug in her heels.

"Why do we have to hide?" she said. "You're werewolves."

"They might be, too," I said.

"Or they might have guns," Reese said. "I can catch bullets in my teeth, but you guys need more practice. And your mom?" He leaned over them and whispered, "Hopeless."

"They're right," Logan said to his sister. "I don't like hiding, but Dad can take care of this. He needs to know we're safe, so he doesn't get distracted worrying about us."

My son. Some days I think he's already more qualified to be Alpha than I am. I kissed the top of his head and gave them both a nudge. They went inside.

Before I followed them in, I turned to Reese. "Stand guard by the door. It's the only way in."

"Got it."

I wouldn't be surprised if there *were* cat-sized spiders in that cabin. Or at least cat-sized rats. I could certainly smell droppings, though nothing scurried away from us.

The cabin was a single room, maybe fifteen feet square. It stunk of rotting wood as well as small animals. I led the twins to the back corner.

There was no cell phone signal in here either. I'd have to wait until I heard Clay or one of the others looking for us. In the meantime—

A figure appeared in front of me. Just appeared, materializing from nothing. The kids lunged, but I was faster, and pounced on the intruder. Kate shouted for Reese. As I pinned the figure to the wall, a vaguely familiar scent almost pierced the stink of the cabin.

"Don't shoot!" he said. "Or, er, bite, claw, punch . . ."

I knew that voice. I grabbed him by the shirtfront and slammed him against the wall again. He was about my age, completely average-looking, except for a thin, curving scar from his temple to his nose.

"Xavier," I said.

"You know this guy?" Reese said as he ran in.

"Unfortunately."

I first met Xavier nine years ago, when he was playing mercenary. *Playing* being the key word, complete with gun, camo, and tough-guy sneer. But the word *mercenary* really only suits Xavier as an adjective. He's a con artist. He can be anything, do anything, say anything if he sees a way to a fast buck.

Reese strode over, glowering at him. "How'd you get past me?"

Xavier glanced at the twins. "Uh . . . I . . . well, you see, I'm wearing really dark clothing, so I snuck—"

"You must be a teleporting half-demon," Logan said. "Tripudio, Evanidus, or Abeo?"

"Evanidus," I said.

Kate sniffed. "No wonder he isn't very good at it."

"Clayton's progeny, I presume?" Xavier said. He'd met Clay shortly before the kids were born. It hadn't gone well.

"Reese?" I said. "Take the kids outside."

"Oh, there's really no need for that," Xavier said. "I'm unarmed. They're perfectly safe."

"That's not why she wants us gone," Kate said. "She doesn't want us watching if she needs to hit you." She lowered her voice. "It's okay, Mom. He deserves it."

"Definitely Clayton's progeny." Xavier looked at me. "Elena, I'm sorry if I surprised you. I was—"

"You followed us from the airport. You and a friend."

"Not really a friend. More of an associate. But I come in peace. I just wanted to talk to you, and a contact who works for the Cortezes gave me your flight info."

That was one employee who wouldn't be working for the Cortezes much longer.

Xavier must have caught the look on my face, and hurried on. "The plan was to speak to you as soon as you got out of town. Just drive up alongside, say hi, find a place to grab a coffee. But I got caught in a traffic snarl, and I didn't want my associate handling this, so he followed you while I caught up."

"So you want to talk?" I said.

"Please. If you'd just let me down—"

I hoisted him higher. The kids giggled. Xavier didn't just teleport out of my grasp, which meant he must really want something.

"You weren't nearly so keen to chat with me last week when I called to ask if you had any information on Gilles de Rais or the Supernatural Liberation Movement," I said.

"Because I didn't have any. And I couldn't ask around because I was in Europe. Do you know what overseas cell phone rates are like?"

"You should have invested in a calling card, because a little assistance last week would have bought you a lot of goodwill right now."

"Er, right. I didn't understand the extent of the threat, see? I'd been in Europe for months. Totally cut off. Then I go home and some guys from this liberation movement try to jump me. Seems someone gave this de Rais guy my name. Told him I was well connected—which I am of course—so I might be useful."

"Uh-huh. So now that the threat directly affects you, things have changed."

"Not entirely. With this virus I heard about, the supernatural world is in serious danger. So I came to help you." He paused. "In return for protection."

"Little late," Reese said. "The threat—"

I stopped him with a look, then turned back to Xavier. "You followed me from Saint Petersburg—and cornered me with my kids—because you want to team up? You've got a strange way of recruiting allies."

He tugged at his collar. "And you've got a strange way of greeting old colleagues. Been spending too much time with your crazy-assed—" He glanced at the kids. "Refreshingly eccentric mate."

I wrapped my fist tighter in his shirtfront, making him cough.

"But it looks good on you," he managed. "I've always said I like a woman who can take care of herself. You could before, too, but you were a little wobbly on the self-confidence when I met you in Winsloe's playroom. You remember that? When we were prisoners together, watching each other's back?"

"I was his prisoner. You were his employee."

"But I still helped you, didn't I?"

"For a chit, which I repaid. Do you remember *that*? You made me steal the From Hell letter while I was six months pregnant."

"But it all worked out. You have two beautiful, smiling . . ." He looked at the twins. Both were staring at him stone-faced, Logan coldly appraising the situation, Kate tensed to pounce.

"It all worked out," he insisted, his voice a little less certain.

"Did it? Have you forgotten that letter released zombies? One of them gave Clay a really nasty scratch."

"Yeah, I . . . heard something like that. But he's fine now, right?"

"After a very long, very grueling rehabilitation. You should ask him about it sometime."

Xavier looked as if he'd rather swallow thumbtacks.

"Point is," I continued, "you haven't won any friendship points with the Pack. Clearly what you're angling for here is protection. But if we're going to protect you, we'll need more than a few tidbits of gossip in return. And this friend of yours, the one who followed us from the airport . . ."

"Not really a friend."

"Right. More of an associate, you said. A supernatural you owe a favor?"

"Something like that."

"And to repay him, you offered to cut him in on this deal. A two-for-one protection plan."

Xavier looked at the kids. "Your mom is one smart lady. You guys are really lucky—"

"Attention on *me*," I said, giving him a shake. "So I'm right. You want protection from this threat for you and your associate. That's going to cost you. I want three chits. Redeemable at any time."

"Three? No. I don't do multiples. How about one? For anything—"

"Three."

"Like a genie," Kate said with a smile. "You'll grant her three wishes."

"They're called djinn in the real supernatural world," Logan said. "They do grant wishes. Usually only one, though." He looked up at Xavier. "But you aren't a djinn. So you'll give our mom three. One for you. One for your friend. And one for sneaking up on us like this. If you don't, she'll make you wait and talk to our dad about his arm." He paused. "He really doesn't like talking about his arm."

"Whoa. You kids are . . ." He looked at me. "Adorable. Absolutely adorable."

"Just wait until they grow up," Reese said with a chuckle.

"So what's it going to be?" I asked Xavier. "Three chits? Or wait for Clay?"

He chose the chits.

In return for those three chits, I promised that Xavier and his "associate" would be under Pack protection until Gilles de Rais was dead and his virus was contained. I didn't tell him both things had already happened. Apparently, whoever gave him our flight information hadn't bothered to share that information.

When Antonio and Morgan returned, they told us they'd

found Xavier's rental car empty and had tried to track him. His teleporting skills made that tricky, and they'd finally given up and come to make sure we were okay. We managed to get to Clay before he went after Xavier's associate. I explained the situation. He was fine with it. The "threat" was over.

I awoke the morning of the Meet to hear the kids whispering and giggling. They'd been sharing our bed, an indulgence we didn't feel right denying them after we'd abandoned them for a week. When I opened my eyes, they were sneaking out the door. I played possum until I heard their footsteps pounding down the hall.

"Sounds like Jeremy's here," I said as I rolled over. He and Jaime had flown in the night before, along with Karl and Hope and the new baby. "We could go greet him. Or we could take advantage of a few minutes of privacy—"

I was talking to myself. The bed was empty.

I rose on my elbows. "Clay?"

He wasn't in the room. His side of the bed was already cool, as if he'd left a while ago. I frowned and checked the clock. Just past seven. Clay wasn't an early riser, and even if he did wake before me, he usually stayed in bed.

I was sitting up, yawning, when the door opened.

"I figured they woke you," Clay said as he slipped in. "Sorry about that."

I slid down under the covers and pulled back the sheets for him.

"Damn," he said, giving me a look that sent heat coursing through me. "I would love to take you up on that, darling, but I'm going to have to ask for a rain check. Jeremy needs to speak to you."

"Ah. Pre-Meet business."

"Yep." He looked at the spot I was offering him again. "But it could wait a couple of minutes . . ."

"No. He's waiting and I just remembered there's no lock on that door. We'll get Nick to take the kids for a walk later." I swung my legs out of bed. "Toss me my clothes."

When I left the bedroom, I caught the distinct smell of pancakes and ham. My favorite breakfast. I smiled and picked up my pace. The others were already in the dining room— eating, I thought. But when I got there, they were just hanging around the table, no food in sight.

I glanced toward the kitchen. "I know I smell breakfast."

"We ate it all," Kate said.

Logan nodded and grinned. No one said a word. They just watched me.

"Okay, what's up?"

No one answered. Jeremy was at the table with his back to me, and turned as I came over.

"Where's Jaime?" I asked, as I bent to give him a quick hug.

"I dropped her off at a spa for a much-needed rest. She'll be here for lunch."

"And there's supposed to be a baby. I know there is . . ."

I looked around and saw Karl. He looked exhausted, partly from the new baby I was sure, but also because he was obviously still recuperating. He stood with one hand braced on the table for support, despite the fact there was an empty chair right beside him.

"Sit," I said.

When he hesitated, I added a growl to it. "Sit."

He sat, eliciting a few chuckles from the others. Clay was right. As pissed off as I was about Karl's disobedience, it did have the added bonus of making him extra obedient now.

"Baby?" I said.

"She's with Hope in the other room."

"Okay, well, I don't know what you guys are up to, but if there's no breakfast on the table, I have a baby to visit—"

Clay cut me off. "They're sleeping. It was a long flight."

As if on cue, I heard a distant gurgle. "Then what's that?"

"What's what?"

"I didn't hear anything," Noah piped in. "They're both sound asleep."

"Uh-huh. Okay, so I don't get breakfast. I don't get to see the baby. What exactly do I . . . ?"

I trailed off as Jeremy shifted his chair and Reese stepped away from the table, revealing a game board.

"Chess?" I said.

Jeremy waved to the seat across from him, and the others moved to let me through. "You're going to play a match against me."

"Why?"

A faint, crooked smile. "Because you always say were-wolves don't settle their differences over a nice game of chess. I think it's time to rectify that."

"Differences?" I stopped in midstep. "What's wrong?"

"Sit," he said, and my feet instinctively started moving again, but my gaze stayed fixed on him, heart picking up speed. Clay reached out to squeeze my hand as I moved past him, but I pulled away.

"Did I do something wrong?" I asked. "In the field?"

"You were perfect in the field. But we have a tradition to uphold, and I thought you'd prefer this to an actual physical challenge."

"A challenge?" My gaze shot from Jeremy to Clay. "What's going on?"

Clay leaned in to whisper, "It's okay. Just play along."

I slid into the chair. Logan had slipped around and was standing on my other side. Kate squeezed past her father to get next to me and leaned her elbows onto the table.

"You can beat him, Mommy," she whispered. "Ask Logan for help if you get stuck."

The others laughed.

"I think your mom will do just fine," Jeremy said.

I looked at the board. "The game's half done."

"Yes, well, everyone's hungry so we're moving this along," Jeremy said. "Reese and Logan set it up. Apparently there's the possibility of a quick victory, and several possibilities for an equally quick defeat. So take a few minutes, then make your move."

I took those few minutes, and a couple more. Then I made my move. Jeremy made his. We made two more and . . .

"Checkmate," I said, moving my piece into position.

"That's it, then," Jeremy said. "I've been vanquished and I will gracefully step aside."

He smiled, his eyes meeting mine, and I swear everyone in the room had stopped breathing. Jeremy got to his feet, grinning now.

"And with that, our first order of Meet business is concluded. Having vanquished her predecessor in a challenge match, Elena Michaels is now Alpha of the North American Pack."

I passed the day in a daze, leading the Meet as best I could, taking care of business and all the fallout of the liberation movement's assault on the supernatural world. I felt a little uncertain, as if I expected Jeremy to take me aside at any moment and tell me it was just a practice run and he was still in charge. He didn't. Jaime, Hope, and baby Nita joined us for a celebration lunch, which lasted well into the afternoon.

We napped after that. It took me a while to drift off, my brain still buzzing, but eventually the big meal did its work and I fell asleep. When I woke, the kids were gone. Clay was still beside me, snoring softly. As I lifted my head, I caught faint shouts and laughter from outside. I slipped from the bed and went to the window to see the Pack out on the lawn playing a game of touch football.

There was no sign of Hope and the baby—it was a little

chilly for a newborn. Jaime must have stayed inside with them. Everyone else was there, even Karl, sitting on the ground and watching, which surprised me. Normally he'd forgo the fun and games unless Hope insisted. When Kate zoomed past, his hand shot out, as if to grab her leg. She screeched and veered off and he laughed, calling something after her.

Morgan was another who usually stayed on the sidelines. Not by choice in his case. I could tell he always wanted to join in. He just wasn't yet comfortable enough to be sure of his place, and hung back during games, rarely touching the ball. He had it now, though, running as Logan guarded him. He made it halfway to the goal before Reese tackled him, sending him flying, the ball leaping from his hands. Kate grabbed it and ran off, chortling as Reese shot her a thumbs-up. She made it down to her end and scored, throwing her arms in the air and dancing.

Antonio got the ball next, only to lose it to Nick, who handed it off to Noah. As Noah raced down the yard, a figure shot from beyond my sight line and tackled him. For a second, seeing only dark hair, I was confused. It wasn't Nick or Antonio or Karl. So who . . .

The figure grabbed the ball and threw it to Morgan and Logan, and as he did, he twisted and I caught a glimpse of his face.

"Jeremy?" I whispered, then I laughed.

Arms wrapped around my waist, Clay coming up behind me. "Hmm?"

"Jeremy's playing. That's not a sight we see very often."

"He isn't Alpha anymore. Things will change."

"Good. He looks like he's having fun." I leaned back against Clay. "I was just thinking that this reminds me of that time in Alaska, after Jeremy told me he wanted me to succeed him. I was watching everyone playing in the snow when I realized this was going to be my Pack someday."

"And now it is."

"And now it is," I echoed.

"You know you're ready."

"As ready as I'll ever be."

"You're ready." He kissed the side of my neck. "That's your Pack down there, Elena. All yours."

I was turning to hug him when Kate caught sight of us in the window and yelled. Logan motioned for me to open up. I did.

"Are you coming out?" he called.

"Yes!" Kate shouted. "We need you! Dad, you're on my team!"

"Then the *Alpha* is on ours," Logan said, looking over at her. "Which means you're going to lose."

"Am not!"

"Are, too."

"We'll be right there," I called.

Clay nudged me aside and yelled, "Give us five minutes." He glanced at me and grinned. "Maybe ten."

He shut the window before they could complain. Then he pulled the curtains and put his arms around my waist again.

"Does my Alpha have any orders for me?" he asked, smiling.

"Mmm, I could think of a few."

"Good." He scooped me up and carried me back to bed.

ACKNOWLEDGMENTS

I'd like to thank some of those who helped bring to life not only this book, but the entire Otherworld series.

Thank you to my agent, Helen Heller, who has been with me from the start. Without you, there would be no Otherworld—just a writer working away in a basement and occasionally thinking wistfully of that old werewolf novel she'd loved writing.

Thanks to Anne Collins of Random House Canada and Antonia Hodgson of Little, Brown UK, who have also been with me from the beginning. I recall that first dinner with Anne, before she bought *Bitten,* when I was so certain I was going to screw up, and she was so gracious and enthusiastic about the project. I also remember Antonia Hodgson's early notes from across the ocean, suggesting that *Bitten* could use a little more gore, which I gleefully provided.

My editorial helpers have been a little more varied in the United States. Sarah Manges of Viking came first, for *Bitten* and *Stolen,* and launched a series. Anne Groell from Bantam took that series and made it a bestselling one. Then Carrie Thornton from Dutton stepped in for the final trilogy and helped me wrap it up.

I'd also like to thank Faren Bachelis, who has been my copy-editor for most of the series. She's helped me see many of my grammatical flaws, but apparently the proper use of hyphens will remain beyond my comprehension.

Thanks, too, to my own team . . .

To Alison Armstrong, who took on the thankless job of assistant for a scattered big sister who often dumps thousands of contest entries into her inbox and stacks of editing work onto her front doorstep . . . forgetting to warn her that it's coming.

To Xaviere Daumarie, who serves in the equally thankless position of "artist of all trades," collaborating with me on graphic stories, illustrating novellas, providing extra covers and art for swag. An artist who can take three photos of Italian male models, some vague and muddled instructions, and give me a picture of Nick is worth her weight in gold Sharpies.

To my beta readers, who've kept me from making some stupendous errors (all of which are far too embarrassing to admit here). Thanks to Ang Yan Ming, Danielle Wegner, Raina Toomey, Terri Giesbrecht, and, again, Xaviere Daumarie, who all helped with this book and many before it, and to Tamara Warden, who came on board for *Thirteen*.

You helped make it happen, guys. I won't forget that. Though I may still forget to warn Alison about new contests before I announce them.

KELLEY ARMSTRONG is the bestselling author of the Women of the Otherworld series, the Nadia Stafford crime series, and the *New York Times* #1 bestselling young adult trilogies Darkest Powers and Darkness Rising. She lives in rural Ontario with her family.

www.kelleyarmstrong.com

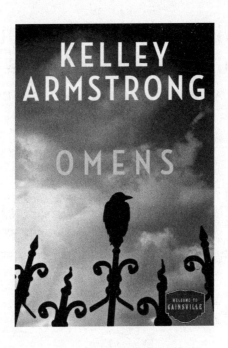

NO WEREWOLVES.
NO DEMONS.
JUST GARGOYLES.

Following the epic conclusion of her internationally best-selling Women of the Otherworld series, Kelley Armstrong launches a brand-new series set in Cainsville, a small town as spookily fascinating as Stephen King's Castle Rock or Dean Koontz's Moonlight Bay.

WELCOME TO
CAINSVILLE

NADIA STAFFORD ISN'T YOUR TYPICAL HUNTING LODGE OWNER.

SHE'S AN EX-COP WITH A CODE OF JUSTICE ALL HER OWN...

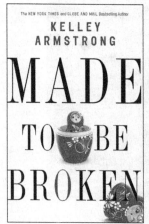

MURDER, ACTION, AND SUSPENSE FROM THE *NEW YORK TIMES* AND *GLOBE AND MAIL* BESTSELLING AUTHOR KELLEY ARMSTRONG.

WELCOME TO THE OTHERWORLD.

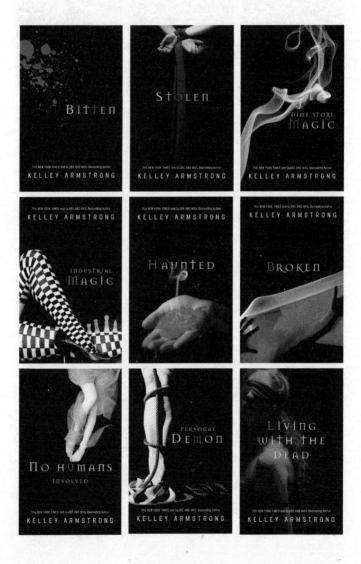